BLOOD AND STEEL

THE COR CHRONICLES
VOL. I

Upcoming Novels by Martin V. Parece II

- *The Oathbreaker's Daughter (Book 1 of The Dragonknight Trilogy)*
- *Wolves of War – A John Hartman Novel*
- *Bound By Flame (The Chronicle of Thyss)**
- *Spectres of the Black Sun – A John Hartman Novel*
- *Advent of Judgement*
- *The Horizon's Edge*

Other Works by Martin V. Parece II

- *Blood and Steel (The Cor Chronicles Vol. I)**
- *Fire and Steel (The Cor Chronicles Vol. II)**
- *Darkness and Steel (The Cor Chronicles Vol. III)**
- *Gods and Steel (The Cor Chronicles Vol. IV)**
- *Blood Betrayal (The Cor Chronicles Vol. V)**
- *Blood Loss (The Chronicle of Rael)**
- *Tendrils in the Dark – Eight Tales of Horror*

*Denotes a novel of Rumedia.

BLOOD AND STEEL

THE COR CHRONICLES
VOL. I

BY

MARTIN V. PARECE II

ISBN-10: 146990196X
ISBN-13: 978-1469901961

To my children, for whom I do everything.
And my wife, without whom I could accomplish nothing.

PROLOGUE

In the southwest of Aquis, there lived a commoner by the name of Pel. Approaching the middle age of thirty, he was a farmer and lived on the land his parents before him had owned and farmed. He was a good man, relatively unremarkable for his race, and he worked his land tirelessly. The land in Aquis was bountiful, and his farm provided him with an ample living, despite its small size. Though a commoner, he was not a peasant; he owned the farm wholly, and during harvest he always hired help to reap and carry his goods to market.

He kept all that he needed to make it through to the next harvest and gave a quarter of what was left to the nearby village to distribute to those who needed it most. The remainder he took to Martherus, the second largest city in Aquis, to sell at the market for a fair price. He used his cash to purchase whatever dry goods he needed and tithed most of what was left to Garod, the ruler of the western gods, and Hele the goddess of fertility and the harvest. Pel did this without fail every year, as he knew it would always pay him a dividend.

In his twenty eighth year, he happened upon a young lady while returning from the Martherus market. She was beautiful to his eye, though many others would consider her plain, and he chose to stop and speak with the man that accompanied her, her senior by twenty or more years. The man was her father, and after much friendly discussion, invited Pel to overnight at their home rather than on the road.

Their home was rather quaint, only two rooms, a main room for everyone to spend their time and a separate bedroom for the adults. The girl's name was Erella, in honor of Aquis' great queen, and she slept on the floor in the main room. Her father apologized greatly for their meager home, explaining they were mere servants to one of the local lords, and they worked his land and helped in the affairs of farming in exchange for a home, protection, and whatever food they needed. Pel waved off such deprecations; it was a home after all, and if it kept you dry and warm, it served its purpose.

Over a fair dinner of stew, to which Pel added some of his own meat as payment for the hospitality, he spoke with Erella's father at great length about all matters of agriculture. The man was quite affable, and after a short while, they felt like fast friends. As the women cleaned the table, Pel took a smoke with the man outdoors sharing from the same pipe. At this point, Pel admitted somewhat forwardly that he stopped to become friends only because he had immediately felt taken with Erella upon seeing her, and he acted somewhat sheepish in revealing this fact. He had recently come to realize his death would come one day, and he was without wife or sons. Pel explained that he would like to make Erella his wife, and he would treat her well.

Unfortunately, it was not quite so simple; as Erella was a servant of a lord, Pel would need to pay a dowry to that lord. It was a rather typical business arrangement, and the lord would need payment for being deprived of an employee. Beyond that, Erella's father gave his blessing, realizing that his daughter would then become the wife of a landowner, not the daughter of a peasant.

That evening, Erella's father offered his bed to Pel, saying that he and his wife would sleep on the floor with Erella. Pel refused to have the man sleep on the floor of his own house, and assuring him that he had no dishonorable intentions, Pel said he would sleep on the floor of the main room. Perhaps, if she were inclined to conversation, he could learn more about the woman he hoped to make his wife. Erella was quiet at first, clearly shy towards a man whom she saw as her elder. Pel kept his word regarding his intentions, but he did explain to her what he hoped he could bring to pass. She somewhat shied away from this subject; though she did not express her fears, she knew there were other duties women were expected to fulfill to their husbands beyond cooking and cleaning. Several of the girls she had known as a small girl were already married, their bellies swelling with child.

In the morning, Pel took his leave of the family, embracing Erella's father as a brother, and clasping Erella's hand in what he hoped seemed a sincere fashion. He returned to stock his home with his purchases from the market, and while repairing his plow, mulled over what he had learned of Erella. In the morning, he sent a message to Erella's master asking what dowry would be deemed appropriate. Pel continued his farm work while he awaited an answer; winter was not far off, and he still had much to do in his home to prepare. Nearly three full weeks passed before he received an answer with a noble's seal upon it. He placed the message on his table as he continued the work for the day, and it wasn't until after he ate a small supper of bread, ham, and cheese that he opened the scroll with no small amount of trepidation.

The noble's writing, if in fact it was his own, was a flowing script, extremely superfluous against Pel's own pragmatic scrawl. The letter rambled on about the need for a noble to have servants to work his land, and they received much in return. The letter finally named a price, and Pel sat quietly sipping mead for several hours simply thinking it over. The letter laid out a formula based on pounds of meat, grain or money, or some combination thereof based on going exchange rates, and Pel calculated that the noble expected roughly two fifths of his annual harvest. It was a high price, but he simply did not see another option; the noble had no need to negotiate.

3

Besides, negotiation, especially in this matter, was repugnant to Pel.

He spent the next year working harder than he had before, and he had much for which to plan. Besides losing almost half of his harvest to the dowry, he also needed to keep more harvest and money for himself and his new wife. He quickly came to the realization he could only possibly increase his harvest by a tenth, which would not leave him able to provide as much charity as usual.

This troubled Pel. He had always made sure the local village received food from him for those in need, and he certainly could not do this and tithe. He chose to take a day of rest and went into the village to meet with Garod's priest there; Jonn was a longtime friend of Pel and his parents. The priest soothed Pel on this matter, explaining that he had always been a good man, respected by the community. Also, the gods knew Pel's piety and would understand one lapse, especially since the joys of spouses were rights to all, denied neither by men nor gods. This lent Pel strength, knowing that all would understand if he did not give his usual, and he worked hard that year during the growing season. Rewarded with a bumper harvest, he gave half of his usual charity and tithe, which was substantially more than he had originally expected.

Pel left the market that year, heading directly for Erella's home. He told her family that come tomorrow, she would be free and married to him, if she so desired it. He promised to be a good husband and that he would honor her; he knew she did not love him but hoped that one day she may learn to. Pel slept the night there as he did the year before, and in the morning, Erella agreed to be his wife. She would respect him as husband, whether love came or not.

She left her home with him, and together they traveled to the noble's estate inside the city, and as per the agreement, Pel brought a great burlap sack of money that

4

totaled exactly to the noble's requested dowry. The man tried several times to not honor the payment, first saying that he made no such agreement. Pel produced the noble's own scroll, leading the man to claim the price had gone up since last year. In one of the few times of his life, Pel's temper flared, and he slammed his fist on the noble's heavy desk, saying that he was no peasant and could not be dealt with in such a way. He would show the letter to a magistrate and ask *him* if the agreement was binding and *equitable*. The noble called for his exchequer, who after three countings agreed the payment was complete, after which he handed one tenth of the silver back, asking that Pel forget the earlier unpleasantness.

Pel thanked him and left with his new fiancée, promising Erella that no man would ever pay anything for her again while she lived. They traveled back to Pel's home, and on the morrow, reached the village near his homestead. He paid the savings on the dowry to his friend Jonn in exchange for a marriage service. The marriage took place in the center of town, just outside Garod's temple, and the entire town witnessed Pel and Erella's wedding.

Over the ensuing days, Erella came to know her husband simply by watching him go about his duties. Again, the harvest was over, and Pel set about preparing the home for winter, and on several occasions, she asked him what she could do to help. He simply shrugged; having never had help before, he didn't know what to do with it. She took on the duties she would normally do with her family, allowing Pel more time to do other things, or sometimes nothing at all. He had never imposed his will on her, nor tried to force her into other things.

Winter came as winter does, and the home became colder, despite a constantly burning fire. There were less daylight hours, of course, and with the frozen ground there was less to be done about the farm. Erella had come to sleep with Pel, as she knew wives did, but only for warmth at first. A month into the winter, she realized her thoughts of him had changed; he made her feel safe, and she realized that working with him about the house and land, she was working for their life, not the life of a noble in a city. Before the winter broke, Erella was with child.

Erella had heard awful stories about pregnancy and childbirth, and it frightened her. She finally told Pel just as spring arrived, and more work was being needed daily. At this, Pel refused to allow her to do any of the chores. He had never needed help in the past, and he could handle the load now, especially since she could scarcely eat without vomiting. While the inevitable sickness passed, her ability to help did not increase, nor would Pel have accepted help even if she were able. He knew he could provide for them both, and he also knew exertion could cause problems with pregnant women. There was no need to risk anything, and he had Jonn come from the village to bless them. A lifelong friend to Pel's family, the priest embraced him and cried with happiness.

It seemed to Pel that harvest approached more quickly than usual, and he hired hands when the summer broke. Erella was well swelled at this point, and he would not allow her to do any work at all outside of cooking. In fact, he preferred that she stay indoors as much as possible, especially once he hired help. He didn't like the way the young men looked at this wife. It was perhaps the first time jealousy had ever touched him, and he wondered at this feeling.

It was about a month before harvest, and over the last several weeks, Erella had felt occasional pains. The midwives had already explained to her that this would sometimes happen, and she shouldn't worry unless they became regular and fast for a period of time or if her water broke. On one particularly brisk morning, the pains

6

came again, but refused to be soothed. She waited several hours, resting as the midwives told her, before telling Pel when he took his midday meal. Pel immediately sent one of his hired hands to the village to fetch the midwives and Jonn. The midwives arrived some time later, but the priest was conducting a funeral ceremony and would come as soon as it was concluded. Pel would not leave his wife's side despite her urgings that there was nothing he could do to help.

As first births tend to be, it was a long labor, lasting until shortly after midnight. Erella showed herself to be a fine, strong woman, and she finally birthed a howling baby boy. He was well made and healthy, and Pel and Erella fawned over him as the midwives worked to set Erella to heal.

"He will be a fine son," proclaimed Jonn, blessing him. "If you have decided on his name, I will perform the Naming now."

"His name is Cor," decided Erella, naming the baby after her father, as it was widespread practice in the Shining West for wives to name their sons, and fathers their daughters.

The priest proceeded with the ritual, declaring the baby's name Cor Pelson before Garod and the other gods of light. After, Jonn took his leave with one of the midwives, and the remaining midwife and Erella stayed in the bedroom, the midwife allowing her to sleep as much as possible. Pel sat heavily in a chair and slept with his head on his hands at the table.

Erella, Queen of Aquis, lay fitfully in her luxurious, silk canopied bed. Tonight, as most nights, she retired just before midnight, well after the moon had risen. Usually, affairs of state left her drained and ready for sleep, but tonight she was restless. Her mind would wander off while she lay starting to doze only to come screaming back to her, bringing her to full consciousness. In her long reign, she had few nights quite like this one. She was not preoccupied with some matter; there was just a feeling of uneasiness, as if a dark storm cloud hovered on the horizon, just beyond her sight. She could feel a change in the world coming, and such changes were as frightful as they were exciting. The advantage to the status quo, whether good or bad, was stability, because things could always get worse.

The ruler of Aquis, the Shining West's largest kingdom, also had the distinction of being the High Priestess to Garod, and He bestowed upon her great longevity. Many would see her as a well-aged matriarch in her seventieth year, but in fact she had been ruler for over a century. Erella's form had thinned over the last thirty years, but she maintained a healthy appearance, despite having shrunk slightly to about five and a half feet tall. She had nearly waist-length hair, once blonde and now white that had not thinned over the years.

Queen Erella closed her eyes and opened them again to find herself on foothills overlooking a great plain with gorgeous purple mountains in the distance, the World's Spine no doubt. The day was dark, the sun obscured by huge gray-black clouds, and the sound of thunder played in the distance. Two great armies faced each other across the plain, one of shining knights, robed priests, and armored footmen. The other consisted of thousands of naked, shambling corpses and men who looked like Westerners, but they were a downtrodden lot with the mark of the whip upon their backs. Behind these men were hundreds of tall figures with unnaturally stretched limbs, many of them cloaked in fine black, red, and purple garments.

Between the two hosts, Erella gazed upon a lone figure; he was not overly tall, standing about six feet in height. In one hand he held a razor sharp, single edged longsword and in the other an evil looking fetish, and he wore a heavy plate hauberk that left his arms bare. Black chain mail fell from a girdle to connect to plate legguards that protected the front of his thighs and shins. His helm struck her most oddly; large and bulbous, it did not appear to be made for a normal man's head, and it had no visor, yet she had no doubt the man could see clearly. Solid black, the armor reflected light off its high shine as it would the body of an insect or spider.

The two hosts charged each other and met at the warrior with a deafening crash, and men screamed as steel rang and blood and gore flew freely. The warrior stood in the middle of the great battle, cavorting wildly in the carnage as his blade hewed its way through armor and flesh from both hosts. Slaves and corpses fell unmoving onto the beaten down plains grass, as did armored soldiers and gleaming knights while the two hosts endeavored to crush each other and the lone warrior. Dark sorceries of black, purple, and red flew from the hands of the necromancers to be met by the white magicks of the priests. The dark necromancers quickly raised the fallen to their cause while the priests healed their wounded as quickly as they could muster.

The warrior suddenly stopped his onslaught and raised both arms above his head, sword and fetish pointed to the sky as he suddenly ignored all of his foes. A dull roar began to rise in the distance. Quiet at first, it gained power before becoming so loud that even the embattled armies took notice, and the combatants slowly ceased their attacks on each other, followed by larger numbers, and then finally both entire armies. The roaring sound had become deafening, and Queen Erella saw they all looked at her, but it then dawned on her that they looked past her, their gazes fixed on something behind her in the distance.

Erella turned slowly, following their gaze and beheld a truly appalling sight. A massive dark tidal wave, a wall of water the deep red color of blood, raged towards the armies. It raced toward her at frightening speed, freezing her in place in momentary indecision before it reached her. It should have crushed her lithe frame with its force, but instead roared past, leaving the queen unharmed. It crashed down onto the two armies with more violence and carnage than thousands of armies could have ever created. It blasted bodies clear apart and crushed both steel and flesh, as it annihilated the soldiers, slaves, priests, and necromancers of both armies in mere seconds. As it subsided, the red waves dissipated, and the blood spread evenly across the plain forming a shallow lake that lay mere inches deep as it slowly soaked into the earth. At the center stood the black steel clad warrior, still lifting his sword and fetish to the darkened heavens.

Queen Erella bolted upright in bed. Sweat beading her forehead, she felt a terror and anxiety unlike any she had felt in decades. A warm, comforting glow appeared in her chamber, overpowering the light and warmth of her fire, and she slowly laid her head back onto her down pillows, allowing the presence of her god to wash over her. The glow faded, and with it went the anxiety leaving her alone in bed.

The queen, with a deftness and grace that belied her great age, swung her feet over the side of her bed and stood. She glided to the door of her chamber and opened it. The guard outside stood slightly more erect as she opened the door and entered the hall beyond.

"Find me Palius. I need him at once, no matter what he is doing," she commanded. Her voice was gentle, but there was no mistaking the sound of authority, and the mailed guard quickly saluted and clinked down the hallway, no doubt headed for Palius' chambers.

The queen turned and considered her chambers briefly before striding purposefully toward her office, leaving the door ajar. A heavy mahogany desk with an upholstered chair sat in the middle of the room, with a smaller desk and a cushioned stool to one side. A fireplace sat cold and empty on the far wall. Her desk was neatly laden with open affairs of state; she sat and began to write on a blank scroll while waiting for Palius to arrive.

"My queen?" asked a male voice from the adjoining room. Palius came slowly through the doorway to her office. He was an older man of nearly sixty with a slightly bent back, but he had managed to keep a full head of white hair. He wore a neatly trimmed full beard, also white. His face was haggard with dark rings under his eyes, and he was dressed in a simple robe he had clearly put on hastily. Palius was the queen's most valued advisor, and his sharp intellect and calm wisdom had aided her often in the past.

"I was uneasy all day," she told him, "and did not know why. Garod has given me a vision while I slept. A Dahken has been born this night." She watched as his face turned from surprise to deep thought as in sank the full weight of her words.

"My queen, I do not doubt your words. What matter is it? The Dahken cult died off nearly a millennium ago with The Cleansing. There is none left to teach this babe how to use whatever power he may have."

The queen leaned her back against her plush chair, sighing. "I know we've long believed that, but I've always had my doubts. Something frightens me about the one I saw; this Dahken may be the most powerful ever. I watched as he summoned a wall of blood to destroy armies of both the Shining West and the Loszian Empire. Do I take it literally, or do I assume it is metaphor?"

"Why should we fear this one boy?" Palius asked his queen, rubbing his eyes tiredly.

"This boy may grow to a man, a man who brings the end of both the Shining West and the Loszian Empire," she answered quickly. At this Palius quit his tired demeanor and stared at his queen. Referring to her

11

notes for details that were already fading, Queen Erella related her dream.

"Perhaps," suggested Palius, "it is not that he will bring about the end of both civilizations. I see many possible interpretations, but certainly we must find this child," he paused, pinching the bridge of his nose, something Palius did commonly when a thought bothered him. "My queen, what do we do when we find him? Do we slay a babe for what he could be capable of? Do we commit a horrific sin for the greater good?"

"Any child may grow to lead revolution, seize power, and commit atrocities. We cannot slaughter children for what they may do. Such an act is a crime for which we would pay with our souls."

"Then, we have no choice," Palius continued, receiving a patient glance from his queen, "we find him, and we watch him."

1.

"Boy, you are too sickly to serve aboard my ship," the captain had said like every captain before him. A light breeze blew in from the bay across the docks where ships of all sizes loaded and unloaded passengers, crew, and cargo. It smelled oddly of salt.

He was an interesting character, from the continent of Tigol across the Southern Sea, which in and of itself was not odd as many merchant captains hailed from that land, but most of them were smaller in stature than Westerners, standing no more than five and a half feet tall with wiry, athletic builds and stylized, pointed mustaches that sprung from either end of the upper lip. This man was a Shet, from the great plains and deserts in the center of that continent rather than the coastal trading cities. Like most of his people, Captain Naran stood tall and wide, extremely well-muscled in core and limb. The epicanthic folds of his eyes were far less developed than the other Tigoleans, causing them to appear more closed from the sun than his fellows, and from exposure to the sun, his skin appeared duskier brown than a shade of yellow. He spoke Western well, though heavily accented, and it took Cor a few moments to decipher his words.

"Sir, I am well. I can work," Cor answered him.

"You look as if you just crawled from the grave. At the least, my men would view a cabin boy of your pallor as bad luck, and I think you would not survive the first voyage."

"I survived working with my father on the farm sir. I'll be fine," Cor replied.

"Why aren't you on your farm now, boy?" Naran asked.

13

Cor paused before answering; he had lied to every other ship captain and met with no success in finding one who would take him. It was time for honesty.

"I ran away, sir. I stole a horse from the barn and rode to the city. It took a few days. I sold the horse when I got here."

"Why run from home? Did your parents ill treat you?"

"No, sir," Cor answered, and he left it at that.

The captain pondered this for a moment before asking, "And why do you look as if you are walking dead?"

"I do not know, sir. My parents said it happened a few days after I was born."

"You are not ill?" he asked.

"I cough sometimes," Cor answered truthfully and with a shrug. "Sometimes, I cough bad, but I'm used to it."

"How old are you, boy?"

"Thirteen this year, sir."

"Very well," Captain Naran said, apparently satisfied. "You seem to be well mannered and able, which is all I can ask from a cabin boy. The wages were posted, and if you are in fact not too sick to live through our voyage south, I will keep you on. Report to the Crewmaster by dawn tomorrow. What is your name, boy?"

"Cor Pelson."

"Westerners," Captain Naran sighed as he wrote the boy's name upon a scroll full of names. "You name your children as if anyone cares whose son you are."

And as such, Cor began his sailing career. With nowhere else to be, he reported aboard ship immediately and was assigned quarters, little more than a small closet, that immediately adjoined Captain Naran's own as well as the main deck. It had just enough room for him to curl up into a ball with a straw pillow and wool blanket, with two

14

makeshift shelves for a few belongings. He learned to be careful not to hit his head on those when he stood.

Tigoleans dominated the crew, and most of these from the northern coasts, though there were also a few other Shet. Mixed in were some Westerners, making about a third of the crew, and they had the typical dark hair, a mix of browns and black, and white skin of their race. Though they were heavily tanned from years in the sun. And what Captain Naran had said seemed at least partially true; some of the sailors eyed Cor with fear and distrust, though the more grizzled veterans carried on about their duties without pause. Cor supposed once you had seen one oddity, you grew numb to others.

Cor was a Westerner of course, with nearly jet black hair and gray eyes, not overly uncommon. Twelve years of age, and well on his way to thirteen, when he first joined Naran's crew, he was about five and a half feet tall and apparently in good physical health except for one notable fact. His skin held the ashen pallor of the grave, solid pale gray across every inch of him without one hint of blemish or variation. Once he had been as pink as any newborn, and at the tender age of three days old he began a horrific coughing fit flecked with blood. The village priest said he saw a great sickness in Cor, and that the babe likely would not survive his first few weeks, much less his first winter. Cor's color changed during that first attack, and he unnerved nearly everyone who saw him.

The coughing attacks still came occasionally but not once during his first voyage, which lasted nearly a month. In fact, in his first week something completely unexpected, to Cor at least, attacked him instead - he could not keep anything at all on his stomach for the first three days. A farmer's son, Cor had never set foot on a boat of any kind, and seasickness was not something he knew about or anticipated. He spent the entire first day voiding his stomach of any and all contents and the following two days dry heaving every time he attempted

15

to stand or move about. By the fourth day aboard ship, his stomach settled enough that he could keep down small amounts of bread. The Crewmaster gave him leave of his duties for those first few days, not out of any kind of sympathy but because seasickness was largely unavoidable with new sailors.

Cor's duties seemed light compared to the others aboard ship; he largely attended to the captain's needs and kept the officers' cabins clean. He took his meals with the captain, and at night all of the officers supped together, an event which he learned to enjoy greatly. The crewmen on the other hand had a hard job it seemed, constantly scrubbing the deck, scraping the hull, and attending sails or any number of odd looking rope contraptions. Cor Pelson was a farmer's son, and he'd never seen a sailing vessel or even how one operated. Watching it up close dispelled any romanticism he may have had.

While at the docks, Cor noticed a striking difference between the fat ships of the West and these slimmer Tigolean vessels. Western ships were wide and heavy oaken things that sat low in the water and required massive, magnificent sails to push them through the water. The shipwrights of the southern continent built long narrow ships that scarcely seemed to touch the water with one large fan shaped sail dead center that could be rotated to better catch the wind. Similar but much smaller sails could also be found at bow and stern. They opened like an exotic paper fan, and when they caught the wind, the ship would spring forth like a crossbow bolt. While Tigolean ships could not carry the quantity of cargo of their Western counterparts, they more than made up for it in speed and the timeliness of their deliveries. This also made them the ship of choice for smugglers, refugees, and criminals.

Over the two month stint across the Narrow Sea to a port in northeast Tigol, it became extremely clear that

Captain Naran was none of these things. He loved life and the feel of the wind in his hair, the misty spray of the sea upon his face, and the sun on his body. He'd left the Shetlands when he was younger than Cor and found the sea, and he discovered nothing in the world to be more dangerous or more freeing. As master of his own vessel, he commanded his own fate and forced the treacherous waters of the Narrow Sea to take him where he willed. These things Cor learned merely by watching and listening to the large Shet; Captain Naran talked to him often about his life, offering stories and wisdom without any real expectation of an answer.

Cor simply listened.

"Boy, tomorrow we will port in Hichima. I assume you have never seen a city beyond Aquis?" Captain Naran asked. They stood upon the deck late in the evening, the night well-lit by the moon and stars. Despite being late summer, the ocean breezes always kept the air cool.

"No sir."

"Tigol is different from your West, boy." The Shet rarely used Cor's name, though he had grown rather fond of him. "Tigol has few kingdoms; every city is its own state and has its own laws. However, there are few of those, and a foreign lad such as you could easily disappear against your will. Does that frighten you?"

"No," Cor said, and the captain fixed him with a long hard look before laughing uproariously and giving the boy a hard slap to his back.

"You are a bad liar boy, but I approve of the brave face! I enjoy you among my crew and expect you to be with me for some time. I need you to stay near me or aboard ship while we're here. I know you want to see the city, but for now it is not safe. The cities we visit will come to know you are under my protection."

They slipped into a bay in the early morning hours. The sun appeared to just break the horizon, seeming to emerge from the sea itself. As they left the open waters for the bay and approached the city, the water changed from a blue so deep as to be nearly black to a brackish brown. From the smell and color, it was plainly obvious that the city's inhabitants disposed of their waste directly into the bay that seagoing vessels passed through to gain access to Hichima. Captain Naran swore with disgust.

Cor could see little of the city itself beyond the docks and the warehouses immediately adjoining them. Two distinctly different docking areas existed, the closest of which was made of quarried stone, and Tigolean ships were lined up bow to stern so close as to nearly touch. The second set of docks had been clearly added much later; off to one side, they were made of wood and extended well into the bay. The graceless, fat boats of Western design moored there.

Cor had visited only two cities in his short life. Martherus, the second largest city in Aquis and the West, was one of course as his father sold his annual harvest there. The other was the small port city at which he joined Naran's crew, and he didn't even know its name. But both these cities had a castle with towers and a fortress that could be seen in the distance, and Hichima seemed to have no such things.

As they slid closer to the great stone dock, the captain ordered all three sails closed, and the men simply folded them into a large upright mast and bound them closed with heavy leather straps. A dozen of the men then went below decks to man oars, slowing the vessel substantially, but allowing the captain to pilot the ship with extreme precision. The ship pulled parallel to a empty place in the dock, sized perfectly for the Tigolean galley, and the oarsmen reversed the direction of their rowing to bring it to a gentle stop. Men on the dock threw

18

four great ropes to those upon deck who secured them to the ship. Cor's eyes followed the ropes and found each of them affixed to spoked steel wheels set into the stone dock so that only the top half of them could be seen. A Tigolean on the dock pulled a lever, and the wheels began to slowly turn. They reeled in Naran's ship like the daily catch. The dockworker set the lever back into its original position when the ship was less than two feet from the dock, and the wheels stopped.

"Boy, I must meet the Dockmaster and attend to business. Do your duties and stay aboard ship until I return," Captain Naran said and crossed a newly affixed gangplank.

The entire area was awash in short stature, thin Tigoleans moving cargo from ships to warehouses and the reverse or conducting all sorts of business. Cor saw no other Shet, making Naran the center of much attention, though there were a few Westerners in the vicinity as well. He turned from the dock to do as he was told.

2.

"Kosaki! My good friend!" Naran beamed.

Captain Kosaki was a true Tigolean of the northern coast. Though taller than most of his race at six feet, he still only came up to Naran's chin. He had shiny, jet black hair that he kept in a long ponytail down his back and a tightly trimmed goatee and mustache. The epicanthic folds of his eyes made it appear as if he could barely open them, but Cor knew he saw everything around him. Even in his warmth with Naran, whom he had apparently known for a long time, he seemed to have a wary bearing, and his muscles looked ready to have him leap into action with no notice at all. Kosaki's ship was a Tigolean runner like Naran's, though longer and narrower. It had arrived under the cover of darkness and moored in a newly available position directly in front of Naran's bow.

The men conversed at length in a bizarre language, seemingly a mix of Western, Shet, and some other tongue, likely Kosaki's own. Cor attempted to follow it with the small vocabulary he'd learned in over two years with Naran, but he found it nearly impossible. After several minutes, the two captains seemed to reach an agreement that pleased them both. They embraced, and Captain Kosaki nimbly climbed over the bow and leapt the short distance to his own ship. Naran shouted for his officers.

"Today is fortuitous!" he announced when they had all formed around him. Naran rarely kept his voice down, and the more excited he was, the louder he became. "My friend Kosaki sails for Katan'Nosh tomorrow. He is here unloading payment for a Loszian lord who will be awaiting him there. It just happens that our next run takes us to the same city! We sail together for safety from pirates."

Loszian Empire? We're sailing to the Loszian Empire? Cor nearly froze to the bone with the thought of it. For two and a half years, he had sailed the coastlines of Tigol with Captain Naran and even back across the Narrow Sea to the West, but never had they business with the dark empire. And now back again in Hichima, Naran sailed directly for Losz. Now fifteen, Cor had worked hard to forget the events that led him to his captain, the events that included strange happenings with strange people, but none as frightening as a Loszian.

The sea made men of boys, Cor learned, and he was no different. He had grown substantially, now closer to six feet than five and learning the ways of the harsh, salty mistress had made his muscles hard and wiry. He was as strong as most other men in Naran's crew and could perform any task aboard the vessel, and Cor often did so with pride. His skin had never browned like the others, always a steady ashen gray. He had even learned some use of a sword.

Cor had been on his third voyage with the Shet captain, a minor affair to be sure, when he had his first brush with combat. A Tigolean alchemist hired Naran to sail to a particular lagoon on a particular part of coastline, and from the jungle there, they would harvest as many of a certain kind of flower as they could find. Captain Naran chaffed at first, the thought of his crew of three dozen hardened sailors picking flowers, but the payment made the task bearable. There was no difficulty in finding the place, and it took only a week or so to reach it.

They had nearly finished the task when a fat Western galleon sailed to the mouth of the lagoon, blocking their exit. At first Naran thought that the alchemist had hired another vessel and crew to do the job or bring back more than Naran's ship could carry. Too heavy to enter the shallow lagoon, the galleon merely waited at its mouth, slowly circling and watching. Naran thought to wait it out, but three days later, the other vessel still waited, and the Shet captain knew he faced privateers.

He decided to make his run at first light, hoping to catch the pirates by surprise. He knew his ship was far faster and nimbler than his opponents, and if he could only manage to get past, they would never catch him. He bellowed orders to the crew to man oars and sail and to the quartermaster to arm every man aboard. Naran told Cor to stay back. When the heavy, dull iron sword was placed in his hand, Cor had never been more scared in his life.

Except for maybe once.

With wind and oar, the ship leapt forward like lightning, making for the far eastern edge of the lagoon's mouth. The pirate vessel was turned the wrong way, and Cor saw its crew working frantically to bring the big, slow ship around. It looked as if they would make it as they passed exactly parallel to the pirates with more speed than Cor had ever seen, the two vessels heading in opposite directions. Cor watched as a half dozen great ballista fired from the other ship's deck, ropes attached to the giant bolts. Some missed altogether, splashing harmlessly into the water, while others bit into man, deck, or hull. The momentum of the two ships pulled the ropes taught, and all this Cor watched in horror as he realized what was about to happen.

The jolt threw Cor and most of both crews to the deck, and he hit the hardwood planks with splinters in bruised palms. The ropes of bolts that had found their mark snapped immediately, but the damage had been done, their momentum broken. Another half dozen ballista fired, and with their target moving much more slowly than before, these all hit their mark, pulling Naran's ship to a complete halt.

"Cut the bonds! Cut the bonds!" Naran screamed, running to aid his men in the task. It was too late as the pirates had pulled alongside and were upon them.

Cor remembered little of his first battle; it wasn't really his battle anyway. He stood stupidly in a corner while he watched men fight and die around him, having absolutely no idea how to use the cold piece of metal in his hand. He watched in fright as a dark haired Westerner came toward him, sword in hand and a wicked grin on his face. The man had not shaved in weeks, maybe months, and his naked torso was browned from the sun and carried several ugly scars. Somehow Cor managed to parry the man's first blow; it was a clumsy defense at best, and the blade was knocked from his hand. The man laughed at this and moved in closer for a killing blow, just as a massive fist carried by an equally massive arm connected with the left side of the man's skull. It emanated a terrific crunch as the man's limp body flew to lay motionless several feet away. Cor tore his eyes from the body to look up on Naran's massive, bloodied form, and the captain shoved Cor into his room.

Cor sat with his arms around his legs, knees up to his chin for some time as the sounds of clanging steel died off into silence. He cautiously opened the door to find that most of the crew lay dead, but more were the bodies of the pirates. Their vessel was several dozen feet off the starboard side, ablaze, and slowly sinking into the deep waters just beyond the lagoon's mouth, while the remainder of Naran's crew tossed the dead offenders overboard to the waiting sharks. Cor stared with horrified fascination at the death around him; blood was everywhere. Naran approached him.

"You have never seen such violence," he said. "This one is a brutal world, boy. You must accept this fact and learn to be of action. He who acts first often dies last."

"I think you should teach me to fight, sir," Cor had said.

"Indeed, but we've won the day, boy! We sail back to port."

Naran himself taught Cor how to fight with a blade, and it seemed that he took naturally to it. He trained daily with a short sword, a weapon of lighter weight and easier to maneuver than Naran's own monstrous two handed saber. Cor had several opportunities to test his fighting skills, and he always managed to come through unscathed. Though, fear always stayed in the pit of his stomach. Naran later told him that it was fear that made men brave; without it they were usually foolish and dead.

Captain Naran paced his deck with an impatience to which he was not accustomed. He rarely agreed to sail with other ship captains, and as such he set his own schedule. Naran preferred leaving port at the moment he saw sunlight, and instead it was halfway to noon before Kosaki's cargo finally arrived. And when he saw it, he swore and spat over the side. Cor came to stand next to the captain.

"Gods be damned! The bastard Kosaki deals in slaves now!" Naran shouted, gesturing his open hand toward the dock.

A lengthy line of perhaps fifty wretched souls made their way across the dock, the first starting up the gangplank to Kosaki's ship. Men, women, and even a few children, the slaves looked filthy and smelled worse. Their ribs projected from their sides, bellies sunken in for lack of proper food, and most had scars of whips upon their backs. Cor could see Westerners and Tigoleans, even a few Shet, and one tall man with skin the color of night.

"That one is from Dulkur far to the east," Naran said, following Cor's eyes. "I will not sail there. It is five or six months, depending on the winds. And you'll be lucky if their rulers do not set you aflame on sight."

"I've never seen slaves before," Cor said quietly. "It's horrible."

"It is and don't forget it," answered the captain. "There is no greater evil than taking the warmth of freedom from a man. It is the only thing I truly have, and the only thing I need in this life."

"The priests of Garod back home told me much the same thing."

"And they were correct in that at least, boy. I live, I sail, and I am free. And I will kill to protect that."

"You won't sail to Dulkur, but you will sail to the Loszian Empire?" Cor asked. At this Naran turned his head to search Cor's face whose eyes were still fixed on the slaves.

"Ha! Fear not, young Cor! The Loszian necromancers would never set foot upon this ship! I fear the sea more than I fear those godless bastards!" Naran blustered and turned toward the deck. "We do not wait for Kosaki to load his 'cargo'. Cast off! We make sail for Katan'Nosh now!"

Cor remembered something of the teachings of the priests at home, and he was fairly certain the Loszians were not godless.

3.

Katan'Nosh was due north across the Narrow Sea from Hichima, a mere ten days sail on a fast ship with an excellent crew. As it turned out, Kosaki's ship was faster, a fact Naran attributed to its narrower design, and Kosaki passed them on the second day, despite a later start. As he came near, Naran made it clear to his friend how he felt about the new business in which Kosaki was involved, and Cor doubted the two would again embrace, at least not any time soon.

The docks in Katan'Nosh were little different from those in the West, but everything had a dark countenance. Instead of oak, sandstone and granite, Cor saw mahogany, basalt, and obsidian. The city's design seemed no different from a Western city, but it felt darker and more dangerous. A great wall of purple stone wrapped around the city and a pair of purple towers stood watch over everything. He saw few people, and most of those walked shrouded in hooded cloaks. Cor shuddered and quickly decided he would not step foot off the ship in this port.

They moored not far from Kosaki's ship, and the entire crew actively avoided interacting with Kosaki and his men. In fact, only Naran and his first mate left the ship at all and only to arrange whatever deliveries and payments were necessary to conclude their business. The entire affair had soured Naran's mood, and he had been dealing harshly with the crew. He wasted no time finishing his business and giving the order to prepare to sail within a day.

"Boy, what does your sight linger on so?" Naran asked with a shout from across the deck at Cor who stood staring across the docks. Naran followed Cor's stare, and it fell on Kosaki and another figure.

"Ah," Naran said, "you have never seen a true Loszian before then have you? Now I know why Kosaki has changed so - conducting business in slaves with a Loszian lord," Naran swore and spat again as he had in Hichima.

The Loszian stood as tall as Naran, but his frame could have been no more than two feet wide, making him appear even taller. His complexion was not so much fair as simply pale white, and Cor could not tell from this distance if he was clean shaven of head and face or purely hairless. He had a long and narrow face, unnaturally so, causing his nose and chin to be thin and pointed. The Loszian wore robes emblazoned with symbols that were black and purple and hid the rest of his form, and he kept his hands tucked within them.

"Come away to my cabin, Cor," Naran said as the Loszian turned his gaze to take a long hard look at them. "It is time that we leave."

They sailed due south to Hichima and lingered for a day before turning east and then south following the coastline of Tigol. It was not the most direct route, but Naran wanted to make a friendly port before starting a long leg of their next journey. The captain watched the horizon behind his ship starting the first day out of Katan'Nosh. He had the sharpest eyes of anyone aboard ship, and if something were to be seen, he would see it. The fourth day out of Hichima, he ordered the ship turned around to the astonished looks of the crew.

"My old friend Kosaki follows us at a great distance, and I will have no more of it," Naran announced. "He follows but does not overtake even with a faster ship. We will go to him and find out why. Men, arm yourselves."

Perhaps if Kosaki had Naran's eyesight he would have realized sooner that his quarry had turned to face him. The two Tigolean vessels crossed the distance between them with such speed that Kosaki had no choice but to continue onward. By the time he realized it, he knew he'd been seen. He had miscalculated, and there was no point in turning back to maintain the ruse. The two ships came upon each other within hours, and they both folded sails to pull alongside with oars. Only a few feet of water separated their decks. Cor noticed the other crew was also armed, and he hoped Naran saw it too.

"Hail, Kosaki! I have watched your scow follow me for over a week. Too much flesh aboard to catch me it would seem. I thought I'd turn about so you could apologize," Naran said, insulting both the man's ship and his pride, which Cor had learned were basically one and the same among ship's captains.

"Naran, we have been friends for a long time. Don't make me end that friendship with a blade. We only want the boy with gray skin," Kosaki returned in a quiet voice that carried easily in the calm wind. Half of Naran's crew glanced at Cor, and some whispered.

"He is of my crew, and not yours to demand," Naran said, his voice dropping to a level Cor had never heard before.

"Naran, be reasonable. He is nothing to you, and there is a Loszian who would reward you heavily for turning him over. On the other hand, you can refuse and make an enemy of the sorcerer, and of me, old friend. Does this make sense?" The edge in Kosaki's voice had softened. Cor had heard merchants use the same tone in negotiations, but Naran only tensed.

"Slavers are no friends of mine, Kosaki! If you want him," Naran yanked his massive, curved blade, "then come claim him!"

Naran leapt across the distance between the two ships and brought his sword down in a great two handed sweep meant to cleave Kosaki in twain from forehead to genitals. Kosaki barely brought his own weapon, a straight Western style longsword, up to defend himself, and the impact knocked him back to the deck. Men from both ships boarded the other, and steel clashed and rang out like thunder.

Cor found himself fighting near his own mainmast, a short and stocky Tigolean attacking him with a pair of long knives. Cor had not truly fought many foes and certainly never one like this. The man weaved under his sword swings and thrusts, rendering them completely powerless. With his intense quickness, he could have struck Cor many times within the first few seconds, but instead used his attacks to back Cor into a corner below decks. With another ineffectual attack from Cor, the man ducked low, and Cor felt his feet fly into the air as his legs were knocked out from under him. His sword dropped, and the Tigolean was upon him. The man straddled Cor's waist, knives still in hand. He struggled, but the Tigolean was stronger. The knives came inexorably closer to be only a few inches from his bare skin.

"Stop fighting," the Tigolean said. Nearly nose to nose with Cor, his breath stank of raw fish. "I don't need to hurt you, but I will if I must."

Naran taught Cor to use a sword, but he also made clear that steel was not a man's only weapon. He knew that, if necessary, every part of the large Shet could be made to kill a man.

Cor didn't think before he acted; he whipped his forehead forward with all the force he could muster and caught the surprised Tigolean right on the point of his nose. Cartilage gave way, blood sprayed Cor's face, and the Tigolean howled, dropping one blade to cup his broken nose. Cor renewed his fight to push the man off, bringing him back to his senses, and in rage, the man brought his remaining knife down with full force into Cor's left shoulder.

Cor screamed as steel pierced his skin and muscle, meeting bone, and he had never felt anything like it, the cold of steel coupled with the hottest fiery pain. He felt his warm blood begin to soak his tunic, and in that moment, feeling the blood that both he and his foe had shed, a strength burst from inside Cor. He suddenly pushed the heavier man off of him, flinging the Tigolean back through the air. The Tigolean's head impacted the ship's inner hull, and he lay still, like a discarded ragdoll. To his credit, the Tigolean never lost grip of his weapon, yanking it from Cor's shoulder.

Cor retrieved the shortsword and plunged it deep into the dazed man's chest. He drove it through flesh and bone and felt both give way as the sword passed through the Tigolean's torso and imbedded into the deck. Cor stood breathing heavy and fast over the short man as the light faded from his eyes. He stood staring for hours, at least it felt that way, as he watched the blood pool, until his breathing finally slowed.

He tried to yank the sword free, but it would not budge from its resting place deep in the deck's planks. Cor felt weak and sank to his knees. He had never fought for his life before, nor had he ever killed a man, and he vomited up his last meal.

After a few more minutes of dry heaving and fighting to catch his breath, Cor picked up the fallen knife and climbed the wide ladder back above decks to find the battle already over. Naran had taken both Kosaki's legs off at the knees, and seeing their captain defeated, most of his crew surrendered. About a dozen men from both ships lay dead, and Naran yelled for his First Officer.

"Staunch this dog's bleeding before he dies," Naran pointed his sword at Kosaki. "Bind the wounded and throw the dead overboard. Kosaki, I claim your ship. Your crew may join me or be thrown to the sharks as well!"

"Cor!" Naran exclaimed as he crossed back to his own vessel. "You are wounded!"

"I…" Cor reached to touch his wound realizing that he no longer felt any pain. The shoulder of his tunic was cut neatly from the knife's blade and soaked with his blood. His fingers lightly touched the smooth skin around his shoulder, finding no wound. "No sir. I think I am fine."

"Good lad."

Kosaki screamed as three strong men held him down, pouring lamp oil over his bleeding stumps; blood had pooled and began to run across the deck toward the rail. His eyes widened in horror as a crewman produced flint and steel and approached. "No!" the Tigolean shouted and pleaded, even until the first spark caught hold and caused the oil to flame. Cor had never heard such a howl as the flesh burned, and the sailors roughly slapped the fire out. But Kosaki no longer bled to death.

Cor turned to see Naran speaking with his first mate outside the door to his quarters. The Shet turned and entered, leaving his officer to supervise the decks. Once everything seemed to be in order, the other officers joined Naran, bringing the half conscious Kosaki and Cor. It took some time to make Kosaki coherent again.

"The Loszian is named Taraq'nok. He's a lord of some power," Kosaki told them haltingly. "I fell in with him last year. He pays well. He asked me to watch for anyone who looks like the boy, skin the gray color of the dead. I arranged to make sure you would have to port in Katan'Nosh so he could see the boy. I was going to follow you until you ported and try to take him in secret. I never intended this."

"I shall kill you for this, Kosaki!" Naran howled.

"No doubt. I am almost there anyway," Kosaki answered unfazed.

"What did the Loszian want with the boy?" Naran asked, his face red with anger.

"I don't know my friend, but he wants him alive."

"Get out and throw this shit over the side to the sharks," Naran ordered, sweeping his hand around the room and pointing toward the door. "Not you, boy."

Cor stopped and turned. As the door to Naran's quarters shut behind his officers, he heard Kosaki screaming again, begging for his life, followed by the faint and muffled sound of a splash. Naran motioned to a chair and waited for Cor to seat himself.

"Boy, tell me who you are."

"I'm no one, sir, the son of a farmer," Cor answered.

"What made you leave home and run to join my crew?" Naran asked softly, his face calm.

"Where do I start?"

"The beginning."

4.

Well into the winter of Cor's seventh year, a massive snow had fallen. Snow was not unknown to southern Aquis, but rarely did this part of the country see more than a few inches at any one time if not over the course of an entire winter. But every so often, a large storm would arrive, and this was one of those times. The snow began falling shortly after the sun rose, and a huge wall of stolid clouds cast a gray light across everything. It began slowly at first, a beautiful light snow that commonly brought joy to children during this season, and as the snow blanketed the ground, parents let their children break from chores and play as they might.

Throughout the morning hours and into midday, the snow fell more heavily with a frigid wetness, and the farmers started to realize that this was not a common snow that would quiet after a short while. They hurriedly went about the tasks of rounding up and provisioning livestock in preparation for an extended stay indoors. The snow continued as the day grew darker, the only sign that the sun was dropping below the horizon, and parents pulled their children indoors before warming fires.

In the evenings of winter, there was little to do, and the storm only added to a feeling of restlessness. It was quiet in Cor's home; he lay on the floor before the fire arranging wooden blocks his father had made for him into the semblance of structures. His mother, as usual, worked on some needlework project or another, while his father sat quietly, no doubt organizing his thoughts for tasks tomorrow, assuming the storm let up. Cor attempted to balance a square block on the point of a triangular block, then stopped to cock his head. Over the

33

crackling of the fire, and the soft sound of falling snow, he thought he heard a horse in the distance. Sitting up, he saw that his father had also heard it, and Pel had stood up to peer out one of the shuttered windows. He shuttered the window again and drifted to the front door, opening it, and half stepping outside.

"For the gods' sake, please close the door," his mother admonished without looking from her work.

"A rider approaches," answered Pel.

Indeed, a hooded rider on a black horse plodded through the snow, which was over a foot deep, the road only distinguishable as a slight depression from the ground on either side. Seeing light spill forth from an open door, the rider turned off the road towards the house and approached slowly. Both the horse and rider were clearly in bad shape. They were exhausted and shivering, and ice and snow clung to them from head to toe, nose to tail.

"Might I stay by your fire tonight? You're the first home I've seen in miles," came a gravelly voice from the hooded figure.

"It is some distance to the village," answered Cor's father. "I couldn't allow you to pass us by. Please put your horse in the barn. You'll find water, feed, and dry bedding for him. Then come in and warm yourself by the fire."

"My thanks to you, kind sir." The rider dismounted and walked his horse to the outbuilding. Pel closed the door to keep out the cold and put another piece of timber on the fire. Erella stood and began warming a broth.

"Father, we don't know him. Should we let him stay here?" asked Cor.

"Don't fear him Cor. He is just a man, and you mustn't refuse help to those in need when you are able to give it. One day it may be you in need of charity."

A few short minutes later, a knock came to the door, and Cor's father allowed the man to enter. He wore a heavy dark wool cloak with a hood and the normal wool tunic and pants with soft riding boots so common to Westerners. Cor's mother bade the man to take off his cloak and hang it by the fire to dry, and he man lowered the hood revealing an aged face, perhaps twice that of Cor's father, with a sparse white beard. His hair was also white, thin, and cropped close to his scalp in a style not uncommon to educated men of the West. Most striking about him was his left eye; it stayed closed while his right was open, and his left eyelid carried a dreadful scar. He unclasped the cloak at his neck and hung it on the indicated hook near the fire.

"I am Portus," he said with a voice like two rocks being ground together, "and again I thank you for allowing me in your home."

Introductions were made, and Portus took a chair, moving it closer to the fire to warm himself. Little was said for some time, and Erella served him a light, hot broth with bread and a small portion of mead. Portus took these with gratitude, offering to pay for the trouble he had caused them, but Cor's parents would hear none of it. As the old man surveyed the room, Cor couldn't help but notice the eye behind the scarred eyelid still moved in coordination. While this made sense, like most children he could not fight the grim curiosity.

"Lad, I was blinded in a smithy when I was younger than your father. That is why I have the scar. The eye is there, but it sees nothing," explained Portus, and Cor hadn't realized he was staring and guiltily turned his gaze to the fire.

"I am not offended, Cor Pelson. I have noticed your oddity as well but choose not to stare as I have seen many oddities in my life," the old man said, noting the boy's gray color, a pallor that never changed.

Significantly warmer and dry, Portus spoke, explaining that he was a merchant of sorts, and that his business had him travel the breadth of the Shining West. He had no set path or destination, and merely went where he felt led. Cor thought little of this, though it clearly seemed odd to his parents, but they allowed their guest to talk as he pleased. They offered little explanation of themselves, as there was no need for any; their life was little different from thousands of others. It grew late, and Cor yawned deeply. His mother had stopped her needlework, and his father was becoming disinclined to conversation. He looked at the stranger and was startled to see Portus staring at him intently.

"I know why I have been led here. It was not clear to me at first," exclaimed Portus, bringing a questioning look from Cor's parents. Then, quite suddenly, the scarred eyelid opened, and the old man stared at Cor with both eyes. The blinded eye was colorless, dead and gray with a horrible rend in it the same size and shape as the scar on its lid.

"This boy is not like you. He is stricken with something you cannot imagine or understand, and he has a destiny to destroy or save. Which path is not clear," he whispered, now looking beyond Cor and into the fire.

Pel jumped from his seat, interposing himself between Portus and the boy, and Erella put her arms about her son, telling him to immediately go to her bed and go to sleep. Cor stood up uncertainly and headed for his parents' bedroom, but the old man's hand shot out and caught the boy as he walked past.

"Leave him be," shouted Pel at Portus.

"No, the boy must hear," continued the old man. "A gray man in steel will come, and you must give your son to him. If you do not, there will be others that come and take him. You must release him wholly to the Dahken and not hope to see him again."

"Release him!" raged Pel. He moved forward to break the old man's grip, and Portus released Cor as quickly as he had taken hold. Erella hurried her son out of the room.

Cor lay down on the bed, barely understanding what was said. All he knew was Portus frightened him, and it was more than the blinded eye. He heard his father shouting at the old man, and Portus replied in a calm, faint voice, though Cor could not understand what was said. The shouting continued for several minutes before being cut off smartly by the slam of the door. Cor heard the muffled protestations of a horse outside, and the sounds of galloping softened by deep snows quickly receded into the distance. His mother then came into the room and held him, crying, until they both fell asleep.

The next morning, Cor asked his parents about the strange old man, wanting to understand of what the old man spoke. He asked why he would have to leave his parents, and it took few questions along this line for Cor's father to tell him to forget about the crazy old man. But Cor was both intelligent and tenacious and wouldn't leave it at that. He ended up with a thorough tongue lashing from his father and spent the next several days sulking indoors because his father would not let him play outside, saying that it was too cold and the snow too deep. Occasionally when his father went outside to check on the livestock or some other chore, he would try to talk to his mother about the visitation. Sometimes she would simply refuse to talk about it or tell him not to speak of it, but other times, she would break out into tears, embracing him.

As the weather warmed a bit, Cor began going outside with his father. He helped where he could and more than once, ended up throwing snow at his father. At times, he was scolded for this behavior, but often his father would reciprocate with laughter. The surreal event never faded from Cor's mind however, and his parents knew they would one day need to answer his questions. They also wanted to teach him more of the pious ways of Garod and explain to him why the sorcery of other peoples was dark and evil and to be condemned. They tried to teach him these things, but found they were unequal to the task. They knew what they knew, but the why of it eluded them.

As winter ended, they spoke to their longtime friend and priest in the village. They explained their concerns and inability to explain things properly to Cor but left out the old man and his cryptic prophecy. Jonn was all too happy to help in Cor's education, saying that few children had such precocious interest in such matters, and that they should be proud of his curiosity. He might even make a fine priest one day. He agreed to teach Cor one day each week for several hours, so long as the boy's mother would bring him to the village temple in the morning and return for him during the afternoon.

The priest found Cor to be absolutely delightful; the boy was happy to converse on virtually any topic. Even at such a young age, he showed an ability to reason, and his vocabulary expanded daily. Jonn read to him from holy scrolls and taught him the values of Garod and the other gods of the West. He explained to Cor that the Western gods were the only true gods, and the others were mythical or charlatans. Cor had difficulty accepting this and argued the point. Surely the other gods were true also, as they endowed their followers with power much like the priests of Garod. The priest gently, but solidly denied this to be true.

Jonn also taught Cor of the great sins of the world. Most of this Cor understood easily; he simply accepted the explanation that certain acts such as murder and killing were evil. Though, slavery was one that Cor could not understand, having never seen or heard of it before. The priest explained to him that slavery was perhaps the greatest sin ever visited upon a people in history. The

Loszians had enslaved the Westerners once, forcing them to serve every whim and desire. Slaves have no will, no desires of their own, and live only to be forced into action by the will of their masters. Nothing is as much an affront in the eyes of Garod as slavery. Cor listened to this, attempting to understand. He had no real point of reference, and the priest hoped that Cor would never truly have to comprehend.

The subject of slavery continued to bother Cor even outside of his studies with the priest, to the extent that he felt a need to discuss with his father that evening while feeding the livestock. He could see his father's naked hostility toward the subject, and Pel could only explain to him that to take another's free will in such a way was appalling and disgusting. Now, Cor knew something of his mother's life before marrying his father, and Cor asked if that was not the same thing. Pel patiently explained that servitude to a noble in such a way was not remotely equivalent; such servitude, while Pel would never enter it himself, was considered a business relationship. Either party could end the agreement if certain conditions were met. His mother's family were paid with a good, if modest home and were able to make a fair life for themselves. Cor accepted his father's explanation, though it seemed to him that the difference was only a matter of words.

Cor grew quickly; he was well over five feet tall by his twelfth summer, and it was on one of these summer days that a rider followed him and his mother home from his lessons. Erella noticed the man on the road behind them, but paid little mind, as he seemed to be keeping his distance. Erella only became sure that he followed them when he passed by their home, then turned around to come back to it. As she saw him coming, she bade Cor go find his father. The man approached the family slowly on his horse, a large black stallion. He was clad in steel plating, breastplate, armguards, sabatons, and legguards, all with a curious blue sheen to them. A shield was strapped to his back, extending out of which the hilt of a longsword could be seen. The man had straight, black, unruly shoulder length hair that he kept restrained merely by a gemmed leather circlet about his head. At first glance, he was clean shaven, but on closer examination, one couldn't be sure he ever shaved at all. A short gray stubble blended with the man's skin, skin gray as a corpse, which could only be seen on his hands and face.

"What do you here, stranger?" Cor's father challenged the man.

"I am Dahken Rael," the man announced as if that answered all questions. They stood in silence for a moment before he continued, "I have traveled far for what I seek, and I was not sure he existed. But now I see I was right. I have come for the boy."

"Be off," Pel commanded, motioning his wife and son behind him with his arm. "He is my son, and no man has claim to him."

"Farmer, this boy is no more your son than I am your father. He is not of you, and there are those who would control the power in his blood. I must show him how to use it," he said in a very matter of fact manner.

"I said be off, Dahken Rael. My son stays with me, and I'll defend myself if I must."

A smile touched the man's lips. "No doubt you will," he said quietly. "I will leave, but know something, farmer. There are those who would take him from you regardless of any fight you put up, and they may not be so respectful of your wishes." He wheeled his horse about and galloped away.

Pel turned and embraced his family. "Tomorrow," he said, "We go to see Jonn. The priest knows more than he would have us believe."

Cor could not sleep that night, every sound pulling at his consciousness just as he may doze off. From the angle of the light coming through his window, he could tell the moon had climbed high into the sky. His mind continued to wander back to Portus; children's memories faded from their mind, sometimes even after only a few years, but Cor had never forgotten the strange and frightening old man. On that winter night years ago, he spoke of a gray man in steel that would come for him. He also said that others would come to take him. Images of "others" came unbidden to his mind, dark shapes of people without detail stealing Cor from his home. They harmed his parents, dragging him from his burning home as he kicked and screamed.

It would not happen. He would leave.

It occurred to Cor that an armored figure on a black stallion watched from far off as Naran's ship left port that first time.

5.

"Will you fuck him, Miri?!" Naran asked the whore boisterously, causing Cor's face to flush.

"I think he is too young, not ready to be a man yet," Miri answered.

She was a Westerner, having left her home years ago to find wealth in Tigol. She had rudely found that she had few talents anyone would pay for, except for one, and that one sailors would pay for mightily. Miri had deep brown eyes and matching long hair that she forced to curl around her breasts. She was generally thin of waist and limb, but buxom and curved in the places that men cared about. She wore a bejeweled brassiere and sheet of gilded sheer fabric that wrapped around her waist, both easily removable. She wore other jewelry as well – gold bangles, rings, a pearl necklace, and silver jeweled tiara. It was all false of course, but her patrons cared little for that.

They had sailed back to Hichima after the battle with Kosaki to port for a few days. Naran spoke at length with Cor on the way back and decided it would be best to take Cor home. Cor needed answers, and he would not find them with Naran on the Narrow Sea; it was time he returned to his parents. Eventually, the Loszian lord would know that Kosaki failed, and more privateers would be sent after the boy. They needed to find that he was no longer with Naran and, hopefully, lost somewhere he wouldn't be found.

Naran decided to have a celebration in a local tavern.

"He's man enough, Miri. I took my first whore when I was younger than he!"

"You Shet," she sighed, "are so very vulgar when you will. All this time, and you have never learned to be civilized?"

"Civilization! Ha! You speak of civilization, and yet I find myself wading through blood amongst civilized peoples. Cor here killed a man with cold steel only a few days ago! Killed him well," Naran said and then continued almost as if to brag, "Only I was strong enough to rip the sword from the deck where it impaled the dog."

"Really?" she asked, perhaps feigning incredulousness. "I'm not sure he is strong enough for that."

"I do not lie, Miri. Does it matter anyway? My coin is good enough for any whore," Naran said as if to end the matter.

"I fuck who I want to when I want to, Naran, not just who has money," Miri said red faced with anger and stormed off.

"Too bad," Naran said wistfully into his flagon. "I'd have paid double for you, my young friend, and the tales of Miri's skills leave men breathless."

Naran slapped Cor roughly on the back, nearly spilling both of their ales. Cor stayed silent throughout the entire exchange and was glad for the way it ended. It wasn't for lack of interest on his part, but rather sheer embarrassment.

They sailed late the next morning, Naran allowing the crew to sleep off the night's revelry; Cor's head pounded. He occasionally drank but never so much, and it seemed pints of ale just continued to appear in his hand. He vomited over the side of the ship at least twice in the early morning hours, and Naran let Cor sleep later than most of the crew. They teased Cor incessantly throughout the day.

"Not quite a man yet," Naran said. "You have to learn to drink like one!"

It was late summer when they arrived. Cor didn't even know the name of the small city, the same in which he had joined Naran's crew, and it had not changed. Naran was not one for goodbyes, and he handed Cor a large canvas bag full of silver coins, claiming it to be Cor's pay. The big man bid him farewell and good luck with a bear hug.

"I will miss you, young Cor," he had said, "But I believe our paths may cross again one day. You know to find me on the Narrow Sea."

Cor endeavored to move quickly; the knowledge that a Loszian lord chased him dispelled any desire to linger. He purchased a horse, only partly to decrease his travel time, but also to replace the one he had stolen from his father's barn. Pondering, he realized that he truly had no idea how to return home, only that he had fled south from his home. But if he could find Martherus, returning home from there would be easy as he'd made the trip with his father many times as a child. Days later when he reached the outskirts of Martherus, he knew exactly where he was and changed direction for home.

Cor spurred his horse to a gallop over the last mile or so near his parents farm. He had no idea what to say to them or where to start, but he knew he wanted to feel his mother's embrace again, see his parents' faces. The place almost hadn't changed at all, but something was somehow different. Everything was where he remembered, and the fields looked as they should for the time of the year. The farm felt subdued, older.

His mother saw him first as he turned off the road toward the small, thatched roof house. She watched as if curious as to the identity of this visitor, and as she watched, recognition came over her face. Her son had grown substantially, becoming tall and his body changing into manhood, especially with the hardships of sailing, but there was no mistaking his face and the obvious coloration of his skin. She held a small wooden bucket that, now forgotten, dropped to the ground spilling water into the dirt. She ran to him screaming for her husband.

When Pel emerged running from his cornfield, an old wooden hoe in hand, he found them kneeling in the dust and dirt holding each other. Cor's mother sobbed loudly, her arms wrapped around her son with fistfuls of his tunic in each hand, afraid to release him lest the illusion suddenly be dispelled. The hoe fell from Pel's hand as he approached the pair, slowing with each progressive step until he stopped, hovering over them. His shadow fell across them, and Cor looked up into his father's face.

"You're back?" Pel asked.

"Yes, father. I've come home. I have a lot to talk about."

"Later, after supper. I still have work to do," Pel said gruffly. He turned and walked back to his field, retrieving his hoe in the process, and Cor could only stare after his father.

"It's been hard on him," his mother said, wiping her eyes. "It's been hard on us both, but your father loves you. It'll be fine. Come inside. I was just beginning to make supper."

His mother listened dutifully as Cor spoke of sailing the Narrow Sea and of the places he had seen. He spoke of the water and the duties and dangers of sailing a vessel, and he prattled on of the differences between Western and Tigolean ships and the people as well. He conveniently left out stories of battle, blood and killing, including his own part in killing a man. He also hadn't mentioned the Loszian lord that clearly wanted him for some design, but he knew he would have to approach it eventually.

"Quite an adventure for a young farm boy," Pel said from behind him. Cor was so wrapped up in his story, he had not heard Pel come in, but he did hear the sardonic tone in his father's voice.

"I guess farming wasn't good enough for you. And what is this?" Pel asked, tapping his boot against the shortsword attached to Cor's belt, and Cor's hand shot to the hilt. He had honestly forgotten about the weapon, so used he was to carrying it; it was the same sword with which he had killed a man a few months ago. Naran had thought it a fit parting gift.

"Sorry father," Cor said, suddenly feeling guilty. "Sometimes you must defend yourself."

"I assume you know how to use it?" his father asked, receiving a slow nod in answer. "Put it in the barn. I will not have it in my home. How long are you staying?"

Cor hadn't expected such a question and as such had no idea what the answer was. "We have things to talk about father. About me," he said.

"Tomorrow around midday it will be too hot to work for a while. We can talk then. Let us enjoy supper in peace," Pel answered.

Throughout the night, Cor started to understand just what he had done to his parents, and guilt came to him with heavy weight. He felt it pressing on him as if he were caught under a huge granite stone like those used to build the massive protective walls found around the large Western cities. Every time he looked at his mother's face, he could see the hurt and the need to understand what she had done to deserve it. There was so much he wanted to say, but he had no way to say it. She looked tired and drawn, and Cor feared he would have to hurt her more before too long.

Pel, Cor's father, showed no such emotion, no signs of how he felt. He remained as impassive as an aged statue.

Cor slept in his old room that night, and it felt huge compared to the veritable closet he'd used on board Naran's ship. His mother kept the room exactly as it was when he had left; it seemed she had even straightened the bedclothes that morning and never again touched anything in the room. Most everything, a bureau, old toys, and small table next to the bed was covered with a fine, thick layer of dust. It made him sad, and he wondered if he could ever make it up to his parents.

Cor woke just before the sun broke the horizon, its rays already turning the sky from black to hues of blue. He found his parents already awake, his father out in the fields and his mother milking cows in the barn. Little was said, but he did what he could to help, taking on whatever chores his mother would ask of him. Cor didn't know how to say how sorry he felt, so instead focused on making himself as useful as possible as if his actions would be their own apology.

Though it was still morning, the day grew hot. Pel had left his fields and busied himself with repairing a damaged fence near the road with the help of his wife. Cor worked in the barn at his mother's request, his father having refused his help, and they had spoken few words to each other all morning. Cor stood at the barn's entrance, taking a momentary break and watched his parents work a rotted fencepost out of its hole several hundred feet away.

A man approached, walking the road from the direction of the village. He had the dark brown hair of a Westerner; long and unwashed, it partially hung over his face. He was above average height with a lanky build, his arms and legs disproportionately long for his six feet in height. The man wore black breeches and soft black boots, both covered in dust from the road, and a gray cotton tunic. Seeing Cor's parents, he walked leisurely toward them, his thumbs hooked into a leather belt. Cor was some distance away, but he could clearly see the man's hands with its abnormally long fingers.

Feeling sudden alarm, Cor frantically retrieved his sword and charged out the door, hoping he could cross the distance in time. His father had stopped his work and turned to talk to the stranger.

"What do you need, neighbor?" asked Pel.

"I'm trying to find a farmer by the name of Pel," responded the man, in a curious accent.

"You have found him, but I'm not hiring hands for a full two months yet."

"Oh fortunately, I'm not looking for employment. I've got that. Farmer Pel, I don't actually seek you, but the boy with gray skin who is your son," said the stranger with his accent that seemed to emphasize words differently. "I see him approaching now. Thank you."

"Go on your way. I've had enough of men troubling my son," Cor's father said, pointing back the way the man had come.

"I'll go about my way once I have the boy."

Pel moved toward the stranger, his mouth open with a forthcoming threat. The man barely flicked his wrist, followed by a gleam of steel flying through the air. Cor skidded to a halt in the dust just in time to catch his father as he fell backward, making a horrific gargling sound. A steel point protruded from the back of Pel's neck, and the steel handle of a small dagger jutted from his throat. His eyes were wide with surprise or fright as he choked and drowned on his own blood that flowed in rivers onto Cor's tunic. Cor fell slowly to his knees, lowering his father to the ground, Pel's head finding his wife's cradling embrace.

"Well, I gave him a chance. But look - he left me a fine woman as well as his son. Too bad I really don't have time to enjoy her," the man said as he slowly came toward them.

Cor leapt to his feet, sword in hand, determined to hack this new foe into bits. He roared unintelligibly as he rushed to the attack. The man reacted with another quick flick of his right hand, and Cor saw the sun glinting off metal just before it impacted his forehead. His forward momentum stopped, and he lost all sense of what was happening, as the man stepped up to him with a clenched fist and knocked him hard to the ground with a punch to the jaw.

Cor lay on the ground, conscious but unable to act, his vision black and purple around its edges. His mother, tears running down her face, took her eyes off her dead husband, first meeting Cor's and then looking up into the sunlight at the blinding outline of their attacker. The man took a fistful of his mother's hair in one hand while running a cruel looking curved knife across her throat. Cor watched a great gout of blood poured from his mother's neck, coloring the ground and the stranger's boots red as it mixed with her dead husband's. It all happened so slowly, but too fast for Cor to will his limbs to move.

"Enough foolishness. You know, I didn't have to kill them. People are just stupid. They don't understand when they don't have a choice," the murderer said, picking up Cor's legs by his ankles to drag him to the barn.

"Let him go Loszian!" boomed a voice. The man looked up and saw a gray faced warrior on a black stallion. He had a longsword in one hand and in the other a shield with a fist sized blue stone set directly in the middle.

"Ah, my master warned me that there may be another!" exulted the man. "Let's make this easy. Come with me. My master would reward me greatly if I delivered not only the boy, but a true Dahken as well. No doubt, you would live like a king in the Loszian Empire. Ride with me."

"The Dahken serve neither your empire, nor the West. We choose our own path," Dahken Rael replied, steel in his voice.

"What we?" the man asked derisively as he dropped Cor's legs and held his arms out from his sides.

"Your people are broken. How many of you are left? The West believes you wiped out completely."

"The boy is leaving with me," Rael said, unfazed.

"I don't think so." He whipped a throwing dagger at Rael in a much practiced maneuver, the same with which he had killed Cor's father.

Unsurprised by the attack, Rael easily batted away the weapon with his shield. He jumped his horse forward, bringing his sword across, parallel with the ground as he passed his adversary. The man deftly ducked the attack just in time, feeling locks of his hair cut free. He turned with his own dagger only to find Rael's sword neatly skewering him from a backhanded thrust. Rael yanked his sword free of the man's belly and brought the sword around to cleave off the man's head. The body tumbled to the ground right next to Cor, blood pouring from the stump of a neck.

Cor struggled onto his side and then to all fours. His head cleared slowly, though it pounded, and every sound raged in his ears. It was similar to the hangover he endured the day he left Hichima for the last time, but far less fun. He touched his fingertips to his forehead, half expecting to find the handle of a dagger, but instead finding only a massive painful knot that was only beginning to form.

"The Loszian threw an iron sap at you. It is a nasty way to stun those who do not protect their head. Are you well?"

Cor tried to stand but found his legs too unstable. He fell back onto his ass, his vision almost clear. He looked around at the bodies of his parents, murdered, their blood merging with the dust and dirt to form red mud. He looked at the headless body of their murderer and felt satisfaction for a moment, replaced by anger that he had not killed the man himself.

"What is your name?" a voice asked him. Cor looked up blinking as if from a dream to see his savior cleaning blood off of his sword.

"Cor, after my mother's father," he replied.

"Cor, I am Dahken Rael, and I am here to protect you and teach you about yourself. This man," Rael pointed at the corpse with his sword, "was a Loszian, an agent of someone who would control you and use you for his own purposes."

"I've seen a Loszian, Dahken Rael," Cor replied. "He did not look like this man."

"There are Loszians, and then there are Loszians," Rael answered vaguely.

Rael dismounted and bent over the body of the Loszian. He pulled from his belt a small utility knife and cut the man's left shirtsleeve clear up to the shoulder and then neck. On the left shoulder was an intricate tattoo, a symbol. Rael carved into the flesh of the shoulder, removing a large flap of skin with the tattoo on it, and he placed it into a saddlebag. He then retrieved Cor's fallen sword and remounted his stallion.

Cor crawled to his parents' bodies, their blood staining his breeches, and sat back on his haunches. He was careful to keep his eyes on their faces. His father, eyes once wide, had apparently died with them closed, and he looked at peace. His mother's eyes were still open and stared unblinking into the sky. Cor softly wept as he reached for her face, closing her eyelids. He didn't know why he did it; it just felt right.

"You must come with me, for others will follow him," came Rael's voice. "I will protect you and teach you how to find your own path. Boy, you must trust me. Look at my hands and my face. See that we are of the same blood and that I only wish to protect you."

Cor stood and turned to stare quietly at this armored man. He looked at the Dahken's hand for a long moment and then placed his own within it. Rael's hand

51

was about the same size as Cor's, and they were nearly indistinguishable from each other. Cor had sailed for over two years and never seen anyone who's skin tone matched his so perfectly that their clasped hands seemed to blend together. It was a sudden and inexplicable feeling that all was as it should be that led Cor to firmly grasp Dahken Rael's hand and climb onto the stallion. In so doing, he caught a glimpse of his mother, lying dead.

"My parents," Cor said numbly.

"There is nothing they can do for you, nor you for them. Your first lesson as a Dahken is that you must embrace death. It comes to everyone eventually, sometimes even the gods." Rael turned his horse around and headed away from Cor's his dead parents and everything he thought he knew.

6.

They rode throughout the day, stopping briefly around midday to eat jerky and somewhat stale bread. In the afternoon, they turned off the road and headed cross country to the south, and they continued until the sun disappeared over the horizon, which was late this time of year. Cor was certain they had traveled a good many miles, and he had of course never seen this part of Aquis. They made their camp near a small stream and dined on yet more jerky and stale bread. Rael refused to make a fire for cooking, saying that they didn't need the warmth at night this far south, but Cor somehow thought he had other reasons.

The next day, they hadn't yet stopped for lunch when Cor finally felt the impact of what happened. He had seen violence and blood, and he'd killed a man not too long ago. But never had Cor imagined seeing those he loved so brutally slain before his eyes, and he was powerless to prevent it. He began to cry.

"What is wrong?" Rael asked without even looking at him.

"I want to go home," sobbed Cor in response.

"At points in life, we all want to go home. It is not possible for you," Rael said, making no apologies.

Cor quieted and forced his weeping to stop, but it blended into a coughing attack, one of the worst he had had in a long time. The mix of coughing and crying kept him from talking anymore, and he bent over in the saddle, coughing blood into his hand. Rael put a hand on Cor's shoulder to steady him. Eventually, the coughing passed as it always did.

"I remember you," Cor said after some time. "You came to our home a few years ago."

"Yes, and that night you ran away," Rael responded. "I realized too late that you had left. I tried to follow you, but I was too far behind."

"I saw you at the docks when Naran's ship sailed out."

"Cor, I am taking you somewhere safe," Rael said, ignoring the observation, "and I will teach you how to use the power in your blood. When you are ready, you may go where you wish, return home and become a farmer should you decide."

"Who sent the man who killed my parents?" Cor asked.

"I do not know, but the mark I removed from his shoulder is the mark of the Loszian lord he serves. I will find out, but one must be careful with such inquiries. What will you do when I find out?" he asked Cor.

"I'll kill him," he replied quietly.

"I am sure. Vengeance is normal, human, but it is also dangerous."

"The priests told me vengeance is a sin," said Cor, "that Garod doesn't recognize revenge against those who have wronged you."

"And yet," answered Rael, "they think nothing of waging war with Losz and slaying its people. Would you have killed that Loszian?"

"Yes," Cor replied quietly.

"Have you ever killed a man?" Rael asked.

"Yes, a few months ago. My captain took us to Katan'Nosh. I saw a Loszian there, and he saw me. He sent another ship to chase us down, to take me back to him. We fought."

"You should assume that the man who murdered your parents was an agent of the same Loszian. If he is a lord, he is also a sorcerer," Rael said, his voice somewhat distant as he thought. "So, your travels across the Narrow Sea have made you a man of action, but it is more important that you are educated so that you know what action you should take."

"The Loszian sorcerers are charlatans, worshipping evil and untrue gods, aren't they?" asked Cor after a few minutes of silence.

"What you believe is what most Westerners are taught to believe. The truth is there are no charlatans, no untrue gods. All the gods exist, some are evil, some are good, but they all exist. When we reach Sanctum, I will teach you all these things."

"Is Sanctum a city?" asked Cor.

"No, at least not anymore," answered Rael, "but it is where I live. It is where you will live while you come to understand who you are. Beyond that, your path is your own choice."

They did not stop for lunch; on their way, they passed a grove of wild apple trees, and Rael picked a sizable number of the fruits. They ate while continuing to ride. They rode for two more days, and Cor detected the faint, familiar scent of the sea in the air. Gulls and other birds floated above on the currents, making their welcome cries. The land here seemed somewhat rocky, and the dirt had a sandy quality to it. They topped a hill, and Rael pointed into the distance.

"Sanctum," he said.

Cor looked in the direction indicated and saw a crumbling stone edifice eclipsing the setting summer sun. It was a small castle, gray with age, with a crumbling outer wall that was completely breached at one point, and the keep and tower did not seem to be in much better condition. The castle had no wall on two sides, as it was perched on a rocky promontory overlooking a cliff. Beyond the cliff stretched the Narrow Sea.

As they approached, they joined a disused road that came from the north and lead straight to the castle. Cor heard great splashes of water sounding in the distance as they climbed the steep hill leading to the castle's gate, waves breaking on nearby surf. A rusted portcullis lay to one side just past the portal; it was so ancient and weather beaten that the iron bars seemed to be literally dissolving. They dismounted inside the curtain wall, and Rael led his horse to one side to let the animal graze while he filled a trough with water from a well. The buildings inside the wall looked little different from the outside; they were mostly stone and dilapidated, and none of them had intact doors.

"Cor," Rael called from the well. "Look around carefully, but do not go into any of the buildings without me. Most of them are dangerous."

Cor walked the grounds warily, not going near any of the buildings. Besides the keep and its tower, he counted six, none of them exceptionally large. As he made his way through the yard, he found a stone wall roughly two feet in height wrapping around the back of the keep, and as he approached it, he realized he was looking over a vast blue body of water.

"I suppose you are used to the sea, more so than me. When we have some time, I will show you how to reach the beach and the water," Rael said, causing Cor to jump as he had no idea the man had come up behind him. "Cor do not go very close to that wall. It is old and waiting to crumble. Follow me inside, and I will show you where you can sleep."

He led Cor to the stone keep, but they entered through a small door in the side of the building rather than the large double doors at the front. Rael explained the front of the keep was not safe, and he also warned Cor to never venture upwards into the tower. During horrific storms that occasionally made landfall, the tower often sounded as if it may crash down at any moment. He showed Cor the larder, where he may help himself to any food or drink he found there, and several other rooms, including a large study. The study was full of books and scrolls, many of them obviously ancient with dust, and a large oak table stood in the middle of the room on a silk rug that crumbled as it was tread upon. On one side stood a large stone fireplace that clearly had been used more recently than most of the castle.

"If you are hungry," said Rael, "help yourself to something to eat. Can you read Rumedian?"

"What is Rumedian?" Cor asked; he had met many peoples in his years at sea, but never a Rumedian.

Rael sighed, "You can read Western, yes? Good, I have to find some volumes for you."

Cor watched as Rael moved about the shelves and decided to head to the pantry while the man looked through them. The room was rather cool and the air dry, and he found it well stocked with aged cheeses, preserved meats, a random assortment of fruit, and stale bread. He chose some of this at random, ignoring the barrel of apples; he felt like he had eaten a hundred apples in the last few days, and he returned to the study, food in his arms.

"Please eat in the larder," Rael said without looking up. "At the least, do not bring food or drink into this room. The texts in here are too old and valuable to risk exposure to an accidental spill."

After eating, Cor returned to the study to find Rael waiting for him. He had selected several tomes and set them in a stack, and he was writing on blank parchment.

"Do you know what a Dahken is?" Rael asked without looking up from his writing.

"No."

"In the days before The Cleansing," Rael said these last two words with no small degree of bitter sarcasm, "you would have been found years ago. There is much for you to learn, and we will start tomorrow, but now let me show you where you will sleep."

He took Cor to a small room. It contained two buckets, one of which Rael filled with water, a candelabra with three new candles, and a cotton mattress. There were several folded wool blankets next to the mattress, and a rug made of animal skins covered most of the floor. All of these contrasted their age sharply with the ancient castle.

"I know it is not late, but the last few days were hard. Get some sleep, Cor."

Rael turned and left the room. Cor sat down on the mattress, finding it quite soft, and looked around the room blankly, and he lay back slowly, the cotton mattress wrapping itself around him. He knew he should feel something, anger, or sadness perhaps, but he didn't even understand how this had all happened. Cor drifted off to sleep, and on some level, he expected to wake up in the morning to his mother's face. Unfortunately, he didn't.

Palius' hands shook as if with palsy as he read the dispatch from Jonn via the lead administrative priest in Martherus. They found the boy through amazing luck within days of his birth; of course, the Queen Herself and many of her highest priests praised Garod. They had him watched closely and even became directly involved in his education at his parents' request. And then he had disappeared, run away it seemed, having boarded a seagoing vessel from Tigol. The priest, Jonn, had just received word that the boy, now almost a man, had appeared near home. Jonn decided to call on the boy's home in the early afternoon and found the boy's parents murdered along with another dead man, who was perhaps a Loszian. The man had a strange wound on his shoulder, as if he had been skinned there, and a gaping sword wound clean through his midsection, not to mention that he had been decapitated expertly. The boy's parents had been killed with daggers the likes of which the headless man carried, so he surely had been the murderer. Who killed the killer? Where was Cor?

Palius knew that this entire matter would chase him into his grave.

Jonn immediately sent word to his superior in Martherus, who then sent his fastest rider with the authority to commandeer the Queen's horses. Garod's priests had no way to communicate through their god's power, and the West had long found birds to be unreliable. To resolve this issue some time ago, Aquis invested a large amount of money in certain highways connecting all the West's capitals and many of its main cities. Outposts were placed at key points along these roads, allowing a rider with the proper authorization to ride his horse near to death and switch to a fresh horse at an outpost.

Palius pinched the bridge of his nose in thought as he stalked the halls of the palace headed for his queen's chambers. She hadn't held court or audience today, preferring to tend to the more mundane matters of ruling from her desk. He entered her chambers without a knock or introduction from the guards; as her highest advisor, Palius always had unrestricted access to Queen Erella. Often, his information could not wait for etiquette, and he found her seated at her desk, leaning against the plush high backed chair. He dropped his hand from his nose in consideration of her as her eyes were closed, and she looked at peace.

"Palius, you are the only person allowed in these rooms without so much as a knock," she said, startling him as she opened her eyes. "So, I know you do not do so without reason."

"I am sorry, Majesty. I was not sure if I should disturb you."

She laughed mirthfully at this. "You weren't sure I was alive you mean. Do not worry; I live through the grace of Garod, and I live as long as he needs me to serve."

"Yes, My Queen," Palius answered automatically, having never been one for religion or mysticism. "I have most disturbing news." Palius summarized the most recent information from Jonn, including his own conclusions he had drawn from the obvious evidence, and he watched as Queen Erella's expression changed dramatically to one of exhaustion.

"I have already dispatched rangers to track anyone who may have taken the boy, but I doubt their ability to help. It has been several days since this happened; the likelihood of them tracking the boy's abductor at this point is slim," Palius concluded.

"We must find him," Queen Erella almost whispered.

"Finding him means finding his abductor. What can we divine about him? He is clearly a trained fighting man; he killed the Loszian with apparent ease. The wound is from a double edged longsword, a common weapon used by all of the peoples across this continent. He obviously isn't a Loszian, which makes him a Westerner or Northman," Palius paused.

"We must also consider that he may be a mercenary looking to collect a Loszian bounty, a man with no real loyalty to anyone," said the queen.

"Yes," agreed Palius, "that's very possible. He let the Loszian do the real work of finding the boy, then slew him and took the boy back to Losz himself."

"Is it possible," the queen met Palius' eyes, "that he was taken by another Dahken?"

"My queen, I see no reason for such a conclusion. The Dahken have been dead for over five hundred years since The Cleansing. No one, *no one* made mention of another," Palius answered.

"They worship a blood god, Palius. They are said to spring from him at any time," she countered.

"Majesty, the Dahken were known for their magic, and there was no evidence of any foul sorcery where the child's parents were found. Besides, if the Dahken still existed, I think we would have seen some evidence. I don't think they could continue to hide their existence for so long a time," reasoned Palius.

"Perhaps," Queen Erella said quietly, closing her eyes.

7.

Cor awoke on his own shortly before dawn, and he wandered out of his small room to find Rael in the larder. The man had already set a number of things out on the table, and Cor sat without saying a word, taking a small share of the food and eating quietly.

"I am not one for niceties, nor am I much for etiquette," Rael said, sitting down. "I am sure it comes from my limited contact with other people over the last number of years.

"Certainly, you know that you are different from other Westerners. Your coughing and the color of your skin are symptoms of this. You are of a race called the Dahken. I know your parents were Westerners, but that means nothing. Dahken are magical, our blood is imbued with power by the god Dahk."

"The priests of Garod say magic is evil," Cor stated, repeating what he had been taught for years by his parents and the priests.

"Of course, they do. Magic threatens them," Rael answered. "But you see, magic comes from the gods. The priests of Garod practice magic, but they call it prayer, divine power, miracles. It is no different. Yes, the Western gods are innately good, just as the gods of Losz are innately evil, but the truth of how the gods work in the world through magic is not taught to Westerners."

"Who is Dahk? I've never heard of him."

"Dahk," Rael proceeded slowly, "is the God of Blood."

"So, you worship a god of evil?" Cor asked. The very idea made him gaze upon Rael aghast.

"I worship no god, nor is Dahk a god of evil. The gods do not need our worship, and exactly how they choose who among us wield their powers is unknown to us. As I said, Dahk is the God of Blood; all men, good and evil, have blood. It is how you use your power as a Dahken that makes you good or evil. It has no reflection on Him."

"So, I can use magic?" Cor asked, puzzled.

"Not so much in the sense of the word as you understand it," replied Rael patiently. "Much of our power is innate, constantly in existence. We do not call on a god to use our powers as the priests of Garod or sorcerers in Losz do. The power is there, and you must simply know how to tap into it. Some of our powers are universal to all Dahken, while others are not. You will have to discover which powers you have on your own. But there is something about you Cor; I have never felt another Dahken as strikingly as you."

"What does that mean?"

"Do not concern yourself with that too much for now. Let me just say, it is how I came to find you, and how I knew you had returned to the West," Rael explained. "It is why you came with me. Our power comes from our blood, and it sometimes tells us what we should do."

After breakfast, they returned to the study where Cor took a chair. Rael handed him a parchment scroll tied with a single silk cord.

"Begin with this," he said.

"What is it?" Cor asked without untying it.

"It is a brief history of the West by the Chronicler. When you are finished, find me outside."

I will not speak of Rumedia prior to the rising of the gods we know. Some of us know civilization existed prior to our gods, but we have no direct record of it.

However, here are signs of the ancients; their tombs and even parts of their cities may be found by a stroke of luck in the dark places of the world. We do not know what happened to those people or their gods, for their gods were not ours. Our gods themselves do not know how they rose to divinity, or at least, they do not reveal their path to us. When they came to be gods, the world was populated with tribes of men with no real civilization to speak of, but they learned to use tools and build rudimentary homes. The Greater Gods watched and decided to each select a people to make theirs.

Hykan, god of fire, and the other elemental gods chose a bronze skinned race in the center of Dulkur, the eastern continent. This land of great jungles and deserts was horrific and untamed, much like the elementals themselves, and they taught these people how to use magic of fire, lightning, and other elemental forces. None of the other gods wanted anything to do with that land, and the godless tribes quickly fell into servitude when faced with their conquerors' magic.

The scholars among the gods took the southern continent, Tigol. They wanted little to do with the others, who were sometimes infantile in their competition, and endowed their peoples with a magic altogether different. They gave these people science, technology, and mathematics, and while they knew that knowledge would eventually filter to other parts of the world, their people would always be the most advanced in the world.

Urso, the Great Bear and God of the Wild and the Hunt, took the peoples who would form the Northern Kingdoms, as they were large and hardy like him. With His presence, the tribes of the north coalesced into a hierarchy led by shamans and great warrior chiefs. Three distinct clans arose to eventually become the Northern Kingdoms.

And Garod, King of the Gods of Light, chose the people we now know as Westerners. A pragmatic lot, they easily adapted to whatever a situation called for, and they spread quickly and easily across the western continent and even established trade with the peoples of Tigol. This gave the Westerners the knowledge of iron and then steel, which they used on several occasions to war with Urso's people of the north. The Bear's people fought terrifically, and even armed with steel, the Westerners simply were not prepared for the ferocity of such wars. Eventually, an easy truce emerged between the two civilizations.

There is yet one Greater God that has gone unmentioned, and that god is Dahk, God of Blood. Dahk did not choose a people to empower; his power was necessary for life to take hold at all, and in many ways, he felt that all the people in the world were his. Sometimes, a child would be born to apparently fall ill to an unknown sickness, and if the child survived, it would eventually take on an unnatural gray pallor, regardless of its natural skin color. Dahk realized that he had inadvertently created his own chosen race, and he revealed himself to one such man. Dahk taught him of the power his blood contained and beseeched the man to find others of his kind, and as such, a race of warriors called the Dahken was born. I should relate the rest of their history in another writing.

The Western calendar starts at year one, Before Cleansing (abbreviated B.C.) with the establishment of a great city that would one day become Byrverus. In one thousand B.C., give or take a few centuries, a great meteor smashed into the eastern part of the continent. It created a permeating darkness, a cloud of ash and dust that settled over nearly half of the land. This meteor brought with it something terrible, and before then the world hadn't known true evil. A new pantheon of gods emerged from the rubble, and those people too near the center were immediately changed, twisted into alien imitations of themselves, tall and gaunt, limbs and joints

65

stretched. They found they wielded great powers of necromancy, control over the dead, the ability to cause death, famine, and plague. The Loszians had arrived.

The West, caught in panic and disarray, had no defense against these sorcerers. The Loszians displayed magic the likes of which the Westerners had never seen, and while Garod's power was equal to the power of the Loszian gods, his people were not ready for an invasion of such terror. The Loszian necromancers enslaved living and dead Westerners alike and swept unstoppably across the continent. Garod's people were forced to flee to the south to Tigol or keep their worship hidden as they toiled to build huge purple and black towers. The Loszian sorcerers were cruel, taking what they wanted and discarding it as quickly. Many of them learned they could breed with the Westerners, creating another class between them and their slaves, and many Westerners also realized the social value of breeding with their masters.

The North remained free for the most part, not for lack of trying by the Loszian Empire. The Loszians found the northern peoples to be indomitable. Certainly, they could conquer portions of the Northern Kingdoms, but even their necromancers couldn't defeat the harsh winters and alpine conditions for long.

The Loszians also learned to leave the Dahken in their strongholds. The Dahken were content to allow the Loszians to conquer as much of the world as they wanted, so long as the Dahken remained free. They met on the field of battle only once, when two hundred Dahken faced three thousand Loszian soldiers, undead servants, and necromancers. The Loszians found almost immediately that their dark sorcery had little to no effect on their foes, and being so reliant on magic, the Loszian soldiers could not contend with an organized and fearless enemy. Combined with the Dahken's own unique blood magic, the Loszian host was absolutely slaughtered. The Dahken returned to their enclaves, and the Loszians let them.

By roughly fifteen hundred B.C., the Loszian Empire reigned supreme over the West. The Westerners never gave up hope and put their faith in Garod, who chaffed greatly at his chosen people being trodden upon. The Loszians lived in evil decadence on the backs of His people. Contrary to many people's beliefs, the gods are not all powerful, nor may they easily affect the lives of mortals. They can make minor impacts by sending visions, bestowing minor blessings and the like, but to make a major change in the world requires them to save up much of their power and loose it at the proper time.

In the year 2994 B.C. this happened. Garod instilled into one unborn child all his strength and power. This child was born knowing of his divine link with Garod, and while he was but a child, he could perform healing miracles of the utmost power. Word of this boy spread quickly, bringing both pilgrims who would follow him and Loszians who would slay him. His name was Werth, and he wielded great powers bestowed on him by Garod; he could heal horrendous wounds and illnesses, even giving life back to those who had just recently died. Loszian sorcery had no effect on him, and through Werth, the West regained its pride and strength. He showed others how to recognize the power of Garod within themselves, and in 3028 B.C. the Westerners launched a holy war against the Loszian Empire, which became known as The Cleansing. The Loszians, though powerful in their sorcery were weak in their decadence, and the empire was not prepared for a massive uprising led by a peasant who wielded awesome and divine powers. In just seven years, the people of Garod had freed a full half of the continent. The Loszians had finally shaken off their fugue and consolidated their power on the eastern half of their empire, and nearly three more years of warfare continued. The remade west, now called the Shining West, held its own, but could make no more headway against the empire.

In the final confrontation, two great hosts faced each other across a flowing plain. Werth, wanting to avoid the massive carnage that would be wrought by a full battle, directly challenged the Emperor of Losz, who was certainly the most powerful of all the necromancers, and the two hurled the power of their gods at one another, meeting in a titanic collision. It dawned on Werth that neither combatant could hope to defeat the other, and he ceased fighting and allowed the necromancer's evil power to wash over him. Werth absorbed the Loszian's power, allowing it to fill his being, and in one final effort, he channeled all of the dark sorcery and the power of Garod directly into the ground below. The ground shook as none had ever felt and split asunder as huge peaks plunged upward, and the two armies fled in horror and confusion as both the priest and necromancer were swallowed by a great crevasse. The World's Spine was born, a scarred mountain range running north to south, fully separating the Shining West and the Loszian Empire.

The next day marked the beginning of year one A.C., After Cleansing. The Westerners tore down all remnants of Loszian power, every purple tower, and every black temple of darkness, and using the knowledge they gained under the whips of the Loszians, they built their own cities and temples to Garod. One large country, Aquis, emerged with three small neighbors. No peace was ever declared between the Shining West and the Loszian Empire, but no large scale war continued. Skirmishes and battles occurred, but neither side ever committed to a full scale invasion. The West thrived in relative peace and prosperity.

Cor set the scroll down; he had many questions about what he read. The priests had never described any of this history to him, not about the gods, the arrival of the

Loszians, The Cleansing, none of it. No doubt Rael could answer his questions or point him to scrolls and texts that would, so he stood up from the table and made his way through the rooms he and Rael occupied. He walked outside into the courtyard and found it to be a beautiful sunny day. It was quite warm, but there seemed to be a constant strong breeze off the ocean, carrying with it the familiar scent of sea air.

Rael was outside, organizing an assortment of weapons and other combat paraphernalia. Cor saw swords of assorted sizes, axes, and several bludgeoning weapons the names of which he wasn't aware. He also saw a variety of shields, ranging from small wooden discs a mere ten inches across to huge steel monstrosities clearly meant to cover the entire body.

"What year is it Rael?" he asked.

"Seven thirty six A.C." Rael answered, turning to face Cor. "You did not know?"

"No, I didn't. Well, I didn't know any of what I just read."

"I am not surprised," Rael commented, scratching his chin. "What you know was taught to you by your parents and by Garod's priests. They conveniently leave out most facts, and I am not even sure most of the priests know the real history anymore."

"I want to ask you some things," Cor said, chewing on a fingernail.

"Of course, but how long has it been since you have wielded your sword?"

"A couple of months at least."

8.

"Combat training," Rael began, "is an excruciatingly long process. Fortunately for me, most of the hard work has been done, but I also have to teach you how to use the power in your blood. First, you must select a weapon."

"But I have a sword," argued Cor, confused.

"Yes, but it may not be the right weapon. You must choose the right weapon."

Cor stood in front of the weapons racks, staring at them uncomprehendingly. Many of them were ancient swords and rusted axes, their edges dulled by time. The bludgeons were bizarre to him, but their use obvious, for there was little question for what a spiked ball at the end of a long handle or chain was meant. The shortsword Naran had given him stood amongst the other weapons; it was plain but clean, sharp and in good repair.

"Rael, I don't understand what I'm supposed to do," Cor said, again chewing on a fingernail.

"Stop thinking about it. In fact, close your eyes and let yourself be guided to one."

Cor sighed quietly, truly not understanding why Rael didn't let him use his sword, but he closed his eyes obediently and simply stood there, trying not to think about the weapons he knew were arrayed in front of him. He noticed an odd sensation in his chest, almost as if there were a string attached to his heart and someone was pulling the other end ever so slightly. Cor stepped forward and then turned slightly to the left, held his right hand out and opened his eyes as his palm settled around the hilt of a longsword. He hefted it off the rack, finding it lighter than he expected. It was old and rusted like the other weapons, and it had a single dull edge.

"Why did you pick that one?" asked Rael.

"I don't know," said Cor, looking at the blade. "It was like someone led me to it."

"That is good," encouraged Rael. "Your blood will call you to things, items, weapons and even people. That is how I found you. You must learn to listen to it. At times, it will lead you to objects that will amplify your strength and power."

"I like my other sword better," Cor said doubtfully.

"Only because it is familiar. You have only begun to feel your power, and you do not trust it. Be patient."

They spent most of the day drilling, allowing Rael to test Cor's skills. He found Cor was indeed an adequate swordsman, clearly taught by one forced to innovate as opposed to any distinct style. Rael found a small wooden shield and strapped it to Cor's left forearm. It was not important that Cor learn to use it now, but only to feel and become accustomed to its weight. They practiced for hours, and after, Rael showed him how to begin cleaning the rust from the sword and sharpen its blade.

That evening, over supper, Rael decided to answer some of Cor's questions. Rael lorded over a pot containing a sort of beef stew, tossing various spices in as he went. He tasted it occasionally, but somehow Cor thought it would likely taste the same no matter what the man added to it.

"Who is the Chronicler?" asked Cor. "You mentioned him when you handed me the scroll."

"The Chronicler is an immortal," answered Rael. "I do not know where he lives, and I doubt there are any who do. The gods gifted him immortality and sight in exchange for recording history."

"So, he could be watching us now?"

"I am not sure, but I think everything is history to him. It is not as if he is using sorcery to spy upon us, he simply sees it all as if it had already happened," Rael said, stirring at the stew which was taking on a burnt odor. "Though, I could be wrong. The Chronicler has been known to make contact with mortals from time to time.

"I must teach you to at least read Rumedian, perhaps speak it. Rumedian is the language of the gods and of the Chronicler."

"I have never met a Rumedian," Cor said, repeating aloud a thought he'd had earlier in the day.

"Yes, you have. We are all Rumedians. The gods call our world Rumedia."

"Why did the Dahken not join the war against the Loszians?" Cor asked, switching subjects.

"There is a history of the Dahken that I will have you read, but the short of it is that it was not our war," answered Rael, scooping stew into a pair of wooden bowls.

"But the Loszians attacked the Dahken once?"

"Yes, and they paid for it dearly," Rael replied as he placed the bowl in front of Cor. "The Westerners had never wanted anything to do with us before, so we did not feel a need to be involved." They ate in silence, Cor organizing his thoughts. He would wait until after Rael was finished to continue with his queries. It was all still somewhat surreal, as if he found himself in a world completely different from the one in which he was a child.

"When we got here," continued Cor, "you called his place Sanctum. What exactly is it?"

"It is the Dahken stronghold in the Shining West. We had one in Losz and a few in other parts of the world."

"Something happened to the Dahken after The Cleansing, didn't it?"

Rael's eyes met Cor's and he paused before answering. When he did, it was by way of a question. "Why would you say that?"

"Well," Cor felt a familiar discomfort; when he was a child Jonn would occasionally pose a question that would make Cor feel like he was being tested. "This castle is falling down, and it doesn't seem like much of a stronghold. There's no one here except us. I've never seen any other Dahken, and you don't talk about them. How many are left?"

"I do not know," answered Rael, his voice a barely audible whisper. "It has been a long time since I have seen another, and you are the first I have sensed in the West." Cor watched Rael's face as he spoke. The man seemed suddenly old and tired.

"Rael, how old are you?"

"Boy, you are terrifically perceptive," he replied loudly, causing Cor to flinch a bit. "No, I meant it as a compliment, though you must be careful with such a skill. To answer your question, I am one hundred and sixty three years old. I was born in the spring of five seventy three A.C."

"Are Dahken immortal, like the Chronicler?"

"No, but once we reach maturity, our aging slows immensely. If you do not die with a sword through you, you may very well live to see three or four hundred years. Look, no more of this tonight. Tomorrow, after breakfast, I will have you read of Dahken history in the West, and that should answer some of your questions," Rael stood from the table. "I must attend to my horse. Please clean up."

Rael stalked away, leaving Cor simply staring after him. He knew he had asked Rael a disturbing question, and he had no doubt it had to do with the absence of Dahken at this supposed Dahken stronghold. He cleared the table and cleaned the pot with some well water before returning to his room. Cor sat on his bed for a few moments, resting his head in his hands, but he wasn't tired exactly. His body was exhausted, and his right arm throbbed. But he couldn't seem to quiet his mind as questions and a burning desire to understand filled his thoughts.

Taking his candelabra, Cor stood and made his way towards the study. He stopped at the doorway, looking down the hall that continued into the darkness. Curiosity came unbidden, and knowing he shouldn't, he continued down the hallway another two dozen paces until he stopped at another doorway. A gaping maw led down a dark stairway into blackness below. The curiosity tugged at him, and the stairway seemed to beckon him downward in a most frightful way. He turned and sprinted back to the study's doorway, slowed as he reached it and turned to look back down the hallway, certain that something followed him. All but one of his candles had gone out.

Cor entered the study, breathing deeply once to clear his nerves. He set the candelabra down on the table, careful to make sure no wax would drip onto the tomes and relit the other candles. He took the scroll that he knew he was to read next – more history, that of the Dahken. He opened it, realizing it was penned in the same hand as the one he read that morning, and the parchment appeared relatively new. Before settling to read, Cor wondered briefly if Rael had translated these from other older texts.

As Chronicler, one finds there are countless subjects and moments in history that must be recorded at some point and discussed with some detail. The emergence of the Dahken as a race is one of these topics, and you will find their history summarized in the paragraphs below. The Dahken first came into being as a race in what is now known as the Shining West, and that is where most of their history is centered. Certainly, they have had a historical impact on the other continents of the world, but I will reserve those stories for other texts.

Around five hundred B.C., the god Dahk manifested to a Westerner named Tannes, appearing before the man as a great iron fountain, bubbling and gurgling enormous amounts of blood. Dahk bade Tannes drink from the fountain so that he may gain full knowledge of what he was. Tannes had no desire to drink of the blood, but he was overawed by the pure power of divinity. Slowly, but deliberately, he lowered his hands into the pool at the base of the fountain and brought them forth again, cupped, blood trickling between his tightly closed fingers. The blood tasted no different from his, and as he forced himself to swallow, he felt as if he had been struck by lightning. He threw his head back, howling in pain as thousands of images filled his mind at once. Stars exploded in his vision and then went dark as he lost consciousness.

When Tannes awoke, his head and body throbbed with soreness. He sat up slowly, beginning to make sense of everything he had seen, and he understood why he was different from other Westerners. He also knew there were more like him, and he must find them. Tannes was deeply aware of the power that coursed through him, power that all Dahken would have if they were only awakened to it, and it was his task to help them find it. He knew Dahk would not be able to aid him, having exhausted much power appearing before him in such a way.

Tannes set about finding more of his race; he found their blood was drawn to each other, which allowed him to find them easily, so long as he went where he felt led. Some he found as newborns, others as children or adults, and many were outcasts. Westerners feared and shunned them, and in the north, where their condition would be seen as frailty, many were killed as babes, left to die in the icy snows. Tannes taught them how to unlock the power within, though some had discovered some small part of it on their own. As they grew more powerful, he bestowed on them the title of Dahken, and they came to call him Lord Dahken.

They built a small castle, complete with wall, keep, and tower on the southwestern coast of what is now Aquis and called it Sanctum. Sanctum would be the center of the Dahken, home, and refuge to all. Here new Dahken would be brought to learn their power and train, and those who died would be laid to rest below.

It became clear to Lord Dahken Tannes that more such castles would be needed. After all, Dahken could be born from parents of any race of the world, and he selected his most powerful six, gifting them with the title of Lord Dahken; their names were Drath, Xalta, Yorina, Baen, Keldin, and Noth. All were set with the task of establishing a castle like Sanctum in other, distant parts of the world. Drath was sent into the north, Xalta and Yorina to the southern continent of Tigol. Baen and Keldin set out for Dulkur across the eastern ocean. Noth went with the latter two but did not join them in crossing the ocean; instead, he stayed to build a castle in what would become the near center of the Loszian Empire.

The Lord Dahken discovered in other parts of the world the same fear and mistrust they were accustomed to in the West. Baen and Keldin found their situation particularly difficult, as it seemed in Dulkur it was widespread practice to kill those who turned to Dahken immediately. Apparently, the elemental gods warned their sorcerers some years ago, and the rulers of that land would not risk anything that threatened their power. As it was, the two Lord Dahken, who had originally planned to establish two separate citadels on opposite ends of the continent, were forced to stay together for each other's strength, and they built their stronghold deep in the jungles of Dulkur.

Drath found he did not care much for the north; the weather was extremely cold and inhospitable, much like the people who lived there. They watched him with great suspicion, and he was forced to stay hidden much of the time. In the first few years, he found only two grown Dahken, and he had limited time to find any newborns. The northmen did not recognize the condition as anything other than sickness and often left the babes to die. Even when he did find a newborn in time, he was no nurse and had trouble caring for the infants. He finally established an icy stronghold in underground caves.

Then the Loszian meteor struck Rumedia less than a mile to the east of Noth's citadel, and in its descent, it sheared off the citadel's great spiraling tower. The falling tower, combined with impact of the meteor when it struck ground, shook Noth's citadel apart and it collapsed amidst great destruction. In the aftermath, Lord Dahken Tannes sent several of his own Dahken in search of Noth and his warriors. The first never returned, and those he sent later came back with reports that the citadel was completely destroyed. There was no sign of Lord Dahken Noth.

The Loszians set about enslaving the West, conquering Garod's people at will, and as I have already described, they battled with the Dahken only once, finding their dark sorcery ineffective. Tannes, some six hundred years old now, led his warriors to a terrific victory over the Loszians annihilating thousands of undead servants, weak soldiers, and necromancers. The Loszian Emperor then sent an emissary to Sanctum requesting peace and making great payment in the form of gold and jewels. Tannes accepted the payment and signed the peace treaty, giving the Dahken full autonomy so long as they did not interfere in Loszian affairs.

Tannes died shortly thereafter. It seemed to the others that the battle had taken all of his strength, and he aged horribly fast over his last few years. What had been a seemingly strong middle aged man died decrepit and ancient only a few years later, his skin stretched across brittle bones.

Over the ensuing centuries, the Dahken found they never numbered more than a few hundred at Sanctum. They could not rebuild their citadel in the heart of Losz without dishonoring their treaty with the Empire, and the messages from Dulkur spoke of constant battles with the people there and began to decrease in length and frequency before they ceased altogether. The Dahken also ceased to care about many things; as a whole, they became enamored with their own abilities, constantly seeking artifacts or other methods to increase their strength. It became a narcotic, and they came to ignore the rest of the world as many of them ceased to even look for other Dahken.

Then The Cleansing began, and Werth and his people pushed the Loszians out of the West. The Dahken were uncaring about this, having long lost interest in the happenings of the world around them, that is, until the final battle of that war occurred. The rending of the world that resulted from Werth's sacrifice led to great earthquakes across the western continent, felt all the way into the Northern Kingdoms. A great gout of lava spilled forth from the caves in the north, completely obliterating the underground Dahken stronghold. The Dahken, so concerned with the power in their blood, felt this sudden cataclysm as dozens of their kind died in an instant.

As the Loszian Empire licked its wounds, the West coalesced into its kingdoms and became the Shining West. It was then that the Westerners realized the Dahken, with their near immunity to necromancy, could have helped them defeat the Loszians from the beginning. The Westerners became incensed, then enraged, and as the veterans of the Loszian campaigns disappeared into history, combined with the apparent absence of the Loszians, the Westerners targeted the Dahken with their ire. The rulers of the Shining West agreed the Dahken must be taught the price of their inaction and that the

Dahken center of power must be Cleansed just as the Loszians were.

In fifty two A.C., they fielded a massive army and marched upon Sanctum. They did not anticipate that most of the Dahken would have a natural immunity to Garod's power, and while their priests had no more luck against the Dahken than the Loszian sorcerers, they could heal their wounded, quickly returning them to combat. The Dahken, having met the Westerners on an open battlefield, found themselves overwhelmed and fled to their keep, losing many of their brethren in the process. The Dahken had never been besieged in history and were wholly unprepared for that type of warfare. The Western army built siege engines, catapults, towers, and battering rams from the surrounding forests and nearly battled down the great tower. They breached the walls and rushed inside. The Dahken fought with all the will of their being, but in the end, a mere one hundred fifty could not hope to withstand a siege against thousands upon thousands. The Westerners left none alive and with the castle nearly destroyed, returned to their kingdoms and homes.

Despite this Cleansing, it is nearly impossible to destroy a race, especially one that quite literally appears through the power of a god. Regardless of attempts by most of the world's rulers to stamp them out, the Dahken do survive in the world, but only in shadow. All but the most learned have never heard of the Dahken, and it is doubtful even they could recognize one for what it is. It is uncertain what role they may play as history unfolds.

9.

Cor awoke to Rael shaking him by the shoulder, his head resting on his crossed arms on the table in the study. Last he remembered, he laid his head down as he organized his thoughts, thinking over the scroll he had read. The history did not make sense to him in some ways, and he, like the Westerners of history, did not understand the disinterest of the Dahken in fighting the Loszians.

"Why did you sleep in here boy?" Rael asked with annoyance.

"I didn't think I could sleep. I wanted to read the scroll you wrote for me. I just fell asleep here thinking," explained Cor. "You did write it, didn't you?"

"I did. I copied it from an ancient Rumedian text, which of course you cannot read. I am also reluctant to allow you to handle many of these tomes, at least until you learn respect for them. In the future, take care not to fall asleep in here again. In your repose, you easily could have knocked over your candles," he motioned at the large stacks of melted wax surrounding his candelabra. "Come eat."

Cor mumbled an apology as he followed Rael to the larder where they ate a breakfast of eggs and pork, and a thought occurred to Cor. "Where does this food come from?" he asked.

"Some of the fruit grows wildly around the castle, but most of it I purchase from a farmer," explained Rael. "The road that leaves Sanctum leads to a fishing and port town a few miles to the north. About halfway there lives a rather prosperous farmer. I pay him well for provisions."

"Does he know you live here?" Cor asked.

80

"I am sure he suspects, but I do not think he overly cares. He is a good man, and as I said, I pay him well."

Cor thought this over for a moment before asking, "Where do you get money from?"

"Cor, you ask too many questions," Rael said with a piercing gaze Cor readily recognized. Rael quickly stood from the table. "Finish your breakfast, then come outside. We have much to do."

Rael always started his day with several hours of practice with his weapons. Though for a hardened warrior it seemed unnecessary, he explained that a man's muscles may forget the actions if not constantly reminded. He would routinely break at least an hour before midday to handle some basic chores, during which time Cor would study whatever texts he had laid out. Cor began to learn Rumedian, the ancient language of the gods and the Chronicler.

Rael also said that it was important that Cor knew how to care for weapons and armor, as poorly maintained equipment could well mean a warrior's death. Aboard Naran's ship, this task was handled by the Quartermaster, or delegated to those who already had the skills. They removed the rust from Cor's sword, and Rael showed him how to restore and maintain the edge. He taught Cor to keep it well-oiled and free from rust.

Roughly once every two weeks, Rael would leave to see the farmer for food and other supplies. The Dahken would not allow Cor to come with him, saying they knew not who else would be looking for the boy. The trip rarely took more than two or three hours; Rael headed north up the road, his horse pulling an old rickety wagon. The stallion's discomfort and injury to his pride were quite apparent in his posture. He clearly preferred travel or even combat to such menial labor. Rael endeavored to leave enough academic exercises or household chores to keep Cor busy.

This did not prevent Cor from occasionally exploring more of the castle. He knew Rael wouldn't approve, but his curiosity was unquenchable. He kept his outings short so as not to alert Rael's suspicions, and he found several more rooms, most of which in perfectly usable condition. More than once, Cor stopped at the stone stair leading down; it was dark and foreboding, but it called to him when he neared it. Once, he edged down the first few steps, only to slip and lose his footing in centuries of dust, nearly falling down the steps into the darkness. Cor scampered back to the top, returning to his studies immediately.

Fall returned, dispelling the extreme heat of late summer, which allowed Rael to focus more of their time outdoors. He was satisfied with Cor's ability to wield his sword, striking in certain ways cleanly and with strength when told, and Rael felt it was time to move forward. On a particularly cool autumn morning, Cor joined Rael outside a bit earlier than normal. The sun had only just passed the horizon, casting long shadows from the decaying walls. The air was crisp, and Cor's breath came in white puffs.

"It is time," Rael began, "for you to learn how to fight as a Dahken does. It will not come quickly. You will have to focus your mind as well as your body. You know how to strike and parry, and your arm is strong, but Dahken do not fence like a noble or strike from darkness like an assassin. Those warriors are afraid of the sight of their own blood. You must let your blood be drawn; a Dahken is most dangerous when he is half dead. Certainly, we wear armor, but that is only to prevent our foes from delivering a killing blow. Most warriors wear armor to avoid injury; they parry and move so their enemies swords do not touch their flesh. You must wade directly into battle.

"Do you understand?" Rael asked.

82

"I think so." Cor told Rael the story of how he killed a man only a few months ago. It almost seemed like it was another lifetime.

"If what you say is true, then you have already started to unlock your strength, and that is amazing. Cor," Rael said slowly, "you must trust me and do as I say. I will not allow you to be truly harmed, nor will I allow you to harm me. Do you understand?"

Cor nodded hesitantly, and Rael picked up a small, battered wooden shield and strapped it to his left forearm. "Strike me."

"What?" Cor asked, completely bewildered.

"Run me through, as hard as you dare!" Cor delivered a weak thrust with his longsword that Rael easily batted away with the shield. "Is that your best? You killed no Tigolean with that attack."

Cor thrust again, and again Rael blocked the blade with his shield. But this time, the point of the sword imbedded slightly into the wood and skidded off the shield's edge, leaving a deep scratch. Before Cor realized what was happening, Rael lashed out at Cor's leg with his own steel, opening a small wound on the front of his thigh. Shocked, Cor nearly dropped his weapon and simply stared at the cut on his leg; it was not deep, but it bled freely. He remembered the feel of the dagger piercing his shoulder.

"Cor, the wound is nothing compared to what your foes would deal you," Rael said, eliciting no response. He stepped forward and slapped Cor across his left cheek. "Focus Cor. See the blood, feel the pain. Immerse yourself in it and control it. Center yourself in the pain and attack me!"

Cor did as he was told, but as an automaton; it was as if he watched the entire scene from above, as if he had no actual control over his actions. He slashed with his sword from the side, again impacting Rael's shield, and this time splinters flew from the solid impact. Rael

83

slashed again, putting another fine wound across Cor's arm near the shoulder. The sudden pain of the strike pulled Cor's consciousness back with extreme clarity. He felt blood soaking his shirt and trickling down his arm. The wounds burned with a peculiar searing sensation, and Cor suddenly felt as if his body were covered with ants.

He attacked again with no command from Rael; this time he thrust forward, the blade's flat parallel to the ground. Rael blocked with his shield, taking the sword's point directly in the middle of the wooden disc. Cor felt the collision, for a moment frozen in time, before the shield gave way under his attack. Rael grunted painfully. Cor stared, realizing that he had imbedded the sword, transfixed it in the center of the shield, and he could see blood dripping from the bottom of the disc, slowly at first, and then freely flowing.

"Boy," Rael said, his eyes wide, "please pull your sword free."

Cor gently pulled at the hilt, but then realized it needed a solid yank to free the blade from the shield, causing Rael to grimace. Cor looked at the sword's point in wonder; it had pierced completely through the three inch wood shield and was coated in blood. Rael busied himself with releasing the straps that held his arm to the shield, and when it fell to the ground, Cor could see the man's hand and wrist awash with his blood. The sword's point had gone cleanly through the shield and Rael's wrist.

"Cor, you have spilled my blood; know it. Do you still feel the pain of your own wounds?" Rael asked him. In his wonder, Cor had forgotten the shallow cuts on his arm and thigh, and it was then he realized they were gone, just like when the Tigolean stabbed him in the shoulder.

"I don't understand," Cor said.

"Let me bandage this. Then we will go inside, and I will explain it to you."

"I am very lucky," Rael said in the larder, pouring himself red wine. "If you had been holding your sword differently, you may have severed my hand from my wrist. As it is, I bled quite a bit."

"I'm sorry," Cor said looking at the man's bandaged wrist. A dark red spot stained it where the sword had gone through, even though Rael had bandaged it twice already.

"No! You do not understand," Rael started excitedly, "You have accomplished with almost no teaching what took me weeks to unlock with an accomplished Dahken training me!"

"I still don't understand. What happened?"

"You felt the pain of your wounds. You truly felt it. When you bleed, if you can find the," Rael paused, trying to select his words, "the center of the pain, it will give you more strength than you can imagine."

"Will I be able to do this every time?"

"It will likely take some time to master it, but again, it took me nearly three weeks to understand."

"How old were you?" Cor couldn't comprehend going through that every day for weeks. Before joining Naran, Cor had never felt real pain before, nothing more than a skinned knee. Learning the ship had caused pain – deeply sore muscles, broken blisters, splinters, and rope burns – the pain of hard work. Having one's flesh opened by cold steel was a pain of a whole different sort.

"Younger than you are now," answered Rael quietly, gulping down the rest of his wine.

Cor sat quietly for a few moments, watching the man as he poured himself more wine. "Why are my wounds gone, but yours aren't?"

"That is simple. You drew my blood after I wounded you and quite substantially at that. When you spill another's blood, your body will heal itself."

"That's why," Cor reasoned, "two hundred Dahken can kill an army."

"Exactly. Is there anything else you do not understand Cor?" Rael asked after the boy had been quiet for a few minutes.

"You can't heal yourself?"

"Only if I inflict a wound on another. There were some Dahken in history that had the ability to heal wounded Dahken, but that power was rare. I would not even begin to know how to access it," Rael explained. Rael sighed as he stood from the table. "Come, you should study for a while."

10.

In the ensuing weeks, Cor shocked Rael repeatedly. He had become adept at tapping the power in his blood, imbuing his own attacks with force that was amazing considering how little experience he had with it. As Rael understood the past, a Dahken's training would have started as a small child, and it took years before they were ready to even try accessing their strength. As Cor grew, Rael was certain that the boy's combat abilities would far outstrip his own.

The season grew late, the days shorter, and the air colder. Rael changed the schedule of Cor's training, moving academic endeavors into the morning while it was still cold, and having combat training after lunch. The training itself had taken a more mundane turn, and with Cor learning to access his powers with increasing ease, Rael focused more on the technical elements of fighting. It was important Cor learned when and how to strike opponents, especially those who may wear armor, and at the same time Rael taught him how to use his own armor to his advantage. While the Dahken gained strength by being wounded, there were times when one need not risk it.

Additionally, the shield turned out to be a problem for Cor; he simply showed no inclination towards using it at all. Rael explained to him on many occasions that it was important to know when to deflect a blow. Often in single combat, it was unnecessary to allow your opponent to wound you, such as when Rael killed the Loszian several months ago. One afternoon, he decided to address the shield problem in a different way. They had just lunched and, after waiting for a suitable time for digestion, went outside. Cor readied his sword and buckler, waiting patiently for Rael, who was clearly organizing his thoughts.

"Cor why will you not use your shield?" Rael asked.

Cor was surprised by the question, which stung of criticism, something he wasn't used to. He had learned to always answer Rael's questions honestly and with consideration.

"It just doesn't feel right," he answered.

"Follow me," Rael said, immediately turning and striding to one of the castle's outbuildings. Upon entering, Cor saw it was an armory, weapons and shields of every conceivable size and type on large racks filled the room. The weapons were in various states of disrepair, and he recognized many of them from his first lesson with the sword nearly two months ago.

"Unstrap your shield and put it over there," Rael said, motioning at a rack of bucklers and small wooden shields. "Cor, do you know what a fetish is?"

"I've seen the word several times in the things you have me read, but I don't really understand it," he answered.

"A fetish," Rael explained, "is a magical object, a talisman imbued with power."

Questions began to flood Cor's mind, as well as a strange sense of familiarity. "What does one look like? How is it made?"

"Virtually anything can be made into a fetish. Some of them are simple, mundane items like medallions, scrolls, or even rocks, while others were crafted specifically for magical or spiritual rites." Rael disappeared around a large rack into the back of the armory as he talked, clearly searching for something.

"But what does a fetish do?" Cor felt curiosity tugging at him. He moved around the other side of the large rack, coming up behind Rael.

"Honestly, I can only tell you what I know Cor. I have never felt the strength of a fetish, but I understand that no two are alike. Some were created by the gods, some by sorcerers and perhaps not even by choice but on accident. Others may date back to the ancients, to the days before our civilization took hold. I know that they grant power to their users, but I can tell you little beyond that, as I neither use one, nor have I ever known a Dahken who did."

Rael pointed to a glass case that sat upon a wood stand against the back wall of the room. It was relatively large, nearly three feet in length, about six inches tall and twice that deep. The bottom of the case was lined with deteriorating scarlet velvet, on which sat four objects that amplified Cor's curiosity.

The first two were simple, as Rael had mentioned, one a gleaming eight pointed gold medallion with a silver chain and the other a weathered parchment scroll. The third was a small cube of mahogany, roughly three inches in each dimension, and each side of the cube had a small gem inlaid into the center, each a different color. The last was a bleached white bone about four inches in length, the ends of which were plated with gold, and it was then Cor realized that it wasn't curiosity or interest that pulled him into the back of the armory.

"Can you feel any of these?" Rael asked, looking at him intently.

"Yes, I think the one on the end," Cor spoke quickly, and he felt energized. He put his left hand out, lightly touching the outside of the glass case, and his palm almost itched to hold the bone fetish.

Rael reached forward, carefully opening the case's lid to lean it backwards against the armory's stone wall. Cor stepped closer, slowly lowering his hand inside, and he closed his eyes as his fingertips lightly brushed each item. He stopped, in light contact with one of the fetishes. Where he touched it, his fingertips were warm, and his digits tingled as if they were asleep. He closed his fingers around it and pulled his hand from the case, and opening his eyes, he found the small, gold plated bone in his left hand.

"When you fight, that is the hand you will hold it in," Rael said.

"Why did I choose this one?" Cor asked, turning it over in his palm.

"Why do any of the Dahken choose anything?" Rael answered. "It is simply meant for you. As you grow, you will find yourself drawn to other items, weapons, armor, and even people. Do not question it."

"What do you think it does?"

"I cannot say. You will find that out for yourself, but I do know you must not think of it in that way. The fetish does not grant you a power or magic; it lends its strength to you in some form or another," he explained.

"This is a pestle," Cor said lifting his gaze to Rael's, closing his fingers around the bone. "It was used long ago by a bent over old man. He used it to grind roots, leaves, and berries in a cow's skull."

Rael nodded, asking one simple question. "How do you know?"

"I don't know," Cor answered, and the fetish grew oddly warm in his hand.

Rael enjoyed talking to Cor over meals; it gave him a chance to lecture the young man without worrying about too many questions. Certainly, he appreciated Cor's inquisitive nature, but every answer he gave Cor inevitably led to another question. He usually ate voraciously, as was common to older boys or young men, and that gave Rael time to speak about things relatively uninterrupted.

"You must learn to feel your blood more strongly," Rael said. "Even now, I feel myself pulled to places, and for the most part I do not know why. But eventually, I will have to answer those calls. That is how I knew you had returned to the West. You called to my blood for years, and when I found you the first time, it was like blazing fire in my veins. That feeling weakened as you sailed further away and strengthened immensely when you returned.

"You have only just learned of your power, so the feeling is weak, and you may not even be aware of it. But as you become more focused, stronger, you will feel it more acutely. And perhaps, as you become more aware of your strengths, they will even change. It is likely, that you will one day give those up," Rael pointed with his spoon at Cor's sword and fetish. "You will feel drawn to something else, another sword perhaps or a fetish which is more powerful, more meant for you.

"The shield I had you using was useless for you, and on some level, you knew that. I began to suspect that you were a fetish wielder, but I had to get you closer to them for you to feel it in your blood. When you selected the sword and the fetish, you felt it. Have you felt anything like that any other time?"

Cor looked down into his stew. Rael unerringly made a stew every second or third meal, and the meat in this one was somewhat unknown. He spooned the stew over itself several times, expecting Rael to become angry with what he would say next.

"I feel it now," he answered, still looking at his dinner.

"Do you know from where?" Rael asked, surprise, not anger showing on his face.

"Further down the hall, there's a doorway and some stairs that go down," he explained, guilt welling into his voice. "I found it right after you brought me here. Sometimes when you are gone, I just go stare at the steps."

"You desire to descend those stairs," Rael stated.

"Yes," Cor paused, "and no. They scare me."

"As they should. That stair is one of the ways into the catacombs of Sanctum. I do not know how safe the steps themselves are, but I doubt a precarious climb is the only thing to fear in those depths."

11.

Winter on the southwestern coast of Aquis is generally a mild thing. The air does get colder, certainly, but rarely does the area see much in the way of frozen precipitation. Cor found it quite nice in fact, as there always seemed to be a warmer wind blowing in off the sea from the south. As he was promised, Cor finally convinced Rael to show him the safe route to the ocean. They left Sanctum, taking the northbound road for about a half mile, then turned west toward the sea, which always lay within sight. When Cor looked back at Sanctum, he realized they had essentially come down the small mountain upon which Sanctum was perched, and they continued descending as they approached the water.

Cor marveled at the beach, an expanse of fine, pure white sand the likes of which he had never seen in his travels; he had only ever seen ports, docks, and moorings. They walked south along this beach, which sloped steadily downward, Cor talking about the Narrow Sea and its difficulties. The sand was strange to walk on; unlike solid ground, it shifted under his weight, making him feel extremely unsteady. He crouched down and dug his hands into the sand. Either because of the color or consistency under his feet, Cor expected it to feel like snow. It did not, and he wasn't sure he cared for it.

The steep hill leading down to the beach finally gave way to a face of rock, which as they continued down the beach, began to tower above them. As they walked, Cor began to notice and recognize the rotten odor of low tide, which meant that this part of the beach was normally under water. This also meant that they could tarry only so long.

They reached what Rael announced was the bottom and was as far as they could go. There was little sand here and the area was littered with large rocks. Cor had no real desire to continue as doing so meant hopping from rock to rock, and he had little doubt that a broken leg could happen easily. He looked upward, craning his neck and saw the top spire of Sanctum towering above him, and the dizzying height of it made Cor want to lose his balance, despite years at sea.

Cor was about ready to start the journey back up when he spotted something curious amidst the rocks further down. Cautiously, he went a little closer, Rael watching him closely, to see the entrance to a cave that was about as large as he. There were puddles of seawater just inside; no doubt the cave completely filled with water at times. Inspecting it from a short distance, Cor could tell the cave opened further in. He wanted a closer look, but Rael called him back, saying it was time to leave before the tide returned.

That night, sleep did not come easy to Cor. He had an uneasiness about his stomach and an anxiousness in his limbs. He felt as if he had forgotten to do something important, and that he needed to do it immediately. Of course, he had no idea what this could be. He had already tried studying, and in addition to everything else, Rael was teaching him Loszian, which by all accounts was an extremely bizarre language. Unable to concentrate, Cor forced himself to stay in bed, constantly tossing in a vain attempt to be comfortable. He would begin to doze, only to be pulled to his senses abruptly by some unknown thing.

He closed his eyes again and lay quite still for several minutes before realizing everything sounded wrong. Crickets and the howling of a wild dog in the distance replaced the ambient sound of ocean waves and wind. He bolted upright, opening his eyes to find his room, the keep, and Sanctum to be gone. He sat on his mattress surrounded by an ancient ruin. Large, worked stones lay everywhere within sight, worn down by weather or covered in moss, weeds, and other foliage. The full moon illuminated the scene with extreme clarity, if surreally, and he stood and made his way through the labyrinth of destroyed walls up a grassy incline, vaguely wondering if he were dreaming.

At the top of the hill, Cor looked in all directions, stopping in awe when he looked to the east. A great trench of upturned soil, perhaps a mile wide, cut its way through the countryside. The trench dug deeper and narrower into the ground as it continued away from him, ending in a fiery pit that billowed black smoke. Littered about the area, he could see hundreds more stones, clearly part of an immense building or even a castle, scattered all about the area. Again, they looked ancient, edges worn by the elements, covered in moss and grass in stark contrast to the fresh trench.

Cor made his way back down the slope to the main ruin, inspecting it quite closely. From what he could see of the ancient foundation, it was smaller than Sanctum, perhaps half the overall size of Sanctum's keep. He found the remains of two sets of stone spiral stairs on the north and south side of the ruin, and they clearly ascended, though there were only a few steps of each left. He made his way back to the middle of the ruin and sat down heavily on his mattress, resting his chin on his knuckles. Clearly, the only option was to wait until the dream ended.

There was a slight sound behind him, like the creak of a wood floor. The sound surprised Cor. He turned abruptly to look around, and the shifting of his weight sent a shudder through the mattress, followed by the sound of cracking wood planks. Too late Cor realized what was about to happen, and the mattress, with him atop, crashed downward through a wood trap door, weak and rotten with age. Cor landed, still on the mattress, with a jarring thud on solid ground. He lay there for a moment and looking up, he could see faint moonlight peering through the hole above. In the gloom it wasn't easy to see how far down he was, but he knew he would need to find another way out.

Cor sat up slowly, taking stock of his surroundings. He was on a floor of smooth stone, caked with ages of dust, and the room or cavern was apparently immense, as he could not see a wall in any direction. He sat in the middle of a wide lane, which was flanked on either side by small stone buildings, none more than ten feet in any dimension. They were gray with heavy oak doors and were largely unadorned, except some had glyphs on the doors themselves. Outside of every second building stood a metal stand, each containing a torch, which burned, giving off black smoke.

The rows of crypts created a wide lane that led off in two directions, and he saw no more rows beyond these two. He looked up and down the avenue, closed his eyes for a moment, and then began to slowly walk. Cor found himself walking between the crypts, east he thought, not that he thought the direction mattered in a dream. The flickering torchlight cast bizarre shadows on and between the crypts, causing him to constantly turn towards shapes that weren't there, and he quickened his pace, paranoia building. After forty or fifty feet, the rows of crypts ended, and with them the torch stands. Still the room continued, and somehow, he knew he was going in the right direction. Cor carefully removed the last torch from its holder, and he was surprised by its weight. Holding the torch as high as he could, he continued in the same direction counting his steps. After about twenty paces, Cor began to panic, as he was surrounded by darkness. He could no longer see the weak light from the other torches, and his illuminated little beyond five or six feet. After looking in all directions, he couldn't even be sure which way he faced anymore. Cor calmed himself, trying to keep in mind this had to be a dream, and he stood quietly for several minutes before continuing on his way, certain that he continued on the same path.

After another ten paces, Cor could see two points of orange light. Uncertainly, he continued forward, slowly closing the distance, and as he approached, he realized he saw a pair of burning torches. The room finally ended, and a solid gray expanse of stone formed a wall leading upwards and to the left and right. Two torch stands flanked a heavy wooden door, and Cor ran to it, certain he had reached his destination. It was of thick oak, banded by heavy black iron, and showed no signs of decrepit age. The door had two glyphs branded into it, which he recognized from the ancient language Rael made him study. The first glyph stood for Lord Dahken; the second was clearly a proper name, but Cor could not decipher it. He knew that he needed a way out, not a tomb, but something drew him inexorably onward.

Cor gently pushed his hand against the side of the door opposite its hinges, but it was solid and unmoving. He added more strength behind his push and made the door give slightly before settling back into its position. Somewhat warily of the dust coating the floor, Cor set his torch down and placed both hands on the door. He braced his feet against the floor and pushed with his legs driving into the door. It began to give, slowly at first, then a little more freely as he forced it ajar.

The opening was little more than a foot wide, but it was wide enough for Cor to slip through sideways into a pitch black room beyond. He bent over to retrieve his torch before carefully passing the door. The next room was relatively small, the ceiling a mere seven feet or so overhead and another parallel wall maybe ten paces in front of him. Inlaid into a wall to his right was a stone shelf, upon which lay three pieces of armor, and he knew it was not a way out that he sought but these.

Cor crossed the room quickly, discarding a burnt out torch from a nearby stand and inserting his own to free both his hands. The armor gleamed solid black in the torch's light and looked as if it had never been used. It was not rusted from time, neither scraped, nor dented from battle. He inspected them each in turn, starting with a set of legguards. They consisted of four metal plates, curved slightly, one for the front of each thigh and shin. The plates were connected in front by black chain mail and had leather straps to secure them around the back of the legs, with two additional straps at the top to attach to one's girdle or belt. The hauberk was similar, made of solid black plate. It was molded to resemble a well-muscled man's torso and would cover from just above the waist to the shoulders on most men. A layer of chain mail hung down slightly from the shoulders, leaving the arms almost completely bare. The front and back of the hauberk buckled together just under the arm.

The helm shocked Cor, for it was unlike anything he had ever seen. Also made of gleaming black plate, it was rounder than a normal man's head. Almost perfectly circular, it had the bulbous look of an inhuman insect monstrosity, and it was bizarre in that it covered the head but not the entirety of one's face. Its protection stopped at the nose, and the plate from the back of the head wrapped around to cover the cheeks and jaw, but the neck and mouth remained exposed completely. The helm had no visor, nothing to allow the wearer sight at all. Cor leaned forward, inspecting it closely, before deciding to try on the helm. He gently grasped it between his hands and lifted it slightly, and despite the solid steel appearance, it weighed almost nothing at all.

Cor raised it from its resting place and suddenly stopped, holding very still. When he entered the tomb, he hadn't looked at the left side of the room and was convinced someone was standing there. He slowly put the helm down and reached for his sword and fetish, but of course, he did not have them. They were in his room in Sanctum, wherever exactly that was. While he had never seen a bear before, he understood very well what they were, and he couldn't help feeling a bear or some other predator regarded him very quietly. Cor haltingly turned to face that side of the room. He didn't know what he would see and was convinced he didn't want to.

An immense clang erupted in the distance, and the room dissolved before him. Cor opened his eyes to find himself staring at the ceiling of his room, lying on his mattress, which had just been on the floor of a great catacomb. His sword leaned against the wall where he always left it, his fetish tucked into the swordbelt. Cor sat up, momentarily confused. He opened the shutter on his window and could see the sky beginning to lighten with dawn's first light. Cor heard movement in the larder, and no doubt, Rael had dropped a pot or skillet. He wiped the sleep from his eyes, belted on his sword and trudged out of his room to join the older Dahken.

In the depths of a dark cavern smoothed by human hands, a form shifted slightly. It removed its hands from their stone resting place and steepled them in thought. It stared at the stone shelf, on which rested three pieces of black armor. The form closed its eyes and returned to its repose.

12.

Cor studied and trained constantly, taking time only to sleep and eat. With Rael's tutelage, he began to learn other languages such as Loszian and became more adept in the ancient tongue. Rael found that Cor had a facility with languages and urged him on in his studies. Cor also continued to read any historical texts he could find in Rael's study, asking Rael to translate certain portions from Rumedian when they became too difficult. After a time, he no longer needed Rael's translations.

They trained several hours each day. While Cor had learned quickly how to use the strength contained in his blood, the arts of fighting themselves took much time and practice. Rael forced himself to be patient, realizing that he had over one hundred years of fighting experience, whereas Cor had learned to fight in unconventional ways. All things considered, Cor took to the teaching well, and Rael began to teach him the art of combat from horseback. Cor found this to be quite a different thing, and it took more practice and care to be sure one did not harm one's mount.

Cor certainly never forgot about his parents, in fact they were always close to the forefront of his mind, but he came to accept Rael as a friend and the closest thing to family he still had. They discussed things beyond Cor's studies, talking easily about a range of subjects. Cor knew that the Dahken was immensely old by normal human terms, and Rael spoke reservedly of his own training as a child and told Cor tales of his travels through the West, the Northern Kingdoms, and Tigol. He explained how his blood had led him back to Sanctum and to find Cor.

However, Rael was rarely inclined to speak about his past, and over time, Cor began to realize that there was a period of perhaps several decades that Rael avoided discussing. However, Rael did enjoy his wine, and on occasion, he would grow too intoxicated and let some minute details slip. Cor was quick to notice these pieces of information, and he eventually concluded that Rael had stopped traveling for a time. Cor was certain the Dahken had settled down, taken a wife, and started a family. What happened to them, Cor did not know, and he was not inclined to push Rael on the matter. The man often brooded late in the evening, and Cor grew convinced that it was related to the years Rael would not discuss.

Cor continued to grow, both physically and in power, and by the age of seventeen, he was nearly six feet tall. His body became well-muscled, lean and wiry from the constant workouts with Rael. Throughout his adolescence, his hair changed color slightly becoming almost black, a stark contrast with his gray skin. Cor had been tall and strong enough to wear a man's armor for a few years, and Rael helped him select some choice pieces from Sanctum's armory. It took the better part of a week to return them to usable condition and teach Cor how to maintain the armor properly.

Rael watched him and marveled, realizing Cor truly was a man now. He knew there was little else he could teach Cor, and combat training at this point was more of a sparring session between the two. Rael had to be incredibly careful as Cor could already best him in combat, though he tried to hide that fact from the young man. Cor easily and readily tapped into the power of his blood and was more than capable of rending straight through steel when so wounded.

And yet there was another problem; the stronger Cor became, the more powerful became the calls to his blood. Rael knew the boy felt a constant urge to enter the catacombs, and he also knew that one day Cor would.

Rael was still uncomfortable with the prospect, and he knew that only his constant presence kept Cor from venturing downward. As such, Rael decided he dared not to leave Cor alone in Sanctum anymore. It was spring, and life outdoors began to blossom when Rael decided Cor would come with him to meet Cade, the farmer from whom Rael purchased most of their food and supplies. When Rael told him, Cor did not ask why; he was pleased to go beyond the walls of Sanctum even if only for a short time.

They prepared a wagon, and Rael had him place their weapons under a wool blanket just behind the wooden bench on which they sat. He always told Cor never to be without his sword, but there were times when you should not display it. Rael never wore his armor on these trips, so neither did Cor. They left after lunch, expecting to be back before supper, and though there was still a slight chill in the air, it was a beautiful day. The winter, as usual in that area, had been mild, and a light rain had fallen the night before, keeping dust down on the road. Cade's farm was about three miles from Sanctum, and they made fair time.

Cade was a short, barrel chested man, standing just over five feet tall with shoulders wider than a bear's. He had a round, jovial face tanned from years of work in the sun and shoulder length light brown hair. His arms and legs were thick from labor and hard as steel. He clasped hands with Rael, taking note of Cor.

"I can't believe Rael never mentioned you, lad. Surely you are his son," Cade said extending his hand, his voice loud but friendly. Cor introduced himself, taking the man's hand; his grip crushed like a vise.

"As usual," Cade said turning back to Rael, "I got everything you asked for. I've a bit to do before sundown, so you won't mind if we get to it."

Rael pulled the wagon around the back of Cade's modest home. A small stack of goods awaited them there, several sacks of feed and other grain, various preserved meats, and a few small barrels. Cor set about moving the goods into the wagon at Rael's direction; the Dahken wanted everything loaded in just a certain way, and he went off to pay the farmer.

Cor was nearly done with the work when he caught sight of something that made him stop. A girl with light brown hair nearly to her waist passed in front of the wagon on her way to water some livestock in a nearby pen. He considered her carefully as he stared at her. He wasn't actually certain if she was beautiful or even pretty, but it was the first girl or woman he had looked at closely since he left Hichima, besides his mother. Cor was keenly aware that most men knew more about women than he did at this age.

"Are you done?" Rael asked, Cor jumping at the sudden interruption.

"More or less," he said with a guilty glance at the older man. He placed the last few items in the wagon.

"Then we should go," Rael said with finality.

They left the farm, Cade waving from his work as they passed. They were nearly halfway back to Sanctum, approaching where a section of road split off to the east when they came upon a man on a horse. He wore light clothes common to travelers and was otherwise unremarkable as compared to most Westerners. Cor started in the direction of their weapons, but Rael subtly lifted one finger as a sign for calm.

"Hello friends," the man called as they approached. "I am looking for lodging for the coming night. Would you be headed to the castle yonder southward?"

"No one lives there," answered Rael, ignoring Cor's glance. "We take this eastern road on our way."

"But there is nothing that direction for perhaps twenty miles or more," the man responded kindly.

"Which means we have far to go. If you seek lodging, there is a farm not two miles in the direction whence we have come, and there is a port town a few miles beyond that. With your good horse, you have plenty of time before nightfall to reach lodging."

"Thank you, sirs," the man nodded his head and spurred his horse north up the road. Rael continued south, and then took the eastern branch of the road.

"Cor, he is watching us?" Rael asked without looking himself.

"He was. Once you turned east, he continued on his way," Cor answered. "What are we doing?"

"We will head this way for a few miles and then cut across country to Sanctum. I want to make sure we are not followed."

"Perhaps next time I should go alone," Rael stated from across the room. They were in the study, scouring the tomes for information on Dahken magic, which it seemed there was extraordinarily little. Apparently, the Dahken had only ever had a few with the knack of incantations and spells.

"Go where alone?" Cor asked, at once understanding what Rael meant. He walked from between two bookcases to face Rael. "Why?"

"The man on the road concerns me. Perhaps I should have killed him," Rael answered.

"He didn't do anything to us. You would've killed him in cold blood? That seems like murder to me," said Cor.

Rael turned and regarded Cor quietly. "Murder is a Western concept handed down by Garod and his controlling priests. It does not apply to us; we are beyond their law."

"Then," Cor reasoned, "we are no better than the Loszians. Perhaps we should rape and slay our way to everything we want? Somehow, I don't think we're meant for that."

"Bah with human sentiments. Regardless," Rael sighed, "it seems likely the man was a spy."

"You'll have to explain that to me later, but what if he was?" Cor asked. "If he works for someone looking for us, then they've found us. We should either leave Sanctum or not. Certainly, there's more safety for both of us if we stay together anyway."

Rael found Cor to become increasingly logical over the last year, and he sighed again before replying, "Be that as it may, there are dangers beyond ambush by our enemies."

"First, I don't know who our enemies are at this point," said Cor, "and second, what are you talking about?"

"I would not have you distracted further by Cade's strumpet daughter," answered Rael.

Leave it to Rael to be blunter than a two handed club, Cor thought. "I just looked at her for a moment. She was only the second person I've seen besides you in what, two years?"

"Perhaps I have made a mistake there but be careful. Women are more dangerous for us than the finest adversary. They will love you, but they take everything you are from you. In the end, they are all whores, and you are better off without them." Rael turned and stalked back to the study's table.

Cor followed him, angry and unwilling to leave the conversation at that, "My mother loved both my father and me. She didn't take anything from us."

"A mother," Rael sneered as he turned back to face Cor, "is just another harlot. A wife forces her husband to pay for her with house and home. She loves him, and he gives her a child. Should he not continue to pay for her, she ceases to love him!"

"I'd rather you not say such things," Cor growled at Rael. His temper rose quickly; he could feel his cheeks and ears burn, and his heart hammered in his chest. "Whatever you think, we were happy, and she loved us. And it's my fault she's dead!" He turned back to continue scouring the bookshelves, and Rael stormed out of the study, headed for the larder and wine.

Cor continued his search, somewhat fruitlessly, for another hour or so. He had found a few promising immensely old tomes but was fearful to even touch them less they simply crumble to dust. He decided it was likely safe to talk things over with Rael; either from time or red wine, the man should be calmer now. He found Rael in the larder brooding over his cup, and he looked up as Cor entered and sat at the table, opposite him as usual.

"Why," started Cor, not seeing the point in exchanging apologies, "do you think the rider was a spy? I don't disagree with you; I just want to understand your reasoning."

"For the most part, he already knew the lay of the land. Had he seen Sanctum from a distance, he would never suspect that anyone lives here; the castle is nearly falling down. He asked us if we were headed here, which means he already knew someone has been living here."

"Was it wise to send him to Cade's farm?" Cor asked. "If he was a spy, he'll ask questions."

"That is likely," answered Rael, "but I saw no other possibility. It was the closest lodging, and it was on his way. Had he chosen to go any other direction, I would have killed him outright."

"If he is a spy, he may come back up here tonight to see if we're here," Cor said, chewing on a fingernail in thought. "Do you think we should stay awake, wait for him?"

"I do not see the point. If he is any good at his job, we will never see or hear him coming. For that matter, if he is any good at his job, he has already come and gone."

The man sat in a plush chair in front of Palius, explaining every detail of his story for the third time. He was a mercenary, one of the rangers Palius had recruited at the behest of Queen Erella. Palius had hired four, and this man was the first to return. However, before Palius handed him an outrageous sum of gold, he wanted to be certain the man's story was true.

The rangers were told the boy they sought was a Westerner, but one with an unnatural pallor of skin, and apparently this ranger had been a bit more interested in this detail and pursued his own research. After years of seeking information that was generally forbidden, he happened upon an historical text discussing The Cleansing. Here he learned of the Dahken, and of their ancient castle, Sanctum. He really could have saved much time if they had simply given him that information to begin with.

The ranger journeyed to Sanctum, which was substantially difficult to find. He knew from the text of its rough location and that it was perched on a rocky promontory overlooking the sea, and he also knew he had found it one afternoon, for no other site he'd located matched so closely. Investigating, he discovered it lived in but momentarily vacant. The road leading from the castle was not well used, but there was a fresh set of tracks made by a horse and a small wagon or cart. He followed the tracks north before coming across the wagon being driven by two men. One was middle aged, the other a young man, and both had the same peculiar skin discoloration. They were unarmed, claimed to be heading east, and they pointed him to a farmer further north for lodging or the town of Hager beyond that.

He found the farmer, a man named Cade, and casually questioned the man over supper. Cade did not know for certain where the men lived, but that the older, named Rael, came every two weeks without fail to buy food and supplies. Today was the first time Cade had ever met his son. The ranger skulked out into the dead of night and returned to Sanctum on foot. While he did not enter the keep, he made out the flickering, guttering light of torches and candles from inside, and he immediately returned to the farmer's home for his horse and rode for Byrverus.

This story the ranger told Palius three times without fail, details never changing to the extent that Palius was satisfied of his honesty. The old counselor removed a map from a large scroll case and had the ranger point out the exact location of the castle, which was on the coast about six miles south of the small port town Hager. Palius scooped up his map and then pointed to a dust covered chest in the corner of his office. Handing the ranger a key, he strode out of the room for the queen's throne room, the hall where she kept public court.

Queen Erella held court today, and she had two diplomats from Akor and Roka, two of the smaller western kingdoms, with a trade dispute she had agreed to mediate. When Palius arrived, the two emissaries were shouting and shaking fists at each other. He couldn't be certain, but he thought he heard war threatened over the quality of figurines carved from semi-precious gems. The queen saw Palius and shot him a pleading glance to which he nodded.

"Councilor Palius," she did not shout, but somehow raised her voice above the fighting bureaucrats, "do you have something you wish to add?" The two men stopped fighting and turned to him expectantly.

"Not about this matter, Majesty, but one of the highest importance," he replied.

"Gentlemen," she said to the two men, "we will take a short recess. Afterwards, we shall discuss this more civilly."

As the queen rose and left the room, everyone bowed, excepting Palius who silently followed his queen. They walked quietly together to her private chambers, where upon entering she unceremoniously dropped her crown around a post of her bed, the gold and jewels marring the finished wood, and sat on the edge of the low footboard. She rubbed her eyes deeply.

"I cannot understand the minds of merchants," she said wearily.

"I quite understand Majesty," Palius replied quietly, lifting her crown from its uncouth resting place to gently and reverently lay it upon its pillowed, marble stand.

"Thank you for saving me from such unpleasantness," she said, watching him. Others always viewed the articles of office with such awe, and it was something else she would never understand. It was only a crown of gold and jewels and had nothing to do with the power she wielded as priestess or queen.

"Do not thank me yet, Majesty. I have come with news about the Dahken," Palius said, facing his queen.

"What is it?" she asked, at once standing.

Palius recounted the ranger's story, detail for detail. "Majesty, I beg your forgiveness; you were correct in believing the boy was not alone. Now, he grows into adulthood with another Dahken, a grown man, to teach him of their black sorcery."

"I see no fault Palius; I had only a feeling," Queen Erella said, straightening herself. "This must end now. Select a dozen men to bring the boy to the palace. Palius, I do not want blood shed over this matter, but I doubt the older Dahken will hesitate to kill our people. Also, we must determine his guilt in the slaying of the boy's parents."

"My Queen, I believe it would be prudent to send Jonn as well, the priest the boy knew as a small child. He was a friend and a teacher, and perhaps if the boy sees a familiar face, it will be easier for him to come back to Byrverus."

"Very well," the queen sighed as she picked up her crown and placed it back on her head.

Jonn despised riding, and he did it as little as possible. Unfortunately, now he rode for a small town on the southwestern coast of Aquis with a group of soldiers, handpicked by Palius himself for their loyalty and professionalism. The ride from Martherus would take a week, and he was simply getting too old for this kind of excitement.

The boy, man he reminded himself, had been found by an enterprising ranger. He was in the company of another, a Dahken, and no doubt had been perverted with their foul magic. Few Westerners knew anything of the Dahken. The Shining West had worked hard to strike them from record and memory, but Jonn understood all too well their god and the evil they wrought with their blood magic.

He must be careful, but he had no doubt he could take the boy to Byrverus, as Cor had been a bright and friendly child. He was not so sure about the other Dahken, but he doubted Queen Erella would be overly concerned if the man chose to die fighting. Jonn had the power of Garod with him, and he was certain that would be enough when combined with a dozen well trained men at arms. Legend had it the Dahken were immune to magic, but what was magic compared to the holy strength of Garod. The Loszians had learned that lesson.

Jonn decided he would reevaluate his plan, if necessary, but it was relatively simple. He learned a long time ago that simplicity added to one's chances of success. They would ride to the town of Hager, and then Jonn alone would visit the farmer. He intended to tell the farmer that the older man was a criminal wanted for crimes near Martherus and that he had abducted the boy from his family. The farmer would divulge the day of the next visit, and Jonn would have them. With any luck, the older Dahken would not bring the boy with him; that would likely make it easier to take him into custody. Then they could easily collect the boy from the castle apparently called Sanctum.

For now, he just wanted his backside to survive the journey on horseback.

13.

The summers on the coast stay relatively cool with a constant breeze, and when the weather was so beautiful, Cor took to simply walking outside to think on many occasions. He wasn't sure what else he could do at Sanctum. Though he kept an eye on Cor, Rael clearly had nothing more to teach him, and it was only a matter of time before Rael would have to let him pursue his own path. Though, Cor wasn't sure what that would be.

He enjoyed the beach on many levels, and as he thought about it, he realized it was oddly paradoxical. He found it calming, soothing, and yet the waves and wind could impact the shore with such terrific force. It was cool and breezy, but the sand often threatened to burn one's feet after midday. Cor would sometimes wade into the sea, sometimes even up to his waist, and sometimes he would idly wonder why that, with having spent so much time at sea, he had never learned to swim.

It was the appointed day to purchase their supplies from Cade, and Cor and Rael left shortly after lunch as they had the last time. They had seen no one else since the errant horseman, and even Rael's vigilance had started to wane. Though beginning to relax into their routine again, they agreed that they should never stray far from one another. The day had warmed a bit more than usual in the afternoon, and it really was quite hot. Cade met them in front of his farmhouse as he did last time, reaching upward to take their hands warmly from where they sat upon the wagon.

"Rael, some men have come for you," he said quietly, never ceasing to smile. "They're from Byrverus, and they say you're a criminal. They're waiting around back, and there's a priest in the house watching us." He paused a moment before adding, "It's strange having a priest lie to me."

"Cade, you have been a good friend to us," Rael said, taking the big man's grasp again. "I never wished to bring anything upon you such as this. We will leave now, as fast as this horse can take us."

Rael whipped the reins, spurring the horse into action to turn the wagon about for the road, and Cade stepped back a few paces to keep out of the way. A shout went up from behind the house, and Cor looked back to see a number of armed and armored men charge from the house, barn, and nearby animal pens. Realizing their quarry was escaping, they turned back to mount horses hidden in the barn. Cor uncovered their swords as Rael drove the horse and wagon up the road wildly.

"Rael, we can't get away from them," Cor shouted over the din of the rickety wagon. "The wagon will fall apart, and it's too slow."

"I know!" Rael shouted back. "The road dips into a small gully after one of these hills. When we are out of sight, we will hide on the side of the road and ambush them."

When they topped the hill, Cor looked back and saw the riders approaching. Rael had taken them by surprise, no small thanks to Cade. His reckless driving earned them some distance, but that advantage faded fast. Rael headed down the hill and pulled the horse to a sudden stop at the bottom. He and Cor jumped out of the wagon, Cor tossing Rael his sword. Rael quickly hacked through his horse's harness and pointed Cor to a thick clump of bushes on one side of the road, as he himself hid behind a thick, moss covered oak on the other side.

The riders thundered over the hill, nearly ending themselves in a disheveled heap as they came to a halt. The wagon sat at the bottom of the hill, the horse idly beginning to wander. The men slowly, cautiously approached it, giving Cor a clear look at them. They were clad in brilliant scale mail for the most part, with plate greaves and sabatons. Some wore plate helms, while others preferred the freedom of chain mail cowls, and every one of them carried the royal crest of Aquis.

"We must find them!" came a voice from the top of the hill, and Cor looked up to see an old man he recognized, the priest Jonn. The sight of a familiar face flooded him with emotions, relief and sadness especially, but then also resentment. This man had the audacity to teach him the rightness of Garod, no doubt knowing all the while what his pupil was, and the thought caused Cor's temper to suddenly flare.

The soldiers dismounted to make a more thorough search of the immediate area. The two refugees were on foot, so they certainly could not have gotten far in the brief moments they were out of sight. Cor stayed as low to the ground as he could, gripping his sword in one hand and his pestle fetish in the other. He wasn't sure what would happen, but he intended to follow Rael's lead.

In fact, one soldier with some degree of skill in reading tracks, headed directly for the tree behind which Rael hid. He was looking at the tracks as he walked and stopped when he reached the edge of the road. The man looked up suddenly to see Rael standing directly in front of him. The soldier, a professional to be sure, reached for his sword without hesitation. He opened his mouth to shout to his comrades, only to have Rael plant the blade of his sword directly into it. The blade burst through the back of the man's skull, but the sword's point did not pierce his chain mail cowl and instead pushed it off the back of the man's head to hang suspended in midair.

Rael yanked his sword free, jumped over the body as it fell and cleaved into the unarmored neck of another soldier who had not even turned around. Cor stood and watched from his hiding place as the other soldiers shook off their surprise and converged on his mentor. Naran had told him to be a man of action, to be the first to strike,

114

but these men were Westerners and soldiers of the Queen Herself. And behind them, dismounting from his horse, was a priest Cor had known for years as a child. He froze.

Rael had taken off the sword arm and a leg of a third soldier but was on the verge of being overwhelmed as the others moved in on him. Jonn dismounted and was moving, a staff in hand, toward the melee shouting for everyone to cease combat and lay down their weapons. Rael had no intention of coming peacefully to be certain, and the soldiers were trained to defend themselves from any threat. The Dahken's blade bit into the groove under a soldier's arm, lifting his forearm to block the soldier's blow with his shield. It was the reflex action of a trained warrior, and Rael realized too late that his shield was back in Sanctum with the rest of his armor. The soldiers sword impacted Rael's forearm, and if it hadn't been for his own blow, the soldier may have had enough force to take Rael's arm clean off. As it was, the sword batted his arm downward, hacking deeply into the flesh, and bones cracked.

It was then Cor realized Rael shouted his name, calling for aid. Rael had retreated with his wounded arm back to his tree, buying himself a few moments as the other soldiers moved in on him. They came slowly, not willing to lose more of their number with a headstrong rush, and Jonn was bent over the one of the fallen, his eyes closed. Rael was the killer of his parents' murderer. He had helped Cor, shown him how to readily use his strength and taught Cor the real history of the West. Cor had already decided to not let the past, the West's or the Dahken's, shape his future, but right now his friend needed help. The fog of indecision cleared.

Cor leapt over the bushes, charging into the soldiers from behind on their right flank. One soldier had opted for a steel breastplate as opposed to scale mail, and this gave him superior protection in front, but left him soft leather in back. A thrust deep into the middle of his back, severing the spine was Cor's first strike. He pulled the blade from the man's back and immediately thrust across his body to the left, sliding his sword between the buckles of another's scale mail hauberk. The soldiers reeled momentarily at this new attack, leaving Rael to take advantage of the confusion.

Cor felt himself struck on the right, but he was in motion away from the attack when the blow landed, so it was only a shallow slashing wound across his ribs. The wound seared with pain, his cheeks flushed, and his fetish warmed in his left hand. He wheeled to his right, swinging his sword before him. The force of his blow knocked his attacker backwards, the blade showering sparks as it rent through scale mail through sheer force alone. Cor recovered quickly and thrust the weapon into the man's body, punching it right through his armor. As he reaved and slew, Cor felt strength he never imagined. His blade tore through armor and shield as easily as flesh and bone and forced his enemies back with horrific force.

Rael had fought free of the soldiers, his arm completely healed, but other wounds bleeding. He saw the priest a few short yards away leaning over one of the fallen soldiers, and the man's wounds were closing, his eyelids beginning to flutter.

"Cor, the priest heals the wounded! We must kill him!" Rael shouted.

Rael charged, and seeing the oncoming Dahken, Jonn broke off from healing the soldier who was attempting to stand. He picked up his staff as he backed away, but Rael came on fast, simply charging through the rising soldier like a mad bull. His arms pulled backward to deal a death blow to Jonn, who suddenly planted his staff into the ground in front of him with both hands. A wall of power struck Rael with a great flash, snapping his head backwards and causing him to careen through the air and into the great oak he had hidden behind only a few minutes earlier. He crumpled to the ground limply.

Cor saw this and nearly bolted to Rael's side, but there were yet two more men in front of him, to say nothing of the priest, Jonn. Cor feinted to the right, and one of the soldiers fell for the maneuver, shooting out his sword to attack Cor, who of course was no longer there. Cor whirled and brought his own blade right into the side of the man's head. The blade connected with the soldier's plate basinet, caving it in to a degree that no man could survive, but the sword broke with the terrific impact, over a foot of its length breaking off to fall and stick into the ground point first.

The second soldier took the opportunity and skewered Cor right below the ribs on his left side. The sensation was extraordinary as the cold steel pierced Cor's body, sliding through his organs, and Cor felt the blade come out his back. He was vaguely aware of Jonn screaming something, and the priest stood transfixed by the scene over fifteen feet away as the soldier slowly pulled the length of his sword from Cor's body. Cor stood staring at the soldier for a moment and felt as if he may collapse as he stared dumbly at the nearly black ichor on the soldier's blade. His body poured blood from the mortal wound, and everything inside his gut felt torn asunder. The soldier lowered his sword briefly, realizing he had slain his foe, a young man or boy perhaps little older than his own son, and Cor struck with the lightning quickness of a snake. He brought his broken blade around and beheaded the soldier. The body fell rigid, a great shock of blood soaking the road, the face on the severed head registering unabashed surprise. Cor fell to his knees, exhausted, but he could feel the wound closing. Arteries, veins, and organs mended as the soldier's body bled itself out.

"Let this nonsense be over Cor," said Jonn. He still had not moved from the spot from which he had thrown Rael, though the staff was back in his left hand. Cor looked over at Rael's limp form, and he could not tell if the man was breathing.

"You tried to kill me," Cor said, locking eyes with the priest.

"The Dahken attacked us first. He is a criminal who abducted you from your family. Come with me Cor; come back to Garod, as your father would will it. Queen Erella has every desire to meet you."

"You know nothing of what my father would have willed. I've my own path, and it isn't with you," he sneered. Cor stood to his feet, knowing that he should be dead already, but his wound, rent flesh, and ruptured organs, were completely healed. His strength returned, and he stepped casually toward the priest, his broken sword in hand.

"Cor, I have known you since you were a boy. I do not want to hurt you. Consider your actions now," implored Jonn. "Who talked to you as a boy when village children would not? Who helped you learn right from wrong? Come. Be the smart, sweet boy I remember."

"You also spied on me for your Queen. I can see that now," Cor retorted. He had stopped.

"Keeping you safe was one of my duties," Jonn appeared to concede.

"Safe? This Dahken," Cor said, pointing his sword at Rael's crumpled form, "kept me safe. Captain Naran, a Shet, kept me safe. Your people killed the only person who ever truly taught me what I am!"

Cor again approached, having closed half the distance between them, and Jonn realized Cor was not going to consider anything he said. He called to Garod for strength and pointing his staff at the oncoming Cor, a ray of pure white light shot from its tip. It hit Cor fully in the chest, causing him to stop and look with awe. The ray pierced him, and he could even feel it's divine warmth pass through him. And it did nothing.

Cor laughed as he approached, faster now and with confidence. The priest gripped his staff with both hands and waited until Cor was mere feet away. Jonn planted his staff before Cor in the same way he had Rael, and the same flash of light burst forth, this time with a sound as of thunder. And Cor still stood in front of the priest, unmoved, broken sword in hand. Cor reared backward, then thrust his broken blade forward. It tore through the priest's robes, met his body, and pushed through it. The blade bisected the priest's heart almost perfectly, blood spurting behind and before him onto Cor's hand. Jonn's life poured from him, and he died quickly, silently asking Garod why he had been forsaken.

Cor drove the wagon south towards Sanctum. Rael's horse hadn't completely taken to him behind the reins at first, but soon realized there wasn't much choice in the matter. Perhaps the stallion still held to his indignance at drawing or wagon, but more likely his disquiet was caused by the body that lay in the back of the wagon, a body with skin the gray pallor of the grave and a broken neck. Cor had covered the body with the bloodied robe of Jonn, the priest of a small village near Martherus. He left the other bodies for the vultures, his broken sword still impaling Jonn's heart.

14.

Cor sat in the larder quietly, chin resting on his palm. He'd never been truly alone before, and the realization that he was completely on his own was beginning to set in. He felt oddly naked, exposed, but he shed no tears for Dahken Rael. Cor had no time for that. He now knew the Queen of Aquis wanted him, though for what purpose he didn't quite understand, and though attacked first, the soldiers were quick to react to he and Rael with deadly force. Certainly, more men would be sent, but it might take some time before the Queen knew what had transpired. The faster he moved, the more distance he could put between himself and whoever came after him.

His mind reeling with the growing enormity of the situation, Cor worked to compile a mental list of the things he needed to do. He needed to gather what supplies he had, and of course, find a new weapon. One way or the other, he would need money. Rael seemed to have no shortage of it whenever it was needed; Cor had to find out from where Rael got his gold and silver.

And then there was Rael. The man deserved a burial of some sort.

Cor stood up with purpose, leaving the larder and heading for Rael's room. On some level, it felt rather ghoulish to rifle through the dead man's belongings, but he knew he needed any and all resources at his disposal. Rael had lived a spartan lifestyle, and there was little here. His armor lay in one corner, surely where the Dahken placed it every time he took it off.

There was one object of note, a large leather bound book that lay next to Rael's mattress, and Cor opened this and quickly realized it was the Dahken's journal. He did not want to invade the man's privacy, even in death, but he needed information. He flipped to the last entry Rael made, in which he discussed some of his recent misgivings over taking Cor to Cade's farm. Cor began to turn the pages backwards, seemingly walking through the last several years. Continuing back, he found a page that made him stop suddenly. Rael had made an entry about the events surrounding Cor's parents, and tacked to the page under the entry was the preserved skin Rael had cut from the Loszian's shoulder. His journal entry explained that the tattoo was the mark of the Loszian's master or lord. Cor lightly ran his fingertips down the tattoo, as if expecting it to impart some knowledge to him, and he stared at it for another minute or so before untacking the flap of skin and placing it in a small pouch on his belt.

Cor continued his search in the book, reversing time as he went, and he found an entry dated nearly fifteen years ago where Rael returned to Sanctum after being gone for nearly fifty years. At the time, Rael hadn't known why he came back, but he apparently spent the next several months reacquainting himself with Sanctum's layout and making notes about parts of the castle that were too dangerous to traverse. In this part of Rael's journal, Cor found the information he sought. The main entrance in the front of the keep opened into the keep's hall, where the final battle with the Westerners took place all those centuries ago. The two doors in the rear of the hall exited into a corridor that ran along the back of the chamber, and there was but one other door in that hallway, a huge oaken door, banded with iron and set into the opposite wall. As he was no locksmith and the door was extremely solid, it apparently took Rael nearly a month to circumvent the door's lock. Inside, he said only that he found the wealth of the Dahken, protected by guardians. He did not say what these guardians were, but only that he vanquished several of them. After, they allowed him to enter and leave at will unmolested, so long as he didn't stay long.

No matter what their form, Cor could not fight guardians without a weapon, but he had other responsibilities first, as Rael's body still lay in the back of the wagon. Many Westerners buried their dead, while others interred them into sepulchers and mausoleums, and in his studies, Cor learned that many cultures burned the dead in funeral pyres. He knew that in his many forays through the study he'd seen a scroll detailing Dahken burial rites. It took him nearly an hour to locate it, and he read it over several times. Cor really didn't understand why, but it seemed right that Rael be interred below Sanctum as the Dahken before him. He would need to collect all of Rael's personal effects and then somehow get them and Rael's body down to the catacombs.

A sudden jolt went through Cor's body, and he went rigid, becoming very still. He hadn't thought of the catacombs in some time, and now his blood felt as if on fire. Gooseflesh formed on his arms, and nearly every hair on his body stood on end. He knew now more than ever, something waited for him down those dark stairs, and Cor found himself at the doorway at the top of the abyssal steps, looking down into the darkness with a lit torch in hand. They were steep and only wide enough for his feet if he went down sideways, and the dust of ages caked the steps, disturbed in places from his one foray years ago. There was nothing to hold onto as he began his descent.

Cor kept his wits about him as he slowly went down. He could see nothing except dust and cobwebs, but the feeling that something hovered just beyond the light of his torch would not abate. He counted twenty one steps, and then the staircase turned around at a small landing. After another twenty two steps, the staircase opened into a large room or cavern. Cor estimated that he was at least thirty feet below Sanctum's ground floor.

An extreme sense of déjà vu struck Cor; he couldn't help but notice similarities between this room and the dream he had had more than once. At the same time, there were many differences. The ceiling was only a few feet above his head, and the catacomb had a horribly musty smell. There were crypts everywhere, but they were made of white limestone, not the same indigenous rock as the room itself. Instead of iron stands, Cor saw sconces on the crypts themselves, some containing ancient unlit torches. The crypts were not organized in neat rows, but were clumped somewhat haphazardly, and nearly all of them were marked with names and a glyph signifying them as Dahken. He also found five marked as Lord Dahken; these contained the remains of various leaders of Sanctum throughout the centuries, and it was one of these he stood before for several minutes. It was marked Lord Dahken Rena. Something begged him to open the door to this crypt, but he eventually pulled himself away to continue his search.

Cor found nothing to fear, though he still could not shake the feeling that a constant presence followed his every movement. At one end of the catacombs, he found a small dark hole, just barely large enough for a man. He looked in, finding a tiny cave that wormed deep into the natural rock, and listening carefully, Cor heard the muffled breaking of waves. He wondered if this was the same cave he'd seen at the bottom of the promontory during low tide. Cor continued his survey of the catacombs and found two other staircases, one a spiral stair that had almost completely collapsed, and the other was a stone stair, not unlike the one he came down.

Cor made his way back to his original point of entry to the catacombs, stopping at an unmarked tomb, and he stood before it briefly before igniting the unlit torch in its sconce, which lit easily. He gently pushed on the door, and it simply opened, and as expected, the crypt was completely empty as he expected, with a large stone slab against the wall opposite the door. Having found Rael's resting place, Cor returned to the ground level.

Cor gathered Rael's meager belongings at the top of the stairs; the man had only his armor and shield, sword, and journal. Cor took the items down to the crypt he had selected and placed the sword in the northeast corner as prescribed, and the armor he laid neatly in the northwest corner. Cor hesitated as he placed Rael's shield, his fingertips lingering on the smooth blue stone in its center before he placed the dead Dahken's journal at one end of the stone slab. He'd seen journals of other Dahken in the study, but he was certain they were copies. The original belonged with the man who penned it. He left the crypt, headed back upstairs, and used his torch to light several others in sconces on the way.

Cor returned to the wagon, which still held Rael's body. He gently pulled the man to the end of the wagon until Rael's head fell of the edge and hung downwards unnaturally. Cor looped his arms under the man's shoulders and pulled backward. Rael was not a large man; in fact, Cor was slightly taller, but the sudden weight of Rael's limp body falling to the ground overpowered him. Cor fell backwards onto the ground, Rael's body lying in a heap in front of him. His failure disgusted him, and silently, he begged Rael's spirit for forgiveness.

Cor steeled himself, certain that if he could just get underneath the man, he could carry Rael's body on his shoulders. Cor sat Rael up against a wagon wheel and crouched down sideways next to him, and leaning, he gripped the front of Rael's tunic with his left hand held over his shoulders. He pulled upwards with his left arm, while straightening from the lean. This let Cor slide his right arm up underneath the man's body, gripping the bottom edge of Rael's tunic on the back. Setting his teeth, Cor heaved the man up onto his shoulders releasing a long, muddled groan while forcing his legs to straighten. He stood still for several moments, feeling the muscles of his thighs burn, and he waited until the sensation dissipated. Cor adjusted the body slightly to make the load more even. His head was pitched forward at an awkward angle, and he was keenly aware that Rael's face rested slightly on his left shoulder facing him. Somehow knowing that he owed this to his teacher, Cor carefully and deliberately placed one foot in front of the other as he headed into the keep.

Once he began moving steadily, Cor found the weight relatively easy to bear. He had a task to complete, and Rael was owed the burial of a Dahken. Cor thought about this as he walked, wondering if he was now a true Dahken beyond definition of his blood. For that matter, was he the only one left? He regained focus, dismissing his ruminations, once he reached the stairs. He had lit several torches on his way up, but the climb down would still be treacherous, as the stairs felt less than safe when one wasn't carrying a body. Cor briefly considered dragging Rael down the steps, but quickly convinced himself that would be unwise. If he dragged Rael by the shoulders, no doubt the weight would cause him to lose balance and tumble down the stairs, and dragging the man by his ankles to slowly bash the back of his head in on each stone stair simply would not do. Cor carried Rael this far; he simply must continue.

Cor took the first step gingerly, stepping down with his left foot, followed by his right. He felt the weight on his shoulders keenly as he took the second step in the same manner. He took each step down the first twenty one steps to the landing one at a time as if each one was a challenge in itself, before turning and starting down the second set. By the time he was halfway down these, Cor had become relatively comfortable with the rhythm of his task, and though his muscles began to complain from the effort, he made it to the catacombs without incident.

Cor carried the body to the crypt he had selected, now containing Rael's few personal items. He reached the door, realizing with a sigh of relief that he had left it ajar, for the closer he got to the destination, the more tired his muscles became. He entered the crypt, lit inside by a single flickering torch and turned backwards laying Rael's corpse onto the large slab as gently as he could. Cor turned around and arrayed the man in repose, legs and arms straight and his hands at his sides.

Cor understood that, typically, one of his fellow Dahken would speak, summarizing Rael's accomplishments, but unfortunately, Cor realized he knew little about the man, except that he had found, protected, and taught Cor of his own strength. Cor hoped that Rael's journal set at the foot of his resting place would serve to fulfill such requirements. There was but one other action to take before closing the crypt, and as the most powerful Dahken present, Cor drew a small knife and lightly pierced the tip of his left index finger. A small amount of blood quickly welled up from the tiny cut, and Cor pressed it to Rael's forehead, thus anointing him. Cor wiped the knife's point on the leg of his breeches and sheathed it. He turned and left the crypt, closing the door behind him.

15.

After the ordeal, Cor needed sleep. Every part of his body began to ache, and he labored to walk, as if he trudged through snow. He stopped in the larder briefly to consume an apple and what was left of a stinky cheese. He barely remembered lying down, and he did not remember anything before falling asleep. He awoke with no idea how long he slept, and looking outside, he found it was yet still dark, at least three hours from sunrise. He had the unshakable feeling that he needed to do something right now, and the anxiety increased as he neared the stairs to the catacombs. Cor remembered the crypt he had felt drawn to before, the crypt of a Lord Dahken named Rena, and he turned for the library, though he felt urged to go into the catacombs.

He reached it in darkness, as he rarely needed much light to simply move around these rooms in Sanctum. Once there, he lit a candle, then in turn lit five more on a candelabra. Cor spent some time searching the shelves before finding a thin tome that looked promising, and opening it, he found an accounting of every Lord Dahken of Sanctum going back to Tannes himself. The tome was clearly modern, and Cor was certain it was written in Rael's hand. In fact, the name of the last entry was Rael's, starting at seven twenty eight A.C. Cor took the book to the study's table and sat down. There was always a quill pen and inkwell at the table, and Cor entered the current year, seven thirty eight A.C., to mark the end of Rael's service.

He continued to search the pages of the ledger, finally finding Rena. She was Lord Dahken for nearly two hundred years before The Cleansing, and there was almost no information about her. Idly, Cor wondered what the Dahken did with themselves for nearly two thousand years. Rena was known as a great warrior; her ability to channel the power in her blood to increase her strength was apparently unmatched in her time. Cor reached a section that gave him a tingling sensation in his right arm and flooded his entire body with warmth. Rena fought with a single edged longsword that she had found in an ancient tomb, but there was no explicit description of the weapon. Regardless, Cor knew he would know the sword the moment he saw it, and he also knew exactly where to find it.

Cor placed the book back on the shelf from whence it came, and candelabra in hand, made his way back to his room. There he strapped on his armor; he wasn't sure that he would need it, but after the incident on the road, he vowed never to be caught without it again. It consisted of a chain shirt he simply pulled over his head, a steel breastplate that strapped over the shirt, and a set of arm and legguards.

Cor walked to the stairs leading down into the catacombs. He had forgotten to extinguish the torches before lying down to sleep, but they had burned themselves out anyway. When he reached the catacombs, the air felt noticeably different from a few hours ago. It was thick and heavy, almost humid, and Cor had to force the breath in and out of his lungs. It almost felt as if the air itself impeded his movement.

His destination was Rena's crypt, of course, but he realized he had forgotten one thing when he interred Rael. He stopped at the crypt and examined the door closely; it was like the others, a heavy oak door banded with iron. Cor drew his knife and quite carefully scarred the door deeply, carving two Rumedian glyphs into the wood, one for Lord Dahken and the other for Rael. He appraised his handiwork and, finding it sufficient, sheathed the knife and continued.

128

Cor had no trouble finding Rena's tomb again, as it seemed he was inexorably drawn to it. Barely breathing, he stood outside the small limestone crypt staring at the marked door. He knew he would enter, but something about the entire matter unsettled him. He supposed it was his leftover sentiments towards the morality of Garod. Reminding himself that what he was about to do would not be viewed negatively by any Dahken in history, Cor set his candelabra gently on the floor and pressed against the door. Déjà vu again swept him as he pushed with increasing force. It likely hadn't moved in nearly a thousand years, and it stubbornly resisted his strength. The door finally budged and, with a screech of rusted iron hinges, swung slightly inward. Cor retrieved his candelabra and cautiously entered the crypt.

Lord Dahken Rena's tomb was no different from Rael's other than its contents. A considerable number of artifacts, trophies from adventures no doubt, littered the floor of the crypt, and many were in varying stages of decay due to their age. The northwest corner contained several pieces of armor, made of a mix of leather, scale mail, and plate, though what protection it would have afforded the wearer he wasn't certain. It seemed to Cor that the armor would leave vast portions of the body uncovered. Time seemed to stand still, and Cor's heart leapt into his throat when he saw a sheathed sword leaning in the crypt's northeast corner, covered in centuries of cobwebs and dust.

Cor wiped the detritus away with his free hand, examining the sword more closely, and as he did so, the air grew heavier. An oppressive feeling built within the crypt. Sweat rolled off his brow onto his face and dripped off the end of his nose. The scabbard itself was made of rigid leather; gold accents inlaid with small gemstones adorned the tip and the mouth of the sheath. The sword's guard, hilt, and pommel were all wrought of a gleaming metal, which Cor was certain not to be steel. The guard itself was relatively plain and unadorned, a straight crosspiece about six inches wide that turned up slightly at either end. The top half of the hilt was leather wrapped, leaving the bottom half naked to flow into the pommel, which was a sort of stylized skull. He longed to feel the weapon in his hand and inspect its blade, but somehow, he knew he couldn't just yet.

Cor turned to the limestone slab that lay against the rear wall of the crypt. On it lay a near naked skeleton; tatters of clothing remained, but most of it had decayed over time with the corpse itself. The skeleton was smaller than him, perhaps only five feet in length, and Cor was certain that in life Rena had been a petite woman. He sank to both knees before the remains.

"Lord Dahken Rena, your sword has called me for years, since I first came to Sanctum as a child," Cor said, and he wasn't even certain why he spoke to this skeleton. Like so many things recently, it simply felt right. "I am young, but I've already spilled the blood of men. Your sword yearns for someone to wield it, I feel it in my blood. I swear to you I will do you no dishonor."

Cor bowed his head reverently to the remains for a long moment, and as he did so, he felt the oppressive weight of the air begin to dissipate as if pushed away by a light breeze. He stood and picked up the sword and his candelabra, and turning from the crypt, he pulled the door shut behind him. Cor ventured back up the stairs, the sword cradled lovingly across his left arm, to find the sky beginning to lighten with the first rays of dawn.

Cor could barely contain his excitement, as he wanted to see the sword in the morning light, but his stomach growled with an insistence he couldn't possibly ignore. He dug through the larder, finding little to eat except for some remaining fruit and vegetables. Rael apparently stocked the larder with extreme efficiency, purchasing exactly what he needed for a set amount of time. Cor laid the sword on the table while chewing through the last few edible apples, staring at it with wonder, and the longer he looked at the weapon, the more anxious he became to use it. Finished with his small meal, Cor stood up and took the weapon outside, again cradling it in his arms as if it were a babe. The sun had broken the horizon, and yellow and orange light filtered in through the open gate and damaged parts of the walls. It was cool this morning, and everything seemed to be coated in a layer of fine, cold dew. He breathed deeply of the spring morning air, smelling the ocean on the wind.

Cor quite carefully and deliberately fed his belt through the sword's scabbard and then buckled it. He took his pestle fetish in his left hand as normal and stood in solemn consideration of the sword's hilt. He could feel something in the back of his mind, as if something were singing to him, urging him to draw the weapon. He only placed his right hand on the sword's hilt and immediately jerked it back, stricken with the sensation of pins and needles clear up to his elbow. After a few seconds, the feeling faded and left him feeling oddly alone in the courtyard. Cor gripped the sword again, and the sensation returned, though not nearly as strong as before. He held his hand there for a few moments, refusing to release the weapon, and the feeling again faded.

Cor drew the sword in a quick, high arc meant to decapitate a foe. It was amazingly light, seeming to weigh no more than the fetish in his left hand and cut through the air with lightning speed. The blade had a single, razor sharp edge that was completely free of rust, and the other side of the blade was dull and strong, designed for parrying. A channel ran up the center on both sides of the blade. The weapon was gorgeous, completely free of notches or scratches, and the blade gleamed with an odd purple shine in the morning light unlike any steel Cor had ever seen.

He practiced for some time with the sword, finding that he could maneuver it with far more agility than his old weapon. This weapon felt more like an extension of his arm rather than a separate thing, and it moved precisely as he willed it with grace and strength. Cor noticed the sword's hilt warmed in his hand as he used it, but not from a sense of exertion. The sensation was both comfortable and assuring, and as he sheathed the weapon to return inside, one word came unbidden to his mind - Soulmourn.

Cor began arranging things he would need for travel. Almost no food remained, other than preserved jerky. He could certainly eat it if that was all he had, but he quickly realized that he knew nothing of living off the land while traveling. He would need to purchase provisions, and his only source for that would be Cade. Of course, that was a hope and could be a completely different problem; if Cade chose not to help him, he would likely have to seek provisions in Hager. Cor gathered two large water skins and fashioned himself a bedroll. There was little else he could do to prepare, so it was time to find what he could only term the Dahken treasury.

Taking several large sacks, Cor walked around the outside of the keep, nearing the front entrance. Two huge wood doors, each about twelve feet tall, stood closed with a bar across them. The bar was little more than a wood plank, but clearly had been added recently, likely to keep the wind from opening the doors. This he hefted off its brackets and dropped to the side, and the doors swung open rather easily.

The immensity of the hall surprised Cor; it was over fifty feet wide and larger than that in depth. Light filtered down from unclosed windows high above, perhaps three times Cor's height from the floor, and as he entered, he found the final resting place of many warriors. Centuries old skeletons, most of them fully armored with weapons lying nearby littered this room, and many of them were contorted in unnatural positions of agony, while others seemed to lay in peaceful resolve. Cor disturbed none of these, determined to let them rest as they were, though his passage did aggravate several birds that fluttered about, chattering angrily before lighting elsewhere or simply flying away.

At the rear of the hall was a great rectangular table, nearly as wide as the room itself with no less than fifty chairs around it. At the center of the far side sat a chair that was larger than the others and carved from a dark wood, perhaps mahogany. The back was nearly seven feet tall, and it had large arms carved into the shape of downward turned claws whereas the other chairs had none. It also bore the remnants of an upholstered cushion, long eaten away by time, rodents, and moths. All of the wood bore the scars and weight of time, and small piles of sawdust lay under them where insects or animals had burrowed into it.

On the back wall, Cor saw the two doors as described in Rael's journal, and he opted for the left one, seeing no real difference between the two. It opened easily into a corridor roughly thirty feet long, at the other end of which he saw the other door leading back to the hall. Set into the center of the opposite wall was another huge door, nearly the size of the main doors into the keep and banded with iron as Rael described. Cor approached it, firming his resolve. He had no idea what guardians lay behind the door, but fear lost its place in his heart a day ago at least.

Despite its immense size, this door also opened easily, and a true horde of treasure greeted Cor's eyes. He had never seen so much gold, silver, and gems at one time. Rael never carried much, and the sums he had seen his father make at market were the tiniest fraction compared to this mountain. His eyes moved over open chests and carelessly dropped sacks that spilled over with gold and silver coins, and gems of diverse sizes and colors glittered intermittently in the horde of precious metals.

Cor stepped into the room, an empty sack in hand, unsure where to begin. There was no light source in the treasury itself, and what minimal light he had came from the hallway behind him. There was a sudden sound of movement from the back of the room beyond his vision, followed by a hail of several dozen coins flung in his direction. Cor covered his face with his hands as most of them missed or bounced off his armor, and he drew his sword and fetish, hearing something in the rear of the chamber that shambled his way. He held his sword before him, ready to strike, but the movement instantly stopped and then started again, receding into the back of the chamber again. It came to Cor's mind that the guardians of this treasure may not know him, but they knew Soulmourn, and the last time they encountered the sword, it was in the hands of a Lord Dahken. That was all the safe passage he needed.

Though fairly certain he was now safe, Cor decided not to tarry long. He had little knowledge of the value of gems, and so he avoided them altogether, focusing on as much gold as possible. By the time he filled the first sack, he realized the flaw in this logic the sack seemed to grow heavier the longer he lugged the sack around. He filled the other two sacks with whatever he could lay his hands on. The silver coins were lighter than the gold, and the gems felt nearly weightless in comparison.

Cor tied one of the sacks to his belt and carried the other two, one in each hand, and the weight of the coinage surprised him somewhat. He set the sacks down in the corridor to pull the door shut behind him and then picked them up again to continue outside. Cor dropped the treasure in a heap with relief and set about gathering his other belongings alongside the sacks, including Rael's saddle. He considered the pile for a moment before his eyes narrowed as something occurred to him. Cor jogged into the keep and into the study; from there he took six blank scrolls, a quill pen, two stoppered glass vials of ink, and several coal pencils. All this he brought back to the rest of his supplies.

Cor found Rael's horse around the back of the keep, the black stallion grazing peacefully. He led the animal back around the building where it eyed his small stack of items, especially the saddle. Cor blanketed and saddled the horse, then went about placing the other items in saddlebags or attached to the saddle itself. Comfortable that all was secure, he mounted the horse and trotted out the gate.

16.

With no wagon to pull, the stallion made short work of the road leading to Cade's farm. Cor had taken one last long look at Sanctum once he'd gotten nearly a half mile away from the castle, and somehow, it looked more decrepit and decaying than it had just the day before. He arrived at the scene of yesterday's battle quite quickly, stopping briefly to survey the carnage. Rigor mortis had set in, and the corpses were unmoved, though some birds and other animals had disturbed them a bit. The day warmed readily under the sun and a stench hung over the area despite the constant breeze.

Cor weaved the horse through the bodies, which lay strewn about and continued. Cade's farm was nearby, and as he approached, he could see a large, covered wagon with two horses hitched to it. He came alongside the wagon to find Cade loading large sacks, barrels, and several cages holding chickens into the wagon. Cor could see the farmer's daughter in the distance near pens containing hogs and cows; she opened the gates and left them open.

"We can't stay here after what you two did," Cade said without looking up at Cor.

"I understand, and I'm sorry," Cor replied. Cade looked up then, apparently surprised.

"Where's your father?" asked the farmer.

"They killed him," Cor answered, not seeing the point in correcting the man about the nature of his relationship with Rael.

"I'm sorry," Cade said, standing to face Cor. "That man never done me any wrong. Where are you going?"

"I don't know," Cor looked over his right shoulder. "I think I'll go east across country. I have plenty of water, but I need food that travels well. I don't know anything about hunting."

"I'd stay away from towns," agreed Cade, scratching at the back of his head. "People tend to remember a face like yours." The man rummaged around inside the wagon for a few moments and handed Cor a pack of salted meat and a huge burlap sack. "The sack's got beans in it. Don't taste for much, but boil 'em in some water and soften 'em up. They go a long way. The meat's good for maybe five days. I got work to do. We're leaving tomorrow morning."

Cor thanked the farmer, clasping his arm. He reached down and untied one of the large, heavy sacks laden with gold and silver and dropped it on the wood planking in the back of the wagon. The sack crashed more loudly than he expected, and when it struck, the mouth opened and spilled coins to bounce out into the wagon and on the ground.

"This is for all the trouble we caused you, Cade. You're a good man, and I hope this will help you start over somewhere," Cor said and turned his horse around, the farmer still staring after him incredulously.

Cor struck out across country due east, keeping the horse at a brisk walk. He had no idea what he was doing, where he was going, or what he would do when he got there. What he knew was he needed to leave Sanctum and in fact put as much distance as possible between himself and the castle without using the main roads. There was little doubt in his mind that eventually someone would find out about the battle, and then a true hunt for him would begin. It also clarified one thing for him – the Shining West seemed to have their own thoughts and plans for him, just like the Loszians.

He thought about the Loszian Empire a good bit. Rael had rescued him from one of their agents, the man an

137

assassin of sorts, Cor supposed. He'd killed Cor's parents, but he had clearly meant to abduct Cor. Cor had shoved the flap of tattooed skin into one of the saddlebags with the scrolls and writing implements. He would need to find out to whom the mark belonged, but he honestly didn't have the slightest idea how to do that. Gallivanting across the Loszian countryside asking who a particular mark belonged to did not seem to be an extraordinarily wise thing to do.

Cor rode for three days, stopping to rest at night of course. He didn't bother tethering the horse because Rael had never done anything to contain the stallion, and he never seemed to stray. Every morning, Cor would wake with the dawn, the horse never far away. The countryside of Aquis was comprised of beautiful green and gold savannahs and plains. It was some of the most arable land known in the world, and many fruits and vegetables grew wildly. Cor would stop as he came across these and fill his sacks and saddlebags with them. It was on the fourth day that he came upon a small town on a low lying plain. It was larger than the village near his home as child, but nowhere near the size of Martherus. Close to sundown, Cor decided to sleep the night outside of the town, and he would decide what to do about it in the morning.

Cor did not make a fire to cook by, but instead ate a cold dinner. The meat was nearing the end of its life, and he'd found wild blackberries earlier in the day. Aquis was a naturally bountiful land and finding freshwater was never a problem. He settled down to sleep for the night, his sword near his hand. He had recently found it hard to sleep at night. The ground was cold and hard, unlike the cotton mattress he slept on in Sanctum, and he also had taken to sleeping in his armor. This added heavily to his discomfort, but he refused to be caught unready for battle.

Cor eventually dozed off to sleep, finding himself in a dream. He was standing before a gray stone shelf, on which lay three pieces of gleaming black armor. They

138

seemed familiar, as if he had seen them before, and he realized it had been in another dream years past. He picked up the oddly shaped black helm and turned it around to face away from him, intending to place it over his head. With a hand on each side, Cor lifted it to his head, and then came the bizarre sensation of being watched. He slowly placed the helm back on its resting place and looked down seeing his sword, Soulmourn, and his fetish in their places on his belt. For a moment, he wondered at the fetish, realizing it was different from the gold plated bone pestle he normally carried. This one had a short handle made of ebony, ending in a skull that was human shaped but no bigger than his fist. Two tiny black wings, like those of a bat, extended from the ebony handle just below the skull. He did not recognize it at all, but he knew it was his.

The feeling did not abate, and every hair on the back of Cor's neck stood on end. In the blink of an eye, Cor pivoted to his left, drawing both his sword and the bizarre fetish simultaneously. Against the wall stood a chair, seemingly carved out of the indigenous rock, and a figure sat upright on the rocky throne. It's skin, stretched thinly over the skeletal head and face, was gray as a corpse, no different from Cor's own. Its head was hairless, and its lips black. The figure wore a robe, gray as the stone on which it sat, that appeared to be disintegrating, and its hands extended from the sleeves of the robe, resting palm down on the stone arms of the chair. At first, Cor thought the figure an ancient corpse, its gender not entirely discernible in the advanced state of its age. Except the figure's wide eyes watched at him with unblinking intensity, and Cor stood very still, returning the stare.

"Why do you continue to come here?" the figure asked, speaking in the ancient language of the Chronicler, its black lips peeling back from pure white teeth.

"I'm drawn here in my dreams," answered Cor, though the explanation sounded hollow.

"This is a dream then," the figure replied. "That is good. I do not have to kill those in my dreams."

"Who are you? What is this place?" asked Cor.

"If this is a dream," said the robed figure, opening his eyes, "then you are I."

"I don't understand," Cor replied, confusion knitting his brow.

"Everyone in our dreams is but a representation of some part of ourselves. I know the answer to your questions. If you must ask, then this is not a dream, and you are not I. Be gone."

He lifted one finger from its resting place, and Cor's sight went black. The shock knocked him backwards, and he lost his balance and began to fall. He hit solid ground with an at once jarring but gentle impact, and once he was certain that he was awake, Cor sat up and looked around. He was still at his campsite, lying on his bedroll, and the horse was asleep a few yards away. His sword and fetish lay where he left them, and his fetish was not the bizarre skull and batwing thing from the dream but his familiar bone pestle. It was still dark.

Cor sat there breathing for a few minutes, before sighing and laying back down to sleep, but sleep did not come easily. He was certain the sky lightened with the first morning light before he finally fell asleep again, and he slept later into the morning than usual. He really had no intention of sleeping late, but he simply couldn't force himself to rise. This led Cor to realize that it didn't really matter anymore if he awoke at sunup, as he no longer had no one to answer to anymore.

As he breakfasted, he decided to enter the town ahead, and though he didn't really want to make his presence known, he needed additional provisions. Also, Cade's comment about his face being one people would remember made him think. He should purchase a hooded cloak, hopefully something oversized that buried his face in shadow. He stroked his face feeling scraggly fuzz that he shaved off using his knife every few days. He should also stop shaving; a beard would help cover his face.

Before entering the town, Cor muscled the two large sacks of gold and silver into his saddlebags, keeping only a small amount in a pouch on his belt. It would not be wise to let either the merchants or local citizens know he had huge amounts of gold. Such a thing would draw even more attention than his pallor. Cor hadn't seen civilization for some time, and though this town was no Martherus, it was wonderful in its own way. It had many of the same sounds and smells, both pleasant and horrid, and the town was laid out in a rational, pragmatic way; a north south road ran through the town, and the markets lined this road. There were merchants everywhere hawking goods to each other and passersby. Most of the merchants did not notice Cor's odd appearance, or at least pretended not to notice, though some of the other citizens did watch him.

Cor had no trouble locating a suitable cloak. It was made of light brown wool and would cover his features well, though he decided not to don it until he was well away from the town for doing so felt as if it would draw additional suspicion. Ignoring the pointed looks and whispering of nearby children, he purchased some other provisions, including another large sack of beans and some very reasonably priced potatoes. Cor wasted no time in the town and left out the south gate as soon as his business was complete, aware that eyes watched him, even if they only belonged to town guards. He continued on the south road until he hadn't seen another person for over a mile and then again cut east across the countryside.

Cor thought while riding, as there really wasn't much else to do. His dream last night disconcerted him greatly for several reasons. Most of his dreams were vague, details blurred into a background of melded grays, but he remembered every aspect of last night's vision, no matter how minute, even down to the thickness of the dust on the floor. Rarely did he recall dreams beyond the first few minutes of waking, and then they would fade quickly. Yet, this one stayed as clear in his mind as if it were a recent memory, refusing to fade into nothingness, and while on occasion, Cor would have a dream that repeated weeks or even months later, he couldn't remember a dream that continued another from years prior.

The fetish he carried in the dream was another matter altogether. He could see it clearly in his mind's eye, and it was bizarre and alien to him. But in the dream, the talisman was familiar to him and warmed in his hand just like Soulmourn. Cor concentrated on that sensation, hoping to discern some other knowledge about the skull headed fetish as he had his pestle, but regardless of how hard he focused on the memory, no new thoughts came to him, making it clear he had not actually touched it.

Cor put the thought out of his mind for some time, but the image of the fetish came back to him later that evening as he sat quietly boiling beans over a fire. Somehow, he knew he had to find it, and Cor considered the fact he felt a call from the east, perhaps from a great distance. The choice to go east had seemed random, yet he had done it twice without real thought. It occurred to him that perhaps the fetish was a Loszian creation, and that would explain his eastern direction.

Cor rested his hand on the hilt of Soulmourn, and instantly he knew that he was wrong. In his mind, he saw a man of regal bearing and in a sheath strapped to his back was Soulmourn. He was humanoid, but shorter than most men at just under five feet tall, which Cor judged easily against the length of the sword itself. The man had brown skin with a shaved head and wore heavy, bulky gold jewelry all over his body. He stood before an empty golden throne on a raised marble dais in a great hall of marble floors and granite columns. He was a king, certainly, his legs arrogantly bracing him in a wide stance.

To the right of the throne was a second golden throne, though this one was slightly smaller. A wonderfully gorgeous woman with perfect white teeth that seemed to glow in contrast against her ebony skin sat leisurely in the smaller throne, legs strewn over one golden arm. She was lithe of limb but with toned and well defined muscles, and she wore only a loincloth of purple silk and a circlet of gold on her shaved head. In one hand she held a twisted scepter, and in the other a wicked looking item that Cor recognized immediately.

As he watched, time began to rush by, and the rulers aged and died, replaced by others who carried the sword, staff, and fetish. The line of rulers ended with the last two remaining dead in their thrones, none to replace them, and as they decayed into skeletons, the entire hall became shrouded in shadow and cobwebs.

The scene did not shift for what seemed like an eternity, though it certainly was no longer than a few seconds. A ray of light burst onto the scene from above, accompanied by a rain of dust, dirt, and small debris. The light grew larger, illuminating the hall, and several ropes fell into view from above. Strangely dressed men and women slid down these ropes to the hall's floor. Speaking a language Cor had never heard before, they began to explore the ruin and scribed notes on bound stacks of thin paper with oddly small implements. There were two men who were clearly in charge, and they directed the others to load loose items from the hall into wood crates packed with hay or straw, including the sword and fetish. As the crate's lid was pounded shut over Soulmourn, the scene went black.

Bright light returned with the creaking of wood and iron nails, and another man lifted Soulmourn out of its crate and placed it onto a cold metal table. Bright white light shone from circular objects set into a gray ceiling, casting their light across the many items were laid out on the table, all of them recovered from the hall turned tomb. The man who stood over the table was of short stature. Also oddly dressed, he was cleanly shaven and bald, and he wore a strange glass apparatus over his eyes that seemed to rest on his nose and over his ears. He looked at every item with apparent interest, examining them with utmost care, and he took measurements, writing many things down.

The scene sped forward at a dizzying rate. People came and went faster than Cor could follow, and the objects disappeared from the table. Eventually a woman picked up Soulmourn and took the sword through a series of doors and hallways. She entered a large room with marbled floors and various statues. Large alcoves were set into the walls all about this room. She walked to one of these and placed Soulmourn into a holder set into the wall. Many of the items and artifacts from the ancient hall were also in this alcove, including the fetish. The woman touched something out of view, and a perfectly transparent glass pane slid down from above, separating the alcove from the larger room with a hiss of air.

The odd light came and went at a fast rate, which was the only way in which Cor could detect the passage of time. Finally, the light returned and with it came the sounds of people. At first small groups of people of every race and age, all of them wearing bizarre clothing with curious affectations of jewelry and hair, filtered into view of the alcove. Time again sped forward, and Cor watched as hundreds, then thousands and even more came through the large room to stop, stare, and point at the various alcoves. Cor was amazed at the vast array of diversity that passed through the scene, but eventually, the masses decreased to smaller numbers and disappeared altogether. The light vanished, leaving the room and alcove in total darkness.

Cor had no sense of how much time had passed before a woman appeared, burning away the webs and dust of ages with a torch. She wore armor that Cor had seen before in a crypt only recently, and it covered too little of her gray skin to be significantly protective. The jerkin had a small bronze breastplate fashioned as an open mouthed skull with leather and iron straps that wrapped her sides like a ribcage. Two other straps went over her shoulders to connect to the back. Cor could see the fullness of her breasts through the gaps in the armor, and her muscled abdomen stood out almost completely exposed. This was Rena, a beautiful and apparently dangerous woman that would one day become Lord Dahken of Sanctum, and just looking at her stirred Cor in ways with which he was familiar and embarrassed.

She sauntered arrogantly and directly toward the glass covered alcove and looked at the objects inside, her final gaze resting on the sword. Rena tapped on the glass with one gauntleted hand, a sound that passed through the alcove's covering ever so slightly. She mouthed a vile oath, reared back, and rammed her steeled fist through the glass in a shatter of shards and splinters. Her arm was cut deeply in several places, but she paid no mind as she grasped the sword's hilt and withdrew the weapon from its place. Rena examined Soulmourn at length, her face alight with satisfaction, before turning and swaggering out of the room. The scepter and fetish had fallen from their places into the bottom of the alcove amidst broken glass and dust.

The vision ended, Soulmourn's hilt warm in Cor's hand. Soulmourn and the bizarre fetish had apparently always been together, the weapons of choice for a line of ancient monarchs, and they had been taken from the hall turned tomb and taken to a place that was indeed very bizarre. Cor had never heard of such a place in existence, even in the writings of the Chronicler, and he could not help but wonder who these strange people were. But regardless, Rena had found the place, and she came for Soulmourn but not the fetish. Cor needed to return to Sanctum's catacombs and search Rena's personal effects, and with any luck, she kept a journal like Rael had that would point him in the right direction of the fetish's resting place.

Cor came to another realization – it was very possible that something else awaited him in the Loszian Empire.

17.

Cor took only three days to return to Sanctum. He turned due west the next morning, crossing the road he'd turned off of the day before and continued. The weather stayed fair, though warm, and the stallion crossed the distance quickly. Cor and the stallion came out of a light wood atop a hill, much like he and Rael had two years ago, to see Sanctum and its crumbling walls, looking just as he had left it a week ago.

On the road leading into Sanctum from the north, Cor saw four hooded figures on foot just entering the castle's gate. From his angle, he couldn't see them once they passed the gate, but he was certain they had not spotted him either. He dismounted and walked the stallion back into the wood, tying the reins to a thin tree. The horse was very displeased by this treatment, but Cor could see little other option. Approaching Sanctum on foot would be much quieter, and he didn't want the robed men to leave the walls and see his horse milling about. He also removed his own hooded robe and draped it over the horse's saddle.

It was about a thousand yards to Sanctum's walls and most of that was uphill. Crossing such a distance quickly on foot while wearing armor took more energy than Cor anticipated, and by the time he reached the castle, he had to lean against its walls to regain his breath for several minutes. As he slowed his breathing, he listened carefully for any sound indicating the men were coming back but heard none. Breathing easily again, he furtively poked his head around the corner, looking through the gate.

Seeing no sign of the invaders, he dashed into the courtyard and hid behind the smithy, which was the closest of the small buildings. As quietly as his armor would allow him, Cor moved around the back of the smithy and again sprinted across open ground to the armory. There was yet no sign of the four hooded figures, but the main doors leading into Sanctum's hall were slightly ajar. Again, Cor skirted the rear of the small building and was about to approach the doors when one was kicked open from the inside. He ducked back behind the armory as three men came out of the hall, the bulkiest of them carrying a fourth.

They wore heavy dark robes, which were too warm for this season, and their hoods were now down about their shoulders. Two of the men were clearly Westerners, one short and weasel like in appearance, the other nearly seven feet tall and almost as wide. It was he whom carried the fourth man, before dumping him unceremoniously on the ground. The last man drew a long look from Cor. He was tall, well over six feet, and narrow of shoulders. Everything about him appeared stretched out along his height, as if every bone in his body had been racked, giving him a gaunt, alien visage, and he spoke to the other two, clearly in charge. Cor realized he was the Loszian he had seen speaking with Kosaki in Katan'Nosh, the one who paid Kosaki to abduct him. Anger flared in Cor's eyes and veins.

"The two of you," he said in Loszian, "return to the library. Start there and make your way back out. Set aflame everything that will burn."

"What of him, milord?" asked the weasel faced man.

"He was stupid like all of you Westerners, dazzled by shiny objects, and he died for it," said the Loszian with a sigh. "But it matters not; he will serve me better in death than he did in life."

Cor stood with his back against the wall of the armory, listening to this exchange. He knew he couldn't let the Loszian burn Sanctum. While the keep itself may stand, the accumulated knowledge in the study was far too valuable to lose. The men were perhaps ten yards away, probably not close enough for him to close the distance while maintaining the element of surprise. The two began to light torches, and the Loszian stood over the corpse, his hands weaving. His fingertips began to glow with a deep purple power, and Cor knew he had no more time for thought.

He rounded the corner and headed straight for the necromancer at a full sprint, drawing Soulmourn and his fetish at once. The Loszian, focused as he was on the corpse, looked up only too late, but fortunately for him, Cor underestimated how quickly he would close the distance. Rather than kill the sorcerer with a blow from his sword then and there, Cor charged bodily into him. The Loszian, bowled over and knocked sideways, hit his head hard on the keep's stone wall while Cor flailed to the ground, sprawling. Fortunately, he held onto his weapons, and not stunned like his enemy, he recovered to his feet quickly. The big man, less surprised than his comrades, hurled his lit torch at Cor, who could do nothing but turn away while ducking to avoid the flames. The small man dropped his torch to the ground, fumbling with two long poignards.

"Go!" shouted the big man. "I'll handle him." He pulled the knot loose at his neck and shrugged off the cloak, revealing an armored torso. His arms were heavily muscled and his legs as large as tree trunks. Cor tried to break for the smaller man who had picked up his torch and was making for the keep's side entrance, but the muscled warrior blocked his way, producing a massive two handed battle axe.

The man grinned and leered as he brought his axe around in huge sweeping strokes. There was little skill in it, but Cor knew, armor or not, one strike would likely end him. The Brute laughed maniacally as his attacks missed Cor by inches and clanged off stone with showers of sparks and debris, living for the joy of carnage. Cor needed only one opening, but his enemy recovered from every swing of his great axe with the reflexes of a tiger. Cor ducked and dodged, sometimes falling, or scrambling out of the way of a blow that would surely kill him.

As the brute swung, he slowly tired, and he finally faltered with a sweep of his axe that swung too far wide; he couldn't bring it back around before Cor struck with the quickness of a snake. Soulmourn cut through the iron thews of the giant's right arm neatly and to the bone. Brute raged and brought the giant axe around with only one arm in a mighty arc aimed at Cor's head. Cor easily ducked this, and again he struck, completely severing a huge leg above the knee. Brute lost his grip on the axe, and it flew for many yards before landing heavily, and he uncontrollably rotated on his remaining leg and fell onto his chest. He tried to turn himself over, but his ruined right arm would not support any weight at all.

"Slay him," came a voice in heavily accented Western, and Cor turned to see the necromancer standing behind him. "I am impressed. Slay him now or not. He will die soon enough, I am sure. Unfortunately, he is not much use to me now. Even risen, he will do me little good so damaged."

"Call your man back. If he burns Sanctum, I will kill you both," Cor threatened in perfect Loszian.

The necromancer's face registered surprise at hearing his native tongue, but only for a moment. "I am afraid it is far too late for that. Yes, look, smoke rises into the air. Come with me, Dahken Cor. You should not live in the squalor of a decaying fortress. You already know the Westerners would use you for their own ends. Come with me back to Losz where you will be treated as a king, if not a god. All your whims and pleasures shall be indulged whilst you train a new generation of Dahken. Together we shall overthrow both empires."

150

"You're the one who sent Kosaki after me in the Narrow Sea," Cor accused, eliciting no denial from the Loszian. "Was it your man who slaughtered my parents?" Cor asked.

The weasel faced man had emerged from Sanctum, tossing his torch in behind him. Acrid smoke began to billow out of the doorway behind him.

"I did not order him to kill them. He acted alone in that matter, but your parents were little more than breeding stock for you. You had less in common with them than they did with insects. Surely you know that," the Loszian said with absolute confidence in the rightness of his words. Cor felt his temper flare, but he needed more information from this sorcerer before he killed the Loszian.

"How did you find Sanctum?"

"I have always known the location of Sanctum. It was only an issue of knowing you were here," answered the Loszian, the corners of his mouth upturned slightly. "Now, let us leave this place."

Cor had no intention of leaving until he found what he came for, but his hopes of that were literally going up in smoke. He could now hear the cracking sounds of fire spilling forth from Sanctum, and he knew he had little time. Cor had less than fifteen feet to cross between him and the Loszian, and he did so in just a few long strides. Before his blow could land, the necromancer clapped his spidery hands together, and a brilliant light flashed in Cor's eyes, forcing him to duck his eyes behind the inside of his elbow. When his vision cleared, the Loszian was gone.

The weasel faced man still stood before him, apparently also blinded. Cor moved towards the man, and he bounded away as fast as a jackrabbit. The man ran straight for the dilapidated curtain wall that protected two sides of Sanctum, discarding his robe in the process. Before Cor could reach the wall's base, Weasel Face was already halfway up, free climbing the stonework faster than a mountaineer could dream of it. Cor knew he couldn't catch the man, and by the time he ran around the outside of the wall, Weasel Face would be down the other side and gone.

Cor picked up a broken stone brick and hurled it at the runaway climber just as he reached the top. The brick missed by inches, bringing a laugh from Weasel Face as he straddled the wall, a leg thrown on either side of it. He waved down at Cor in a manner of goodbye, just as the stone he sat upon shifted and tumbled down the wall with Weasel Face still sitting on it. Cor leapt aside as the two landed in a jumbled heap at the wall's base, Weasel Face broken and beaten to a pulp by the journey.

Cor rushed back to the keep but stopped short of entering. He needed to get down into the catacombs, but there was one thing he had to see first. Sheathing his sword, he half ran to the big man who lay still alive, but only barely. His eyelids were heavy, and his chest barely moved while a huge puddle of blood at the end of his severed leg slowly soaked into the ground. The man's armor did not cover his shoulders or arms, and on his left shoulder Cor found the emblazoned image that matched the tattoo of the man who killed his parents. He then knew for certain he must hunt down and kill the Loszian sorcerer, but a more pressing matter was at hand.

Cor sprinted into the burning ruins of Sanctum, the main room he had occupied with Rael full of flames and black smoke. He quickly realized he couldn't breathe and fought the stars that threatened to black out his vision. The timbers comprising the ceiling had caught aflame, and Cor could hear them creaking in complaint, likely to give way at any moment, and he charged through the fire into the stone hallway beyond. With nothing here to burn there was little fire, but the smoke thick smoke still threatened to choke him into unconsciousness. He ran past the rooms he and Rael had slept in, the mattresses, in fact anything flammable, burning hotly. The study was awash with flame, and Cor had to stay on the side of the corridor opposite the doorway due to the shear heat of the blaze.

Cor quickly lost his momentum, his run turning into a staggering gait as he could no longer find clean air to breathe. He came to the stairs leading down into the catacombs just as he was certain he could go no further. He half staggered, half fell down the first set of stairs to the landing, where he coughed horrendously for several minutes. With the cooler, cleaner air, the smoke in his lungs cleared, but the coughs gave way to one of his chronic coughing fits, one of the worst he'd had in years. He hacked up several large globs of crimson streaked phlegm, as well as pink and red masses he dared not contemplate.

Cor lay there for some time, the fire raging overhead, before he could move again. He finally made his way down the rest of the steps into the catacombs, and the air here, though stale and stagnant, was clean and cool as smoke and heat tend to rise. Cor realized he had another problem; though some ambient light filtered down the stairs, he could walk little more than fifteen feet without being in total darkness. He yanked a torch out of the sconce on the nearest crypt and gingerly made his way back up the stairs. A piece of flaming detritus had fallen onto the steps little more than halfway up, and Cor used this to light his torch.

Returning to the catacombs, he set out for Lord Dahken Rena's tomb yet again. Hopefully, Rena would be as understanding about this intrusion as she had his first. As he walked further into the catacombs, he could still hear the fire above; in fact, it seemed to rage more strongly than before, and occasionally he would hear large crashes. Cor found and entered the tomb with little difficulty. He had no desire to stay here long, somewhat concerned with the fire above him, and he knew that as it was, getting out of the catacombs may be nearly impossible. He used his torch to light another inside the tomb and set them both in sconces on opposite walls to provide him ample light. It didn't take Cor long to find what he needed; Rena had an extensive journal, and it seemed she obsessed constantly in recording the details of her life.

Cor unrolled two scrolls, made of some type of leather, and wrapped them around the thick tome. He quickly removed his breastplate and chain shirt, followed by the sweaty tunic underneath. He turned the tunic into a sort of sack, inserted Rena's leather wrapped journal into it, and then tied the tunic's sleeves around his belt. Cor pulled his chain shirt back on and buckled on the breastplate; the steel was extremely uncomfortable on his bare skin, and the chain links continuously pinched him painfully as he moved. He quickly bowed before Rena and exited the crypt, closing the door behind him.

Cor carried one torch with him; the other he'd left burning in the crypt, but he was unconcerned as it would burn itself out shortly. He knew he couldn't exit by way of the stairs he came in, so he made for the matching set he had seen on the other side of the catacombs. He found it easily enough, but it was blocked only a few feet up by an ancient cave in. The stone, some of it hewn and shaped blocks, some not, was well settled and wholly unmovable. Cor had no doubt some of the natural boulders that blocked the staircase weighed more than ten men could lift.

As Cor contemplated this new, somewhat grim discovery, he noticed a low rumble over the other signs of the fire above. The sound quickly built into a roar as the entire catacombs began to shake violently. Cor struggled to keep his footing and began to sprint, realizing he may have but one chance to exit these catacombs alive. He could see the hole in the wall of the catacombs and just as he approached it, a great quake rocked everything around him and sent him sprawling. The cave that comprised the catacomb's ceiling burst inward as huge blocks of masonry and stone tumbled through the opening. Cor struggled to his hands and knees and scrambled the remaining feet into the cave. An enormous impact exploded from the catacombs behind him. It threw Cor forward into the cave with great force, and then he knew nothing.

18.

Cor awoke slowly, his head throbbing as if it had been beaten in by a rock wielding giant. As it turned out, this wasn't far from the truth, as whatever had thrown him through the air had brained him against the rocks in the cave. On some level he was sure that he was lucky to be alive. His torch was gone, and the cave was completely pitch black. Cor checked himself over and found Soulmourn and Rena's journal still attached to his belt, but his pestle fetish was gone.

He searched his surroundings by feel and found that the cave had three apparent walls. Two were rough and solid, but the third seemed to consist of blocks of masonry, large boulders and much dirt and other debris. It seemed Cor had been very nearly crushed alive by a cave in, and he nearly panicked with the thought that he may not have a way out. He calmed himself and quieted his breathing; listening intently, he heard the sloshing sounds of water, like that of waves within the cave.

With little other option, Cor focused on the sound and slowly felt his way through the cave on his hands and knees. The cave was dry, though the air was fetid, and at times the cave closed in suddenly to add to Cor's unease. More than once, he crawled face first into what he believed were stalagmites, jostling his already pained head and mounting his frustration, but he moved forward, always forward, the cave beginning to dampen, until he reached a point that the cave clearly opened up to either side. He reached outward several feet in each direction, unable to follow the cave walls. The entire cave stank horribly, but Cor had found the source of the sounds of waves he had been hearing; somewhere nearby, this cave opened into the sea. Uncertain as to where to go now,

Cor continued forward ever so slowly, finding that the cave floor sloped suddenly downward and was very slick with slimy, wet scum. He noticed that a dim light shown far below; it was an eerie, pale blue light that seemed far away, but it certainly did not emanate from fire, which meant he went in the correct direction.

Cor turned around, intending to lower himself down the slope feet first, and he hoped to use the heels of his boots to help him gain purchase on the uneven, slick cave floor. The flaw in this plan became quite evident; as soon as Cor's hands were no longer on the level part of the cave floor, he immediately slid downward, and his boots did nothing to slow him or give him purchase. His hands received many abrasions in his vain attempts at slowing his momentum, and after several long seconds of sliding uncontrollably, he came to rest through none of his own efforts. The cave floor simply and suddenly leveled. Cor lay there for a moment, relieved, before a small wave washed over his legs and then pulled away.

Cor sat up and yelled in triumph at what he saw, raising his fist into the air. The cave closed into a small tunnel, large enough for a man that clearly led outside; sunlight filtered through the water, seemingly turned blue. Waves occasionally came through the tunnel, but when they receded, Cor could see clearly through into the open air out the other side. The tunnel couldn't possibly be more than twenty feet in length, and it appeared just tall enough to stand in if he hunched over.

He was convinced that this was the same cave he'd seen at the bottom of the promontory, which meant the tunnel would be empty of water at low tide. Cor had no idea how long he had been unconscious or in the caves, which meant he had no idea when low tide would occur. Also, it was easily conceivable that high tide would completely flood the cave, drowning him. He had no other option but to chance the tunnel now.

The ocean frightened him in many ways, and Cor had no idea how to swim. Aboard ship, one had the illusion of control over the sea, but in the water, the sea herself was the master. He decided to acquaint himself with the feel of the water and the rhythm of the waves for a few minutes before committing himself fully. He removed Soulmourn and the tome from his belt and sat them on the cave floor where the gently rolling water would not reach them. Cor slowly lowered himself into the pool of water at the end of the tunnel; he'd always had the impression that the sea was a cold place, and this water surprised him with its warmth. He stood there and allowed a few waves to impact him; the water tasted of salt and stung his eyes, but he found the force of it manageable. However once he moved into water nearly up to his chest, the weight of his armor pulled down on him frightfully, and he was glad the water was shallow.

Cor lifted himself back onto the cave floor, his muscles beginning to protest the constant abuse. He unstrapped his breastplate and legguards, allowing them to clang on the stone floor, and he pulled off his chain shirt in relief and tossed it on the pile. Last, Cor loosened the buckles on his armguards and let them fall as well. He again belted Soulmourn and tied the arms of his tunic together, hanging Rena's journal around his neck. He hated to expose the book or sword to the saltwater, but somehow, he knew it would not harm Soulmourn. As for the journal, he could only hope that his improvised wrappings would protect it.

Cor looked at the armor wistfully before again lowering himself into the pool of water; the book did not float up to his face as he expected it to, but in fact hung heavily against his chest in the water. The saltwater stung the many small cuts and nicks he'd received from the chain shirt, but after a few moments it cooly soothed the miniscule wounds. Movement was easier without the heavy armor, and Cor was certain he could manage this last task.

Cor stepped into the tunnel immediately following a wave, crossing several feet in the tunnel while the water level was low. He walked with his neck and shoulders uncomfortably hunched over and had to be careful he didn't knock the back of his skull on the ceiling. The tunnel was shockingly smooth under the touch of his fingers and somewhat slick under his booted feet. When the first wave came, Cor braced himself, pushing his arms and legs away from his body with as much pressure as he could manage. The water washed over him and into the open pool behind him, and again, it was not nearly as violent as he imagined.

He continued forward without hesitation, only to have his feet ripped out from under him as the wave receded back out to sea. Cor went down under the water, his hands immediately grasping the journal to his chest and the hilt of his sword. He felt himself dragged out of the tunnel for a panicking moment, and then the pressure eased as the tunnel emptied into the sea. Cor stood up in the tunnel, coughing and gasping for breath, but fortunately, the coughing passed quickly and did not lead to an attack as the smoke had before.

Feeling stupid, Cor blinked the water from his eyes and cursed himself for a fool. He had anticipated the strength of the wave coming into the tunnel, but not going back out to sea. As his vision cleared, Cor could see that he was only mere feet from the exit. Cor waited for the next wave to wash over him and immediately ducked through the cave's mouth. He stood in three or four feet of water at the bottom of a rocky cliff, the late afternoon sun shining down warmly on him. Cor couldn't easily see below the surface, but his uneven, fumbling steps found the bottom was strewn with rocks as he remembered. He saw a wave beginning to rise, heading to break against the rocks and cliff face, and he clambered across the rocky bottom, using the cliff itself to steady himself. By the time the wave broke, Cor stood in only about a foot of water, and it lapped gently against the back of his knees. He walked a few feet up the rocky beach and collapsed in exhaustion, allowing the warm summer sun to wash over him.

Cor lay there half asleep until the sun began to sink into the horizon. He forced himself up and moving north up the beach, realizing it had been at least six or seven hours since he left Rael's horse tethered to a tree. He turned east, nearly asleep, knowing that he had nearly a mile to reach the edge of the wood and the stallion, and by the time Cor crossed the distance, the horse grumbled its annoyance, tail swishing in irritation at being so restrained for so long. Cor tossed his bedroll on the ground and then released the animal to graze at his will, before removing his sword and the journal from his belt and lay down to sleep dreamlessly.

19.

Cor slept late into the morning, a habit that seemed to be forming in the last week or so, but on the other hand, he was certain that he had not dealt with this much hardship ever in his life. He immediately fished Rena's journal out of his tunic and laid the tunic out to dry in the sun. Between the cotton tunic and the leather scrolls he had wrapped around the journal, he was pleased to find that the tome seemed perfectly dry and undamaged, and he breakfasted and flipped through the journal while waiting for the sun's warmth to dry his tunic.

Rena had lived three hundred years and was Lord Dahken of Sanctum for nearly two hundred, having died before The Cleansing. She apparently started keeping her journal during her teenaged years, at which point she came to Sanctum and went through a training and education regimen like Cor's. Rena wrote her entries with almost obsessive detail, recording nearly every blow in combat and describing sunrises in poetic prose. As he scanned the pages, Cor found she even recorded her sexual encounters with exceptional detail, evoking feelings that Cor simply wasn't sure how to handle.

It was just before Rena became Lord Dahken that she had found Soulmourn in a bizarre and ancient edifice. The building seemed to be made of steel with accents of precious metals, and one side was wide open to the elements as ancient, shattered glass littered the area. Though known, the building was avoided by the Westerners of the day and ignored by the Loszians. The sword called to her blood, just as it had called to his, and she found the strange building easily enough. Rena had even drawn a rough map showing its location, and it was

161

that which bothered Cor significantly. Based on other landmarks, he was certain the building he sought was in the southern portion of the World's Spine, though her description said nothing of mountains. With the violent creation of the mountain range during The Cleaning, did the building even still stand?

Cor closed the volume, and deciding it was time to get moving, he collected the stallion from where it grazed nearby. He gathered his belongings and slipped the journal into a heavy sack, which he hung from the saddle. His tunic was mostly dry, and he pulled it over his head, followed by the hooded cloak he had purchased. It was going to be a sweltering day, but Cor intended to go into the town of Hager a few miles to the north. He did not want to announce who he was to every soul in the street.

Before Cor turned north, he walked the horse to Sanctum; yesterday, in his exhaustion he noted that something about it looked odd. Today, it was plainly obvious that the tower had come down from the fire, as no doubt, the wood spiral stairs leading upward contributed substantially to its support. The fire likely had spread into the tower, and the ancient, worn stones could simply no longer keep the tower aloft. When Cor reached the gate, the total devastation astounded him, and he stood staring in disbelief. The tower had indeed come down, and the huge mass of stone and masonry crashed down with such force that it punched through the keep's floor into the cave below. The catacomb's ceiling gave way, and the entire keep had collapsed into its depths. Only a few of the smaller outbuildings survived, and Cor had no interest in testing the strength of the ground within the walls. Sanctum was gone, a smoking hole in the ground as the remnants of the fire still burned down within. All of the recorded history, the treasure, and the remains of Dahken before him were gone.

Cor turned his horse north for the town of Hager just past Cade's farm. The necromancer may have vanished in a flash of light, but he and his servants hadn't arrived that way. If they had simply used magic to transport into Sanctum instantaneously, they would have arrived before Jonn and his soldiers. This meant that the Loszian may have discovered Cor's location at the same time as Aquis' queen but took much longer to arrive through normal means of transit. Did that indicate a spy in Queen Erella's palace? And why that should concern him?

Hager was a small port, and being the nearest settlement, it followed that the Loszian had come by sea through that town. Of course, a Loszian necromancer would not exactly be welcome in Aquis, so Cor needed to find a captain who would have been willing to smuggle the four men. The intrigue of it all made Cor's head hurt; the realization that the world was so much more complex than what he'd been taught as a child continued to grow. And he wanted nothing to do with any of it, outside of killing the Loszian.

Hager was little different from the town Cor had visited a few days ago, at least on the surface, and he kept his hood drawn about him, which drew less attention than his deathly pallor would have. It made sense that the Loszians would have wasted no time seeking him at Sanctum, so they must have arrived on a ship that morning or just the previous day. It took only one inquiry, which he paid well for with a local merchant, to find out two ships had arrived in the timeframe. The first, a galley from Tigol arrived at dawn, while the other ported in the afternoon. By that point, Cor was already in battle with the Loszians, so he set out for the docks in search of the foreign galley, which took minimal effort.

About a dozen men, sailors by the look of their calloused hands and bare feet, unloaded several wagons, carrying sacks, crates and barrels up a gangplank and disappeared below the ship's deck. A Tigolean stood on deck shouting orders while talking to a Western merchant.

He handed the merchant a small, but heavy sack and with their business concluded, he followed the merchant down the gangplank to oversee the final cargo. The ship's captain was dressed in silk finery, and he had no shortage of gold jewelry about his body. Clearly, business was good.

"Sir, you are the captain of this vessel?" Cor asked, raising his voice as he approached. The captain turned to face him.

"I am Soko. We leave today for the north coast of Tigol if you are seeking passage," the man replied.

"No, Captain Soko, I seek information."

"I deal in goods, not information. Look elsewhere," Soko said turning his back to Cor. He resumed his conversation with the merchant.

"I believe," Cor said loudly, "you have the information I need, sir. I'm looking for a ship that arrived early yesterday and carried four Loszians." The captain's head turned quite suddenly, shooting Cor a sidelong glance, and the merchant shifted uncomfortably with this news.

"My friend," Soko said to the merchant, "my men will finish this work, and they will bring the wagon back to you. Allow me to see if I can point our hooded friend here to the correct vessel. Perhaps you would like to discuss this matter aboard ship?"

Cor watched the merchant rush away before answering, "I'd rather stay in the open. Enough people have tried to kill me in the last week for my taste."

"Certainly, you do not think I'm to blame for this?" asked the captain, genuinely incredulous.

"I believe you smuggled four men into this port, three who appeared as Westerners and a fourth who was a Loszian sorcerer."

"It would mean death for a Loszian to enter Aquis, and anyone bringing him would at least lose the right to trade here. I certainly have done no such thing," Soko

164

replied dramatically, inflections on his words matching the raising of his eyebrows.

"Perhaps," said Cor, lowering his voice nearly to a whisper, "you merely provided transport to four men who paid you fairly for their passage. You had no need to know their business here or where they hailed from."

Cor jingled his fingers in a small pouch at his belt and dropped two blank gold coins on the dock. The captain bent over and picked up one of the coins; he attempted to bend or break the coin in his hands and satisfied as to its composition, Soko picked up the other and placed them both in his own pouch.

"I did provide transport to four … pilgrims," Soko said the word with emphasis, "wishing to journey through Aquis visiting its temples. They purchased passage from Sarrap on the northern coast of Tigol. They were quiet and stayed to themselves the entire voyage, praying no doubt."

"No doubt. Do you know where they came from? They were not from Sarrap."

"No, they weren't, and I do not know. I have work to do, if you have what you need," said Soko eyeing his sailors, who were beginning to idle.

"Thank you, Captain Soko," Cor said, dropping two more gold coins at the man's feet. "But perhaps in the future, you'll look into your passengers a bit more before taking their gold." Cor turned and rode away from the docks.

Cor needed a map of modern Aquis, which he purchased at an abhorrently superfluous price at another merchant before leaving Hager. He wanted to compare it against the rough map Rena had drawn about one thousand years ago, but he knew that finding the hall buried in the mountains would be a wild stroke of luck at the least. Cor rode from Hager, continuing north for several miles to make certain he wasn't followed. He then turned east and rode throughout the day before stopping at sunset. By the light of a small cooking fire, Cor compared his new map to the hand drawn map in Rena's journal. He was certain that the hall lay in the southern part of the World's Spine, near the Western kingdom of Roka. Worh, the capital of Roka and a huge port city, lay just over a thousand miles to the east, on the southern coast of the West. Cor could only estimate that the place he sought was perhaps two hundred miles or so from Worh, into the mountains to the northeast of the city.

He would ride to Worh and carefully ask around. Surely, there would be mountaineers there who could guide him up into the mountains, and Cor doubted that would be looked on oddly. No doubt, prospectors, adventurers, and other treasure seekers went into those mountains all the time. Hopefully, once he was closer, Cor would feel his blood calling him to the fetish, for the more he envisioned the thing, the more he knew he needed it. Cor used the water in one of his water skins to put out the fire for the night. There was a freshwater stream nearby, from which in fact his horse was drinking, that he would use to refill it in the morning.

20.

Palius was convinced that this issue would be the death of him; every time there was news, he felt a regular pain in his left arm that shot to his jaw. Two weeks after dispatching Jonn there was absolutely no sign of the priest, his men, or the Dahken. Palius had his men track down the enterprising ranger who had found the boy, as it turned out the man was still in Byrverus. He paid the ranger well to ride to the town of Hager with all haste and find the priest. He gave the man a signet ring with Queen Erella's seal so that any local official or bureaucrat would know he came with the highest authority, using the queen's horses as needed. The ranger returned in two weeks, having stopped little to even sleep, and he had killed several horses in so doing.

In the town of Hager, he learned that Jonn and his men had gone south towards the farm; their intention was to ambush the Dahken at the farm from which they bought food and other supplies. Having been here recently, the ranger knew the area quite well. He found the farm completely deserted, with nothing but a few sundry items in the house itself. Some weather had come through recently, and there was little evidence or traces for him to follow.

The next obvious step was to continue south on the road to Sanctum, and he hadn't gone far when he came across a scene of pure putrefaction. Thirteen corpses, some with severed limbs or even heads, lay in the sun with their skin turning black, and a truly foul stench hung in the air. The ranger inspected them as closely as he dared, not terribly interested in disturbing the considerable number of insects and larvae that were infesting the bodies. The priest, his robe missing, lay on

167

his back impaled by a broken single edged longsword, and some of the soldiers had wounds from this weapon, while others had been slain by a double edged sword. The ranger continued to Sanctum to find the castle a victim of some catastrophe, completely obliterated and fallen into the promontory upon which it was built.

Palius listened to the ranger's story twice, concentrating on keeping down the anxiety which threatened his calm. He had already paid the man well in advance, but Palius excused him with another small pouch of gold coins. As the ranger left, Palius told him to stay available should the queen have further need of him; she appreciated his efficiency.

Palius slumped in his chair, staring off into space, and for a moment, he looked upwards wishing Garod would simply strike him down and make this someone else's problem. He quickly recanted this line of thinking, mentally asking Garod for forgiveness. He wasn't suddenly finding religion, but he saw no value to tempting fate. He closed his eyes in thought, needing a course of action to suggest before giving this news to Queen Erella.

How was it possible this boy thwarted every attempt they made at controlling, capturing, or containing him? Aquis was the greatest kingdom in the Shining West, and yet they had found and lost him thrice! The fact another Dahken, an older Dahken, was involved had been extremely disquieting, but he had had no doubt that a dozen well trained soldiers led by a venerable priest would have no difficulty subduing them one way or another. Palius, though not the most pious man, was not one to blasphemy, but he couldn't help the feeling that some other power worked against them. He stood from his desk and left his office. It was time to talk to the queen, and he had no idea what he was going to recommend now.

It took Cor over a month to reach the city of Worh, and it was becoming plain to him that Rael's stallion, his stallion, was an older animal. Though prideful, the animal's best days were likely behind him, and the extreme heat of late summer caused Cor to slow the pace a bit. They rested more during the day, usually stopping for several hours shortly after midday and continuing until sunset. The slow pace ate into Cor's provisions, and he had to spend more effort than he would have preferred finding food growing wild in the countryside. On more than one occasion, he cursed the fact that he didn't know how to hunt. He avoided towns and villages as much as possible, and when he had no choice but to stop and purchase provisions, he preferred to buy from the farmers living away from the towns. Most were friendly, offering the same hospitality his father would have, but Cor lingered nowhere, not even to occasionally sleep on a soft bed as opposed to the hard ground.

As he approached Roka and its capital, Cor became acutely aware of stirrings in his blood. He felt two distinct forces pulling him, both to the east. One was close by, and though it was weaker, the proximity made it more urgent. The other pulled at him from far to the east, past the World's Spine in the Loszian Empire. Cor knew he had been feeling this call for quite some time, and he didn't know how much longer he could resist answering it.

Additionally, he couldn't help the feeling that he was being watched or followed for most of his journey across Aquis and into Roka. After the first couple of weeks, he took to the roads more often; the going was faster, and it was easier to purchase provisions, when necessary, as the roads always led to a town or village. While he saw other travelers on the roads, Cor never spotted anyone specifically pursuing him. This didn't

169

ease his suspicions however, and at times he was certain the horse felt it too.

The city of Worh, being the only true city in the kingdom of Roka and a prosperous port as well, was massive, and from a mile off on a hilltop, Cor took in the enormous vista. The city was set on a gorgeous blue bay, and large trading ships came and left from its harbor. It looked as if it had been built and rebuilt upon itself as it grew outwards, giving it a tiered look, and as one moved closer to the city's center, the buildings towered over the outer areas. A stone wall surrounded the city, and Cor saw interior walls further enclosing other parts of the city. As he approached, he could see the outer wall, over thirty feet tall, was comprised of huge granite blocks. Unlike Sanctum's, this wall was topped with battlements, and Cor noted many soldiers standing atop it, keeping a lookout. The huge wall had multiple gates set into it, each with two huge iron banded double doors, and traffic of all types moved freely through these gates, each manned by armored guards.

The press of people, mostly merchants, coming and going was amazing to Cor; he hadn't seen such a metropolis since visiting Martherus in Aquis, and then he'd been only a boy. It seemed to him that one's memory tended to fade over such a time, and all Cor could remember of Martherus were flashes and images. He controlled himself, keeping his eyes off the impressive sights as he entered the city. At the least, he was still carrying a large sum of gold, and he did not want to invite thievery by looking like a country bumpkin.

The bazaars and merchant stalls seemed to be centered around the outside ring of the city, closest to the gates, though it many of the more prosperous merchants had warehouses and other facilities near the docks. As Cor worked further into the city, the general bazaars gave way to more specialized shops and tradesmen. Smiths of all types, glassmakers, weavers, and other professionals kept their shops here. They were close enough to the merchants and bazaars, but far enough away to avoid most of the noise.

The crowds were thinner here, and Cor noted several taverns and inns. He selected one with a large stable and paid the stable boy to feed the horse so long as he remained there. Cor entered the inn with his possessions and found it to be quite comfortable with one main room littered with tables and chairs, and shortly after noon, that was mostly empty. A portly man with a grease stained apron waddled up to Cor from a back room that smelled of cooking meat.

"Young sir, you have recently arrived? I do have some private rooms available, though sleeping in the main room is friendlier to your purse," solicited the innkeeper.

"I would prefer to be alone. What is the cost?" Cor asked.

"Well," the innkeeper scratched at his belly, "one solid gold piece per night, five for a week. You pay for meals separately. Also, one silver per night to cover your horse, or a gold for a fortnight," said the innkeeper, motioning at Cor's saddle. The price seemed exorbitant, and Cor knew he was expected to negotiate, a skill his father was adept at despite his preference against it.

"I despise haggling," he confided in the innkeeper. "I'll pay it, but I want a hot breakfast every morning." Tired of beans, berries, and dried meat, he reached into his pouch and fished out six gold coins.

"Thank you, sir," said the innkeeper as he took Cor's gold, a look of satisfaction on his face. "If you'll follow me."

The innkeeper took Cor up a small set of stairs and down a hallway. The inn was much larger than it looked from the outside, and this hallway alone had four rooms on each side before making a right turn. The man stopped before reaching the turn and pulled out a small copper key, which he used to unlock a door. He then handed the key to Cor explaining that there would be a one gold piece charge should Cor lose it, and that there were no other copies of that key. The only other person who could open his door was the innkeeper himself with his master key.

Whistling, the innkeeper strode back down the hallway and downstairs while Cor entered the room, dropping his belongings in one corner. The room was small, but it was spotless and appointed with two basins, one filled with clean water and the other empty, a large bed and a trunk that sat with the lid open. Cor closed the chest's lid and saw that it was designed to take a padlock. The room was windowless, and the one door was the only entrance or exit.

Cor lay down on the bed, finding it soft and smelling of down and organized his thoughts. He needed to do a few things before starting his search for a guide to take him into the mountains; for one, he'd felt naked for the last month without armor of any kind, especially any time he saw a bow. He wasn't afraid to fight without armor, but he knew a well-trained archer could prevent him from even getting close. Cor also considered paying for the room in advance for quite some time, which would allow him to use the inn as a sort of base of operations. This also meant purchasing a fine lock for the chest at the foot of the bed. Thinking over his options and next actions, Cor drifted off to sleep.

Cor hadn't really meant to sleep, and he awoke to the sounds of activity below. He stood, rubbing the sleep from his eyes and made certain Soulmourn was belted securely, allowing his hand to linger on the gleaming hilt. He put most of his belongings in the chest, including Rena's journal and his two sacks of gold, which were a bit lighter than when he left Sanctum. Cor added no small sum of gold to the pouch at his waist, and then closed the chest's lid; it had no lock, but he would rectify that soon.

Making sure his cloak was quite secure and the hood keeping his face in as much shadow as possible, Cor left his room, closing and locking the door behind him. He walked to the end of the hall and stood at the top of the stair, looking down upon a gay scene in the main room. The room was completely full of merchants, soldiers, and travelers, eating, drinking, and sharing various stories, while serving girls carried platters of food about the room. A few women wearing clothing that left little to the imagination mingled solicitously amongst the patrons, clearly attracted to those purchasing the more expensive food and drink. Other figures sat furtively in various corners, interacting with no one but watching everyone, and Cor knew his appearance did not go unnoticed.

Cor's stomach grumbled with the smell of meat and spices that filled the room, and he descended the stairs, looking for an empty seat, preferably at a less populated table. This proved no easy task however, and Cor quickly decided to enter the street instead. He had slept for several hours, and the sun was just beginning to set, casting a pink glow over the city streets. The bustle was clearly gone as all manners of business were being concluded for the day, and Cor knew he had little time if he wanted to accomplish either of his errands tonight.

Skilled tradesmen populated this section of the outer city, and Cor entered the first smithy he found. The blacksmith's assistant inside explained that in a city this large, the smiths specialized in specific goods and pointed him in the right direction. Cor entered a locksmith's shop just as the man prepared to close. He took little of the man's time, purchasing the most expensive lock that would fit the chest in his room, and as usual, Cor did not bother to negotiate the price. By the time he left and found the recommended armor smith, the shop had closed, and though he was still inside, the smith refused to reopen. Cor returned to the inn, the sun dipping below the horizon, and returned to his room. Finding everything in order, he fitted the padlock to the chest and dropped the iron key into his pocket with his room key.

By now, Cor hungered mightily, and he knew he would simply have to brave the main room. It had cleared out a bit. Most of the patrons, having finished eating, had moved on to the taverns or other amusements, and Cor had little trouble finding a table where he could sit alone. A girl about his age brought him a rich platter of steaming beef and potatoes that had been fried in some sort of oil with a pint of ale. He made certain not to lift his face to hers, but Cor knew she saw the gray color of his hands. He watched her with keen interest as she receded into the kitchen.

Cor concluded that the ale was perhaps the vilest liquid he'd ever had the misfortune of drinking, darker and headier than what he'd had in Tigol under Naran, but compared to his own nearly nonexistent culinary skills, the meal brough great satisfaction. He gorged himself, sighing deeply when finished, and he leaned back to simply enjoy not traveling. The girl returned, and he paid for his meal with both silver and thanks, allowing his eye to linger on her figure.

As the girl turned to serve other patrons, a feminine form slipped into the chair next to him, sliding it closer. She was at least six inches shorter than he, although while sitting the disparity was less noticeable. She had long dark hair and green eyes, a color that was very uncommon among Western women and added to her other, interesting assets. Her body was supple and firm, and her satin clothing provided some modesty, while at the same time making her offer plain.

"A man shouldn't be alone," she said, "especially when fine company is available."

174

"I don't want any company," Cor said, staring straight ahead.

"Oh, I doubt that's true," she said, laying her hand on his arm. "You see, I was watching you. I saw the way you looked at the girl, but I promise you she has little to offer compared to me."

"You're a harlot," Cor said simply, at which she laughed heartily; he did not expect such a reaction.

"Yes, I am. And I'm sure a fighting man such as yourself has plenty of experience with women such as me," this she said, allowing her hand to trail down from his arm and laid one finger on the pommel of his sword.

"Or perhaps not. I'd say you're barely a man. Tell me, how many men have you killed?" she asked, her hand moving lower, and Cor was acutely aware of her closeness.

"None today. I'd prefer it if you leave me alone," Cor said, hoping to sound ominous. She leaned forward so that her mouth was near his ear, despite the hood.

"I don't think you would. Take me upstairs, and for what you paid for your room, I will be yours for the night. I'm worth more than any ten serving wenches in this inn."

Cor, with no experience in these matters, was unprepared for the strength of the feelings this woman evoked within him. Eventually, he allowed her to lead him upstairs to his room, and she locked the door behind them. She was concerned neither with his lack of experience, nor the pallor of his skin. She loved him and taught him how to love. Later, Cor thought he understood Rael's apparent hatred of women, and that it was perhaps derived from a fear of them. Cor now understood how easily a woman could enslave a man's soul.

21.

The harlot left him early, no doubt shortly after sunrise, though without a window, Cor couldn't be sure. She left with no promises and no expectations, and it had been quite an education for him. He slept awhile longer, dozing in and out of sleep for some time, but he eventually roused himself and washed a bit in the basin, which he then sat outside the room for one of the inn's employees to refill. He double checked the chest and his purse to be sure the woman hadn't robbed him and then went downstairs into the main room. As promised, the innkeeper had the kitchen make him a warm breakfast of eggs and pork.

After eating, Cor sauntered outside into the warm morning air; it was late summer, and Roka seemed, as it was south of Aquis, to get much hotter than what Cor preferred. It was almost like being in the ports of Tigol again with the salty, sea air. The large buildings and concentration of people did not help the heat, and activity already bustled in Worh's streets as people of all professions went about another day's business.

Cor headed directly for the armor smith, who was more than happy to speak with him today. In fact, the smith apologized for not being more accommodating; he had another engagement for which he simply could not have been late. Somehow, Cor thought the weight of his purse was responsible for the apology, but he accepted it, nonetheless. Cor explained that he did not plan to wear the armor long, and he did not have time to await the making of custom fit pieces. As such, he purchased what the smith had available, namely a scale hauberk and armguards and a set of mismatched plate legguards. He considered purchasing a basinet but decided that the large helm would likely draw attention, which was the opposite of his intent.

Before leaving, he asked what the smith knew about hiring a guide to go into the mountains. The smith explained that it wasn't his business, but he knew it was somewhat common; the Spine was known to be extremely dangerous for many reasons. Regardless, Cor should seek a man named Kamar in one of the taverns near the docks. While he no longer ventured into the mountains himself, doubtless he could find Cor a willing mountaineer. Cor thanked the smith and left.

Cor asked no one for directions to the docks; he knew the bay was on the southern side of the city, so it was only a matter of time before he found the docks. He took careful note of the path he trod, so as to make certain he could find his way back, and slowly made his way through the city. As he continued deeper, the buildings grew apparently older and significantly taller, having been rebuilt on top of themselves over the centuries. He passed through another gated wall, much older than the outer wall he had entered yesterday. The older buildings and walls were made mostly out of limestone, as opposed to the granite blocks used in the newer areas. The business districts gave way to affluent estates, which eventually turned to homes of those who worked hard for their living. After passing through a second gated wall, he found himself surrounded by warehouses and other holding facilities used by merchants, and as he expected, it was only a short walk from there to the docks.

The docks of Worh looked much like the docks he had seen in other Western cities, though on a substantially grander scale. A forty foot wide boardwalk, made of poplar and elm, curved its way in a slight crescent for as far as he could see, and twenty foot wide wooden piers jutted into the harbor, each at least one hundred feet in length. Vessels of all kinds from the Shining West and the continent of Tigol were moored at these piers, many of their crews involved in the loading or unloading of cargo. The sounds of seagulls, raucous laughter, barked orders, and the occasional whip filled the air, and sailors roamed about everywhere, some involved in ship's business of some sort or another. Most ignored everything but their own tasks.

As was common in bustling ports from his experience, Cor counted multiple taverns off the boardwalk; there had to have been at least half a dozen in plain view, not to mention any others hidden in the streets or back alleys. One of these he chose at random and entered, finding himself in a dark room with a large bar and a few small round tables. The entire establishment had an extremely seedy air about it, and Cor had the distinct impression that he did not want to stay too long lest he invite trouble. The barkeep, who would only talk to Cor after he bought a drink, knew Kamar, but said he was not there. He suggested that Cor continue checking the taverns, and he would find Kamar eventually.

Cor found every tavern in the area to be basically alike, and he searched three more before he finally found the man he sought. It seemed Kamar drank constantly, and his method of choosing today's drinking establishment was relative to which ones he owed money. The bartender of this particular tavern pointed Cor to a man who was short in stature, but solidly built despite the constant influx of alcohol. His hair was light brown, almost to the point of blond, and his skin was tanned brown by the sun and elements. He sat on the far side of the room, his head lying flat on the tabletop, drool seeping from his gaping mouth.

Cor could only rouse the man with the help of the bartender and a cold bucket of water, which awoke Kamar in quite a fury as he hurling curses, insults, and threats at Cor with every breath, ignoring the fact that he couldn't even stand on his own. Cor easily calmed Kamar's ire with promises of more drink, but it was only after the second round that he would hear anything Cor had to say beyond alcohol.

"Aye, ye're a fool," Kamar told him between gulps. "Why in Garod's name would ye want to go to the Spine?"

"I understand you used to go there often," Cor answered.

"Aye, used to. Not now. People die up there, between monsters, animals, Loszians and, just dangerous mountains," Kamar said, again burying himself in his mug.

"I'm not asking you to go," Cor explained. "I just need a mountaineer to guide me into the mountains. I know nothing of climbing."

"Ye're looking for some great treasure no doubt," Kamar stared at him, somewhat bleary eyed. Cor's hood covered his face well in the gloom of the tavern. "Where exactly in the Spine ye needs to go?"

"I'm not sure, but I'll know when I get there," Cor answered, a spittle ridden laugh erupting from Kamar. "Just tell me who I should talk to. I'll pay well."

"Ye're needing a madman like yerself, methinks. Tell me what it is ye seek. I say nothing else until ye do," Kamar said, and Cor recognized the ultimatum. He stared back at the man and took a long breath.

"I'm looking for a building," Cor explained, "Perhaps two hundred miles to the northeast from Worh, somewhere in the mountains, is a strange place made of steel and glass. It is ancient, surely dating back hundreds of years. The inside has marble floors, statues, and items of all sorts that come from before our time."

"So, it is treasure ye seek," Kamar said, deep in his cup.

"Not exactly, not treasure of gold and jewels at least," answered Cor.

"There is only one man who can take you where you want to go. He's actually been to the place you seek," Kamar said. He seemed instantly sober, and his odd accent and inflections were gone.

"What's his name and where do I find him?" Cor asked.

"He's me."

Kamar agreed to take Cor into the mountains, swearing that he'd seen the building Cor sought, and in fact, it was the finding of that building that made Kamar give up the World's Spine altogether. Two years ago, a lifelong friend of his had found ancient writings in a tomb in the mountains. The writings were in an old dialect of Western and spoke of a great building filled with the treasure of many kingdoms. Oddly, the location of this hall had to be in the mountains, though the writings spoke of sweeping plains and other strange ruins.

Kamar, his friend, and three others set out looking for the treasure, expecting to be rich for as long as they lived, but instead they found only death. The climb was more treacherous than they expected, and one of them died in an accident on the mountain before even finding the building. They were running low on provisions and decided to turn back when another simply lost his footing and fell down a steep incline. When they reached the bottom, he was dead, but there, only a few hundred feet away sat the most bizarre edifice they had ever seen, disguised from above by an ancient rockslide and nestled in a tiny valley. They rushed into the building, through an open side of shattered and dangerous glass, anxious to lay eyes on the treasure for which they had already sacrificed much.

They stood in a large room, millennia of dust caking the floor. Natural light filtered in from the outside, and they could see two large doorways leading further into the building at the rear of the room. There were four perfectly round marble columns arranged as the corners of a square near the center of the room, and there were several other portals shaped like doors that seemed utterly sealed and impassable.

It was then that Kamar's friend met his end. A black spider, with legs and body as shiny as polished steel and twice as wide as a man is tall, dropped out of shadow from the ceiling and picked the man up. He screamed, pleaded, and begged for help as the spider rolled him in silk while climbing its own line back to the ceiling. Kamar's final companion, all sanity lost, ran screaming deeper into the building, and Kamar with no intention of dying, left as quickly as his feet could muster.

The tragedy of it all became even more pronounced over the next few days. Kamar, most of his climbing equipment lost or otherwise used, spent days trying to find a way out of the mountains. He knew this part of the Spine well, all things considered, and he had never come across this building or any pass leading to it. However, the hall had been completely disguised from above, and it stood to his reason that there may be trails to this place that were likewise hidden. He investigated every nook and cranny leading from the tiny valley, mapping each route on a flat boulder, writing with indigenous chalk. On the second day he found a path, a mere crack that squeezed between two cliff faces, that eventually emptied onto a well-known pass through the mountains. The crack was hidden from plain view by a massive boulder.

All of this Kamar related to Cor in complete detail after Cor had agreed to the price. Kamar would take him there, so that he may find whatever it was he thought was so important, and then Kamar would lead him out. In addition to provisioning the trip, which they would undertake on foot, Cor agreed to pay Kamar a handsome sum of fifty gold pieces as well as pay all of Kamar's drinking debts.

Kamar estimated that the journey would take four days on foot at a brisk pace to reach the mountains, followed by an additional one or two days in the mountains. Cor paid up his room and the horse's board for an additional two weeks, as well as a separate room for Kamar for one night to allow the man ample time to sleep off his hangover before leaving the next morning.

22.

They ate a hot breakfast shortly after sunrise and then entered the markets to provision the trip. They would carry everything they needed on foot, since once in the mountains, a horse or mule would be unable to follow them. Kamar explained to Cor that it would be hard enough at times for them to squeeze through the route they would take, and he also expressed his concern that should an errant rockslide have blocked the passage, they would have to climb over and down as he had done with his earlier expedition. Cor hoped this wouldn't turn out to be the case, having about as much interest in the concept of climbing as he did falling.

The trek to the mountains was absolutely miserable but uneventful. The summer was fully in effect, reaching sweltering temperatures in the afternoon as the sun beat down upon them, and the air never really cooled even in the middle of night. They started at sunrise, resting for several hours during the hottest part of the day, and walked until the sun was fully down before stopping. They encountered several short, summer rains that did little to cool them off in the oppressive heat, and in fact, the rain simply amplified the discomfort, bringing an extreme humidity that made it hard to breathe.

Kamar tried to convince Cor to leave his armor in Worh, but Cor would not, explaining that he refused to be without protection. The armor became burning hot to the touch in the summer sun, and Cor's tunic and other undergarments soaked through with sweat before midday. By day's end, his clothing would begin to chaff against his skin in the most uncomfortable ways, and at night, he would remove his armor and clothing and sleep naked, allowing his skin the opportunity to breathe and his clothing to dry.

The mountains could be easily seen on a cloudless day from the city of Worh, and Cor had the distinct impression that no matter how far they plodded, he and his companion never seemed to get any closer. By the fourth day, he could finally see that the mountains loomed larger now than ever, and ground became hilly, but with an overall constant incline upwards. On the fifth day, the going became noticeably rougher as the ground became rockier, and the hills gave way to boulders, rocky outcroppings, and mountains themselves.

Kamar explained that there were many paths and passes in the Spine, and he knew of none that would lead one all the way into the Loszian Empire. Though he wasn't sure why someone would want to go there anyway. At this Cor said nothing, very aware of an unseen force that pulled him in that direction. It was also quite plain to Cor that they were nearing the hall and the fetish in his visions, for his blood tingled in his veins, and he felt increasingly restless. They walked north up a small ravine on the mountains outskirts, before Kamar, clearly finding the path he sought, turned them east into the mountains.

The going became slow now; the mountains of the Spine contained enormous amounts of basalt and granite, and loose rock could be seen everywhere. The two tread carefully, keeping their eyes on the ground to avoid missteps that could lead to twisted or even broken ankles. Kamar, familiar with the mountains and their environment, also kept a watchful eye about and above, and he was extremely concerned with potential rockslides or the occasional denizens of the Spine, such as huge brown bears.

The sunset in the mountains was unlike anything Cor had ever experienced. In the pass, they could not see the horizon, and the sunlight seemed to pass over them with an odd orange and red glow, while the pass itself seemed shrouded in blue shadow. Kamar announced they would stop for the night, and he pointed, saying that the final leg of their journey started right behind a large boulder. Cor protested, saying they may as well finish if they are indeed that close. Kamar explained that they still had about two miles left to travel, and that was through a tight squeeze that would likely take them several hours. Cor acquiesced, but he simply could not force himself to be still.

No sleep came to Cor that night; he knew the bat winged fetish was close by, and this gave him a nervous energy, almost an anxiety that he could not manage to calm. Additionally, the night in the mountains was an extremely nerve wracking experience. When he camped in the plains of Aquis, he could see in all directions for miles, but in this mountain pass, Cor could see little beyond twenty feet. The moon rarely shined directly into their campsite due to the immense size and shape of the mountain formations, and every sound echoed between the rock walls to sound as if it were right behind him. He quickly concluded that he would never venture into the Spine again if he could avoid it, but the inherent mistruth of that belief nagged at him.

Cor woke Kamar early, much to the man's disgruntled chagrin. Cor was eager to finish this expedition, and he could no longer ignore the need to wrap his fingers around the fetish's ebony handle. He didn't bother to breakfast, though Kamar made it clear that he was not continuing on an empty stomach. Cor paced like a caged tiger the entire time glaring at the man, who it seemed took a bit longer than usual to finish his meal.

Behind the massive boulder was a triangular crack in the rock face less than five feet tall. It was wide at the base and tapered at the top, and the claustrophobia of it reminded Cor of the round tunnel through which he had escaped the catacombs of Sanctum, though this was even smaller. Kamar said it would be best to leave all the gear and provisions here, and with any luck they would be back shortly after midday. Cor could not deny the wisdom of this, though he refused to leave his armor or Soulmourn behind, especially following the story of an easily twelve foot wide spider.

Kamar led the way into the rocky crevice that apparently wormed its way between two mountain cliffs. The crack consisted of two rock faces that came flush together just below head level. It was less than three feet wide at the base, which forced the men to enter it sideways and shuffle with their backs to one rock face, while hunching over or bending their legs to avoid banging their heads on the top. Once inside, Cor realized the tunnel he had made his way through underneath Sanctum really could not compare to this crevice. Rock jutted out at odd angles, sometimes forcing the men to contort in strange ways to pass. After a short distance, Cor stopped and took off his sword belt, as the sword tended to get stuck at awkward angles. He wrapped his belt around the scabbard and carried Soulmourn in his left hand to keep it out of the way. Roughly halfway in, Kamar had found a pile of loose rock that had apparently come down in his absence; it blocked most of the way through, and the men had to crawl over it while on their sides. Kamar would have been happy to turn back, but Cor forced him to press on with reminders of payment.

It took the pair nearly two hours to push through the crack, and when they emerged into the open air on the other side, no amount stretching seemed able to relieve the fiery aches in their muscles. While attempting to work the kinks out of his sore neck and back, Cor saw they had emerged into a small valley or gorge. Mountains and cliff faces rose on all sides for several hundred feet, preventing the sun from shining into the depression except for when it was most directly overhead. Like the rest of the mountains, the gorge was desolate and rocky; no vegetation grew here, indicating the obvious absence of water.

And there it was – a large edifice stood only a minute's walk from the crevice. The building's façade was made of crisscrossed beams, of steel perhaps, and shattered glass still hung in places, suspended from the steel and giving it a skeletal countenance. From Cor's vantage point, it looked as if the entire roof of the building was covered with boulders and other debris from an apparent rockslide. The detritus was ancient and well settled, which would explain the virtual invisibility of the building from above. Cor immediately set out for his destination, leaving Kamar behind to his surprise. The man followed Cor, but he kept his distance and only approached at a slow pace, in sharp contrast to Cor's meaningful and measured strides. To withstand millennia, as well as some unknown number of years with tons of basalt and granite on its roof, the building was an amazing feat of engineering if not magical prowess. No doubt, the kings and queens that ruled in the days this building was erected were incredibly powerful.

Cor passed through the building's shattered facade and found himself within the room Kamar described. It was impressive and awe inspiring, walls, floors and four massive columns of marble. Centuries, if not millennia, of dust and debris littered the hall, and huge webs hung suspended from the ceiling and columns. Cor quickly reminded himself to be wary; he was not overly interested in becoming a meal for an enormous spider. He cautiously walked deeper into the hall, ignoring that Kamar had chosen to remain outside as he explored. The guide was clearly unwilling to enter the building, and Cor did not urge him to do so. Kamar had done his job.

At the end of the hall, Cor could make out the vague outlines of the two massive doorways that Kamar described. They were obscured by a huge mass of webs that was centered between them, which lent credence to Kamar's tale. This made Cor uneasy, and he found himself looking about almost frantically in all directions. He had fought and killed men, but an unnatural spider was something different. Cor knew he needed to pass by the webs to access the part of the building that housed the fetish, and he felt an enormous pressure urging him forward. Getting to it would mean hacking through or even burning the webs, and in his experience, the smallest spiders tend to respond to such disturbances. He stood in place, contemplating the situation; the obvious answer would be to somehow draw the spider out of its hiding place and even perhaps out of the building itself. Of course, he didn't know exactly where the creature was at this moment, if in fact it still existed. Cor turned, following with his eyes the webs that reached out to columns and the ceiling, and he realized the entire hall was one giant spider lair, culminating in its center directly between the two doorways.

It was then Cor saw movement in his peripheral vision, and shifting his gaze back towards the open entrance, he froze in horror. A truly enormous creature, taller than he, headed towards the portal leading outside, the legs and body shining with reflected light as brightly as the most polished plate armor. Its eight segmented legs were longer than described by Kamar, excepting the front two, and were as thick as Cor's upper arms. The arachnid's body was huge, with a disgustingly bulbous abdomen, which hung only a couple of feet off the ground, and it shocked Cor how quietly the thing moved; it was nearly silent, despite its bulk.

Cor realized the thing stalked Kamar, who sat on a small boulder outside the building staring out over the gorge. Too late, Cor shouted a warning to the man, who turned just in time to be punctured by the creature's giant fangs. Kamar screamed, either in pain or terror, for a long second before his voice was cut off, and Cor stood silent and still as the huge spider pulled the front half of its body back through the doorway and began to ascend a nearby web. Once closer to the ceiling, it used its rear legs to begin rolling Kamar's body into a wrap of silk.

Cor needed to move quickly, and he had little doubt that once he began hacking his way through the webs, the spider would come for him. He also had doubts as to whether his sword could cut the webs without getting caught in the sticky silk, but grasping Soulmourn's hilt filled Cor with a warm confidence. He moved deeper into the room, close to the heart of the massive web, noting several clusters of bones caught up in it, many of them not human. He kept one eye trained on the monstrous arachnid, not totally certain how he hadn't spotted it sooner, and he felt the thing return the gaze with its many black eyes.

Cor was amazed at how easily Soulmourn passed through the first swath of webs, and by his second swing, large sections of the web fell to the room's marble floor. Cor hacked through a third time before the spider even moved. It came frighteningly fast, dropping Kamar's half mummified body to the hard floor with a sickening thud of broken bone, and if Cor held any hopes that his companion still lived, they now dissipated.

The thing charged, coming down one of its own webs, and Cor knew he had mere seconds before it reached him. The web it traveled danced and waved wildly, and Cor's eyes followed it to end at a cluster directly next to him where several strands met. This he cut through and watched as the web holding the spider gave way, the end rebounding back towards the thing. The monster landed heavily on the floor with its own web wound about its body and legs.

Cor wasted no time; he charged the spider while it struggled to extricate itself from its own web, which had it temporarily restrained. He ran across the creature's right flank, swinging his sword in a wide stroke that severed two of the spider's legs immediately, and purple black fluid spouted from the stumps, while the amputated legs jerked spasmodically on the floor. The spider's other legs began to work with a speed faster than Cor's eyes could follow, and if Cor hadn't struck as he did, the thing would likely have freed by itself quickly. Soulmourn grew warm in his hand as he struck the spider's other two right legs in alternating blows, and again, the sword sliced through as if it met no resistance at all, severing the legs with more disgustingly colored blood. The monster fell to the floor again, unable to support itself on one side; it scrambled in panic with its left legs to simply get away from the man who had wounded it so grievously.

Cor moved around to the rear of the creature, not wanting to be anywhere near its mandibles even if the thing was wounded. He thrust Soulmourn directly into the beast's horrible abdomen, nearly to the crosspiece. The creature convulsed greatly, and its rearmost left leg shot backwards, catching Cor squarely in the chest. He had no time to notice the pain, as the blow pushed him into the air. His back smashed into a marble column several yards away, and he crumpled forward onto his chest. He never lost his grip on Soulmourn, and the sword came out of the spider with the force of its blow.

Cor lifted himself to his hands and knees, trying to breathe; the punch of the spider's leg, combined with the impact into the column, made every breath a painful struggle. If not for his armor, Cor was convinced he would be truly injured, if not outright impaled on the end of the segmented limb. He struggled to a kneeling position, his breath coming easier, and he realized the spider had disappeared. A wide trail of its purple black blood led away from its four severed legs deep into one corner of the hall. Cor gathered himself and followed the trail, finding the spider on its back with its remaining legs rolled up tightly. He brought Soulmourn down in a great blow, severing the monster's head, which brought only a slight convulsion from its frame.

Like most people, Cor shared a general distaste for spiders, and the fact that he had just fought a virtual spider god was not lost on him. He shuddered as he considered the fate he very nearly shared as he ventured close to the right doorway. Cor began to hack his way through the thick webs until he reached the doorway itself. It was not a simple doorway, but an actual passage, though it was short at only five or six feet in length. He continued to cut through the spider webs, but found they ended immediately on the other side of the short passage.

As soon as he entered the next room, light snapped into existence from above. It was pure, bright, and white, not unlike the power he had seen Jonn wield against him, though it was not blinding. Looking up, Cor could see that it emanated from the same circular objects Soulmourn had shown him in the vision, set into the ceiling in a recessed fashion. Clearly not all this magic still functioned after these unknown millennia, as there were dark recessed spots that didn't erupt light as he passed, but there was more than enough light to guide Cor's way.

The room was approximately twenty feet across and proceeded forward for another ten before branching in either direction to the right and left. The floor was thick with dust and debris, but Cor saw no more evidence of giant spiders or any other kind of beast beyond the more mundane insects and normally sized arachnids. Alcoves lined the walls, all of them with gleaming plaques below them with inscriptions in writing that Cor could not comprehend. They were filled with all manner of items, such as pots, weapons, jewelry and even bones. Many of them were damaged, their glass coverings shattered and their contents spilled onto the floor and damaged or even destroyed.

Cor simply walked through the room, heedless of direction, but he was certain that the fetish was here somewhere and intact. He walked for an indeterminate amount of time, passing hundreds if not thousands of artifacts. He glanced at them as he passed, as he had seen the people of his vision do, but he did not stop to thoroughly inspect any of them. Cor noticed that the light above seemed to anticipate his movements, illuminating areas just before he reached them and darkening others as he left them behind.

He finally stopped, having no desire to move further into the building. There were four alcoves set into the wall in front of him, all of them united by one massive plaque that no doubt told an ancient, long, and involved story. The first was still sealed but contained a mass of jumbled bones that had fallen out of place. The second alcove's glass covering was shattered, remnants of glass still hanging in place and on the floor, and amidst the glass and cobwebs in the bottom of the alcove, Cor saw the item he sought.

Cor took the fetish in his left hand while removing wisps of cob and spider web from its head. The thing looked exactly as he remembered it from his dream and Soulmourn's vision; the eight inch long handle and neck was made of ebony, and the end of the handle itself was leather wrapped. The neck ended in a bleached white skull that looked perfectly human, though was about the size of a cat's. Two tiny black batwings extended from the fetish's neck just below the skull and extended in the opposite direction of the skull's face.

While holding it, Cor felt the peculiar sensation that he had come to associate with Soulmourn – pins and needles enveloped his hand and ran most of the way up his arm. He rested his right hand on the hilt of Soulmourn, and the feeling intensified and spread up his right arm until the sensations met in his chest. He drew Soulmourn, and it was as if a jolt of lightning shot

192

through him from one hand to the other, then back again. Cor felt, knew these artifacts were meant to be together, and so long as he lived, they would never again separate. They were Soulmourn and Ebonwing.

23.

Cor could not leave Kamar there in the ruins to rot; the man had done exactly as he promised, and he deserved some sort of burial. Cor dragged the man's body out of the building and into the gorge, where he selected what he felt was a suitable location and built a cairn of rocks over him. Cor thanked Kamar sincerely and hoped that he rested peacefully with whatever god he held dear.

Cor made excellent time back to Worh. Even the tiny crack he had to shuffle and crawl through to pass back into the main gorge slowed him down little. It was only midday, and his belongings were as he had left them that morning. He gathered what he needed to make the return trip, leaving most of Kamar's belongings where they were. He was well out of the mountains and nearly out of the foothills before stopping to sleep for the night. Cor felt amazingly energetic and could barely contain his desire to continue on his way to Worh. Once out of the mountains, he ran most of the way, despite the weight of his remaining provisions and armor.

Cor returned to his room in the inn in the afternoon of the third day, finding everything as he had left it. He half expected the innkeeper or some other enterprising individual to enter his room and attempt some form of thievery or another. Cor opened the chest and reviewed his financial situation; he had taken three large sacks of gold, silver, and some gems from Sanctum. One he gave to Cade, and over half of a second was depleted. Though thus far, he had only used gold and silver, and Cor knew he had several gems in these sacks. He fished a few of these out; in a city the size of Worh there had to be shops, perhaps a jeweler of some kind, whose owners would purchase gems.

He left the inn with three gems in his belt pouch. He truly knew nothing about them, but assumed if the Dahken of Sanctum felt the need to protect the gems, they must have value. Cor had never been one to haggle, but he was quickly realizing that gold was in fact finite, and he doubted anything was salvageable back in Sanctum. Or even recoverable.

Again, skilled craftsman seemed to set up their shops in this section of the city, so finding a jeweler was relatively easy. Cor waited patiently while the shop owner waited on a young couple – a pretty, young woman and a professional soldier. The man fixed an odd looking apparatus to his eyes and inspected Cor's gems at length. Declaring them to be of little value, the shopkeeper offered him a relatively paltry sum. Cor pushed the gems back into his pouch, receiving hurried exclamations from the jeweler, who asked to look at them one more time. In so doing, he apologized for making a mistake, finding the gems to be much higher quality than he previously realized and offered Cor nearly three times the former amount. Cor thanked the man and said that he would come back should he choose to sell them. Cor continued up the street, finding another jeweler only a few shops down. The shopkeeper here was a plain looking man, and he examined the gems briefly before leaning back on a stool staring at them where they laid on the wooden counter. After several minutes, he leaned forward again in the stool, its front two legs thudding on the shop's floor.

"Sir, at your age, I really do not want to know where you came across these, but I assume they are not stolen? I can offer you fifty for these two. But this one," he indicated the smallest of the three, "I cannot pay you for today.

"This gem," he said, picking it up carefully between his thumb and index finger, "must be worked into a special piece. It is fit for nobility, if not the king of Roka himself. I will write you a receipt and contract, paying you one third of the price of the jewelry I work it into. I do not doubt your share will allow you to live well without lifting a finger for the rest of your life." With that, the jeweler brought out several sheets of parchment and began writing with a quill pen.

"Thanks for your honesty, but fifty silver is less than what I was offered by the last man," Cor told the shopkeeper, reaching for the gems. The shopkeeper looked up, his gaze locking with Cor's, and he placed his hand over the three gems.

"Son, fifty silver? My offer is a hundred times that. Fifty gold."

Cor left the jeweler, headed for the docks, with a comfortably heavy purse and a contract that promised to pay him well. It crossed his mind that if the gem truly was so valuable, he may never see the shopkeeper again, but the man's directness provided him some comfort. The docks, as was apparently the norm, bustled with activity, and Cor couldn't help but compare the sailors and workers loading and unloading cargo to a colony of ants. He entered every tavern he could find and paid every one of Kamar's tabs; even with the man's death, Cor needed to uphold his end of their bargain just as Kamar had.

"I grow tired of asking, why do you continue to come here?"

Cor turned to see the skeletal figure still sitting in its stone chair, just as he had seen it over a month ago. He stood clad in the armor he had purchased in Worh, Soulmourn and Ebonwing secure at his sides. At this point, Cor wasn't sure how to answer this question; it was the second time it had been asked, and he didn't know the answer. Or even where here was.

"I don't know," Cor answered.

"Yes, you do," replied the figure, its black lips curling back from its teeth in a disturbing grimace.

Cor turned to his right and saw the black armor that he knew would be sitting on its shelf, in the same place it was every time he dreamed of this place.

"You have come for my armor. You cannot have it," said the figure.

"It calls to me," Cor whispered. "It begs me to wear it and use it in combat." Cor lifted the helm in both hands, feeling the familiar tingle in his blood.

"You cannot have it!" screamed the figure in a voice that rose terribly in pitch, and Cor half dropped the helm back into its resting place. He turned to face the ghoulish figure, which stood from his chair of stone, causing inches of dust to puff upwards and float frenetically throughout the air, and parts of his robe began to fall apart from rot.

"How long have you been here?" Cor asked in a whisper. The rage faded from the ghoul's face as it realized a question had been asked.

"I do not know," he said, returning to his seat. "But I will remain here always. Tell Tannes to stop seeking me."

"Tannes?" asked Cor in confusion with a slight shake of his head. Realization dawned on him, and he gently replied, "Lord Dahken Tannes has been dead for almost two thousand years. You've been here that long? What is your name?"

"Two thousand... my name," the figure whispered. He began to stare at Cor, but Cor had the distinct feeling that he was being stared through not at. "Yes, I had a name once, and I was revered among many. I built a great citadel on the eastern side of this continent, and it became a beacon for generations of Dahken. They came here to learn of their own power from me, the greatest of the Lord Dahken.

"Then fire came from the sky, and our great citadel crashed down upon us. My great Dahken screamed in the destruction, their bodies rent asunder from the fire and rain of stone. Few of my warriors survived the carnage, and those who did died shortly after. Their hair grew gray and fell out. Their skin darkened with strange burns. They refused to eat, vomiting if they did, and they wasted away to die, their bodies wracked with pain. Only I was strong enough to survive the aftermath, and I have never left here. This place will be my tomb until death finally takes me."

"That happened nearly three thousand years ago. Your name is Noth, isn't it?" Cor asked. The skeletal man's eyes focused on Cor, pulled back into the present.

"Yes," he whispered. "Yes, Noth was my name. I know not what my name is now, for surely, I am no longer Lord Dahken Noth. Why do you covet my armor?"

"I believe your armor covets me Noth, not the other way around," Cor answered. "I feel its call every day through my blood. How long has it been since you wore your armor?"

"I have not worn it since after the citadel fell and the last of my warriors died in agony," Noth answered. "I wish you to be gone, but I know you will return. This is no dream, but neither do you truly stand in front of me. I do not understand these visitations, but I do know that one day you will truly come, as others have. Come prepared for death, for I will not release my property so easily to you."

Noth made a flippant backhanded wave with his left hand, and Cor bolted upright in his bed in the inn. Wide eyed, he looked around the room, which was exactly as he left it when he lay down in bed. He threw himself heavily onto his back and tightly pulled the down pillow over his face. Cor never really went back to sleep, tossing and turning in bed for an eternity.

He dozed off on occasion, only to be awakened by his own thoughts. This latest dream, or visitation as Noth had called it, lit his mind aflame with questions and ideas. Lord Dahken Noth was the ghoulish figure he had now seen twice, and the armor belonged to him. It was inconceivable that Noth still lived in the ruins of his citadel; he would be nearly three thousand years old. Many of the Dahken survived two or even three hundred years, and Tannes, the first true Dahken, lived to the oldest age of any recorded. Noth described the Loszian meteor and the ensuing cataclysm with an oddly detached expression, as if he remembered it from a dream. If Noth truly lived in the catacombs where his citadel had been, then he truly had no understanding of the amount of time that had elapsed. It also meant he knew nothing of The Cleansing or the current affairs of the West.

Noth had mentioned Tannes, and that others had come to him before Cor; Cor remembered from his readings that Tannes did send Dahken in search of Noth, or any survivors, over the years. Cor saw in his mind's eye Noth's face, the black lips of his mouth saying, "*Tell Tannes to stop seeking me.*" Noth said that others had come, perhaps not sent by Tannes, but also seeking his armor. Cor thought of Soulmourn and Ebonwing, and it seemed that these artifacts sought out new masters when their current ones died, assuming Noth was indeed dead.

Cor had decisions to make, but he needed more information. Sanctum was a smoldering ruin, its wealth and treasure, history and knowledge destroyed by the Loszian necromancer. The Loszian said the location of Sanctum was no secret to him, which meant it was likely he knew the location of Noth's citadel as well. The Loszian may have far more knowledge at his disposal, and perhaps it was time to take him up on his offer. Cor opened the chest and removed one of the small scrolls he had taken from Sanctum. He considered it briefly before penning a letter to Queen Erella of Aquis.

24.

Palius ran through the palace for his queen's chambers, an exercise he was not used to under any circumstances. Servants, courtiers, and guards watched him with astonishment as he ran past them, shouting his apologies to those he ran down or nearly collided with. They were certain they had never seen the queen's chief advisor act in such a way, and seeing the old man, who was nearly eighty years old, so fleet of foot created fervent discussion and debate. The main doors to Queen Erella's chambers were open, and she sat at her desk signing various papers and orders. He stopped before her and struggled for several minutes to catch his breath.

"Palius, perhaps you should consider taking a run every morning; perhaps run one mile with one of the guard captains," she said, without looking up. "When's the last time I mentioned how difficult I find the more mundane aspects of my position? As Queen of Aquis, I am High Priestess of Garod, and yet I spend far more time signing orders and releases of permission or negotiating disputes with our neighbors than I do leading Garod's faithful. Perhaps I should create a new advisory position, High Signer of All Things Mundane sounds nice.

"Are you able to breathe yet?" she asked, now lifting her eyes to Palius' face.

"Yes Majesty," he responded. He still puffed a bit, but it was manageable. "This small scroll was brought to me by a rider from Martherus this morning. A lad on a black stallion delivered it to the Temple of Garod in Martherus yesterday. He said that he rode from the town of Hager, but we believe that to be a lie."

"What is it Palius?" she asked, though she knew there was only one matter that had ever shaken Palius.

In answer, he merely handed her the scroll; it was made of parchment and no more than five inches wide. An unmarked red wax seal was broken open, and inside was a brief letter, written in a concise block style of handwriting. It was specifically addressed to her, and the tone of it was one that the writer clearly considered respectful. According to the date, the letter had been written approximately three weeks ago.

Queen Erella of Aquis,

I believe you have looked for me since the day I was born. Your priests taught me the ways of Garod. Of course, I have come to understand these to be true only from a certain point of view. After my parents were slain by a Loszian, I escaped with a man of my own kind, a man who taught me how to be what I am. With information from a spy no doubt, your priest Jonn came after me with armed men. He killed my mentor, and I repaid him in kind.

I will be coming to Byrverus, and by the time you receive this letter, I will be well on my way. I come to see you Queen Erella, and I come in peace. Expect me within two weeks.

Dahken Cor

"Well Palius, it appears we no longer have to look for the Dahken," she said, placing the scroll on the table before her.

"Majesty," started Palius, a sense of urgency in his voice, "this boy, man, has already caused the death of a dozen of your loyal subjects, including a respected priest. He admits to the murder in this correspondence. He says he comes to see you. We can have the entire royal guard awaiting his appearance, and we can end this now."

"Palius, he also says he comes in peace. This letter is no different than a request for formal parlay. I

202

cannot order his murder, regardless of the harm he has caused," responded the queen.

"Majesty, years ago you confided in me a fear that this one man could destroy both the Shining West and the Loszian Empire. He has shown a willingness to kill the servants of Garod. I respectfully suggest –"

"I will not," shouted the queen, slamming her fist on her desk, then suddenly quieting her voice, "commit a murder, regardless of his crimes. We have our honor Palius, and I would extend the same courtesy to the Emperor of Losz. Leave me, and I will pray to Garod for guidance."

"Yes Majesty," Palius said with a bow. He turned from the queen and left her chambers. Palius was as loyal as any of Queen Erella's subjects, and he would not go against her will. But that did not mean he wouldn't prepare for the worst.

Cor had paid a courier, a boy only a few years younger than himself, very well to deliver the scroll to the temple in Martherus. He also gave the black stallion to the boy as an incentive for discretion, that is, lying about where he came from. He hoped to use Worh as his home for as long as possible; he had stayed another week after dispatching the letter, during which time he struggled to stay busy. Before leaving Worh, he purchased a new horse, a gorgeous palomino mare; she had a dark gold coat and a mane and tail of platinum. Cor was taken with her the moment he saw the horse, and her name was Kelli.

He took his time riding to Byrverus, keeping Kelli at a leisurely pace, as he wanted to be certain that his scroll reached Queen Erella about two weeks before he did. The boy had told him how long it would take to reach Martherus, and once there, Cor knew one of the more senior priests would read it and immediately dispatch it to Byrverus with all haste. The summer heat had broken, much to Cor's delight, as he had found that wearing steel armor in the summer sun to be a most uncomfortable experience. The days still tended to the warm side, especially after midday, but the oppressive heat of the sun had faded. Cor was vaguely aware that he would arrive in Byrverus within days of his nineteenth birthday. He felt much older than that somehow. More had happened to him in the last three months than perhaps his entire first eighteen years, and it amazed him how things changed.

Cor had formulated what he hoped was a clever scheme. He knew the Loszian did not want him dead; the necromancer's first agent had come to abduct him. In their second encounter, the Loszian offered him power, luxury, and pleasure, that he would live as a king. Cor needed the location of the Dahken ruins in Losz, and he had no doubt the Loszian necromancer would either know or be able to divine their location. Cor also needed to learn anything he could about Noth. He would go along with the Loszian's plans as long as necessary to get what he needed. Then he would slay the necromancer in vengeance for his parents.

The Loszian knew Cor could be found at Sanctum. He had not divined this information from sorcery, or he would have come for Cor long ago. No, he had to wait for the knowledge to come by mundane means, and then he came by ship, smuggled into Aquis. It was possible that the Loszian had sent his own spy to Sanctum, but it simply seemed too coincidental. The Loszian arrived very shortly after Jonn and his soldiers, making it likely that Queen Erella had a spy in her midst.

He had little doubt that the queen would choose to meet with him in open court. It seemed that she feared him, for what reason he still could not summon, and keeping the meeting in the open would prevent him from attempting some sort of assassination. He certainly had no intention of harming anyone, but he somehow doubted the queen would trust him. Cor saw little reason to trust her either, but he hoped to placate the queen by making it clear that he harbored no ill will toward the West. Thoughts of reestablishing the Dahken began to swirl around in his mind, mostly when in the state between sleep and wakefulness, but this was another matter altogether. Regardless, he would announce to the queen his intent to enter the Loszian Empire in search of the necromancer responsible for the death of his parents. During their short expedition, Cor learned from Kamar that there were few passes that completely crossed the mountains between the West and the Empire, and these were heavily defended at both ends. Cor would ask for safe passage through Aquis' checkpoints, and beyond that, he would be left to his own devices.

On some level, Cor felt this plan was daring if not clever; he was counting on the logical deduction that the Loszian had a spy near Queen Erella. But even so, he didn't know exactly what the Loszian's plans were for him. The necromancer was a noble or lord of some sort, however the Loszian system worked, but he was no emperor. The emperor would never come himself, even with protection. *"Together we shall overthrow both empires,"* he had said. That made his intent plain enough, but how Cor figured into his plans remained to be seen. Regardless, Cor had little doubt that the necromancer's agents, if not the man himself, would intercept Cor shortly after he left Aquis behind. In fact, he counted on it.

Cor expected the Westerners would consider his plan suicidal, and hopefully would view allowing it to go forward as an effortless way of ridding themselves of him. It was most definitely dangerous, but since reuniting Ebonwing and Soulmourn, Cor began to feel a proud confidence. He felt the artifacts bolstered his strength. He had energy whenever he needed it and simply felt stronger and more agile than ever before. Somehow, he knew his blows would rend steel as easily as flesh and bone, and regardless as to the why of everything that had happened, he would not die at the hands of the Loszians. Of this, he was sure.

Once he crossed into Aquis from Roka, Cor chose not to wear his hood as he had for the past two months. He had announced his coming to the highest authority in the kingdom, and the hood now seemed inconsequential. He did not hide from villages and towns, but instead rode through them on the most direct path to Byrverus, even staying the night at a small local inn if he was near one at the end of the day. Cor drew looks from nearly all the commoners he came across. It was curiosity, pure and simple, as Garod's priests had eliminated any history of the Dahken from common knowledge, and he did not mind the inquisitive glances or even the long stares. Cor had already decided that everyone in the Shining West would come to understand that the Dahken were neither evil nor to be reviled.

Byrverus could be seen from miles off, a great white beacon shining brightly in the early autumn sun. The entire city seemed to be made of gleaming stone, and when the sun was low to the horizon, the city reflected the sunlight with so much brilliance that onlookers had to avert their gaze. Byrverus, the most populous city in the Shining West at over fifty thousand persons, dwarfed both Worh and Martherus, and rich farmlands extended outwards for miles from the city itself.

An immense wall, larger than anything Cor had ever seen, surrounded the city proper. It was perhaps twice as tall as the city wall around Worh and made of the same gleaming white stone as the towers protected within. Even from a distance, Cor could see ballistae and catapults topping the wall, and armored figures glinted as they walked the battlements. Though the West's premier center of learning and culture, Byrverus was clearly designed with war never far from its mind. The wall had enormous gates much like Cor had seen in Worh, and passing through them, Cor saw the walls themselves were nearly twenty feet thick.

Cor noted more soldiers around the gates, both inside and outside the walls, and they were all professional soldiers, clad in chain or scale mail, and paid him no more mind than they did most of the others who passed through the gates. Even so, Cor knew there were eyes on him, no doubt many of those people were shocked by his pallor. More importantly, Cor was certain the queen would have placed spies specifically on the lookout for him, surely using his marked skin color as the defining characteristic for identification.

Once inside, Cor could not help but stare in awe at Byrverus' magnificence. Every building was made of the reflective white stone that was like marble in appearance, but the stone was pure white with none of the swirl associated with marble. Even the common homes were built of this material, and basalt paved the streets, which were kept impeccably clean. There were small temples to the lesser Western gods throughout the city, amid businesses as well as homes, but Garod had no temples among them. At Byrverus' center stood two massive complexes; one was the palace of the reigning monarch, who was also the highest of Garod's clergy, and the other was the largest temple to Garod in the world.

Cor decided he would not see those buildings today. For now, he sought a well-appointed inn with stable to sleep off the day's travel and allow Kelli some well-deserved rest. He had little doubt that by now the queen was aware of his arrival in the city, and surely Cor was being watched at every moment. He idly wondered if only Queen Erella's agents had their eyes upon him, or if Loszian spies watched him as well. There was one thing of which he was certain – fighting one's enemy with a sword was far more honest than matters of intrigue.

Finding a suitable inn turned out to be an easy task in the wealthiest city of the West. The building was wrought of the same white stone as everything else in the city, except the stable located around the building's rear was of a normal lumber construction. Late in the day, he secured his room and lodging for the horse, as well as a hot meal. It seemed to Cor that every innkeeper in the West must look alike; either that or there was but one man with awesome powers of transportation who ran them all. Cor dined amongst the inns other patrons. He ignored the stares, some of which he was certain were more than mere curiosity, and he retired to his room in a vain attempt at a restful night's sleep.

25.

Apparently, no one in the city of Byrverus slept much beyond sunrise, for once the sun rose high enough to shine over the city's walls, the rays of sunlight reflected off every surface of every building. The entire city lit up almost instantaneously, casting near blinding light through curtained windows. Cor had not slept well, and he was not pleased by the early morning light.

His room was more than well appointed, containing a bed that he was certain was big enough for three or four people, and which he did not doubt it occasionally contained. The room was impeccably kept, exceedingly clean and with not a single fold of linen or blanket out of place. It was also the most advanced room he had ever seen, with a small side room containing basins and a sort of hand driven contraption that produced water from a spout. There was a second basin, low to the floor and physically attached to it for relieving oneself, after which one could pour water from the spout into it and wash away the waste through a round hole in the bottom of the basin. Modern engineering was clearly its own kind of magic.

In the bedroom itself, a floor to ceiling mirror hung on one wall, clearly for those merchants, diplomats, or members of other professions in which it was necessary to always look one's best. Never prone to vanity, but with the mirror available, Cor looked at himself at length while buckling on his armor. He surely looked like death's messenger; deep black and purple rings under his gray eyes from lack of sleep accentuated his corpselike pallor and straight, near black hair. Ebonwing, with its skull and batwings, did nothing to dispel the image, and Cor's scale mail hauberk and armguards, polished to a high shine the night before, added hardness to his appearance.

Hopeful that his appearance denoted someone not to be trifled with, Cor retrieved his palomino from the stable. He would ride to the palace, hopefully adding to the image of strength he wanted to project, and his silver armored countenance contrasted well with the golden horse. Cor rode through the paved streets of Byrverus, not completely certain of his destination, but he knew both Garod's temple complex and the palace were both near the dead center of the city. Again, he knew he was being watched and followed, and those who monitored him did little to hide themselves at this point.

Garod's temple and the palace of Byrverus were the two most astounding buildings Cor had ever seen. Made of the same white stone as the rest of the city, both buildings stood incredibly immense over the surrounding city. The palace had one tall spire that rose at least one hundred feet in the air, as well as two smaller ones, all of them accented with silver and gold. Banners and flags of rich silk hung from every window and spire with the heraldic symbols of Aquis.

The temple was even taller than the palace, no doubt because Aquis was truly a theocracy as opposed to a hereditary monarchy. The giant structure was geometric and unimaginative in design, appearing as one huge block of white stone standing on end, with squat cubic towers at each corner containing huge, polished copper bells. The temple complex stood on a white stone platform with a dozen basalt steps leading up to it; whether this was a natural formation covered with stone or something specifically built to elevate the temple above the other buildings Cor did not know. Twelve foot tall marble statues of Garod in various poses, a fair young man in robes, lined the steps leading up to an open portal.

Plate clad soldiers wearing royal blue surcoats with the emblems of Aquis and robed priests of Garod filled the plaza around the two buildings, and access was unlimited to the public areas of the complexes. Keeping his horse at a slow walk, Cor headed straight for the palace's main entrance, and eight soldiers in two columns of four with a ninth at their head marched directly towards him. Citizens endeavored to stay out of the soldiers' way, while priests watched warily, some of them likely aware of what was to transpire. The soldiers, all of them clad in highly polished steel plate armor with royal surcoats and who carried pikes, shields, and swords, stopped ten feet short of Cor, and he pulled Kelli to a halt facing them.

"Dahken Cor," said the leader, his voice rose in a tone practiced at addressing crowds, "Her Majesty Queen Erella of Aquis welcomes you to Byrverus. We are to escort you into the palace, and her Majesty shall receive you in court presently. This is to be a peaceful meeting, is it not sir?"

"As stated, I come peacefully," Cor answered.

"Perhaps you would surrender your sword, sir. It will be returned after your audience with the queen is concluded."

"And will every soldier in Byrverus also lay down his sword? I somehow doubt I could escape the city were I to commit violence," Cor reasoned. "I go as I am."

"Then sir, I beseech you to maintain your honor," the captain concluded, motioning for his men to take up flanking positions on either side of Cor, and the fact that he was surrounded was not lost on him. He idly wondered if he could defeat them all should it come to that.

The small contingent continued to the palace, Cor and his horse at their center, and guards opened the double doors as the group marched into an antechamber. The interior of this room was not made of the same stone as the palace's exterior, but sandstone with marble floor instead. Inside two more royal guards opened doors allowing Cor to ride Kelli forward at a walk, still surrounded by his escort, and the mare tossed her tail from side to side in annoyance at the soldiers' proximity. The antechamber opened into the great hall in which the ruler of Aquis kept court. The room was immense, roughly eighty feet wide and over twice as long with a domed ceiling nearly forty feet in the air, and easily a half dozen passages led away from it. The hall was also made of sandstone and marble, and a rich burgundy carpet led from the entrance straight ahead to a raised dais, centered on which was a single throne. Cor wondered at the need for architects, or perhaps monarchs, to place thrones on raised platforms.

Perhaps forty or fifty people, mostly priests and soldiers, milled about the room at a respectful distance from the throne, and they all froze as soon as Cor rode his palomino into the hall. The silence in the room was palpable, and Cor could feel every eye fixed upon him. He walked Kelli until she was about ten feet from bottom of the steps leading up to the dais, and then he dismounted, bowing to the figure on the throne in what he hoped seemed a respectful manner.

The woman on the throne was ancient, older than any person Cor had ever seen before, and everything about her seemed to be a badge of office. She wore white robes marked with symbols of Garod and Aquis, a heavy gold and jewel crown, and a scepter lay across her lap. Queen Erella had pure white hair and extremely fair skin that seemed stretched across her face, and the image of Noth appeared unbidden in Cor's mind. The queen regarded Cor intently, and he allowed her to inspect him as long as she liked. He stood before her, just an inch or so shy of six feet tall, and he had no doubt he would tower over her should they stand alongside each other. The pigmentation, or lack thereof perhaps, of Cor's skin blended somewhat with steel shine of his armor and gray eyes, but contrasted sharply with shoulder length near black hair that he made no effort to restrain. He became suddenly aware of somewhat scraggly growth on his cheeks and chin and began to think he should have shaved it off with his knife before coming to the palace.

"Dahken Cor, for years you have avoided my rule, even to the extent of slaying my subjects, and yet now you come before me willingly, with a plea for formal parlay. What do you here?" asked the queen, her voice surprisingly strong for her obviously advanced age. Her face remained impassive as she spoke, and there was hardness in her gaze. Cor knew he was expected to show all manners of respect and deference to this woman, but Rael and his death had driven those sentiments out of him.

"I've come hoping to end any hostility between us. I am not evil and wish no harm to anyone in the West. I don't want to have to avoid your spies any longer," Cor answered, though somehow it seemed inadequate.

"I cannot help but question your honesty, Dahken Cor. You are responsible for the death of twelve of my soldiers as well as a venerable priest, a priest that you knew and that served Garod faithfully for over sixty years." The queen's manner remained impassive, but her voice developed an edge. The accusation brought a sense of guilt that Cor pushed away with his response.

"Your soldiers were obviously under orders to take me regardless of whether or not I was willing. You would have people believe that they in Aquis live in freedom from tyranny under the care of Garod, but apparently that freedom from tyranny only exists for those who accept Garod's care without thought. Your priests have changed history over the last seven hundred years, and I doubt even Her Majesty knows the true history of the West or especially the Dahken."

He challenged her with his tone, and though he used the title, his words contained no respect. This brought fire into the queen's eyes, but she allowed him to speak his piece; extreme silence had come over the crowd.

"You blaspheme," she said, quieter now than before, "and you dare to throw accusations at the god to whom you and all Westerners owe their freedom. You come before me, showing no respect before Garod. You worship an evil god who did nothing to end the enslavement of the West at the hands of the Loszians, and your people allied themselves with the sorcerers. Were it not for your letter announcing this parlay, I would do as my advisors recommend and have your life ended here and now."

Though the queen's face was honest in her dire warning, Cor could not help but smile at the threat. He was keenly aware of Soulmourn and Ebonwing's presence at his belt and could almost hear them urging him to do battle and shed blood. And for a brief moment, Cor considered whether he could in fact reach Queen Erella to slay her before her guard fell upon him. He felt a mirthless laugh well up within him, but he stifled it and pushed these thoughts away.

"I see the need to discuss neither history nor epistemology with you, Queen Erella," Cor replied with contempt. "Suffice it to say, almost everything you know and teach about the Dahken is untrue at best. I'm here for a specific reason, and I would have it heard.

"I ask free passage through the Shining West at my will, and I will harm no one except in my own defense. I require access through one of the mountain passes into Losz and safe passage back into Aquis when my business is concluded." This created quite a stir and some guffaws amongst the small crowd.

"Entrance into Losz is strictly forbidden to all," the queen replied succinctly.

"Majesty, I don't need your permission," he said, beginning to clench his teeth; his defiance was clearly appalling to both the priests and soldiers. "I have traveled the breadth of the West and avoided your spies for months. I will find a way into Losz without you, if necessary, but frankly I require the fastest path available."

"What *business* could you possibly have in the Loszian Empire that does not involve harm to the West? The Dahken and the Loszians have long stood against us."

Cor unbuttoned one of his saddlebags and removed the preserved tattoo Rael had cut from the Loszian assassin so long ago. He held it up for Queen Erella who motioned with her right hand, and a plated soldier stepped forward, took it from Cor and brought it to the queen for inspection. She looked at the design on one side for a long moment, before turning it over; her impassiveness turned suddenly to recognition, and she cast it back towards Cor with revulsion.

"You dare to defile my hands with a trophy cut from human flesh!" she very nearly screamed at him. "Perhaps the honor of peaceful parlay is not for you; you are no more honorable than the Loszian necromancers who slay at will in their own orgies of evil."

Her guards and soldiers, including the nine who still flanked Cor, rested hands on weapons, their weight shifted to the balls of their feet. Should she order it, they were ready for combat, and Cor heard the weapons at his belt singing in the back of his mind. They wanted blood. He willed them from his mind, and Cor made certain his voice reflected level calm as his next words could mean his death.

"My apologies, Majesty. The marking is a tattoo cut from the arm of the Loszian who murdered my parents two years ago. The Loszian lords mark their servants so that other lords know whom they serve. The Loszian necromancer who claims this mark came into Aquis by way of a smuggler in the town of Hager, and he utterly destroyed Sanctum, the old Dahken castle that was my new home. While the three servants he brought with him did not live to return to Losz, he unfortunately escaped me through magic." Cor paused a moment, holding the queen's gaze and hoped she would come to the same logical conclusion as he. "I would like very much to meet him again."

"My Queen, may I speak with you?" asked a voice from the periphery of the hall.

Cor looked to the left where an old man, though not as old as the queen herself, stood in a doorway of an adjoining corridor. The man had stark white hair and beard that looked as if it had begun to thin only recently, and his back was bent in a way common to those of advanced age. He approached the queen with a speed that was unexpected for his apparent age and physical condition and leaned over her in a most familiar fashion with his back to the assembly. He whispered at an inaudible level, and Cor could not see the man's lips for he kept his face pointed directly away. After only a few seconds, the man stood up and planted himself to the side of and slightly behind Queen Erella.

"Dahken Cor, I see little reason to grant you this request, and I have even less doubt that you will turn out to be treacherous like those Dahken before you. However, provided you leave Byrverus without incident, I will allow you access through the mountains. I will send two of my guard captains with you to ensure your safe passage, and they will cease to accompany you once you reach Fort Haldon in the mountains.

"Dahken Cor, I do not expect I will ever see you again. Either the Loszians will slay you or pervert you to their wills, assuming they haven't already. If by some chance you are a man of honor, and by even less chance you survive your endeavor, I expect you to present yourself before me once more."

Queen Erella stood, turned, and walked slowly, but not without strength, exiting through a corridor to the right of the throne and dais. Two armored guards followed behind her, while the old man selected two armored men, one of whom led Cor into the palace, and spoke with them in hushed tones. Cor stepped forward to the bottom of the steps leading up the dais and picked up the tattooed skin, placing it back in a pouch at his belt. He patted the horse, deciding the entire affair went about as well as he could have expected. Now, he only had to hope he was right.

Palius knew what every Westerner knew and many things beyond common knowledge. He had no idea what the Dahken referred to as the "true history" and neither did he care. The older Dahken who abducted him clearly had corrupted the young man, who now styled himself Dahken Cor. The Dahken proved himself to be blasphemous, disrespectful, arrogant, and remorseless; he was everything history had taught Palius the Dahken were.

He had advised the queen to allow Cor his request. Evil the man may in fact be, but Palius was not certain he was a liar. Cor's desire to meet, and perhaps slay, his parents' murderer seemed genuine. If the Dahken truly was in league with the Loszians, as Queen Erella seemed to suspect, he would already have a route into the empire. With all likelihood, the Loszians would kill Dahken Cor on sight, and that would resolve the matter completely.

26.

It took the better part of three hours for the two captains to prepare for their new responsibility. They had to secure horses, gear, and supplies, as well as official letters from the old man explaining to any official what their specific mission was and where it ended. Cor waited impatiently with Kelli's reins in his hand. He didn't understand the complications; when he wanted or needed to go somewhere, he simply went.

The ride to Fort Haldon would not take long, perhaps a week, as the captains intended to set a brisk pace. The fort did not show up on Cor's map, which didn't completely surprise him. Fort Haldon was a military installation only, little more than a wooden stockade with tall archer's towers, whose sole purpose was to guard one of the few passes that led completely through the mountains to Losz. Approximately five hundred men stayed there, almost all of them archers, and the force was changed out completely every six months.

The first two days were ridden in near silence, with what little conversation passing only between the two captains. They did not interact with Cor whatsoever, preferring each other's company. They clearly did not care for the duty and obviously had their own misgivings about the man they traveled with to Fort Haldon. The captains ate their own food, not partaking of anything Cor ate or prepared, and offering him nothing of theirs. Cor knew that one day he would have to address mistrust as well as curiosity, but for now he was content to allow the two soldiers their own misguided thoughts and beliefs.

As the ride continued, the men began to talk more freely of various things ranging from their families and extended families, the weather, battle, and what they will do when they choose to be done with the army. One of the captains was a career soldier and had already decided to die in the queen's service, one way or the other, while the other only did the job to help pay his father's debts. In another few years, he would leave the queen's service and return to the farm. Cor began to take part in the conversations and was at first met with a distrustful silence. As the soldiers came to realize that he and they were different only in minor ways, they began to speak with him more easily, though they often would end conversations in awkward silence. It would not be fair to say that by the time the three men reached Fort Haldon they were fast friends, but perhaps the two captains had a slightly different view of the Dahken. At the least they understood Cor's desire to locate his parents' killer.

Cor recognized the terrain as they rode closer to the ever present mountains on the eastern horizon. The ground changed into foothills the closer they journeyed, and it was no different than when Cor went into the mountains with Kamar. The memory brought him a hint of sadness, as that man did not deserve his death, and Cor always wondered why the spider hadn't attacked him first. Perhaps the thing had a memory of the meal that had escaped it once before.

Fort Haldon was nearly one hundred fifty squat wooden structures behind a fifty foot tall wooden stockade that measured a hundred feet wide and ended on either side at an impassable rockface. It looked more like a military camp than an actual fort, and only the wooden shacks as opposed to canvas tents gave the fort an air of permanence. Six towers, roughly twenty feet taller than the wall itself and currently each manned by four men with longbows, were interspersed at even intervals from one end to the other. A walkway ran between these towers, providing nearly four feet of cover for any defenders standing upon it, and it was ten feet wide, barely offering just enough standing room for two ranks of archers if necessary. Should a massed attack come down the pass, roughly half of the fort's defenders could man the walls in defense. Additionally, eight catapults with large piles of boulders beside them stood at the center of the fort, surely with the ability to toss copious amounts of rock several hundred feet beyond the stockade. While Cor was not skilled in the arts of war, he was sure that Fort Haldon's five hundred could easily slay thousands of attacking troops before falling.

Pickets met the group a quarter mile from the fort and held them until the commander and several of his men arrived. He was a tall Westerner, several inches taller than Cor, and was of a lean and wiry build. He wore leather armor, designed for ease of movement, and carried a shortsword at his side and a full quiver on his back. The commander inspected the captains' orders, written by Palius with the queen's seal, and then dismissed the soldiers to return to Byrverus with fresh horses to speed them on their way. Cor clasped the men's arms, and they bid each other farewell. The commander welcomed Cor into Fort Haldon and offered him all manners of hospitality, which Cor declined saying he wished to get on with his journey. The commander expressed his concern over Cor's intent to enter Losz, but the queen's order was clear in the matter – if Cor intended to cross the mountains into the Loszian Empire, the commander would send him on his way.

Cor merely accepted some additional provisions such as extra water, for water is nearly impossible to find in the Spine, before announcing he was ready to leave. A dozen men were called to the wall's center where they took up positions grasping thick hemp ropes. The men heaved and a pair of near seamless doors, almost indistinguishable from the rest of the wall, opened inward. Cor looked out the open gate into a desolate but wide mountain pass. He thanked Fort Haldon's commander one last time before riding through at a trot, and he could hear the men heaving behind him as the doors closed with a booming thud. Cor turned Kelli around to see that the doors, when completely closed, were almost invisible from the outside.

Cor knew the mountains were as wide as seventy miles in places, and he couldn't be sure how long it would take him to pass through them. Nor was he exactly certain where he was located, as Fort Haldon was not marked on his map, and he could only make an educated guess based on the direction they had traveled from Byrverus. The ground was simply treacherous, inclining alternately upward then downward with a fair amount of loose rock and rubble, and he kept Kelli to a walk and even walked alongside her at times.

It was little more than a month ago that Cor promised himself that he would never again enter the World's Spine, and yet here he was, not only passing through the mountains but well on his way into the Loszian Empire with the intention of playing a very dangerous game with a necromancer. Cor couldn't help wondering why his blood had been tainted with the power of Dahk. He could have been happy as a farmer; while the work was not easy, he believed most farmers likely underestimated the happiness of such a simple life. Cor's life hadn't been simple since the winter night when he was a boy that an old man requested shelter from a horrible snowstorm.

Cor endeavored to put such thoughts out of his mind, for in truth, the why or what could have been did not matter at all. The only thing that mattered was the reality that here he was crossing the border between the moral but revisionist West and an immoral decadent nation of necromancers and assassins. Cor needed to take utmost care in remaining perceptive of his surroundings. The Loszians would have scouts in or above the rocky pass, but he could not know how close to Fort Haldon they would be. Cor reasonably assumed that the fort's commander would have his own scouts in the area, which made Cor wonder if the opposing scouts would confront each other or simply keep their distance from one another.

The days had begun to grow noticeably shorter, and in the mountain pass Cor could not push too far with the light fading so quickly. With the rough, rocky terrain, he could only guess that he traversed perhaps ten miles in the few hours since leaving Fort Haldon. He set out fresh water and some oats in a feedbag and tied the horse to a large rock outcropping. Kelli was somewhat free spirited, and Cor was not yet comfortable with leaving her unattended. He did not sleep well, neither for the discomfort of the ground or sleeping in armor for he had grown accustomed to those, but due to the disquieting sensation of being watched.

Cor spent the entire next day looking over his shoulder or up on the ridges around him. He still could not ignore the nagging sensation of being observed, though he was certain that the spy was not above him. Throughout this day, Cor saw many mountain animals on the various ridges, goats being the most common. He had also seen two bears, huge shaggy brown animals that watched him with curiosity, no doubt wondering what he tasted like. The pair were also above him and obviously not curious enough to make their way down into the pass. Cor assumed that whoever watched him would also draw the attention of animals if they were in fact above him on the ridges, and this led him to the conclusion that the spy stayed a safe distance in front or behind him. Or perhaps it was simply his imagination.

Misery reigned on the third day. The air never warmed to a comfortable level, and a storm had moved in the night before, bringing cold driving rain from morning through the afternoon. At points Cor had to stop as the rain became so hard that he could not see, and Kelli had trouble keeping her footing. Their breath billowed like hot steam in front of them, and though the rain stopped in

222

the afternoon, the sun did not appear from behind the dark gray clouds. Cor had no choice but to sleep almost naked; the garments he wore under his armor became so soaked with the near freezing rain that he could only warm himself by removing them. The night was no colder than the day, and the next day warmed under the sun quickly. Cor, his clothes still wet from the previous day, decided to wait a few hours before moving on, allowing them to dry against the rocks warmed both by the sun and his meager campfire.

It was that afternoon that Cor caught sight of a small group of men coming from the other direction. In the sloping, twisting gorge it was hard to tell how far away they were or how fast they moved, but they came on foot toward him up the pass. Once he was perhaps forty feet away, Cor quickly dismounted and double checked the buckles on his hauberk and legguards. He hoped these men came at him with purpose and were not just sentries come to intercept an intruder, but he was taking no chances. He tethered Kelli and then stood a few yards in front of her, waiting for the men to approach.

There were five of them, all wearing black leather jerkins and breeches with heavy wool cloaks. Four of the men were relatively nondescript as compared to typical Westerners, but the fifth, their leader, reminded Cor of the man who killed his parents. He did not look like the Loszian necromancer, but his limbs, joints and fingers looked slightly distended, slightly out of proportion with the rest of his body. He signaled for two of the men to stay back, both of whom carried loaded crossbows, a significant fact that was not lost on Cor. The other two and the leader approached closer. All were armed with a sword of some type or another, but they kept their weapons sheathed and close at hand.

"Are you Dahken Cor?" the leader asked, bringing his men to a halt.

"I am."

"Why would you seek entrance into Losz? To do so means death for a Westerner."

"I am no Westerner, and I answer to no monarch or god of that realm." Cor reached into his belt pouch and tossed the tattooed skin at the leader, who caught it one handed. "I seek the Loszian noble who owns this mark. He and I have met before, and we have much to talk about."

"I am Wrelk," said the man, folding the flap of skin and placing it in his own pouch, "and I serve the lord you seek. I have been sent to bring you safely to him. You are lucky he knew you were coming. Had you reached our gate, the men there would have slaughtered you without asking questions. No Westerner enters the Loszian Empire without a dozen crossbow bolts in his chest, and it was expensive to secure your access through the gate.

"Hand over your sword," Wrelk commanded him.

"You are the second person to demand my sword in the last few weeks. Will you be as wise as the last in letting me keep it?" Cor asked him.

"It would not do to have you assassinate my lord once I bring you to him, Dahken Cor."

"If I wanted to assassinate him, I'd have paid a Loszian to do the job. At the least, I would have myself smuggled in aboard a ship from Tigol, not have walked in plain sight through the Spine. I go with you, but I keep my sword," Cor said, his tone making it clear that it was his final word on the matter.

Wrelk rolled his eyes and stepped back. He motioned at Cor with his right hand, and the other two men stepped forward, hands on their swords. The first made a clumsy reach for Cor's sword hilt, and Cor, in a much practiced manner, drew Soulmourn and took the man's left hand off at the wrist before he even realized what had happened. Grasping Ebonwing in his left hand, Cor plunged Soulmourn through the man's breastbone while he, still clearly in shock, slowly attempted to draw his own sword with his right hand.

Cor heard the smooth sound of steel pulled from a sheath behind him, and he kicked the dying man from his sword. He turned just in time to catch a two handed blow on his right armguard, and had he not turned, the stroke's angle would have likely led the sword to sever his sword arm just below the shoulder. As it was, the heavy blow knocked him sideways and bent the armor painfully into his upper arm. As Cor recovered his balance, the man brought his bastard sword back around in a stroke meant to hack deeply into Cor's shoulder, scale mail hauberk or not. Cor weaved his upper body back away from the blade and, using the flat edge of Soulmourn, pushed the passing blade faster in its arc down and to Cor's left. The swordsman was suddenly off balance with the massive weapon and realized too late he was overextended. In a backhanded stroke, Cor whipped Soulmourn up and to his right, hacking diagonally through the man's head, and it shattered as if it were a melon, chunks of bone, brain, and gore blasting out in an arc away from where the body slumped to the ground.

Wrelk stood about ten feet away from Cor, a longsword in one hand and his other hand held in a fist at head height. Though urged to lunge at the man, Cor saw the crossbows trained on him from twenty feet away, and he couldn't be sure as to how much protection his armor would afford him against a weapon with such power at that range.

"Enough Dahken Cor," Wrelk said. "My master would be very upset with me should I bring you back as a corpse. Though he has powers to make you his slave after death, I believe he has other intentions."

"Don't think you'll live long enough to experience his displeasure," Cor growled back menacingly, taking a measured step in Wrelk's direction. The man laughed and sheathed his own sword, lowering his raised fist.

"Very well, Dahken, keep your sword then. My lord did not actually order me to take it, so he is clearly not concerned about you. Let us go. We have some miles to go before you meet him."

"You sacrificed two men over an issue of no matter?" Cor demanded, disbelief plain in his voice, and Wrelk merely shrugged his lack of concern.

Cor wiped the blood off Soulmourn onto the wool cloak of one of the dead men and then sheathed it, and he could feel an odd melancholy settle over him at the prospect of no more bloodshed. He walked back to Kelli, who had watched the entire exchange wide eyed, and unbuckled his right armguard. Inspecting it, he hoped he could repair it easily enough, and he placed the piece of armor into a saddlebag. His arm, which was in immense throbbing pain moments ago, no longer hurt, and Cor knew not even a bruise would show itself. Bruises were nothing but bleeding under the skin, and like all his wounds, they healed as he slew his foes. Cor untied Kelli and walked with her, following Wrelk out of the mountain pass.

27.

It was not much further to the Loszians' end of the pass, only about another hour on foot. Clearly, Wrelk had been watching Cor and waited until he was certain the Dahken would make it that far. The Loszians had their own wall and fort, theirs made of a curious black stone that shined purple with reflected sunlight. Western walls and buildings were always made of limestone, granite, and sandstone, perhaps even marble, and this black stone was unlike them all. He vaguely recalled the Chronicler mentioning in his writings the black and purple towers of Losz on several occasions, and Cor remembered those he saw in the distance while briefly moored in Katan'Nosh. The stone wall was roughly the same height as Fort Haldon's wooden stockade with battlements and four large square towers, all made from the same black rock. An iron gate with portcullis was set in the center.

"Halt," a voice called from above when they grew near. "Wrelk, you have found the Westerner for which your master sent you?"

"Yes, Lord," Wrelk replied, shouting to make his voice heard above.

"You left with four men. What happened to the other two?"

"I'm afraid they met an unfortunate and unexpected end. You see, a large boulder simply fell down the mountain and crushed them." Wrelk lied with ease; the tone of his voice was light and reasonable, as if no other occurrence could have possibly happened.

"A most unfortunate end, indeed. Perhaps they should have been more careful."

Cor heard the mirth in the voice from above, and he suspected the speaker knew Wrelk's words were untrue but would make no issue of it. He wondered why they even bothered with the pretense at all; surely, it would be easier to simply tell the truth. The voice shouted for the gate to be opened, and the iron portcullis began to lift with the sound of scraping metal and heavy chains. The group advanced, passing through the gate to the other side of the wall.

The Loszian fort looked surprisingly little different from Fort Haldon, with a mass of buildings for the assembled troops, though these were all made of basalt instead of timber. However, the Loszians did have one large square building at the center of the others to which the group was led. Forced to leave Kelli outside, and with a warning of violence should anything happen to her, Cor and Wrelk were ushered into this building through a heavy oaken door.

Inside was a single room, the length and width of which were the same dimension, roughly forty feet by Cor's eye. In the far right corner sat a massive plush bed, on which sat two stark naked women chained by the throat to the headboard itself. The back wall was adorned with a giant map of the area, apparently showing a span of about five hundred miles in every direction from the center of the mountain pass, and a huge round mahogany table sat in the center of the room. Gold and loot of all kinds lay in a massive heap in the other rear corner. Smoky torches burned in sconces at even intervals around the room, and several others were placed in iron stands around the table.

At the table, his back to the map sat a man writing on parchment with a charcoal pencil. Though sitting, Cor could tell that the man was at least a foot taller than he, and he was impossibly narrow of frame. His fingers, each six inches or more long, reminded Cor of the enormous spider he fought and slew to the south. This man was a true Loszian, and he was even more alien than the first Cor had encountered. His head and neck alone made up

228

two feet of his height, longer than his shoulders were wide.

"Approach, Wrelk," the Loszian said in an oddly deep voice. "I assume you have found the Westerner."

Wrelk did not answer right away and shot Cor a meaningful look, which Cor took to mean he was expected to approach as well. He walked alongside the man, stopping a few feet short of the table's end, about ten feet from the Loszian. This close Cor could see the Loszian had extremely pale skin, quite unlike his own pallor, and blue veins spidered their way across his hands and face. He wore black and blood red robes of silk adorned with various symbols Cor could only assume were magical in nature, and something warned him against touching this Loszian.

"Yes lord, and my lord thanks you for your consideration," Wrelk said.

"To the abyss with his thanks Wrelk. I have his gold, and that is what matters." The Loszian stopped his scribblings and looked up at the two men, staring at Cor intently. For just a moment, a subtle squint came over his visage and his eyes glinted in the torchlight.

"If this man is a Westerner, then he is a walking corpse as he looks as if he comes from the grave. But no, I see his chest rise and fall, and I can see the rhythm of a strong heart. Wrelk, I know not what your master plans, but his gold is not enough for me to hold my tongue. Inform him that he owes me a great boon for allowing this abomination to pass."

Wrelk and his two underlings had horses in the Loszian stable, and the four men left the mountains behind heading northeast. They rode swiftly with the few hours of daylight that remained, and Cor was pleased to let Kelli stretch her legs on less treacherous ground. They did not use roads, clearly on a more direct path to their destination, and they rode until the sun had completely dipped below the horizon, Wrelk declaring it too dark to continue.

After a warm supper, Wrelk set a watch order, explaining to Cor that it was not wise to sleep unprotected in Losz, and he took the first watch himself. Cor had a few questions he wanted answered and said he would stay up for a bit, so long as Wrelk did not mind the company. He did not trust Wrelk, and he doubted Wrelk trusted anyone, possibly not even himself. Cor waited until the two crossbowmen were asleep, or at least pretending to be so, before slowly sauntering over to Wrelk, who sat on a small rock a few feet out of camp.

"You should sleep, Dahken Cor," he said without turning. "You may soon need your rest."

"I'm restless. Wrelk, where do we ride to?"

"My master's stronghold is a day and a half's ride to the northeast."

"I have met him once, and it wasn't under the best of circumstances. How do I know he won't just kill me when we arrive?" Cor asked.

"I suppose you don't, but I imagine if he wanted you dead, he would have let the border guard kill you," Wrelk answered. He never looked at Cor, always keeping his eyes attuned to the darkness beyond the camp.

"I owe your master a debt for killing my parents. What's to stop me from killing him?" At this question, Cor saw a slight, wry smile touch the corners of Wrelk's mouth.

"It's none of my affair, but I wish you luck in that endeavor," Wrelk replied, his voice dripping with sarcasm. Cor waited a few minutes in silence before deciding to change the subject; he had some other questions he wanted to ask.

"You are part Loszian, aren't you?"

"My grandfather was half Loszian; his father was a noble who took liberty with peasants and slaves."

Though the West had no shortage of peasants and indentured servants, in all cases it was purely a business transaction that either party could leave at any time without fear of retribution or recrimination. Outright slavery was illegal and considered to be one of the highest crimes in the Shining West. Cor had a hard time fathoming misery of such an existence, especially with the knowledge that one's oppressors may "take liberties" at any time. The thought of his mother being subjected to such an atrocity came unbidden to his mind, and suddenly his blood began to boil.

"You must hate the Loszians," Cor said, receiving a puzzled look from Wrelk.

"Why would I? It's my Loszian blood that makes me better than the slaves or peasants. Over the centuries, the Loszians created a ... sub nobility I suppose you might say. Those of us with mixed blood have more freedom and power than the masses. Our lords select us for tasks, and we work to make ourselves more useful to them. I have no wife or daughter, but if I did, I would happily allow a full blooded Loszian, even halfblooded, to take her. Any child from that union would live better than I."

Cor listened incredulously to Wrelk continue about the social and economic advantages of allowing the rape of his hypothetical daughter or wife at the hands of a Loszian lord. Wrelk contentedly viewed it as a means to an end, an attempt at raising one's status, and the man's detached matter of fact perspective appalled Cor. His mind whirled with the disgusting logic of it and that the people of Losz had simply come to accept this as the way of things. Again, Cor allowed the discussion to simply die out before asking another question.

"Who was the Loszian that spoke to us back in the mountains?"

"Lord Menak. He was once a powerful noble and sorcerer. I do not know the entire story, but I know he chose to leave his lands in favor of the border, away from the center of machinations in the empire."

"He's a full blooded Loszian, isn't he?" Cor asked, knowing the answer.

"Yes, like most of the lords."

"Most," said Cor slowly, watching Wrelk's reaction, "but not all, like your lord. When I saw him, I only assumed he was a true Loszian, but after meeting Menak, I know that's not true. What's his name?"

"Taraq'nok, and I will not discuss my lord's birth or his private matters," Wrelk said, turning his face to Cor. "I serve him, and it is his business what he shares with you. Go to sleep, Dahken Cor. Ee have much riding to do tomorrow."

Cor had heard that tone in a person's voice many times over the years, and it always came when he had asked one too many questions. It carried a note of finality that his parents had taught him meant to drop the issue lest he pay the consequences. He returned to his bedroll and forced himself to sleep.

Cor found that the Loszian countryside looked little different than that of Aquis. It was rather boring and uneventful, and Wrelk kept to himself the rest of the journey. Cor did not even attempt to engage the man, or his cohorts, in conversation. They kept up their pace, and they reached their destination before noon on the second day since leaving the mountains behind. The group gained a small hill and upon looking down into the valley, Cor knew where they were headed. In the center of the small valley stood a small black castle, similar in size to what Sanctum once had been. A black curtain wall surrounded the castle with towers at each of the four corners; it was a relatively unimaginative design, but Cor didn't doubt its effectiveness. A cluster of small buildings stood directly outside the walls, and farms extended outward for several miles around.

As they descended into the valley and passed through the farmland, what Cor saw shocked him. The various crops were not well tended, and he doubted that even half of the impending harvest would be edible. The people, mostly men, he saw working the fields were filthy and emaciated, driven only by a lack of anything else to do or the whip of an overseer. The workers looked no different from other Westerners, but the armored overseers clearly had varying amounts of Loszian blood.

As they approached the castle, Cor saw that the wall and castle were made from the same black stone he had seen at the Loszian side of the Spine. The stone shined dark purple with light reflected off it, and it clearly had some special significance for the Loszians. Cor idly wondered if they somehow made the stone themselves through their sorcery or if it was something quarried on the eastern side of the Spine. Just outside the curtain walls stood several squat buildings; a few were made from timber, but most of them were clay and mud huts. He could see into some of the huts, as they had no doors except perhaps an animal skin, and they were stark and filthy inside. Children ran freely here playing, but not with the same joy Cor remembered as a boy, while teenaged girls sat or stood nearby idly watching.

A wide, deep moat surrounded the walls, though it was empty, and a ten foot wide drawbridge crossed it allowing entrance into the castle. As they passed through the gate, Cor noted the heavy black iron portcullis drawn up overhead, clearly another affectation popular with the Loszians. The wall's interior was far larger than Sanctum's had been, but the spaciousness was lost to many black stone buildings. He spotted the usual services a castle would need, such as a blacksmith, armory, and cooper, but there were many nondescript buildings with closed doors. Wrelk explained that Taraq'nok's captains and agents of Loszian blood lived within these, while his lieutenants and direct servants stayed within the castle.

The castle itself looked little different from Sanctum outside of the color and one large tower that was completely open to the outside at the spire.

The men dismounted, and their horses were led away by stable hands, with yet another warning from Cor regarding Kelli. He had grown rather fond of the palomino and had long decided he would violently eviscerate anyone responsible for mistreating or harming her. They entered the keep through double doors of iron banded oak, and it seemed to Cor that nearly every door of every large building he had ever seen was made in the same manner. They stood in a small room, the walls of which were the same black stone with sconces holding torches. A guard wearing a suit of black chain mail conversed briefly in hushed tones with Wrelk before turning and passing through the next set of double doors.

"We wait now," Wrelk said. "When we are summoned, I will walk ahead of you and my men behind. Kneel when we do."

The wait was brief, though it didn't seem that way to Cor. Anxiousness gnawed at him, and it took all his willpower to not pace the room or climb the walls like a trapped animal. He forced himself to keep in mind what he needed from this Loszian. The man's servant had murdered his parents, and his men had lit fire to Sanctum, eventually causing its complete destruction. The necromancer was his only link to information about Noth and his citadel. To risk that through rash temper, likely leading to his own death, would be exceptionally irrational, and the slight tingling sensation where Soulmourn hung at his hip did not help the situation.

The double doors to the antechamber opened from the other direction, and the black mailed guard, with another, stood at attention to either side. Wrelk began a measured pace into the room beyond, with Cor trailing several feet behind and the other two men from their short trek just behind him. Again, Cor marveled at the similarities in architectural design; the antechamber opened into a large hall with an open windowed ceiling perhaps forty feet overhead. The hall was about eighty feet long and about thirty feet wide with eight large columns, four on each side. The room was made of the same black stone, of which Cor assumed the entire castle would be built, and many torches illuminated it. Again, there was a raised platform at the far end of the hall, though not nearly as large as in the palace in Byrverus, and six black steps leading up to a high backed throne apparently carved of pure ebony.

Cor certainly had no difficulty recognizing the figure sitting on the throne, for it was the Loszian that faced him at Sanctum, the same he once saw in Katan'Nosh. There was no question he was tall, and even sitting flush against the back of the ebony throne, his hands hung off the end of the armrests, and his knees jutted out from the throne by several inches. He had long fingers, similar to Lord Menak, and Cor still couldn't help but compare the Loszian to a spider. His head and face were shaved completely smooth, which combined with his pale complexion, added to his abnormally gaunt appearance. The Loszian had a small but pointed chin, an angular face with a seemingly tall forehead and understated ears. He wore silk robes similar to those of Lord Menak but in black and purple.

As they approached, he stood from his throne, standing at a full height easily six inches over Cor, and on the raised platform he appeared as a giant. Wrelk and his two men immediately dropped to both knees, their heads hanging from their shoulders so that their faces pointed to the ground. Cor did not kneel or bow in any way; he would go along with this Loszian so long as he attained the information he needed, but he would not show any degree of fealty to him.

"Lord Taraq'nok, I have found the man as Your Excellency has commanded," Wrelk said without looking up, his voice raised to be heard.

"You serve me well, Wrelk, but where are my other two servants?" The Loszian's voice was smooth as ice and moderately pitched.

"My most humble apologies, Excellency. Dahken Cor eliminated two of them in a misunderstanding regarding custody of his sword. I did not anticipate he would be so protective of it."

"No doubt he was," the Loszian paused, looking Cor over with interest. "Why did you not bring the corpses back to me so they may continue to serve?"

"My lord, I did not think Lord Menak would allow us to pass had he known there was violence."

"There is truth in that, Wrelk. Fear not, you are absolved from blame."

"Excellency," Wrelk paused, as being the bearer of unwelcome news to a Loszian lord was not advisable, "I relay a message from Lord Menak as well. He says that your payment in gold is not enough, and that you owe him a great boon for allowing the Dahken to pass."

"Yes," Taraq'nok said with a quiet sigh, "I expected as much. You see, Dahken Cor, it is policy of the Loszian Emperor to kill Dahken on sight."

"You haven't killed me yet, and your servants, like poor marksmen, can't seem to hit the target," Cor said. He knew he could push the Loszian too far, but he couldn't help making sure Taraq'nok knew this would not be one sided. This was the second such game Cor had played recently, and though he wasn't totally sure of the rules, Cor obviously had an asset that made even a queen think twice.

"Killing you was never my intention, Dahken. Though, I must say I am perturbed at you; that is now six of my servants for whose deaths you are responsible."

"Three Loszian," Cor corrected. "The first, Dahken Rael killed, when he saved me from being kidnapped. The second died inside Sanctum, which had nothing to do with me, and the weasel you left at Sanctum died from a very unfortunate fall off of a decaying stone wall. But I don't think the score is even. Your man killed my parents, and they were worth all of your men's lives, if not yours as well."

"I don't believe you have come all this way in a misguided attempt to slay me," Taraq'nok responded, a slight smile touching the corner of his lips, though his voice had quieted slightly.

"You have spies in the palace in Aquis," Cor said; it was a statement not a question, and the Loszian laughed at it.

"Of course, I do. I suspected, as the highest in Garod's order," this Taraq'nok said with venom, "the queen would have some knowledge of you. The West has tried valiantly to eliminate all history of your race, but only where common knowledge is concerned.

"However, now I must rectify another problem, for I am not the only Loszian with spies in Byrverus. By now, the emperor knows there is a powerful Dahken in Losz. Lord Menak knows Wrelk is my servant, and if forced, he will divulge that to the emperor. I will have to provide proof of your death, perhaps your severed head carried by your reanimated corpse."

Cor instinctively drew Soulmourn and Ebonwing, bringing reactions from guards in various positions in the hall, including Wrelk and his two men. It surprised him that Taraq'nok would go to this much trouble only to kill him, especially as he had just said that was never his intent, but Cor would not stand idly by and allow it to happen. He would kill as many of the Loszian's servants as he could. He felt an urge to begin the slaying with Wrelk, but Cor held his ground, awaiting the next move.

"Put your weapons away, Dahken," Taraq'nok said. "I have other ways to make the emperor believe I have killed you, and I will show you those in due time. For now, let us end this nonsense. I have had an adequate set of quarters arranged for you here in the castle. Please make yourself more comfortable, and then we shall meet for supper. I am sure it has been at least a week since you have had a decent meal.

"Dahken Cor, welcome to the Loszian Empire and your future."

28.

Cor was led by a small man, thin and short of stature with close cropped hair and goatee beard, out of the hall through a doorway. They climbed a flight of stairs and turned down another corridor before stopping at a set of average height double doors. The doors had no lock and opened easily; they were extremely light, likely made of pine with a reddish stain. To call the quarters adequate was a gross understatement. There were two rooms, the first of which was extremely spacious and contained the bed, a huge four poster frame of solid mahogany. The posts were octagonal and as large around as Cor's thigh, connected at the top to form a canopy from which purple silks hung around all sides of the bed. A large desk of cherry, with a matching plush armchair, stood to one side of a large window with an open interior shutter. The floor of the bedroom was covered in animal skins of various kinds.

Something else in the room drew Cor's attention; a naked teenaged girl sat dejectedly on the edge of the bed. She had long dark hair, near black as is common to most Westerners, which hung loosely and unkempt about her shoulders, partially obscuring the view of her breasts. She immediately stood upon Cor's entry into the room, and he endeavored not to linger with his gaze. Though after looking at her for a moment, Cor was certain she couldn't be much younger than he. Despite her obvious position of degradation, she was comely and had an extremely well-shaped body.

"This room," said the man, "and everything in it is at your convenience, sir. The next room contains a large bath, also at your convenience. I am Lord Taraq'nok's House Steward, and I handle all the castle's domestic

239

needs. Should anything here not please you, I will rectify it immediately." The man looked pointedly at the young woman. "His Excellency asks that you make yourself at home and relax. I will return at sunset to bring you to the dining room." The steward turned and closed the doors behind him.

Cor had no intention of taking advantage of the girl; she was a slave, in a life of degradation, and he would not add to it. Even with his limited experience, Cor knew that paying for a whore was a completely different affair. Throughout history, the Dahken clearly had their own sense of morality. He didn't recall slaves ever being mentioned in any of the historical texts one way or the other, but he refused to accept it as moral or acceptable. If there was one thing the Shining West understood, it was that slavery was a vile, disgusting practice to be stamped out. Unfortunately, surrounded by the Loszian Empire there was little he could do about that just now, but he did not have to partake in it.

"What is your name?" he asked her in Loszian, carefully keeping his eyes off her body. She seemed shocked by the question and looked at him uncomprehendingly. "I'm not going to hurt you," he reassured her.

"Ania."

"Ania, please put on some clothes."

"Do I not please you?" she asked, seemingly disappointed. "If you prefer another girl, or a boy, the steward will oblige you."

"No, not at all. It's just that you are a slave. You do this because you must or you will be punished," Cor stumbled over his words. Her naked flesh distracted him, but her reaction surprised him to the point of confusion. She seemed completely accepting of her role in life, and Cor suddenly found difficulty explaining to this admittedly attractive girl why he wouldn't do as she expected.

240

"As a slave, you have no will, wants, or desires, and I won't take advantage of that," he explained. "If you were here of your own will, that would be a different matter."

"But my lord, I do desire you. I am a slave, and I am here as I was told. But this life is far better than working in the fields and being forced to breed more slaves. This is what is expected of me, and if I don't meet your desires, I become useless to my master." She slowly walked from her position, crossing the room to approach him. "If I am exceptionally good at providing you enjoyment, I have food, warm shelter, and a bed to sleep in. Perhaps, I will even bear your child, making myself more than just a slave."

She was close to him now, and her scent, perfumed and so vastly different from steel and sweat, found its way into his nostrils. Cor struggled with her rationalization, fighting his urge to simply take her as she came closer. It amazed him that she had such acceptance of her place in this society, and he wasn't even sure she would know what to do with freedom if it were given to her.

"Please clothe yourself, Ania."

"I don't have any clothes, my lord," she answered, standing mere inches from him. He pulled his eyes from her and strode over to the bed, ripping down some of the silk hanging from the bed's canopy. He turned back towards Ania and held the silk sheet before him at shoulder level.

"Please Ania, cover yourself in this. I'm tired, and I don't have the strength for this right now."

"Yes, my lord. Rest now, and perhaps later you will allow me to serve you," she said while wrapping the silk cloth around her torso under her arms. The shear material only slightly hid her supple form, and Cor could easily see her firm breasts and thin waist through the silk. The fabric only dropped about one inch below the meeting of her legs, and somehow, the entire effect was far more seductive than her fully naked form.

Cor turned back toward the bed and began unbuckling his armor, allowing the pieces to simply fall to the floor. Once down to his tunic and breeches, he sat on the edge of the mattress and unbuckled his swordbelt, leaning Soulmourn against one of the bed's posts. The mattress was rich with plushness, and he felt his weight settle down into it. The linens were of burgundy satin, smooth and cool to the touch, and Cor lay back in the bed and dozed off.

Cor woke confused; he lay in an extremely comfortable bed with smooth satin bedding, and an attractive dark haired woman lay almost naked cuddled up next to him. On top of that, a plain faced man with a beard hovered over him. The sunlight coming through the open window slanted at a steep angle, and Cor knew he'd been asleep for several hours. He had not meant to sleep so deeply, and it took a moment for the last day's occurrences to return to him.

"Sir," said the steward, "I apologize for waking you, but it is very nearly time to serve supper. Lord Taraq'nok has of course requested your presence for a fine meal. Please prepare yourself, and I will wait outside until you are ready." The man turned and again closed the door behind him.

Cor slowly sat up, throwing his legs over the side of the bed, and rubbed his eyes with both hands. He panicked for a moment, realizing that he had slept heavily, but the few belongings he had brought into the castle were still right where he left them. He stood and stretched his back, realizing that he felt more rested after this brief nap than he had in months. Ania did not stir, and he watched her sleep briefly, noticing that she really was an attractive girl. Cor began to wonder what her soft body would feel like pressed up against his.

These thoughts he put out of his mind as he focused on what was to come. He knew that the girl, while she may be part of the accommodations, was also an attempt by Taraq'nok to distract and sway him. Cor needed to make sure the Loszian knew that his will was unbreakable, and he could not be diverted from his task. He must show no deferment to the necromancer; as such, Cor decided it would be best to appear as if he would leave or kill at a moment's notice. He prepared himself with both armor and sword, the sound awakening Ania. He favored her with a kind smile and exited the room. The steward waited outside, as promised, and Cor took note of the two mailed and armed guards that stood on either side of his doors.

"Thank you for sir for your alacrity," said the steward. "Pardon these gentlemen. With no locks on the doors, Lord Taraq'nok uses them to make certain his guests are safe."

"I don't doubt it."

"Follow me please sir," said the steward, going back the way they had come a few hours ago. It was not lost on Cor that the two guards followed them.

"Sir, I hope you found the rooms accommodating to your needs?" the steward asked, and Cor was certain the man looked at him through the back of his head.

"I am satisfied, thank you," Cor answered.

Somehow the steward's civilized tone and manner of speech was beginning to grate on Cor's nerves, to the extent that Cor wanted to ram Soulmourn down his throat. Perhaps it was the fact it was expected that Cor would have raped Ania until he was sated, as was apparently the custom in Losz. Once, Taraq'nok had told Cor they would overthrow both the Loszian Empire and the Shining West. Cor was concluding that, at the least, he would destroy the Loszians one by one, castle by castle and block by block if need be, as they disgusted him already. His mind headed in this direction, he could feel Soulmourn and Ebonwing suddenly warm at his side, and he suppressed the urge to hack the steward into pieces. He wondered if he would ever get used to that feeling, or if one day it would overwhelm him.

They progressed back down the stairs to the castle's main level and crossed the hall in which Cor had met his host. They entered another corridor, this one directly across from the last, which ended at a tall door after only a few feet. The door was of a dark, solid wood, and the steward opened it, motioning Cor inside. He then closed the door, leaving the guards outside in the corridor. The following room was a large dining hall with a thirty foot long mahogany table in the dead center. There were multiple windows, but they were all shuttered, no doubt to keep cool autumn air outside. A small fire blazed in a stone fireplace at one end of the room, adding unnecessary heat to the air. The table had eight comfortable looking armchairs on either side, as well as another on one end, which stood three feet taller than the others and had carved arms that were at least six inches wide.

"Sir, if you would please?" While Cor had been looking around the room, the steward had moved to the other side of the table and pulled out a chair immediately to the left of the large chair at the table's head.

"Does he always entertain as many as this table will seat?" Cor asked while moving to take his seat. He removed Soulmourn from his belt, leaning the sword in its scabbard against the left side of his chair as he sat.

"No sir, I am afraid not," he answered. "Lord Taraq'nok sometimes dines with his officers, but you have his full attention tonight. Sir, please wait here."

The steward left the room the way they had come, and Cor sat quietly for several minutes, questioning the wisdom of his entire plan while he looked around the dining room. It was quite large, and light from the few torches and candles did not illuminate the far corners of the room. Cor looked at the ceiling, which was about twenty feet overhead, and marveled at the construction; it was made of black stone blocks with no support beams or timbers of any kind. The Loszians must employ magic of some kind in their buildings.

The door opened again, producing the steward, but it was who followed behind him that made Cor hold his breath. He walked into the room and held out the chair immediately to the right of Taraq'nok's for the most exotic and beautiful woman Cor had ever seen. She was three, maybe four inches shorter than he with a lean, muscular frame. She had hair of gold that was held in a ponytail high on the back of her head with a black silk cord and hung halfway down her back. In fact, her attire was made entirely of a black silk that seemed to have a slight shimmer but was not at all translucent. She wore a tunic and pants that were completely formfitting, and she walked with a slight sway that made Cor wonder what she looked like when walking away. Her pants ended just below her knee, and on her feet, she wore a set of soft soled sandals with black silk cords that ran around her shins. As she came closer, Cor could see her face had an angular, almost feline look, and her bronze skin was not a trick of the torchlight.

He had never seen anyone of the ruling class from the continent of Dulkur, but it was plainly obvious that she hailed from that land.

Before sitting in the offered chair, she unclasped a thin black leather belt that ran from over her right shoulder to under her left arm. Cor realized it was a kind of swordbelt, and attached to it was a sword of roughly the same length as Soulmourn. The weapon curved along its length in a bizarre arc, and the leather wrapped hilt bent slightly in the opposite direction. The blade narrowed noticeably where it met a strange guard, roughly hexagonal but with six sides of irregular length. She placed the weapon nonchalantly on the table to her right and sat down.

The steward walked in his ever purposeful way to a sideboard, which Cor had to turn his head to see as it was slightly behind him and returned with three gold goblets and a decanter of wine. He placed the goblets on the table, one each in front of Cor and the woman, and the third in front of the large and yet unoccupied chair. He poured a red wine from the decanter into each of the goblets and then returned to the sideboard, clearly waiting. Cor did not touch the wine, though he did not fear it poisoned; it simply made little sense for Taraq'nok to poison him when the Loszian had several opportunities to kill him already. Again, if he wanted him dead, he would have let Cor simply walk up to the Loszian wall and filled him with crossbow bolts.

While waiting for their host, Cor made a conscious effort to not stare at the striking woman, though she did not return the favor. He felt her watching him the entire time they waited together, which felt interminable though it could not have been more than a few minutes. He reverted to staring straight ahead impassively, and he met her eyes one time and felt himself enraptured by her unwavering gaze. From only a few feet away, he could see her face more clearly. Her eyes were slightly almond shaped from epicanthic folds at the corner, and her irises were silver, not gray but truly silver.

Cor could not have been more relieved when the Loszian finally arrived, coming from the same corridor from which Cor and the woman had arrived. He crossed the room, approaching the large chair at the table's end, his robes making it appear as if he glided rather than walked. As he sat, the steward exited the dining room through a smaller door on the other side of the room.

"I apologize for my tardiness," said the Loszian. "I was held up by a matter that required my immediate attention. I assume the two of you have become acquainted."

"In truth no, Lord Taraq'nok. Your guest here seems to prefer silence," said the bronze skinned woman, her voice soft and melodious with an underlying strength. She spoke Loszian mellifluously with a strange accent that seemed to linger on certain consonants, and Cor wondered if all of those from Dulkur sounded the same way.

"How rude of him, though I imagine if he is still trying to decide if he wishes to kill me or not. My dear, our silent dinner partner is Dahken Cor, originally of Aquis, though I understand he no longer pays Queen Erella any allegiance.

"Dahken Cor, allow me to introduce Lady Thyss of Dulkur," Taraq'nok said motioning with his right hand. At this she laughed heartily in dulcet tones, leaning back in her chair. The Loszian sat impassively with his hand frozen in the air, apparently not understanding the humor.

"My Lord," she explained, stifling her laugh, "I gave up any claim to titles or worship long ago. To call me Lady is only accurate in the purely feminine sense of the word."

"Indeed, that is likely so," agreed the Loszian, "though I must point out that in your case, there is more than enough reason to recognize your femininity." At this, she laughed again, deeper and richer than before, just as the steward returned with several slaves in tow. The first course, a light concoction of vegetables and some pork, was served.

"So Dahken Cor, you intend to kill Lord Taraq'nok do you?" Thyss asked, the bluntness of the question surprising him. He looked up from the plate to see her again looking at him, a facetious half smile lifting one corner of her mouth.

"Honestly, I haven't decided yet. I'm still waiting for him to give me a reason not to," he answered, eliciting another laugh from the woman.

"In due time," the Loszian said, leaning back from the table. The steward appeared seemingly out of nowhere and refilled everyone's goblets. Without realizing it, Cor had started to drink the wine and found it to be far more appetizing than the stuff Rael drank almost daily, which meant he had to be careful that he did not imbibe too much.

"I've never seen a Dahken before," Thyss said as slaves removed plates and delivered what was apparently a main course involving beef and an oddly orange colored sauce. "I understand their resilience in combat is unmatched. Is it true you are immune to the effects of Loszian sorcery as well as Garod's?"

"Garod's yes, but as far as Loszian," he answered with a sidelong glance at Taraq'nok, "I have not yet had the opportunity."

"I believe," interjected Taraq'nok, "that resistant is the proper term. No one is completely immune to our necromancy."

"I wonder how resistant he is to my magicks. What do you think Lord Taraq'nok? Do you supposed I could light his hair on fire as easily as one of your slaves?" she asked, leaning back in her chair again. Her head was slightly turned towards the Loszian, but she kept her gaze locked on Cor.

"I invite you to try," Cor answered her, his eyes narrowed and his voice low and with a hard edge to it.

She lifted her right hand and held it in front of her face with the back of it facing Cor, and he realized the woman held something that seemed to flicker, splashing light across her features. She tipped her hand his way and opened her fingers slightly, revealing a small ball of blue flame that did not burn her, and in fact, it caused her no discomfort at all. Cor was not sure what her next action would be, but he hardened his jaw and returned the threat in her eyes, completely unblinking. After a seemingly long moment, Thyss' eyes opened slightly, and Cor could see the humor within them. Yet again, she laughed loudly and closed her hand around the flame, extinguishing it. Cor relaxed slightly, knowing that he had passed some sort of test she had devised.

"My dear Thyss, I must warn you," said Taraq'nok, "Dahken Cor has proved himself to be a man of iron will, defying not only myself, but Queen Erella of Aquis at many turns. I would suggest that you not push too far, for you may find that even you are unable to break him.

"And Dahken Cor, I would issue a similar warning to you. Lady Thyss is an accomplished warrior, perfectly capable of slaying with her steel, but the elemental gods have gifted her with powers quite different from Loszian necromancy. I would not antagonize her, lest she in fact sets your hair aflame."

The two looked at each other intently while the Loszian spoke, sizing one another up and surmising what they could of each other. Cor had read some history of Dulkur in his time at Sanctum, though the knowledge there clearly leaned towards the West. He had long assumed that the Dahken repositories in other parts of the world also focused on their areas, but he knew that those blessed with the powers of the elemental gods were priests and rulers in Dulkur, revered, worshipped, and feared among the masses. Also, she clearly favored powers of fire, and the god of fire, Hykan, was considered the leader of the elementals. What could possibly entice someone with such power to leave her homeland behind? Cor realized that they had been staring at each other for several minutes, while the Taraq'nok merely sat watching them. He could see a slight, enigmatic smile touching the corners of her mouth and had the distinct impression that a great predator was about to eat him.

"I am still waiting to hear why I shouldn't simply cleave your head from your shoulders," Cor said, turning to Taraq'nok. He could hear Thyss laugh softly.

"Ah yes, Dahken Cor, you truly are of a one track mind. However, I mean for this to be only a relaxing occasion. Should we not be able to come to an understanding, there is plenty of time for us to kill each other tomorrow. I simply assumed you would appreciate good food, a soft bed, and fine company for one night at least."

Cor sighed disgustedly, pushing his plate away. He couldn't understand how this Loszian could be so infuriatingly calm about this entire situation. Yes, Cor did come seeking information, but he also came to kill this man, who seemed completely at ease or even oblivious to the fact. The two exchanged looks, and it was then that Cor knew he had grossly underestimated Taraq'nok. The necromancer had thought through this entire encounter years ago, and it was playing out no differently than he expected. The plates were cleared, and a cold dessert of some type was served.

"Do not be petulant, Dahken Cor," Taraq'nok said. "This is a social occasion, and you can at least attempt to enjoy yourself. Do you see, Thyss? We all strive to hold onto youth for its strength and virility, but as we grow older, we forget the flaws of youth such as fervor, inflexibility, and rashness. I suppose Dahken Cor will one day learn as we have."

Cor sat back in his chair and watched the two finish their meal, wondering just how old the two sorcerers were, as they appeared no more than ten years his senior. The more he thought about it, the more disgusting the Loszian and his entire lifestyle became to Cor. Cor now knew that no matter how antagonistic he became, Taraq'nok would not rest until he got what he needed from Cor, and he realized that if he played by the same set of rules, he would get what he needed from the

Loszian that much faster. Cor leaned forward and tried the dessert, and finding it delicious, he ate most of it. Taraq'nok did not fail to notice, despite his continuous small talk with Thyss.

The dinner lasted a little longer, the steward producing a heavy citrus flavored liquor of which Cor consumed little. Following promises from Taraq'nok that tomorrow they would discuss how they could help each other, Cor returned to his set of rooms, with his guard escort of course. He found Ania, clothed, though scantily, lounging carelessly in the bed, and she immediately sat upright upon his entrance. Cor waved her off, saying that he would simply like to relax, and he removed his armor noisily.

Looking for some sort of basin, Cor explored the next room and found a huge marble tub inlaid into the black stone of the floor. Two round holes about half the size of his fist were set in the deepest part of the bottom, and four silver ropes hung from a pulley system down to a level where someone in the tub could operate them easily. Ania had followed him into the room and explained that pulling the first and second ropes controlled how much hot or cold water filled the tub. Pulling the third rope slowed or stopped the filling of the tub, and the fourth rope, when pulled, would drain the water. Cor marveled at the ease with which one could take a bath and wondered if it was a feat of ingenious engineering, magic, or both.

Cor had not left Soulmourn and Ebonwing with his armor. He put them down gently on the floor and completely oblivious to modesty, Cor removed his clothes, stepped into the tub, and began to work the rope system. Steaming water began to fill the bottom of the tub from one of the two holes he assumed were drains. Once the water was above his ankles, Cor sat down in the tub and rested his arms on its massive sides while leaning his head back with his eyes closed.

A soft splash and disturbance of the water made him open his eyes to see that Ania, completely naked with her garments in a heap on the floor next to his, had climbed into the tub with him. She leaned over him on her hands and knees, kissing his neck, and her closeness evoked a sudden reaction in him of which she was quick to take advantage. He allowed himself to enjoy it for just a moment, letting his mind wander. It wandered to the filthy, beaten, and whipped people sullenly boarding Kosaki's ship in Hichima.

"Ania, please don't. I can't let you do this," he said softly. He gently but firmly took hold of both her wrists, at once removing her hands from him and receiving a confused and dejected look from her. "I'll make you a promise. I'll free you one day, and then you can do this of your own free will, if you like, but not because it's your lot in life."

She did not understand his unwillingness, and Cor wasn't sure he could make her understand. On some level, he didn't understand himself; it wasn't as if *he* were forcing her to do anything. She left the bath and dried herself with wool towels before putting back on her less than concealing garments. She made certain that there were two towels ready for him and even brought him a fresh set of clothes, and when she finally left and stayed in the other room, Cor let out a long sigh.

He didn't doze off in the tub exactly, but hot water has a tendency to relax one's mind as well as the body. Cor stayed comfortably in the bath for some time. He finally roused himself when he could feel the water was only a little warmer than the air, and he pulled the last of the silver ropes. The water slowly drained out of the tub by way of the other hole in its bottom, and Cor forced himself out of the bath. The marble was slick with the water, made even more difficult by his well relaxed muscles. He carefully dried himself and dressed in the clothes Ania had left out for him – soft cotton breeches and a tunic that buttoned all the way up the front, a fact that Cor found annoying.

He walked into the bedroom, his hair still dripping, and found Ania lying naked on the bed. He sighed quietly, wondering what it would take for her to understand that he would not be taking advantage of her hospitality. Before he said something, Cor noticed that his belongings that he had left with Kelli were laid out on top of and next to the large desk in the room. He walked over to it, taking a mental inventory to make sure nothing was missing.

"My Lord, the steward had them brought up while you were at dinner," Ania called across the room. He didn't remember the steward ever leaving the dining hall; the man must have made the arrangements ahead of time.

Without warning, the doors to his quarters opened forcefully, and Thyss stormed in, seemingly ablaze with purpose. She looked at the naked Ania and jerked her head hard at the open door behind her. Ania leapt off the bed, picked up her few thin garments, ran past Thyss, and a guard closed the door behind her. Cor's armor of course laid in a heap between he and the golden haired woman, but he suddenly realized he had left his weapons next to the marble bath in the next room. Thyss carried her curved sword by its scabbard in her left hand, and he highly doubted he could dart in there to retrieve Soulmourn before she could strike. With no other options, he simply held his ground, hoping to overpower her should she come that close.

She strode right up to him, dropping her sword on an animal fur several feet away and embraced him with a kiss harder than he thought possible. Thyss tore away his clothes and, fondling him, pushed him down onto the floor. Caught up in the ferocity of her assault, Cor grabbed a hold of her tight silk tunic at the neck and tried to tear it open, only to find that the material was strong as chain mail, and his muscles strained against it. She laughed at his shock and pulled the tunic over her head, revealing her naked breasts and her well-toned, strong upper body. She laid her half naked body across his muscled chest and kissed him fiercely, moving her mouth to his right ear.

"I *will* break you," she hissed.

Cor allowed the bronzed skinned woman with the golden hair and silver eyes to do as she willed, taking pleasure from it all. She did things the harlot in Worh had not even dreamt of, and he accepted her fully. Cor did everything she ordered of him, but he did not surrender himself to her. She could not break him.

29.

"Sir, it is morning and time for breakfast," said the steward, again hovering over Cor. He groggily opened his eyes, seeing morning light filter through his window. It faced south, so the sun always cast some amount of light through it regardless of the time of day. "I should expect you downstairs when you are ready. Also, sir, I have had the liberty of sending your armor to be repaired and shined, and yes sir, your sword is still in the next room." The man turned and left.

Cor rubbed his eyes and wondered at the propensity of that man to be everywhere at once. It was certainly possible that there were copies of the man all doing the same job, and in a bizarre way it made more sense than the concept that the one man could do everything that was clearly expected of him. *Or*, Cor thought still rubbing his eyes, *perhaps he takes efficiency to new extremes.*

Thyss was nowhere to be seen, and the steward certainly did not act as if he had seen her in his room. This was the second woman he had lain with, and the second woman who was gone in the morning before he woke up. Sitting on the edge of the bed, Cor couldn't help but wonder if this was standard practice among the species known as women. He had often heard talk in the bars and inns that they were never as pretty in the morning. He had always thought that a joke, but now he could not help but wonder.

Cor stood and found a freshly pressed set of clothes had been laid out for him, not too different from those Ania had given him last night, though this tunic simply pulled over the head. The thought of Ania pained him, and he genuinely hoped she was well. His old

255

clothes, as well as his riding boots, were gone, and he found a new pair of hard leather boots awaiting him as well. The entire set of attire was black, and it dawned on Cor that every Loszian he had ever seen seemed to wear black as their primary color. He wondered about the idiosyncratic nature of people as he belted on Soulmourn and secured Ebonwing at his waist.

Cor left his quarters, noticing that the guards were no longer there, and made his way to the dining room. The steward had laid out an excellent warm meal, and Cor endeavored not to enjoy it too much, remembering that it came from the labors of slaves. While eating, his thoughts wandered to Thyss and the night before, and he wondered where she could be found. Then the oddity of the thought struck him, that he should be so interested in her.

"Sir, I understand you did not find the accommodations completely to your liking last night," said the steward as he cleared Cor's meal. "Please tell me how I may rectify the situation for you."

"Accommodations?" Cor asked, at first not comprehending. "You're talking about Ania. No, she was fine. I just don't have need of her… services."

"Perhaps another girl would be more to your liking, or if you have other tastes?"

"No, thank you," Cor answered quickly. "What happened to Ania after she left my room?"

"She has been reallocated to other parts of Lord Taraq'nok's service, sir. If you are finished, My Lord wishes to see you in his library."

The steward led Cor back through the main hall of the castle and into a corridor that exited the rear of the room. The library was very little different from the one at Sanctum, prior to its destruction, though substantially larger. There were several plain oak tables and chairs near the room's entrance, and Cor counted eight oak bookcases, each about twelve feet tall, that ran parallel to each other deep into the room. They were all packed tightly with volumes, mostly leather bound books, but he could see that one entire bookcase was committed to scrolls. The steward left the room, closing the door behind him.

"Taraq'nok!" Cor shouted. "I'm here!"

"One should not shout inside a library, Dahken Cor," said the Loszian's voice as he came around the corner of the furthest bookcase to the left. "Someone may well be inside trying to read."

"Enough of this, Loszian. What is it you want from me?" Cor asked.

"I sent one of my men after you when you were but a boy. It took me years to get a spy deep enough into Byrverus to find out that they knew where you were. Of course, I did not realize that my man would meet his end at the hands of another Dahken. It is really quite unfortunate; he would have lived the rest of his life in extreme luxury having brought me two Dahken at once, especially one that was trained and experienced."

"So, you weren't after me specifically. You are supposed to kill Dahken on sight, but you wouldn't risk coming to Aquis to kill one or even two Dahken. Why are you trying to find Dahken?" Cor asked.

"The Dahken," Taraq'nok patiently explained, "are perhaps the most dangerous warriors on the western continent. You are highly resistant to both the powers of Garod's priests and Loszian necromancy. Yet your predecessors squandered their chance at greatness, refusing to take a side in the ancient conflict."

"So, you want me to join the Loszians and help you conquer the Shining West," Cor said, inferring the logical conclusion.

"With such a powerful ally at my disposal, why would I have interest in only the Shining West?" Taraq'nok asked, the last two words said with a sneer.

"Yes, Queen Erella and her allies will fall, but only after we dethrone the Loszian Emperor."

Cor laughed in the Loszian's face and asked, "What makes you think that I by myself can destroy both empires? And even if I could, why would I? Garod's people are misled, certainly, but in the end their leaders are good people."

"Good people?" Taraq'nok closed the book he had been holding and placed it on the table. "Would it shock you to know that they considered killing you as an infant? I can tell by your face you did not know that.

"The Shining West is just as corrupt and enslaving as Losz. Our slaves at least are free to think as they will, so long as they serve us well, but Garod enslaves the minds and wills of his people. They do nothing without consulting the clergy and the temples. You were the son of commoners. Tell me, did your father tithe away his hard earned livelihood? Did he teach you total submission to the will of Garod and his pantheon of do-gooders? Does that not immediately revert to total submission of the mind to the priests, and therefore the Queen of Aquis herself?

"Look at the hypocrites they are. They have outlawed sorcery, though they practice it, and are willing to kill Loszians on sight, though any individual Loszian may have never done anything to harm their rule. They turned on the Dahken, murdering hundreds of them for no cause, and then virtually erased them from history.

"You have in front of you an opportunity to liberate the minds of Westerners."

"Only to enslave them bodily to you," Cor interjected.

"Let's not quibble over semantics and social structures," Taraq'nok answered calmly. "When we overthrow the emperor and reunite Losz with the Shining West, we can create any system of rule we see fit. I will accede to some of your outmoded moral sensibilities if that is what you wish."

"You still haven't explained to me how I would accomplish all of this," Cor said impatiently.

"*We* cannot overpower Aquis and the other Western kingdoms without the strength of the Loszian Empire behind us," Taraq'nok explained. "The Loszian Empire selects its ruler by one simple criterion – he or she who is most powerful controls the throne. Maintaining the throne means showing that no one else in the empire can defeat you.

"Once we put you on the throne of the Loszian Empire, it will be easy to rally the empire to attack the Shining West. For over seven hundred years we have made no moves against those who rebelled against us. Many of the Loszian nobles are becoming restless. They have watched the last three emperors choose to live in decadence and study with no ambitions towards reclaiming the continent. With that as our intent, the nobles will quickly fall in line with us."

"And if they don't?" Cor asked.

"Then we will begin killing them until they do," Taraq'nok said with a most unsettling smile.

"You still haven't answered my question. Why am I so pivotal to all of this? I understand that I have a resistance to your sorcery, but I am one Dahken. How can I make such a difference?" Cor asked.

"Yes, you are only one Dahken," agreed the Loszian. "The Dahken used to find their own, but since The Cleansing they have basically disappeared. Surely, more Dahken are born every year, but with no one to find them, protect them, and train them, the Dahken as a race have vanished into obscurity. Let me show you something, and then perhaps you will understand."

Without saying another word, Taraq'nok led Cor between a set of bookcases, and as he followed, Cor couldn't help but notice the truly massive wealth of

259

information the Loszian had amassed. At the rear of the library was a spiral stair of black stone that wound upward into the castle with no support structure of any kind that he could see; the steps seemed simply suspended in midair. The Loszian stood several feet away from the stairs and worked his fingers in a complex pattern that Cor could not seem to follow. He spoke a single word, that Cor was certain to be in Loszian, though it was not in his vocabulary, and ceased his somatic movements.

The black stone floor underneath the spiral steps dissolved into black mist, revealing more steps leading down into darkness. Cor followed Taraq'nok, who had to bend to avoid hitting his head on the steps above, down a dozen black steps into a pitch black room. The Loszian spoke another word, which was followed by a booming thud over Cor's head, and a final word from the sorcerer brought bright light, causing Cor to shield his eyes for a moment while they adapted to the change.

The room was small, nondescript, and perfectly square, and a single door of iron stood set into the wall in front of them. The Loszian unlocked it and the door swung open easily on oiled hinges. The next room was perhaps as large as the castle's main hall and divided up into small cells by iron bars that ran from floor to ceiling. The cells all had doors also of iron bars, and Cor could see no way to unlock or open them. Many contained an unmoving figure.

"Look closely at them, Dahken Cor, and tell me what you see."

Cor did as he was bidden and began walking between the cells, looking closely at the forms. He saw young men and women, none who appeared older than himself and children of various ages, some as young as toddlers. Every one of them was completely unmoving, seemingly frozen in a disturbing caricature of life. He found one that shook him to the core, an infant perhaps no older than a few months whose face was frozen in midscream. The sight filled him with fresh hatred and loathing for the Loszian. One other fact did not escape Cor – they all had the same gray pallor that he did.

"Dahken Cor, what you see before you are those who will become our generals and commanders, those who will lead our armies to victory over both the Loszians and the Shining West," Taraq'nok said, raising his voice slightly for it to be heard across the room. "You will make them strong, powerful, and they shall follow us to glory. Before you is the rebirth of the Dahken."

"What have you done to them, Loszian?" Cor's temper flared, and it was all he could do not to kill the necromancer then and there.

"The best explanation I can give is that they are paralyzed, suspended in time if you will," Taraq'nok answered. "They are unaware of all around them. They do not age, nor do they need sustenance. They remain here until I awaken them."

"You will release them," Cor growled. He was filled with sudden hatred as he imagined the fear these people must have experienced before being frozen in time.

"Soon, Dahken Cor. We are not ready."

"You will release them now!" Cor shouted, turning on the Loszian and drawing Soulmourn. The necromancer seemed unsurprised and made no move away as Cor took a fistful of his robes and threw him painfully against a set of bars, Soulmourn's edge just under his throat.

"Or what, Dahken Cor? Will you kill me now? Then how will you free them?" asked Taraq'nok. "*I* saved these people. Most of them, and all of the children, are from Losz. I discovered them before other lords and nobles, who would have surely killed them as per imperial edict. I also knew I could not teach them how to use the power of their blood, which is why I needed you. Dahken Cor, I have saved your race, not destroyed it. I had no

261

choice but to suspend them, for I could ill afford to have them running freely around my lands while I waited for a true Dahken to come along. These people should be dead twice over. Kill me, and they will never live again.

"Kill me, and you will never find what you seek either," the Loszian said, looking at him pointedly. Cor released the necromancer's robes and sheathed Soulmourn, again knowing that Taraq'nok had thought through everything that would happen between the two of them. He knew everything to say and when to say it, and Cor doubted that he would be able to out subterfuge the Loszian.

"Despite your youth," Taraq'nok said smoothing the front of his robes, "you are a rational man. You must learn to govern your passions, however, lest they be your undoing. I mean no harm to any of these people. The Dahken are gods in their own right, much like sorcerers and even the priests of Garod, but they need you to unlock their strength.

"Shall we return to the library?"

"What was the name of the Dahken who took you to Sanctum?" asked Taraq'nok. They had returned to the library and sat in a pair of high back chairs, separated by a table.

"Rael. He found me just as your man had come to take me from my parents, just as your man had murdered them."

"It is unfortunate he did not simply join me; we could have started this years ago. What happened to him?" he asked.

"A priest named Jonn and a dozen soldiers came after us near Sanctum. Rael was killed in the battle."

"Such a loss," the Loszian sighed. "Dahken Cor, I know you hate me and because you hold onto some ridiculous morality taught to you by Garod. You hate

262

everything the Loszian Empire is. Honestly, I hate most Loszians myself, and you know as well as I do that the Westerners are deluded and betrayed by their rulers. Together we can remake the entire continent."

"What part does a warrior sorcerer from Dulkur possibly play in your scheme?" Cor asked.

"Ah," Taraq'nok's eyes lit up before he laughed softly. "Honestly, I do not know; whatever part she chooses, I should think. Hopefully, she would consent to be my queen. I can only wonder what kind of sorcerer a mix of her blood and mine could produce. At the least, she is a powerful ally, but I do not yet understand what motivates her."

Hearing the Loszian speak of Thyss in such a way, Cor wished he had not asked the question. He felt suddenly angry or perhaps jealous, and he didn't understand why he suddenly ground his teeth and wanted to strike the Loszian. Cor was certain of one thing however – that Thyss would never submit to the will of Taraq'nok in such a way.

"Where is she today?" Cor asked. He wasn't sure why he wanted to know, but Taraq'nok took no notice of his interest.

"I do not know actually," he answered, staring into space. "Likely riding a horse through the countryside or burning some hapless peasant to a cinder because she likes to watch them dance or some other such nonsense. She seems somewhat prone to flights of fancy, much like her gods."

"So, what is next in your grand plan, Taraq'nok?" Cor asked, bringing the Loszian's gaze back to him.

"Well, we have two small issues to be addressed. The first is how do we begin training the Dahken without it taking years for them to reach their potential. While neither of us are in any danger of dying of old age in the near future, it would be preferable if we did not take twenty years."

"I don't even know if I can train them," Cor answered. "All I can do is try to teach them the way I was taught, but it could take months before they unlock the smallest part of their power, ignoring the fact that you have children and even a babe down there. Some may not be ready to learn for ten years or more. Besides, what makes you think any of them will even go along with it?"

The Loszian shrugged, "What choice do they have?"

"They have every choice," Cor answered, eliciting a humorous look from the Loszian. "We'll argue over that later. How many people know of your little Dahken prison?"

"Only you and I. The steward will eventually have to be informed once they begin needing provisions and such. I had one lieutenant who knew, but unfortunately your mentor killed him for me. It was likely for the best."

"What is the second problem?" Cor asked.

"It is a relatively minor thing," Taraq'nok answered with a shrug. "By now, the emperor knows you came through the gate, and he will interrogate Lord Menak as to why he didn't kill you. Lord Menak will throw me under the horse's hooves to save himself, and the emperor will expect proof that I killed you. I have an easy solution to the entire problem, but you will have to do everything I say. It will be a true test of trust on both of our parts."

"Then we are doomed," Cor nearly blurted, laughing uproariously. The Loszian waited until Cor's laughter quieted, before making a statement that further proved to Cor that he was not in control of the situation.

"Well, my friend Cor, now you might explain to me why *you* have come to Losz."

30.

"Tell me about the Loszian meteor," Cor said after thinking a moment.

"What specifically do you want to know?"

"I know it hit nearly three thousand years ago. What exactly was it?" Cor asked.

"The meteor," Taraq'nok began slowly, "was a vessel, a repository for the consciousness of the Loszian gods. Eons ago, our gods left their world; the peoples there had almost completely destroyed each other and left nothing. The gods had little choice but to wait millions of years for men to rise again or leave in search of a new home. They searched the skies of the universe and found a suitable world in which men were beginning to again climb from the muck of barbarism. They placed their consciousness into a meteor and hurled themselves across the universe. Unfortunately, when such a large thing hurtles with so much force, there is little to stop it without inflicting destruction, and the meteor crashed into the eastern side of this continent in a great ball of flame.

"Upon the collision, the meteor broke apart and released the souls of our gods. Having been caged for so long, they let loose their power across the land and changed the people they found into the first true Loszians. These Loszians had been followers of Garod, but with the power granted them by our gods, they found true freedom. They learned how to manipulate the dead, spread disease, and cast spells of unnatural cold on their foes, cold completely different from the elemental gods. They were superior to the followers of Garod."

"I know well the rest of the history," Cor said. "Is it known where the meteor impacted?"

"Of course," answered Taraq'nok, a glint in his eye. "Why?"

"There was a Dahken citadel there established by a man named Lord Dahken Noth. The citadel had a great tower, and it came down when the meteor struck it."

"Less than a mile from the crater created by the meteor, the first Loszians found the destroyed citadel of which you speak," explained Taraq'nok. "The rubble was strewn very nearly to the crater itself, and the few Dahken that were found were dead or dying. My ancestors left them to their fate."

"I need to go there," Cor said, with more urgency than he would have preferred.

"The place is dead," Taraq'nok said. "Nothing but weeds will grow within miles of the crater, and what few animals live in the area are predatory and unnatural. The meteor still resonates with power deep in its crater, and living things that come in contact with it are corrupted. Even we necromancers avoid it. What could you possibly need from that site?"

"The Dahken citadel was destroyed when the meteor impacted, but the Dahken built catacombs under their strongholds in which they interred their dead. The tower may have fallen, but I know the catacombs are still intact," Cor said. He hoped that this was explanation enough, but Taraq'nok only sat and stared at him waiting.

"I must go into the catacombs and find Lord Dahken Noth," Cor finished.

"Perhaps I was wrong earlier," Taraq'nok said, and Cor shot him a questioning look. "Perhaps you are not a rational man, you are a fool. There is nothing there but death. If the meteor's energy does not sicken and kill you, you may just as easily fall victim to the area's predators. Regardless, Noth cannot possibly still live."

"He does," Cor nearly whispered. "I have spoken with him more than once. He is down there, and he is waiting for me."

266

At this, the Loszian became silent, at first staring at Cor with his eyelids half closed. After a few minutes he clasped his hands, looking at the ceiling, apparently lost in thought. Cor did not move from his seat, and nor did he offer any more information, though he grew restless. For some reason, he did not want the Loszian to know that he sought artifacts rather than Noth himself. After several long minutes, Taraq'nok finally spoke again.

"Well, Dahken Cor, I have no reason to believe you to be a liar, though I think you have tried your amateur hand at it. I believe you when you say you have spoken to something claiming to be Lord Dahken Noth, but even you know that is entirely impossible.

"I agree you must go and soon. The exact location is not far from here, perhaps a mere three days hard ride to the east. I will send some men with you for additional protection, but you must wear some type of helm and gauntlets to cover your features. If Noth lives, he would be a most powerful ally in our endeavor. He would likely see that we offer an excellent opportunity to return the Dahken to greatness, but if he does not live, then you will have to face whatever dwells in those catacombs.

"We should discuss it in more detail over a meal this evening, but I see no reason why you should not leave tomorrow."

"I am going with Dahken Cor," Thyss said, "I will not continue to stalk within these castle walls like some sort of caged tiger."

"My dear, Thyss," said Taraq'nok, "I am not sure what a tiger is, but I would rather not risk something untoward happening to you."

"I am not some asset that you control at your will, Lord Taraq'nok," replied Thyss. "I could wait years for your scheme to be ready, and I cannot possibly make you understand how bored I am here."

Taraq'nok fumed over his meal. He and Cor began to discuss plans for the Dahken to leave tomorrow in search of Noth, and the woman had listened with interest. Of course, he had attracted the woman to his side with talks of war, combat, and power to be had, but he had not calculated how quickly her patience would wear thin. And of course, she was right; he couldn't possibly expect to control her. To do so would mean Thyss would leave him and his plans entirely, or worse.

"I do not think it is wise," said Taraq'nok, making his displeasure clear, "but I would not stop you, Thyss. Go with the Dahken, as he may very well need your help should he find what he is looking for in those catacombs.

"I will send Wrelk to guide you as he knows the area well. Cor, I will have the steward provide you with appropriate armor of my house, including a helm to cover your rather obvious defining characteristics. It would not do at all for you to run into a Loszian noble or his servants without something to hide your true nature. Should that occur, I would allow Wrelk to do the talking. The obvious story should be that Thyss here is my guest from Dulkur, and the two of you are merely escorting her to a vessel that will take her back to her homeland."

"Sounds like an adventure," Thyss said over her meal, throwing a slight smile at Cor that made his stomach turn over slightly, but not in an uncomfortable way.

"I think," Cor said nodding, "it sounds easy enough. Taraq'nok, there is something I'm curious about. How is it none of the other Loszians know I am here?"

"I am certain they suspect, and it is something we will have to deal with," replied the Loszian.

"That's not what I mean. You aren't the only Loszian with a spy in Byrverus. What's to stop them from spying on us here?" asked Cor.

"Ah, I understand. Steward, come here please and roll up your sleeve so that we may see your left shoulder," called Taraq'nok. As he approached, the steward did as he was told, showing the mark Cor had come to recognize.

"You are of course familiar with my mark. It is more than a simple tattoo. When I place it upon my servants, my living servants, it binds them to me, and they become completely unable to betray me. So, I do not have to worry about one of my own servants spying on me for another master.

"You of course by now have noticed the stone with which all Loszians build their abodes and most defensive fortifications. I know of everything, living or dead, that sets foot in this castle at all times, and the two of you are the only persons here who do not bear my mark."

"So, the same holds true of all other Loszian sorcerers then?" Cor asked.

"Naturally."

"So, it forces a race of liars to keep their intrigue somewhat in check," Cor concluded. Taraq'nok's eyes flashed angrily for just a moment before his calm, calculating exterior returned.

"Precisely, Dahken Cor."

The door leading to the dining room opened unexpectedly, and Wrelk strode in with nervous purpose. He crossed the room, almost at a run, and evaded the steward's attempts at intercepting him. Wrelk came up alongside his master's chair and knelt before him, his face low to the ground.

"What is it Wrelk that you must interrupt my meal?"

"My Lord, a messenger has brought this from Ghal," Wrelk said, handing the Loszian a scroll. Taraq'nok impassively broke the seal and read it, his face an unreadable mask as his eyes moved across the parchment.

"Thank you, Wrelk," Taraq'nok said, excusing the man. "Your search for Lord Dahken Noth must wait I am afraid. I have been summoned before the emperor to answer for the crime of treason."

31.

"Ghal is the capital of Losz, and I will have to go there tomorrow and face the emperor. He accuses me of ignoring imperial edict and housing a Dahken, which is a capital offense. I shall go there tomorrow and present my defense and return immediately, and the two of you should be able to start your journey the next day," Taraq'nok explained.

"Where is Ghal?" Cor asked.

"Five hundred miles east, northeast of here," the Loszian answered, smiling.

"And how would you travel there and return in one day?" Cor asked, though he was sure he knew. He looked across the table at Thyss, who listlessly ate her meal, clearly bored.

"The same way the messenger arrived here so quickly from Ghal," answered Taraq'nok. "If you recall, when we first met, you had apparently decided to kill me, and I disappeared right before your eyes. Perhaps two thousand years ago, a Loszian sorcerer discovered the ability to transport himself over any distance, so long as the destination was predetermined with a sort of magical beacon. All nobles have access to the beacon in the palace in Ghal, and most of us are smart enough to establish our own beacon in our own castles and towers. Unfortunately, that also allows Emperor Nadav to find us quickly."

"With such power, why haven't you conquered the Shining West?" Cor asked. "Could you not transport an army instantaneously into Byrverus?"

"Not exactly. It requires a massive amount of energy to send oneself and perhaps one or two servants," he answered. "I myself will be able to cast no other spells

271

tomorrow should I wish to return. If all the sorcerers in Losz combined their power, I doubt we could transport more than a thousand soldiers, and even then, we would be powerless to lead them into combat. No, the power is not meant for war.

"Cor," the Loszian hunched over slightly in Cor's direction, as if preparing to tell him a great secret, "you need to come with me to Ghal. I need you to see the man that you will help me slay."

"How's that possible?"

"I will bring two servants with me, men clad in my chain mail and helms. You will be one of the two. You must not speak and obey every order I make without hesitation or question. Else, we will be found out," explained Taraq'nok.

"Won't the emperor know who I am as soon as I step foot in his palace?" Cor asked, tapping the black stone floor with his foot.

"No, he will only know that you are not bound to him," he explained. "The emperor is arrogant, and he would never debase himself to look at or speak to a noble's servant.

"Cor, I see the doubt in your face, but you must do this. You believe me evil, immoral, and decadent, and perhaps I am, but I pale in comparison to the Emperor of Losz. Come with me to Ghal, and I promise your moral sensibilities will scream for you to kill the man."

"Why must I do this?" Cor asked. "Why shouldn't I search for Noth while you deal with your emperor?"

"So that you can see that there are those far worse in Losz than I, but also, you need to see for yourself that I will not betray you to the Emperor, despite the opportunity to do so.

"Thyss, I am sorry, but I must ask you to stay in the castle tomorrow," the Loszian said, bringing a disgusted hiss from her as she pushed her plate away. "It is but one more day, and I am certain you can find something to amuse yourself for one day. Peruse and explore my library. Perhaps you will find something of interest to your own powers?"

"Loszian," she said, and it was the first time Cor had ever heard disrespect in her voice, "your magic is based on knowledge and thought. Mine is a function of desire, emotion, and strength. Our powers are as incompatible as we are, but I will wait one more day."

She stood from the table and stormed from the room, slamming the door behind her. The two men, united in their lack of comprehension of women, could only sit and stare after her as the echo boomed through the room. The Loszian sighed audibly and leaned back in his heavy chair.

"As I said Dahken Cor, she is as unpredictable as her gods, and like an open flame, she can be as dangerous as she is beautiful."

The next morning, the steward awakened Cor immediately at sunrise, providing him with a full suit of polished black chain mail, sabatons, gauntlets and a slightly oversized helm with visor and chain mail cowl. He also carried a black silk surcoat emblazoned with Taraq'nok's emblem, and the steward asked that Cor ready himself with all speed to meet the Loszian in his library. Cor had always thought chain mail was the easiest armor for a warrior don, for it simply went on much like normal clothing, and having only ever had mismatched bits of armor, Cor never realized just how much the steel could weigh once he was fully encased in it.

Ready, Cor made his way to the library, carrying the helm under one arm. Upon entering, he found Taraq'nok, his steward, and one other soldier who was completely clad head to toe in the same armor. Taraq'nok was on his hands and knees in a most undignified position, drawing a large circle and intricate patterns within it on the floor. The steward immediately walked over to Cor and began straightening the armor and surcoat, saying that Cor had put it on in a most unkempt manner. The steward commanded Cor to put on the helm so that he could make certain everything was in its proper place, and satisfied, the steward announced that Cor was ready to leave. Taraq'nok, also finished with his task, stood up and looked Cor over.

"Dahken Cor, you must leave your sword and the fetish here. If the sword's obviously magical nature does not draw attention, I am certain that would," he said, pointing to Ebonwing. "Besides, bringing weapons to such a gathering would be… frowned upon."

"My weapons?" Cor asked in surprise. He hadn't realized he had actually belted on his weapons, and he supposed it was just his nature at this point. He removed Soulmourn and Ebonwing, but suddenly found himself quite reluctant to give them up. With great reassurances from the steward that they would be protected with utmost care, Cor finally released them.

Taraq'nok bid Cor come stand in the circle behind him and slightly to the left, while the other soldier flanked the Loszian's right. The Loszian explained that transporting oneself was relatively easy, if consumptive of power, but to transport multiple bodies required them to stand inside an emblem such as the one he had inscribed on the floor. The larger the circle, the more people could be sent of course, but the spell became an exponential draw on the sorcerer's power. Taraq'nok reminded Cor to follow him wordlessly and to obey his commands without hesitation.

The Loszian weaved his hands in the somatic movements of a spell, though he intoned nothing. His hands moved about for several seconds, and Cor could feel the hair all over his body stand on end, or at least try to as it was hampered by his armor. The Loszians fingertips began to glow with a soft purple light, followed by the entirety of his hands, and then he clapped them together sharply. As he had seen months ago, a brilliant flash of light filled Cor's vision, and he felt disoriented, sure that his feet no longer touched solid ground.

The sensation passed almost as quickly as it had come, and Cor found himself standing in position in a small room with an arched open doorway, in which a man stood considering them. He was of Loszian blood, though clearly mixed, and likely not as pure as Taraq'nok as he only stood about two inches taller than Cor. He had short kept black hair and wore a tunic and breeches of silver silk.

"Lord Taraq'nok, we have awaited your arrival. Please follow me to await trial," he said.

They followed the Loszian down a narrow corridor into a small room lit by two torches, and Cor walked in measured step behind Taraq'nok, careful to keep the proper place. The visor on his helm obscured his vision, but he noted that whatever structure they were in was made of the same stone as Taraq'nok's castle. Taraq'nok had said that all Loszian lords used this material, and again Cor wondered as to its origin. The room had another door, which the short Loszian ducked through into a room beyond that was much larger. Cor paid little attention, as his gaze was on the near giant form of Lord Menak.

"Ah, Menak," sighed Taraq'nok, "So you are my accuser in this trial."

"No, I accuse no one," the taller Loszian replied. "The emperor is your accuser. I am merely here to testify as to what I saw."

"And what was that, Lord Menak?"

"One of your men paid me to allow him access to the mountain pass, saying that he was sent by you to retrieve a Westerner. As it turned out, this Westerner was in fact a Dahken, and I allowed your servant and the Dahken free passage into the empire.

"Taraq'nok, I could care less about your schemes. I moved to guard the mountain pass as I wished to be away from my fellow Loszians and their constantly entangling plans. I testify only because I have no choice if I wish to avoid the emperor's wrath," explained Menak.

"Fear not, Lord Menak," Taraq'nok answered, placing his right hand on Menak's shoulder. "I understand your motives, and I am not angry with you. However, I owe you no boon as you suggested as the Dahken is dead."

"Very well then. Hopefully, this will not take long."

The man in silver returned, opening the door, and allowing the small group to leave into the larger room beyond, but to say it was larger would be a gross understatement. They entered a hall that, architecturally, was little different from the several he had seen already, but it was absolutely enormous, dwarfing even the palace in Byrverus. The floor, walls, ceiling, and dozens of columns were all made from the same Loszian stone, and many of the columns carried graven images of Loszians, presumably past emperors. Cor struggled to keep himself under control as he marveled at the sheer size of the hall. They were led to the bottom of a dozen black steps that led, in typical fashion, to a large platform upon which sat an empty throne. The throne gleamed in the light, which had no source, and Cor was certain it was made of solid platinum. On each step, flanking a gold carpet that led up to the throne, sat two slaves, one male and one female. They were mere children, none of them out of adolescence, and all of them completely nude. The children were chained together by their necks in a long row down the steps, and the display made Cor's blood boil. It took all his willpower to maintain his calm.

276

A door opened from behind the throne, and in walked another Loszian, this one as tall as Lord Menak. He was completely bald, adding to the completely inhuman look the Loszians had, clad in silks of silver and black. He walked forward and stood in front of the throne, and the small group, Cor included, bowed in the customary manner. The emperor sat on his platinum throne, and the group rose to its feet.

"Sovereign," said the shorter silver clad Loszian, "Lord Taraq'nok has come to answer for his crimes. I also present Lord Menak who will testify against him."

"Taraq'nok," the emperor's voice boomed unnaturally through the hall, and Cor was certain that the Loszian chaffed at the lack of his title, "you are accused of ignoring imperial edict. You actively sought a Dahken from the Shining West and bought his access into Losz. Lord Menak, deliver your testimony."

Menak recounted the same story he had told Taraq'nok, though this time with more detail. He described the Dahken to the best of his knowledge, explaining that he was an apparently young man and clearly skilled in the ways of combat. Taraq'nok listened with his practiced impassiveness and did not interrupt Menak at any point. When Menak concluded, the emperor again spoke to Taraq'nok.

"Lord Taraq'nok, is this true?"

"Yes, Sovereign."

"Then you admit to a crime for which the penalty is death."

"No, Sovereign," contradicted Taraq'nok.

"You dare call a Loszian of true blood a liar?" the emperor asked with an edge to his voice. Taraq'nok's eyes flashed momentarily, and Cor was certain an insult had been hurled at him.

"No, Sovereign," Taraq'nok answered, his calm returned. "The events as they occurred to that point are true, but I am in no way harboring the Dahken. In fact, I have brought him as a gift to you Sovereign."

Cor's eyes widened in alarm behind his visor, and he realized he had been trapped. A hundred thoughts flashed through his mind at once, unfortunately leading him to a total lack of action. He simply stood there, also realizing that he had no weapon with which to fight anyway. Taraq'nok turned around, and Cor could see a faint smile on the necromancer's face as he motioned toward the other soldier.

"Take off your helm," he commanded the armored form, who reached up and slid the helm up over its head. Cor recognized him; he had seen this young man underneath Taraq'nok's library. He was about Cor's age and of similar height, with the dark hair of a Westerner. There was no ignoring the man's deathly pallor, but his eyes were glazed over and unseeing.

"Taraq'nok, you would have me believe that this walking corpse is the Dahken?" the emperor's voice boomed with anger.

"Yes, Sovereign," Taraq'nok said, turning back to the emperor. "I have slain him and raised him as a gift to you. He has several most unfortunate wounds under the armor, but he is completely functional."

"Lord Menak is this the man you saw?" the emperor asked.

Menak stared at the armored figure for a long moment and cut his eyes at Taraq'nok, something the emperor could not have seen as Menak's back was to him, before answering. "Yes, Sovereign."

"Very well. Lord Taraq'nok, your gift is accepted, but in the future simply bringing the Dahken's head would be just as appreciated."

Cor followed Taraq'nok back to the side room, where the necromancer again drew the complex symbols surrounded by a circle on the floor. Cor said nothing and simply waited, though it appeared they were alone, until he had completed the spell, and they arrived back in the library. Cor immediately kicked his full weight right into the Loszian's back, knocking Taraq'nok sprawling across the floor. The steward immediately stepped forward and Thyss, who had apparently been sitting in the library with her legs casually crossed over each other on a table, jumped to her feet.

"Damn you, Loszian!" Cor shouted. "You didn't think I would recognize that man? Why did you kill him?" Cor's every pore was ablaze, and his palms itched for Soulmourn and Ebonwing.

"What would you have me do, Dahken Cor?" Taraq'nok asked as he sat up, rubbing at his lower back. "I had to present a dead Dahken to the emperor. I could have easily presented a live one in you. Then you would be dead. Would that have been preferable to you?"

"You didn't have to kill him!" Cor raged.

"Didn't I? What else could I have done? If I had given him to the emperor alive, he would not have corroborated Menak's story, and all our lives would have been forfeit. Think Cor, and you will realize it was unavoidable without killing you instead."

"It is not noon yet," Cor said, slowing his breath by enunciating each word clearly and deliberately. "Thyss and I leave at noon to find Lord Dahken Noth, and I expect we'll be back in a week. When I return, I want those bars removed from the cages and every person down there restored. I want them to be made comfortable, especially the children. Do what you have to do." Cor stormed from the library, collecting Soulmourn and Ebonwing on his way out.

32.

Cor fumed in the small yard outside the castle, furious at the Loszian, and he swore to himself it would be the last time this man pushed him. Cor hadn't been outside yet this morning, and it was a miserable autumn day, rainy and cold. His breath came in small white plumes, and he stood in the cold black armor with his helm in his hands, allowing the rain to freely splash his face and the chain mail cowl. It seemed foolish to stand outside in the weather, but the damp cold helped calm his temper and focus his mind.

After a few minutes, Thyss joined him outside clothed in her usual garb with her curved sword strapped to her back. She hissed between her teeth, a sound Cor had come to associate with her displeasure, as she looked upwards with obvious disgust at the falling rain. Thyss closed her eyes briefly, and when she opened them, Cor could see that she was totally dry. As the rain continued to fall on her skin, hair, and clothes, it sizzled away as if on a frying pan over a hot fire.

"Useful," Cor said.

"I cannot wait to stretch my legs," she said. "I've been cooped up too long. There is nothing in this castle to interest me."

"Until I showed up?" he asked, seeing that slight smile he had become accustomed to. "Why are you here?"

"I just told you. I need to do something other than read moldy books and stare at black walls."

"That's not what I meant," he said, uncertain how to phrase the question. "I know something of Dulkur, and you would be someone important there. You have all the physical aspects of the ruling class, and the power of the

280

elements runs through you. Taraq'nok introduced you as *Lady* Thyss."

She turned to meet his eyes, and Cor swore he could see fire burning in her pupils as she spoke, "A life of luxury, spending every day lying on satin cushions while strong naked men with beautiful ebony skin feed me exotic fruits stolen from the villages of the masses. Wearing gold and jewels to exemplify my wealth and power over people with no hope. A different lover every night, or even every hour if that's what I want. An existence with no passion, no fear, no excitement. All order and no chaos. Decadence and no risk. Hykan damn it.

"I go where I will and do as I will when I will," she said, raising her voice to the heavens. "I create enemies only to slaughter them and bathe in their blood, should I so desire. I shall challenge the tallest, strongest peak with my blade and force it to submit to me. I bow to no kings, no queens, and challenge even the stars themselves to shine brighter than I. I shall force the chaos of entropy upon the world and laugh as those who would rule struggle vainly to contain it. I live for my own desires, here and now, for as long as I live, and no one shall take that from me, lest they take my life!"

Cor stared at this woman in amazement, and for the first time in his life, understood himself. His entire life, forces across the continent had tried to make him as they would have him. Even Rael, the Dahken who taught Cor how to use his power and strength, had attempted to mold Cor into a shape that he would prefer. Cor looked upward into the falling rain and vowed that no longer would he allow any to seek his destiny for him, and nor would he determine another's except by his sword. Cor turned and kissed Thyss, embracing her with his steel clad arms and crushing her body to his. She fought against him, her body rigid and almost as strong as his, but she returned the kiss with no less ferocity.

The trip deeper into Losz was uneventful, though the weather stayed miserable well into the next day as a cold, driving rain beat itself on them. Ignoring Wrelk completely, Cor and Thyss took to bedding down together, as much to share her warmth as any other reason. Even after the rain stopped, the air kept its chill as winter was approaching, and Cor wondered somewhat if there would be early snows this season. They had seen a few other travelers, but always in the distance, and none of them ever turned to intercept the trio, paying mind to their own business. While the countryside itself was remarkably like Aquis, Cor noticed that Losz clearly lacked the large number of villages and independent farms found in the Shining West, doubtless due to the empire's social structure.

Starting the third morning, they eased their pace somewhat, Wrelk declaring that they weren't far from the crater and that it would be better to allow the horses a slower gait. There would be nothing safe for them to eat or drink within several miles of the crater, and it would be best to conserve their energy. The walking tore at Cor's patience; the less miles between himself and their destination, the harder he felt the unseen force pull at his blood. He felt like a piece of iron affected by a massive lodestone, and the burning flow in his veins excited him further with each step.

Cor estimated that they had crossed nearly two hundred miles since leaving Taraq'nok's castle, and the landscape had changed somewhat. The slightly rolling hills and prairies with tall grass and wild fruit trees had given way to scraggly shrubs, weeds, and crabgrass. The very ground itself seemed less lush, harder, and drier, the closer they traveled to the meteor. It was shortly before noon when they reached a point where Wrelk would go no further.

"The meteor is about two miles that way," he said, pointing slightly north of east. "I and the horses will stay here. I will not risk them or myself any further on this errand."

Cor shrugged and dismounted his horse, giving instructions for Wrelk to wait two days; if he didn't come back by then, he was not going to. He checked his gear, also making certain he had an ample supply of fresh water and some dried meat. Cor pet Kelli's forehead and fed her a sugar cube before turning to leave, and he found Thyss standing impatiently in front of him.

"You are coming, then?" he asked her.

"I am certainly not staying here with him for two days," she answered, lifting her chin towards Wrelk.

Cor began walking at a quick pace in the direction indicated, and Thyss fell into step next to him. They had not even covered a mile when most of the foliage had disappeared; there were no trees or shrubs of any kind, and the grass had given way to intertwined vine-like weeds and moss. Cor had not seen any signs of animals at all since the previous day, and he doubted Taraq'nok's claims of unnatural creatures. They ventured up a sloping incline, which seemed to have a vague familiarity to Cor, and stopped upon reaching the top.

Cor removed his helm and dropped it on the ground to get a more thorough view of the landscape that lay before them, feeling a very complete sense that he had been there before, but at a different point in time. They stood looking down at a wide track that was completely devoid of any plant life at all. Weather had changed it substantially over nearly three thousand years, but Cor could still make out a slight depression nearly a mile wide that narrowed at the far end of the track as it made its way deeper into the ground. It stopped quite suddenly in a deep crater, also overgrown by thick vines.

"Where do we go from here?" Thyss asked.

"I'm not sure," Cor said, surveying the land. "I was here once before, and I climbed a grassy hill to see this same stretch of land, but it was more of a trench with upturned dirt and small trees that were on fire. When I went back down the hill, I was in the midst of the ruins, and I fell into the catacombs on accident."

"I saw no ruins before we came up this hill. I would not think they would disappear even after three thousand years." Thyss said.

"No," he said, squatting down on his haunches, "something is not right. I don't think we are in the exact spot that I stood in the dream."

"Dream? We are here to find something you saw in a dream?"

"It's here," Cor replied certainly, without looking back at the sorceress.

Cor stood up and headed south along the hilltop, which he realized was a sort of ridgeline. As he walked, he kept his eyes on the ancient trench dug by the meteor, watching for when his perspective matched what he recalled from the first dream nearly ten years ago. Thyss simply stood, watched, and waited. Cor's foot suddenly hit something with a hard thud, and he sprawled face first to the ground, barely throwing his hands up in time to catch himself. He was uninjured physically, though he looked sheepishly at the hard mound he had apparently tripped over. Cor looked up to see Thyss jogging over to him slowly; he had walked several hundred feet without realizing it. He sat up and began scraping away hard packed dirt, weeds, and moss to find a large rectangular gray stone, well weathered and half buried in the ground.

"This came from the tower," Cor said, looking up at Thyss. "The entire building was made of stone blocks just like this one. It must be nearby."

"Then let's find it quickly. This place is beginning to unnerve me, and try watching where you walk from now on."

Cor closed his eyes and attempted to clear his mind, focusing on the sensation that had been building in his veins and arteries for days, if not months. He was right on top of it, but he just couldn't seem to find the place. He stood up and again surveyed where the meteor impacted, and then he turned his back to it looking west. The slope back down the hill was less smooth here, as if the weeds and moss had overgrown numerous objects. Cor's gaze followed down the slope, and at the bottom he saw a tangled mess of weeds and scraggly growth that seemed to be obscuring shapes he could not clearly make out.

"This is it," he said and immediately started down the hill.

"How did we not see it before?" Thyss asked, and he heard her start down the hill behind him.

Cor didn't answer the question. He didn't know at first, but the answer became apparent the further down the hill they went. The site was obscured from view on all sides by other hills, and one would likely only see it if standing directly above it. The slope was somewhat treacherous, as it was a bit steeper than the path up had been, and the plant growth here was comprised of short, tangled weeds that threatened to trip those who made a careless step.

Cor stopped when he reached the bottom of the hill, looking around carefully and trying to envision the ruins he saw in his dream. He could just barely see the outlines of crumbled walls and piles of rubble under the foliage. Cor did not move into the ruin, as he remembered crashing through some kind of wood planking, perhaps a trap door, and this time he had no mattress to break his fall. He walked to the north side of the ruin, looking for the remains of a stone spiral stair, and he found a large pile of weather beaten rubble, grown over with moss. Seeing no other likely options, Cor asked Thyss to stand next to it, as he walked back to his starting point and took a circuitous route to the south side of the ruin. After a few minutes, he found the remains of three stone steps; while they were only two feet high and covered in weeds, Cor was certain he'd found the second staircase.

"The entrance into the catacombs should be right between us," Cor shouted, partially from excitement, but also because the wind seemed to whip coldly through this slight depression.

They walked towards each other and closed the distance quickly at first, and as they neared each other, they walked more slowly and watched the ground intently for any sign of the entrance. They stopped nearly ten feet away from each other, and Cor drew Soulmourn. He moved slowly towards Thyss, thrusting the sword into the ground every few inches. He had gone several feet when the sword met no resistance, passing right through the weeds without striking anything solid. If Cor hadn't been looking for exactly such an effect, he likely would have lost his balance. He sheathed his sword, and the pair dropped to their hands and knees, clearing away the weeds with daggers and fire Thyss produced from thin air until they had defined a mouth that was roughly four feet square. The noon sunlight shined down into a room below, showing a dust caked floor less than twenty feet below them.

"I fell through some sort of trap door. It must have rotted away hundreds of years ago," Cor reasoned.

Thyss found a small piece of wall nearby that was still mortared together and kicked at its foundation several times. Satisfied that it was solid, she uncoiled a rope that she tied around the hunk of masonry and then threw it down into the open maw. Cor felt the rope for a moment and looked at Thyss doubtfully. It was made of the same black silk as her clothing with slivers of silver running through its threads.

286

"Are you sure this will hold me?" he asked, eyeing the silk rope.

"Would you like to again try ripping the clothes from my body?" she asked by way of reply, laughing deeply at the look he gave her.

Cor really had no idea what he was doing, and he was sure that he couldn't grip the thin cord well enough to lower himself to the ground below. He removed his gauntlets for a better grip on the smooth material and wound it twice around his armored right arm in the hopes that he could control the speed of his descent. It crossed his mind that he would still have to get back up the rope, but he knew he needed to focus on one problem at a time. Gripping the rope tightly in both hands, Cor slowly lowered himself over the edge and fell like a stone. Fortunately, the distance was short, and at the last moment he figured out how to control the fall very slightly. If it hadn't been for these two facts, he might have broken both of his legs on impact; instead, he crumpled into a heap of black steel armor with a huge plume of dust.

Cor had gotten to his hands and knees and was coughing heavily when Thyss landed lithely next to him, having slithered easily down the rope. The dust had triggered a painful attack, and he could feel things moving in his chest every time he was wracked with a cough. Thyss found a torch nearby and lit it ablaze with her fingertip while waiting for Cor's coughing to subside, which took several minutes. Finally, he stood, hacking a glob of blood streaked phlegm to the floor.

"What was that about?" she asked him.

"It is something the Dahken live with, though I'm not sure why. Sometimes it just happens."

As he looked around, Cor's mind superimposed his memory of the dream onto what his eyes saw. He could see the torches lit and billowing smoke, even though they were dead and covered with dust. The crypts themselves looked the same though somehow older, and now he could read the names of the Dahken whose glyphs were inscribed on the doors of their tombs. Cor knew precisely where he was and immediately set off down the lane between the crypts, again drawn by some force that made his blood now feel as if on fire. Thyss followed, using her abilities to light a torch every so often, further lighting the catacomb.

In his dream, Cor had walked seemingly forever between never ending rows of crypts before they disappeared entirely, and he had to walk with no sense of time or direction before reaching a stone wall. In reality, the pair passed about a dozen crypts, having walked not even two hundred feet. The wall was in fact natural, part of a cave that had been smoothed by human hands, and a heavy wooden door stood directly in front of him, set into the cave wall. Cor could now read the glyphs on the door when years ago he could not decipher the name.

"Lord Dahken Noth," he whispered.

Thyss glanced at him before placing her lit torch in one of the two stands that flanked the door, discarding the dead torch that the stand held. She lit the torch in the other stand and then drew her sword from its scabbard on her back. It was the first time Cor had ever seen the weapon unsheathed, and it was quite wicked and beautiful at once. The blade was as long as Soulmourn and curved down its length dramatically; he believed it was known as a scimitar. The weapon had one razor sharp edge on the outside of the blade's curvature, and the steel seemed to have a green tint to it, just as Soulmourn occasionally gleamed purple.

"Impressive," Cor said, a word that he seemed to use regarding Thyss increasingly often, and some part of him hoped she felt the same of him.

"This is Feghul's Claw," Thyss said, virtually preening the sword. "One day, I will trouble you with its story."

Cor again regarded the door, seeing little other option at this point but to open it. Every urge within him screamed to delay no longer, but he knew that some confrontation or another awaited him on the other side of the heavy wood door. He knew Noth lived, and the man, or whatever he now was, would not relinquish his property so easily. Cor removed the chain mail from his body and left it in a pile on the floor, stripped down to his black tunic and breeches.

"What are you doing, Cor?" Thyss asked him.

"I won't need it in there."

Cor braced himself against the large door and nearly fell into the room as it opened smoothly on hinges that made not the slightest sound. Thyss followed behind him and immediately lit the first torch she saw which was on the wall opposite the door. Cor, his balance regained, saw Noth's armor directly in front of him on a stone shelf, exactly where he knew it would be. He could feel the helm, hauberk, and legguards singing to him, begging to be worn in battle. He coveted them more now than ever, but Cor knew something else must be dealt with first.

He turned to his left and was not shocked to see the ghoulish figure in a decaying gray robe staring at them intently. Noth was exactly as Cor expected him with skin as gray as Cor's stretched across his skull in a disturbing caricature of humanity. His think lips were black and slightly pulled back against his white teeth, and his scalp was completely hairless. He sat in the stone chair, carved right out of the wall, that Cor had seen him in twice before. Thyss turned slowly, looking around the room, and gasped when she saw the ghoul.

"Why do you return again?" Noth asked. He jerked the fingers of his left hand towards Cor, and an unseen force buffeted him, forcing him to take a step backwards. Noth cocked his head sideways, his unblinking eyes considering the situation. "So, this is real then. I knew one day you would come."

289

"Lord Dahken Noth," Cor said, dropping to one knee as he felt was proper, "I have come to request a great boon. The Dahken are scattered, and perhaps we are the only true Dahken left. Your citadel was destroyed by fire from the sky, and the Westerners turned on and destroyed the Dahken of Sanctum two thousand years later. I have no wish to quarrel with you, but I covet your armor and it me."

"You cannot have it," Noth responded.

"I need its strength to return the Dahken to the world."

"What care I for the Dahken now? We were aberrations, mistakes of the gods. Let us be destroyed." Noth spoke with venom, and his vision seemed clouded with darkness only he could see.

"Then stay here in your tomb, Lord Dahken Noth, and allow me your armor so that it may once again go forth into the world."

"You cannot have it!" the ghoul screamed at him, rising to its feet. Parts of Noth's gray robe disintegrated with the sudden movement, revealing dead gray skin underneath that was stretched thinly over his bones.

Cor stood, holding the ghoul's gaze, and shrugged. "You will have to stop me," he said, turning toward the black armor that gleamed in the torchlight.

Noth howled in fury and pumped his left fist in the air, and another unseen force hit Cor squarely in the back, nearly knocking him off his feet. Noth curled the near skeletal fingers of his right hand into the shape of a claw, and Cor yelled in massive pain. He crumpled over, feeling as if someone were crushing the organs inside his ribs. Thyss extended her hand out towards Noth, her fingers extended and palm up, and blue-white flames shot from her hand and enveloped the ghoul. Engulfed, the remains of his robe disappeared almost instantaneously, and his eyes, ears and thin skin began to melt from his body. Noth turned toward Thyss surprised, as if seeing her for the first time. He released Cor and turned his ire on her as the skin of his fingers peeled back from his bones.

The pain gone, Cor leapt from his position, closing the distance between himself and Noth almost instantaneously with his weapons drawn. Soulmourn came down swiftly, and cleaved through Noth's right forearm, which was now little more than bone, crackling in the flames like a dried log. His right hand and wrist fell to the ground, and Noth looked at it slightly confused. Before Cor could strike again, Noth pushed the flat of his left palm at the Dahken, and he flew across the chamber and landed with his head hitting hard against the wall.

Thyss came at Noth, whose skin was completely gone and his bones beginning to blacken, and she brought her scimitar around to strike. The skeletal thing lifted his remaining hand as if to grasp her neck, and an invisible grip of steel took Thyss' throat, physically lifting her off the ground. She dropped her sword with a clang, and her arms and legs flailed as she felt her throat crushing under Noth's mystical grip. Just as the blackness overtook her sight, she was suddenly released and fell to the ground fighting for breath, the horrific pressure around her throat gone. Thyss' vision was clouded over, but she could make out the shape of the still burning ghoul. Cor stood, sword in hand, over Noth's other severed arm.

Cor looked at Noth in amazement, wondering how to defeat the former Lord Dahken. There was no flesh left of the man, and what stood before Cor was a mass of horribly blackened bones, animated by some disturbing power Cor did not understand. But with both arms severed, Noth was apparently powerless, and he merely stood before Cor making no move whatsoever. Noth's skeletal jaw opened and moved as if he attempted to speak, but with no flesh, he could not vocalize his thoughts. The skeletal remains took a step back and once again sat upon its stone chair, and he did not move again.

Cor backed away from Noth and kneeled next to Thyss, who was beginning to breathe more easily.

"What now?" she asked, her voice somewhat quiet and ragged.

"I take what I came for and leave Noth in peace," Cor answered.

"It was never about finding a Lord Dahken, was it?"

"No," he admitted, putting on Noth's armor. If the skeleton reacted at all, Cor could not tell, though he did keep one eye fixed on it. "There has not been a Lord Dahken here for nearly three thousand years, not since the meteor struck and he became something else. We'll leave him to whatever perdition awaits him."

33.

The armor was incredibly light, to the point that Cor could easily forget he wore steel of any kind. The plate hauberk did not restrict his movements in the slightest, and he didn't feel weighed down as he did in Taraq'nok's chain mail. It was the helm that gave him the greatest shock, however, as it had no visor of any kind. It was simply solid plate steel that had been molded in a rather bulbous fashion and resembled the head of a beetle or large insect. When Cor placed it over his head, it amazed him that he could see right through it as if it were not there. He even touched his hand to the face of the helm and could see his hand encounter something that from his perspective was invisible. The longer he wore Noth's armor, his armor, the more he knew it belonged to him, and new strength and power coursed through his veins. Who could have crafted such?

They left the remains of Noth in his crypt, uncertain if any consciousness remained within his bones as he did not move again and ran their way back through the catacombs. Thyss snaked her way up the silk rope with impressive agility, and apart from her well-formed biceps flexing as she pulled herself up, the task seemed nearly effortless to her. After a moment, his body remembered its sailing days with Captain Naran, and he climbed his way out with ease.

Cor wasted no time standing to begin the walk back to where Wrelk should be waiting with the horses. He wanted to return to Taraq'nok's castle as quickly as possible, though the urgency of his mission had somewhat abated. Thyss stared at him somewhat on the walk back, and several times he nearly asked her what interested her so but stopped himself remembering that his head appeared encased in steel.

"You look like something that crawled out of an ancient abyss," she said. "You appear as a beetle that walks upon two legs. And you see?"

"Yes," Cor answered, "it's as if I have nothing on at all."

"I will never understand the need to wear steel," Thyss sighed.

"Protection isn't enough reason?"

"If there is no risk of death, then why fight?" she shrugged in response. "I am curious. I wonder if Taraq'nok will have fulfilled your demand by the time we return."

"Which demand is that?" Cor asked.

"Your demand that the Dahken in his magically hidden cellar be released from his spell."

Her words brought Cor to a halt, and he turned to face her. "You know about them?"

"Of course, I stumbled upon them before you arrived, though Taraq'nok does not know it," Thyss answered him. "Honestly, it was a poor piece of magical trickery that hid them, and he is lucky none of the higher nobles have paid his little library a visit."

"I need to ask you something," Cor said, and something in the gravity of his words brought a question to her eyes. He gently placed his hands on either side of her face as if he were about to lean in to kiss her and asked, "Can you release them from the spell if he doesn't?"

"No, it's a magic based on charms and enchantment, something I have no control over," she answered. "But I assume he would, considering that both you and they are pivotal to his plan for conquest. Eventually, he has to start giving in to your wishes."

"How do you know that?"

"I am no imbecile, Dahken Cor," she said, shrugging off his touch. "He needs you because no Loszian's necromancy will affect you. And what would be better than one Dahken except an army of Dahken? His plan is transparent and simple, yet quite feasible, assuming you intend to go along with it."

They continued walking in silence, meeting Wrelk in precisely the place in which they left him only a few hours ago. Wrelk made a point of not looking at Cor's new armor, and he did not ask what transpired. With plenty of daylight left, they began the ride back, Wrelk wanting to put as many miles between himself and the place as possible before it became too dark to travel. The weather remained fair, though a chill remained in the air, and they made good time. They rode at a slightly slower pace, but they arrived at Taraq'nok's courtyard close to sunset three days later. In a way Cor was happy to be done with the ordeal.

Wrelk took the horses around to the stable, and Cor and Thyss entered the castle, finding that Taraq'nok awaited them for dinner. They entered the dining hall, the Loszian in his usual chair sipping wine, and he appraised Cor's new armor with an interested gaze. Cor did not care what this man thought of him at this point. The room was even more darkly lit than usual, only a few candles burning, and the fireplace cast flickering shadows about the room's floor and walls. Off to the side, Cor could see a white form lurking about the sideboard where the steward kept the wine, but he could not see who it was.

"Dahken Cor, it seems that I was wrong, and you are somewhat practiced in subterfuge," the Loszian called to him as they approached. "You return wearing armor you did not leave with, armor that does not hide your somewhat obvious nature. Perhaps you did not seek Noth after all then?"

"Lord Dahken Noth," Cor said slowly, "has been dead for nearly three thousand years. I don't know whom or what we fought within those catacombs, but it was no Dahken."

"I am not surprised," Taraq'nok said with a sigh. "Regardless, perhaps we may dine together? I doubt Wrelk's provisions did much to sooth hunger." Thyss took her customary chair and leaned back, kicking her feet onto the table to receive a pained look from the Loszian.

"Did you release the Dahken?" Cor asked, not moving to sit.

"We'll discuss it in due time, Dahken Cor. First, we eat."

"Did you release the Dahken?" Cor asked again, nearly shouting the question.

"Yes, damn you. Dahken Cor, you are as relentless as a rhinoceros, or at least based on what I know of a rhinoceros. I will take you there after we dine, and I have no doubt that my steward is working hard to attend to their every wish right now. Now please, take off that ridiculous looking helm. Ania, please bring Lady Thyss and Dahken Cor some wine."

Cor had forgotten about the helm, as he had done since placing it on his head. The thing impacted his senses not at all and weighed nothing, and often, he only remembered it when he lay down to sleep. He removed the helm, taking a small joy in Taraq'nok's grimace as it scratched the tabletop, and turned to see Ania shuffle from the sideboard to the table in a slowly deliberate fashion. Ania, her hair thinned and falling out and her skin as gray as Cor's, stopped next to the table and poured red wine into the goblet in front of him. He stared at her, in open mouthed shock at the mechanical movements and the unblinking eyes that always looked ahead levelly with no spark behind them. As she poured, Cor saw that gaping gashes rent open her wrists, and his goblet full, she shuffled to Thyss' side of the table.

Cor dove out of his chair and around the table, knocking over both his and Taraq'nok's wine, and he clenched the necromancer's robes in his fist. Cor pushed with his momentum, driving the Loszian and his large chair over onto its back with a crash of wood on stone. He had drawn Soulmourn and had the point of the blade hovering mere inches from Taraq'nok's face. Thyss watched idly but did not move while Ania continued to pour her wine, taking no notice of anything.

"Release her!" Cor shouted at the Loszian.

"Cor, why does it seem that we always end up in this position?" the Loszian asked, calm though somewhat jarred by his impact with the floor.

"What have you done to her? Release her from this!"

"She clearly was no use to me living. She couldn't even seduce a boy barely out of adolescence. She was no good as a whore, so she will serve me in other ways," Taraq'nok answered, his voice perfectly level and matter of fact.

"You do know I am going to kill you," Cor growled at the Loszian.

"Perhaps, Dahken Cor, but first let us eat. After that, I will show you how I completely acceded to your demand in regards your fellow Dahken, and then you may kill me if you wish." The Loszian smiled at him, and Cor sheathed his sword then righted the necromancer, chair and all.

"Is it safe to assume you have told Thyss of the Dahken below and completely informed her as to our plans?" Taraq'nok asked.

"No," Thyss interjected, the Loszian turning his head toward her, "I discovered them well over a week ago, and it took little to divine their purpose."

"Indeed. I apologize for underestimating you," Taraq'nok said with a slight bow of his head.

Dinner commenced, and Cor neither ate his food nor drink his wine; he sat and watched the fire as Thyss and Taraq'nok ate and talked animatedly. She discussed their journey to the meteor and the catacombs, and Taraq'nok listened with rapt attention to every detail. He was particularly interested in the encounter with the thing that had once been Lord Dahken Noth. He hypothesized that the Loszian meteor had a different effect on the Dahken as it did other humans, and only Noth had been powerful enough to survive the metamorphosis. Noth had apparently been turned into some form of undead creature, though extraordinarily unlike the reanimated corpses that Taraq'nok created. Noth's use of an unknown magic, some sort of force of will telekinesis Taraq'nok hypothesized, was also most interesting. Cor listened to all this showing no reaction at all; he was tired of the Loszian and had no more use for his interests or pleasantries.

"You would not be willing to await time for digestion, would you Dahken Cor?' Taraq'nok asked once the meal was concluded.

In answer, Cor stood from his chair and replaced his helm, drawing an exasperated sigh from the Loszian who pushed his plate away and led the way to his library. Cor followed closely, somewhat annoyed at the Loszian's leisurely pace, and Thyss came last with her arms crossed over one another. Taraq'nok dispelled the illusion hiding the stairs, and the trio made their way down. The Loszian simply stood aside, allowing Cor to investigate the dungeon himself.

Wrelk and two other guards stood just inside the entrance, facing the room itself. Cor walked past them and into the large room, which he saw was still broken into cells by floor to ceiling bars, but the doors were now completely gone. Every cell now contained clean bedding and a water filled basin, and Cor saw the steward with several slaves moving through the area with meals.

The children had gravitated to one another, regardless of age differences, and a wet nurse attended to the infant. He looked over the group, briefly counting over two dozen, and several of the erstwhile prisoners looked upon him with interest and perhaps fear. Cor hadn't considered that, especially in his new armor and helm, he was likely quite imposing.

"Dahken Cor, I assume this meets your expectations?" asked Taraq'nok, who had come up directly behind him. "I needed some odd components, and it took until yesterday to work the spell necessary to free them. The steward has been working since then to make them more comfortable and provide care where necessary. You see they are healthy, and we intend to keep them so. What else do you require of me?"

Cor's movement was so fluid to be nearly instantaneous, but all who saw it would remember as if it were mystically slowed, almost as if time came to a halt. He whirled to his right, Soulmourn in hand before he had even turned halfway, and Cor saw Taraq'nok's face with its smug, ever present smile and calculating glare. A sphere of black light surrounded the Loszian as Cor's sword cut through the air toward its target, and the sword passed right through it effortlessly. It was not until the blade's edge met the soft tissue of Taraq'nok's neck and the torchlight reflected from the blade danced across his face that the Loszian realized all his calculations were for naught. Before his instinct of self-preservation recognized what occurred, the sword had already cut through flesh and bone, veins and arteries. His knees crumpled underneath him as a spray of blood shot through the air, and Taraq'nok's head bounced on the ground to rest next to iron bars, a look of wide eyed, open mouthed surprise on his face.

The two guards gaped momentarily in shock, but Wrelk, a consummate professional leapt to the attack. His first blow was parried away easily by Cor, who suddenly felt more empowered than ever before in his life, and Cor drove his sword deep into Wrelk's body near the heart. Impaled, Wrelk limply struck again with a blow that Cor took with his left forearm. Though weak, the blow still cut deeply through tissue and muscle to the bone, but Cor ignored the wound, allowing the pain to fuel him. He kicked Wrelk in the chest, twisting his sword while he yanked it out an angle, rending the man open, and the body fell to the ground, a huge well of blood forming underneath him.

The shock worn off, the two guards attacked Cor with short swords, and Cor allowed one blow to carom off his helm carelessly. He was vaguely aware of a muffled clang, but otherwise did not notice the attack. The other man attempted to thrust his blade through Cor's middle, just underneath the hauberk. Cor parried the attack with the dull edge of his sword and came around backhanded, Soulmourn hacking through the man's black chain mail as easily as Wrelk's leather armor. He impaled the man twice through his chain mail while ignoring two more sword blows, one of which penetrated his side just under his own hauberk. Cor pivoted to his right, whipping Soulmourn around, and the second guard's right arm, chain mail sleeve and sword in hand fell to the ground uselessly. Cor again plunged his sword deep into a foe, pushing him hard against the iron bars as the sword sank to its hilt and came out between the bars on the other side. He pulled Soulmourn from the dying guard's body and turned to see Thyss still leaning against the doorway with her arms crossed.

"I just wanted to see if the stories about the Dahken are true," she said. "I figured you could handle yourself."

Cor looked around the barred dungeon, finding mixed looks of dismay and horror, but also satisfaction from some of the Dahken prisoners. The steward stood quietly, a completely impassive look on his face, and the slaves stared at Cor incredulously. Cor looked down in quiet consideration; the floor was slick with the blood of the four men he had killed in a matter of seconds, and it suddenly dawned on him that his own wounds were no longer bleeding and in fact were completely healed. Cor motioned to the steward, who approached him quickly though with some reservation.

"What should I do with you?" Cor asked the man.

"My Lord, I am the steward of the house. I serve the house in all manners required of me, regardless of its lord," the man answered.

"Then I want this mess cleaned up immediately and be certain these people are cared for and given whatever they require."

"Yes, My Lord, but if I may point something out? You may have little time before you must deal with the rest of Lord Taraq'nok's servants," the steward said before going about his business. Cor waited for the man to return upstairs, and then he stalked up to stand mere inches from Thyss, heedless of blood and bodies. She uncrossed her arms and set hands balled into fists on her hips in a pose that smacked of defiance.

"And what about you?" he asked her.

"Oh, I am with you, Dahken Cor, so long as you keep life interesting," Thyss said, followed by the laugh that he had heard so many times.

Cor turned again to face the rabble that Taraq'nok had gone to such lengths to assemble. The Loszian had believed Cor would train them into a force that neither the Loszians nor Garod's priests could harm with their magic, making them the avant-garde in his army to conquer both nations. As he gazed around the room, Cor realized that slaying Taraq'nok had been truly the first moment in his life that he had done something explicitly for himself. Everything else he had done had been a result of other forces that would control him, even if he didn't completely understand their motivation to do so. Cor looked at the faces turned to him with some expectation, whether for good or ill, and decided that he would not be the decider of their paths. Cor removed his helm, allowing them to see his face for the first time. The young men, women, and most of the children did not fail to notice the similarity between themselves and this slayer of the Loszian who had imprisoned them.

"My name is Cor Pelson. I have slain your captor and now offer you freedom to go where you will. I know nothing of you, where you come from, or how long you've been here, but you are free to leave if you wish. But before you go, look at me well, and you will see that we are the same. We are a race called the Dahken, born of Dahk the Blood God, and we are hated and feared by nearly all the peoples of the world because we represent something they cannot control. Each of you has great power in your veins, power that you must learn to awaken and tap. It will make you strong, if not indomitable. You are now free to go where you will, but if you stay with me, I will help you find that power. I will help you find the strength you need to make sure no one controls your destiny, and I ask nothing in return. Regardless of your choice, your life will not be easy. There are those who will hate you and even kill you on sight, but I can offer you the chance to fight them.

"Make no decisions now. We have some time before the Loszians realize that the man who imprisoned you is dead. Stay here for now to think over the decision, and if you decide to leave, I will make sure that the steward provides you with anything you need. I will return in the morning."

Cor left the room with Thyss just ahead of him, and he could hear the people behind him beginning to talk to each other. It was interesting to him how it was extremely improbable that any of them had known each other before this place, and yet they seemed to speak freely to each other, united in their predicament. He could only hope he made his intentions clear to them. In the library he most literally ran into the steward and several slaves returning to retrieve the bodies and clean the blood and gore.

"Steward," Cor said, catching the man by the arm, "I am going to dine now."

"Yes, my lord, I will have the kitchens cook a meal."

"No, there is a cold meal on the table, and that's fine. When you are done, I want all the guards and soldiers removed to outside the keep and the doors secured. I will inform them of Taraq'nok's death when I am ready," Cor said, pausing. "Also, we will have to do something about the slaves."

"I do not understand, lord," the steward said with a quizzical look.

"Slavery is a disgusting evil, and I will not allow it," Cor explained. "Not tonight, maybe not tomorrow, but soon we will have to change their circumstances."

Cor strode from the library, leaving the steward behind him with an astonished look, and Thyss kept pace beside him, the entire time with her slight, enigmatic smile. He returned to the dining hall and prepared to sit down to eat his cold meal when a sight caught his eye near the sideboard. He slowly walked over to the table, finding Ania's body cold and motionless on the ground, lying in the remains of a broken decanter of red wine. Cor kneeled and reached out to caress her thinned hair, but hearing Thyss walk up beside him, thought better of it, and instead closed the dead girl's eyes.

"When you killed Taraq'nok, his power over her was broken," Thyss explained. "I do not doubt there are many more elsewhere in the castle."

"Well, she is at rest now," Cor said, standing up. "I will have to ask the steward to prepare her whatever burial rites are proper."

Cor returned to the dining table and ate ravenously at the meal of chicken and some sort of soup. The food was cold and greasy, and the soup congealed; the meal was simply awful, and Cor wasn't certain it would have been much better hot. But it was the most satisfying meal he had eaten in months, and he chewed his food staring with relish at the empty chair just to his right at the end of the table. Thyss sat across from him, leaning back in her chair with her legs crossed, her feet pushed against the table. As he ate, he felt as if something had not occurred to him, or he was missing an important fact; it was as if he had forgotten to feed his horse.

"Do you really intend to train those people as Dahken?" Thyss asked. Her face was hidden in the shadows, but Cor could hear her smile.

"If that's what they decide."

"And what will you do when the Loszians come for you?"

He stopped chewing and focused his gaze in her direction. "I suppose I'll offer them a choice. They can leave us alone, or I will kill them."

"All by yourself?"

"I thought you said you would stay with me as long as I keep life interesting. Have you deserted me already?" he asked her by way of reply, causing her to laugh.

"Of course not," Thyss said, taking her legs off the table and causing her chair to fall forward onto all four of its legs with a thud and scrape of wood on stone. There was a mischievous glint in her eyes. "It will be interesting to see if Loszian necromancy can stand up to the power of my gods."

Later that night, Cor and Thyss made love vigorously for hours on the satin sheets of his bed. Clearly, Thyss enjoyed the challenge of exerting her dominance over her lovers and enjoyed it even more when her dominance was met with forceful resistance. It

304

was not until after, when they lay entwined, their bodies and the bedding still moist, when Cor started with an epiphany. He looked at Thyss; her eyes were closed, and her naked chest rose and fell with her breathing, but Cor was certain she was not yet asleep.

"You said something before. I want to ask you about it," he said.

"What is that?" Thyss asked, opening one eye lazily.

"You said that the spell over Ania was broken when I killed Taraq'nok. That would have broken the spell over all of his raised servants?" Cor asked.

"As I understand such enchantments, yes. In fact, all of his spells would cease to function," she explained. She then shifted to her side, resting her head on one arm. "Why?"

"Taraq'nok," Cor sighed, "He killed one of the Dahken and then raised him. He gave it to the emperor as a gift, to show his loyalty."

Thyss rolled onto her back, laughing, which confused Cor, as he did not see the humor in the situation. She then climbed atop him and kissed him fiercely.

"Life is about to become very interesting," she said, still laughing.

Sovereign Nadav, Emperor of Losz, was busy amusing himself when something completely untoward and unexpected happened. The mixed blood bastard Taraq'nok had given him a gift, a raised servant that had once been a Dahken. Nadav did not completely trust him, but with Lord Menak's testimony could find no reason to hold Taraq'nok accountable without causing revolution amongst the other nobles. To vent his ire, he had taken to nightly sodomizing the corpse in a most violent fashion in the vain hopes that every time he thrust, Taraq'nok just might feel it. He was almost at the point of release when the damn thing went limp and simply collapsed in a heap on the floor. Regardless, Nadav finished, though he was not terribly pleased with the situation, and it aggravated him that Taraq'nok was a noble when obviously his power was so pathetic that he could not even keep a corpse animated for more than a week or two.

Sovereign Nadav stood drinking a glass of wine in consideration of whether or not to reanimate the thing himself when the obvious fact dawned on him, and he smiled wickedly. Taraq'nok was dead, and surely there was little question about whom was responsible. The noble had lied to him. He dropped a tablet into his wine, the purplish liquid effervescing, and he swirled the glass until the drop fully dissolved. For now, Nadav would rest in a meditative trance, and tomorrow, he would assign a small force to ride to Taraq'nok's castle bring the Dahken back to Ghal. He would thank this Dahken heartily for ridding Losz of a noble prone to trouble making, and then Nadav would have him beheaded right in the throne room.

Sovereign Nadav's limbs grew sluggish and his eyelids heavy as the entrancing drug took effect in his blood. He lumbered slowly to his plush bed, his eyes unable to focus on any nearby object. He was just able to seat himself in a lotus position before his mind drifted into the cosmos.

Epilogue

"We do not have to fear immediate attack," Thyss said. She reclined somewhat lazily in a high backed chair, her feet elevated and resting on a large, plush ottoman. "I believe the emperor cannot use the power of transportation to send anyone here."

Cor had risen before the sun and immediately began making an inventory of everything he thought a group might need for a journey. He knew that he would not think of everything, but this didn't concern him. Cor was sure that the steward would have advice on the matter. Thyss had stayed in bed for a while and only grudgingly awoke and dressed after the sun had been above the horizon for a solid hour.

"Loszian sorcery is heavily based on enchantment, and their transportation spell requires a magical beacon," she continued. "Just as their animated corpses cease to function, so should their beacons. It only stands to reason that Taraq'nok created the beacon in this castle, and if it still functioned, the emperor would have already sent someone to investigate."

Cor listened, though neither reacted nor responded to her statements. The logic seemed sound as far as he understood magic, but it did not change the current predicament. Thyss stood from her chair, clearly aggravated. She was not used to not being the center of attention, and she suspected she could make her presence felt more clearly. She lightly approached his seated form from behind and leaned over him so that her breath would caress the back of his neck and ear.

"So, what now, Dahken Cor?" she whispered.

"I must lead the Dahken from Losz to a place of safety," he answered, struggling to keep her presence

307

from distracting him. Thyss hissed her disgust, and she stormed back to her chair, throwing herself into it heavily.

"Where will you take them?"

"I see little choice except to take them west, back through the Spine into Aquis." Cor leaned back and stared at the ceiling as he talked. "While the Loszians wouldn't dare invade the Northern Kingdoms in chase of us, they are too far away. I doubt we could reach them in time, and I doubt that the children are prepared for such hardship. I could attempt to reach the southern coast; it isn't as far, and I could hope to hire a Tigolean smuggler."

Thyss laughed loudly, drawing an injured look from Cor. "The Loszians are not friendly merchants like Westerners. They inspect their ports too closely for you to escape them there."

"Again," Cor responded with a sigh, "I have little choice but to travel west."

"And combat Lord Menak and his entire garrison?" Thyss asked. Her voice registered doubt or disbelief, but Cor could see something else burning in her eyes.

"I can't be sure how many soldiers are there, but no doubt it is a force roughly matching that of Fort Haldon on the other side of the pass. I cannot defeat five hundred men in a direct confrontation. It's a problem I will have to work out between here and there."

"Maybe you cannot," Thyss agreed, stretching languidly, "but it will be a gloriously bloody battle, I think. When do we leave?"

After a checking his list several times over, Cor sought out the steward, who was in the process of laying out a meal for him and Thyss. The steward looked over the provision list, agreeing that it was well made, though lacking in a few items. The steward agreed to handle the task and would have it ready by noon. In the meantime, the steward informed him that three of the Dahken, all

308

boys in their teenaged years, had already struck out on their own in the dead of night. While this troubled Cor, he saw little he could do about it at this point.

Just after the sun reached its zenith, twenty-six persons on horses set out from Taraq'nok's castle. At the head of the group was a black armored warrior on a beautiful palomino, the horse's coat in stark contrast to the man's countenance. At his side rode a beautifully dangerous woman from a far away, eastern land. The middle of the group was made up of children, riding two to a horse, and the smallest of which had larger children to help them. The rear of the column was brought up by two young, adult men who looked over their shoulders at the peasants, slaves, and occasional guard who took great note of their passing. They rode west, the sun overhead, towards the Spine.

END OF VOLUME I.

TO BE CONTINUED IN *FIRE AND STEEL*

WHO IS MARTIN PARECE?

I'd really rather you not ask me questions like this! Well, are you asking who I am or "Who am I?", because the latter is a completely different question that forces one to look deep into the heart and mind. It is the question humankind has been asking since there was humankind.

Who I am, on the other hand, is just some guy who loves to read and tell stories. As I look back, I have always been a storyteller, from my first short stories to my first faltering attempts at playing Dungeon Master. I still love TTRPGs, all sorts of fiction, heavy metal, and horror movies. In fact, this last will be readily apparent should you read my anthology Tendrils in the Dark. A lot of shout outs, homages and influences there...

I returned to my creative endeavors around 2009 as my business of seven years began to burn down around me during the recession. I suppose adversity causes growth, and though I shelved my projects for a few years, I returned to them with the publication of Blood and Steel in 2011. Regardless, people seemed to enjoy the world of Rumedia, and I returned to it with five more novels.

In the end, I'm just a guy who loves to tell stories, read other persons' stories and head bang in the car. I have so much more to come, and I hope you'll join me on the journey!

Turn the page for an excerpt from

FIRE AND STEEL

THE COR CHRONICLES
VOL. II

Available Now!

"This is it," Cor said to those behind him. He turned his horse about so they could all see him and spoke in a loud whisper. "We'll be riding as fast as we can. The horses are tied together so just hold on and don't fall off. Once we get the gate open, we'll ride through and into the mountains as fast as we can."

They started towards the fort at a walk, and Cor slowly urged the horses onward, faster. He had the group almost to a full gallop as they reached the first outbuildings. Cor risked one look over his shoulder to see how his charges were handling the rough gait and decided that he dare not push the horses any faster, as many of the smaller children held on only with the aid of the larger. The baby, strapped to the wet nurse's chest, had begun to cry, awakened by the terrific bouncing motion of her horse. Cor pushed it from his mind as he focused ahead.

They moved quickly through the clusters of buildings, and he saw the immense gate clearly ahead of them. It seemed that the huge stone doors were each opened and closed by large upright wheels interlocked with some sort of gear system below the ground, similar to the mooring mechanisms he'd seen at the docks in Tigol. Cor hoped they would not be difficult to operate, though he realized he only needed to open one door. One man guarded each wheel, and he counted four more upon the wall's walkway, just as Thyss had reported.

It was then that the alarm went up, not from in front, but from behind them. A black mailed guard, likely on his path patrolling through the buildings, shouted in Loszian that intruders rode through the compound, and Cor looked over his shoulder to see the man running for a large building he assumed to be one of the barracks. Cor pushed his horse faster, causing some of the children behind him to bounce dangerously close to losing their holds on their mounts, but he saw little option. At any moment, Loszian soldiers would come pouring out of their barracks.

The guards in front had turned their attention to the oncoming group, and the first volley of crossbow bolts fired their way. Cor could waste no look behind him to see if any of his charges had been hit by the attack, and he charged his horse in a full gallop towards the men guarding the gate mechanisms. To an observer, it would have looked as if the Dahken intended to ride by the first guard, but just as he was about to pass, Cor half leapt, half fell from his saddle into the unsuspecting soldier. The impact jarred both men as Cor landed on top of the guard in a heap of arms, legs, and steel.

The Loszian received the worst of it as Cor's helm slammed into his face, breaking his nose and splintering his teeth. Cor quickly scrambled to his feet, drew Soulmourn and ran the man through while he was still fighting for breath. A weak blow clanged off the back of Cor's hauberk as the other guard had attacked him poorly from behind. He quickly glanced to his left to see one crossbowman screaming, arms flailing as he fell off the wall fully engulfed in flames. Another lay burning, his body still and on the battlements, while the other two frantically reloaded their weapons. Thyss charged up the steep stone steps, curved sword in hand, and thinking Cor's attention diverted, the guard launched another attack with several high, broad, sword strokes. Cor easily ducked the first two, before parrying away the third. The poor man had no chance of regaining his balance before Soulmourn rent its way through his left arm near the shoulder and into his midsection.

Cor looked around and knew his situation was about to deteriorate quickly. Thyss had torn through the third crossbowman, and the fourth had closed in on her with twin daggers. He felt a twinge of fear and wanted nothing more than to run to her aid when he saw the fletched end of a crossbow bolt jutting from her left thigh. But he could not afford to help her, for only a few hundred feet away the first Loszian soldiers were charging toward the group.

Dropping Soulmourn, Cor gripped the spokes of the closest wheeled device. He heaved his weight into it one direction and found it completely unmoving. He shifted in the other direction, and the massive wheel began to turn, spokes interlocking with a large gear set into the ground. He could hear a great clicking as the gear teeth interacted with metal, no doubt other gears beneath the ground, and there was a mild vibration as one black stone door began to swing open. He pushed the wheel until the door had opened perhaps three feet.

"Keth, Geoff, get them through!" he yelled at the two older boys while sheathing Soulmourn, and nodding, they began to herd the horses out the great door. "Thyss, we leave now!"

The fourth crossbowman dispatched, Thyss lithely jumped from the top of the wall, landing in a roll. She screamed once in pain, clutching the crossbow bolt embedded in her leg, as she made impact with the ground, but she forced herself to her feet and limped to her horse. Cor looked back at the oncoming soldiers, counting that he had mere moments before they were upon him. As the crowd of horses quickly filtered through the open gate, Cor saw the shape of a small girl lying face down in the dirt two dozen paces away.

"Dahken Cor," Thyss shouted, now on her horse, "leave her!"

This girl was here now only because of him, and he ran to her unmoving shape without hesitation. Behind him, he could hear Thyss swearing eloquently in her native tongue. Scooping the girl up, he noticed a large knot forming on the side of her head. She must have fallen off her horse when they came to a stop. Something whizzed by Cor's left ear, and as he turned to run to his horse, white hot pain lanced through his left hand. His palomino anxiously awaited him, her eyes wide as her tail swished back and forth.

Just as he reached her, a wave of immense heat nearly knocked him off his feet. Thyss sat on her horse, arms raised to the heavens, and a wall of orange flame over twenty feet tall and twice as wide separated them from the oncoming horde of soldiers. Crossbow bolts were shot into the flame, only to be incinerated, and Cor slung the girl's limp body over his left shoulder as he stepped into the saddle's right stirrup. Soldiers with crossbows flanked the wall of flame by climbing the stone wall's steep steps, but just as the first men reached the top of the wall for a clear line of fire, they fell, suddenly punctured by long Western arrows that arced over the battlements.

Turn the page for an excerpt from

BOUND BY FLAME
THE CHRONICLE OF THYSS

Coming July 2024!

"I do not understand. How have you yet to find her? I have paid you well. You are the best tracker in my lands, and yet you have no news?" the priest questioned angrily as he stared down at the man who stood before him.

Mon'El eagerly awaited news for weeks, and so had no qualms about interrupting breakfast with his wife, demanding his servants bring the tracker up to their suite atop the palace straight away. As King, High Priest and Chosen of Aeyu, He whom ruled the air and winds, Mon'El could have commanded the man to locate his daughter without any compensation at all, so the priest felt extraordinarily generous in offering a sum of gold that would buy the tracker an estate on the river itself.

Much depended on Thyssalia's safe return. Thyss, he reminded himself.

The suite sat atop Mon'El's massive pyramid that stood in the center of his city and consisted of a large, central room with four open archways that led to others at each point of the compass. These all had grand balconies to allow Mon'El to look down on his people and to allow the currents of his god to pass freely through his abode. He and his wife maintained separate bedrooms to the north and the south, though they seldom slept alone, and the room to the east comprised Mon'El's private temple to Aeyu. His wife Ilia kept the room to the west, there indulging in whatever her heart desired.

Standing three or four inches taller than Mon'El, the ranger known as Guribda had smartly dropped to his knees upon being brought before the priest and king. It would have done him no good to physically overshadow a man who could send him to his death with a mere flip of a hand, but even kneeling, he felt himself shrink before Mon'El's ire even as the king seemed to grow and darken.

Guribda feebly replied, "Well, Highness, I have some news, and I will find her. I swear it."

"What news, then?" Mon'El demanded impatiently.

"Your daughter recently was seen in a village to the north, bordering on the great jungle there. I tracked her to the edge of it where she was joined by at least six other people before they entered the jungle," he explained, leaving out the part where he was sure Thyss had been accosted and taken prisoner.

"And what of the jungle?" Mon'El pressed, idly adjusting his robes. He had been told that Guribda returned to the city alone, so he opted for more blue in his robes than white, hoping that the calm wisdom of Nykeema would embrace him in the face of bad news.

"I… I did not pursue them."

"What?!" Mon'El's voice smashed the interior walls, carried by a gust of wind as thunder cracked in a cloudless sky. Silk tapestries blew from the walls to the floor, and the plates of food on the table behind him rattled and moved about. One fell to the floor with a shatter, causing his wife to sigh. He lowered his voice to a dangerous growl as he pressed on, "Explain carefully."

The tracker's eyes shot quickly around, lolling almost like that of a panicked animal as he assessed his chance of escape should he choose to run. There were four very large, heavily muscled men at each corner, excluding the one who had moved up to be but six feet behind him. All were armed with the best scimitars the city of Kaimpur could produce, and while the tracker was no stranger to swordplay, he doubted he could take out one before the others were upon him. And then he had the priest-god's magic to contend with. No, escape was not an option.

With hands open before him, almost in supplication, he responded meekly with a bowed head, "That jungle is well known to be cursed, Highness. There are monsters in that place that defy time, that predate the rise of men, and I admit to being a coward. Surely, you would have no fear with your immense power. You are blessed of the gods, but I am but a man. I beg your forgiveness.

"Highness, I have other taken steps, however. The jungle borders the sea to the north, and a vast, lifeless desert stretches from its southern edge all the way to your lands. If she doesn't return to the village, she has little choice but to travel to King Chofir's city on the other side. I have paid for eyes in both places. She will not escape me."

Mon'El's anger seemed to abate as the man spoke, for the priest did remind himself that most men were in fact weak and powerless. So few of Dulkur's people wielded the power of the gods, and Mon'El was one of those Chosen few, arguably the greatest of them all. The tracker's words placated him enough, and he nodded at the mention of Chofir. He knew the king well, and a smile touched the corners of his mouth at the thought that the fat merchant-king might try to impose his will on Thyss.

"Very well," Mon'El replied calmly after a moment. "See to it that she does not. She has been gone too long, this time, and I demand her presence. She must be at my side in one month or much may be lost. Go."

The tracker turned to leave, just as the guard returned to his post in the corner, and as Guribda made his way down the steps that would lead him down the outer wall of the pyramid shaped palace, Mon'El surely heard the tracker issue a relieved sigh. Mon'El clenched his fists, anger brewing again, but not aimed toward the man who had just left. No. Yet again, his daughter tested his patience and his will, as she had for the last ten years or more, and it could no longer be allowed. What was soon to happen would have repercussions throughout all of Dulkur, and she was the integral piece on the gameboard.

"Must you scheme so?" Ilia, called from behind him as he began to pace.

Turn the page for an excerpt from

The Oathbreaker's Daughter
The Dragonknight Trilogy
Book 1

Coming March 12th, 2024!

Every time the swords struck each other, the ringing of steel carried on the subtle wind currents of the warm summer day. Training for one to two hours per day, three days a week for the last two years had wrought tough, lean sinews in Jenna's arms and legs. While other girls her age mooned and obsessed over boys, many of whom noticed certain differences between the genders, Jenna crossed swords with the one armed teacher of the village's children. She was the only one among them Brasalla took the time to mentor in swordsmanship and, to a lesser extent because she left it to Jenna's mother, archery, and Jenna swelled with silent pride even as the other girls jeered at her. Two years of training to help her gain strength and then learn the basic forms of fencing had finally led to sparring with real swords, though with dull edges and blunted points. Brasalla had several of these weapons in her cottage, as well as a number of wooden practice swords and other such weapons, so as to avoid any real wound besides bruises and damaged pride. The one armed woman had taught Jenna so much, and yet every time a new lesson was unveiled, Jenna found herself bested once again. She had never once defeated the former Protectress, despite the woman having but one arm, or even landed a single point. But still she fought, knowing that one day...

Brasalla attacked with a downward stroke meant to slash down and across Jenna's body starting at her right shoulder, and Jenna knew her opportunity when it presented itself. Bringing her own sword around, she easily parried the blade to her left, and scraping steel on steel, thrust her blade forward in such a way that it would skewer her opponent, if not for the spherical mound of steel that made the weapon's point. But her sword met nothing, and in her hurry to take advantage of Brasalla's careless attack, Jenna stood suddenly off balance as her arms extended well forward. Brasalla's weight came to bear on her parried blade, forcing the point of Jenna's sword down to the ground as she could contest neither the woman's weight nor strength, to say nothing of leverage.

"You over extended your thrust, little dear. You're dead, I'm afraid."

"I know. Damn it all," Jenna swore angrily.

With a disapproving glare, Brasalla eased her weight and lifted her sword from Jenna's, allowing the girl to recover her blade, and she said, "If I were your mother I'd likely tell you to watch your language."

"Then, it's a good thing you're not, huh?" Jenna shot back, but the tone held more playfulness than challenge.

"I suppose."

"Just once, I want to kill you. Just once," Jenna complained.

Brasalla chided, "Don't do that."

"What?"

"Whine," Brasalla explained. "It's unbecoming of you. You're strong and brave, and you're growing into a beautiful woman. Such bellyaching is unacceptable, especially among the Protectresses."

Jenna's eyes narrowed, and she immediately returned, "I don't want to be a Protectress."

"Is there something wrong with being a Protectress? Something wrong with being a trusted defender of Abrea and our way of life?"

"No," Jenna replied quickly, noting her teacher's suddenly solemn tone and emotionless face. She chose her next words carefully so as not to give further offense, "It's just not what I want to do."

"You cannot do what you want to do, Little Dear," Brasalla gently reminded the girl, and it was now Jenna's turn to grow silent. "Anyway, do you know what your mistake was?"

Jenna sighed quickly, puffing a snort of air out of her nostrils in annoyance as she clenched her draw and turned her head from side to side, looking at nothing. After a moment, she answered, "I assumed."

"Assumed what?" Brasalla asked with slightly raised eyebrows.

"I assumed that you, a trained warrior, someone who has killed people far more skilled than me, made a basic mistake."

Brasalla prodded, "And?"

"And I tried to capitalize on it."

"As you well should've, but that wasn't the fatal mistake."

"No?" Jenna asked, looking up at her mentor, and her face betrayed a mix of impatience at the drawing out of the lesson and aggravation at her own ineptitude.

"You did the right thing, but you're right in that you assumed. Never assume your enemy has made a mistake, but be ready to take advantage of it if they did."

The impatience turned to more annoyance as Jenna worked to unravel the riddle in her mind. "How does that work?"

"Even the best trained warriors make mistakes," Brasalla explained calmly, indicating her missing arm with a pointed look, "and you must take advantage when they do. You parried my poor attack perfectly, but you were so certain of victory that you telegraphed your thrust badly."

"What does that mean?"

"I knew the attack was coming because I was testing you, but most trained warriors would have seen it coming, too. You pulled your sword arm back just a few inches to give more force to your thrust."

Jenna breathed in a slight hiss of air between her teeth as understanding dawned on her. "So," she reasoned, "by doing that, you saw the attack coming and had more time to react to avoid it."

"Exactly! We're fighting with swords, not clubs or staves or some other weapon that we have to bash each other's brains in with. Your father's sword came from Vulgesch. It is so strong, can hold such an edge that it can easily punch through most armor, except maybe

Vulgesch plate. Fight with grace, finesse, dexterity, not force."

"I..." Jenna began, but she suddenly wasn't sure what she wanted to say, so she nodded and replied softly, "I understand."

"Maybe a little, but I think you'll understand more in time. There's one more thing I'd like you to consider, just keep it in mind. As a woman and not particularly tall, people, especially men, will underestimate you. Take advantage of that. Lure them in, and do something they don't expect. Remember what I told you before – fair fights are for suckers."

Jenna nodded idly at this, her eyes downcast as she mulled it over. Without warning, she shot her left foot out, hooking her soft leather boot right behind Brasalla's right knee while giving the woman a sudden push with both hands. Caught completely unaware, Brasalla's legs bent as she tumbled backward and landed hard on her back, only the thick grass behind her cottage slightly cushioning her impact. Even so, she felt the wind painfully knocked from her lungs as she struck the ground.

"You mean like that?" Jenna asked with a wide, proud grin. She pointed her practice sword at her mentor and said one word, "Yield."

"You little shit," Brasalla spouted angrily as she struggled up to one elbow, and then she noticed the tip of the sword, blunted with a sphere of steel as it hovered only a half foot away from her. Laughter took the woman for a moment, and she tipped her head backward, answering, "Yeah, something like that. Here, Little Dear, help an old woman up."

Turn the page for an excerpt from

Wolves of War
A John Hartman Novel

Coming October 2024!

Darkness filled the ancient woodland, permeating everything around Hartman just as much as the frigid air chilled him to the bone. Nothing about his slow, quiet trek through the forest felt pleasant, and a sense of foreboding hung heavily in the air, tempting him to abandon his mission and start hoofing it back to France. It wasn't the first time he longed to be back with the regular Army, taking it to the Jerries in a straight fight, but this was different. John just couldn't shake the pervasive dread he felt as he ventured deeper into the German wood.

He shouldn't be alone out here. It was one thing to undertake a solo operation, a task he had accomplished many times in the past. But this time, he was supposed to have a guide with him who knew the woods better than he, but his contact failed to show up at the designated rendezvous. Maybe the he had gotten held up by German soldiers, or maybe he had to hunker down somewhere. After a while, John decided he couldn't wait any longer, steeled himself and went on with the operation.

For the fourth or fifth time, John wished he'd procured a heavy coat to keep the damp cold at bay. He found a tiny break in the eldritch canopy, through which shined a beam of pale light from the full moon overhead. He stood in this welcome dispeller of darkness long enough to unfold his map and become certain of his bearings. He had only a few miles left to traverse until he broke from the forest into the open where he would have little protection from watchful German eyes, and yet, he would breathe more easily once free from this place.

A shiver ran through Hartman, and he thought, *Damn, it's cold!* He began to fold the map back into itself, but his hands seemed to slow with each progressive crease. Surely, they were cold, but it wasn't the near freezing night air that made them react so. He slipped the map into a jacket pocket, and his motion slowed to a complete halt. He stood perfectly still, and the hair on his neck and arms would have stood on end were it not for his appropriated German uniform.

Narrow set, disembodied red eyes materialized out of the gloom some distance in front of him, seeming to glow with an inner, baleful light. They hovered perhaps a foot off of the ground, but Hartman couldn't for the darkness be sure if they were five feet ahead of him or twenty five. He knew only that he stood transfixed by that hellish glare, apparently frozen to inaction while they regarded him. He needed to act, draw a pistol and shoot at those eyes, ready a knife, something, but his limbs wouldn't obey his brain's commands. The entire encounter felt eerily familiar. He had been in some freezing German wood at some point before and had seen those eyes there and then as well, but this was also different. Hartman was alone, and the darkness and cold were all pervasive, not simply offensive to the senses. And there was only one set of eyes, though he remembered, on that other occasion that other attackers had come at him from the sides.

Hartman broke his paralysis just in time to see a silver and black streak from the right as it caromed off of the back of his legs. The energy from the blow knocked him off balance, and it was only his superb athleticism that kept him from tumbling to the forest floor. Just as he regained his footing, another rush of dark motion attacked from the other direction, but this one drew blood. A fierce snapping of unseen jaws severed tendons in his left leg, causing Hartman to collapse, and as he clutched the wounded limb, warm, steaming blood coated his hands.

Either out of a preternatural sense or pure luck, he managed to get his left forearm up just as a huge wolf of silver and black lunged at him. A mouth of wicked, yellowed teeth opened wide in anticipation, and Hartman wedged his arm as far into the mouth as he could. Like a dog whose chewing bone had gone too far backward, the wolf chomped its jaws trying to dislodge him. The power of those jaws wrought tremendous pain, and Hartman felt the teeth puncture the skin of his arm even through the layers of his jacket and sleeve. But it also bought him precious moments. His free hand reached for his knife, but before he could find it, another beast charged from his right. This canine minion of Hell he caught by the neck, and it took all of his might just to hold the thing at bay as it snapped at his face, rancid carrion breath caressing his face. If he could somehow manage to get his legs underneath the creature in front of him, perhaps he could launch the beast just far enough to access his knife or gun. Then, he could turn this fight around.

This glimmer of hope flickered in his mind only to be extinguished in an instant as a third monstrous wolf stood less than a foot away to his left, mouth agape and tongue hanging low out of its mouth. It panted softly, but seemingly out of anticipation rather than exhaustion, and Hartman knew he couldn't hold this one off; he was simply out of arms. It lunged toward his face, and all he could see was teeth and then darkness as the wolf's jaws clamped around his face.

Hartman bolted upright, his clothes and the bedsheets of the hospital bed soaked in sweat. As his heart and breathing gradually slowed, his head cleared so that he could regain his bearings. Two nurses moved around the room, drawing back curtains to allow in the first rays of the autumn sun, which told Hartman it was around seven in the morning. There were only six men in the score of beds in the room, and of them all, he was the only one unwounded. He was vaguely aware of a rifle toting guard that stood in a gray uniform next to the room's entrance.

One of the nurses glared his direction as he watched them, and as she made her way across the room to his bedside, he reached down and rubbed at his ankle, which was shackled to the metal frame of the bed. She stood to his right in her uniform - a dress of narrow, vertical white and blue stripes under an apron of white. Her collar, also white, contrasted against the dress, and was pinned closed severely by an emblem of the Third Reich. A black German eagle clutched a red cross in its talons, though the cross had been extended and resembled an inverted Christian cross.

"Gut morning. Nachtmares?" she asked in a hodge-podge of English and German. She wasn't pretty in the least, but she hadn't been unfriendly to him despite their nations' adversarial nature.

"*Es ist nichts*," Hartman replied in perfect German, "*Danke*."

"Nothing? It's nothing you say? You come into my country, my Fatherland, and kill my sons and brothers, and it is nothing?" she asked, her English becoming clearer though accented. Her eyes began to glow with an unholy red light as she continued, "You come here to fight a war that doesn't belong to you. You kill thousands of good men and deprive the Fatherland what we are owed by right. You do not know what you face, what this Old World can unleash upon you!"

She seemed to grow as she spoke, her uniform tearing at the seams as her bones popped and elongated. By the end of her tirade, her words were nearly unintelligible as her human mouth reformed to that of a wolf's toothy maw under bright red, demonic eyes. Hair, fur of silver and black had sprouted across every inch of her, and razor sharp claws extended from each of her fingers. The room grew dark, as if her very presence alone blotted out the light of the rising sun.

John shouted in alarm and leapt out of the bed as if a great spring had been compressed underneath him, except the shackle around his ankle prevented him from going too far. His back slammed hard onto the cold floor, and he would've cracked the back of his skull as well were it not for his flailing arms somehow breaking his fall. His leg remained suspended in the air, attached as it was to the bedframe, with the hospital bed acting as the only barrier between Hartman and the monstrosity.

"Captain Hartman?" a worried voice said in his ear, and cool hands cradled his sweaty face. "Captain Hartman, wake up."

John Hartman blinked his eyes and shook his head once to dispel and clear away the fading image. He indeed lay on a cool floor, but it was that of the Army field hospital in France. His left leg was propped up on his bed, his ankle wrapped up in bedsheets so twisted to be as strong as thick rope. The room was dimly lit, except for the warmth of a soft glow emanating from the hallway beyond the door. Somewhere in the next room, he heard a muffled announcer's voice calling a baseball game. It sounded like the World Series that just ended two days ago with the St. Louis Cardinals beating the St. Louis Browns.

"Captain Hartman are you all right?" the brown haired night nurse asked.

"I'm fine," he replied with a hardened face as she helped him stand and get back into bed.

"You know, I could find something to help you sleep," she offered, likely referring to whiskey or some other such spirits; being an officer had its privileges.

"No, thank you very much," he replied as he laid his head backward to stare wide awake at the ceiling. "I've slept enough."

Made in the USA
Middletown, DE
28 July 2024